TALES FROM CHINA

OUTLAWS of the MARSH

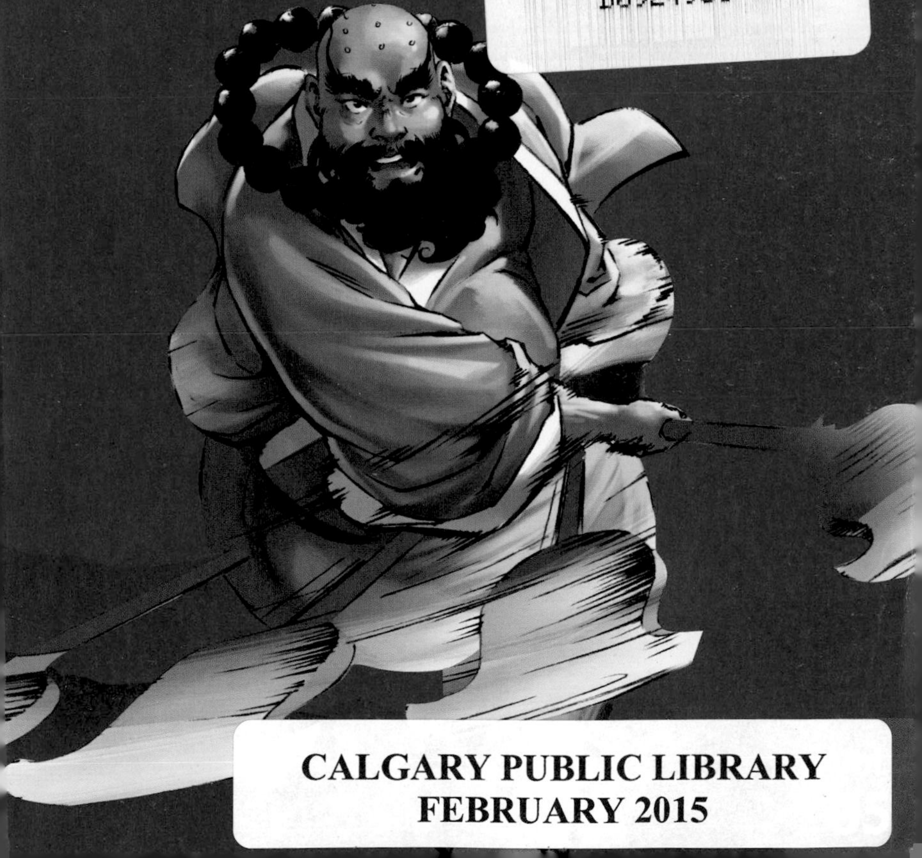

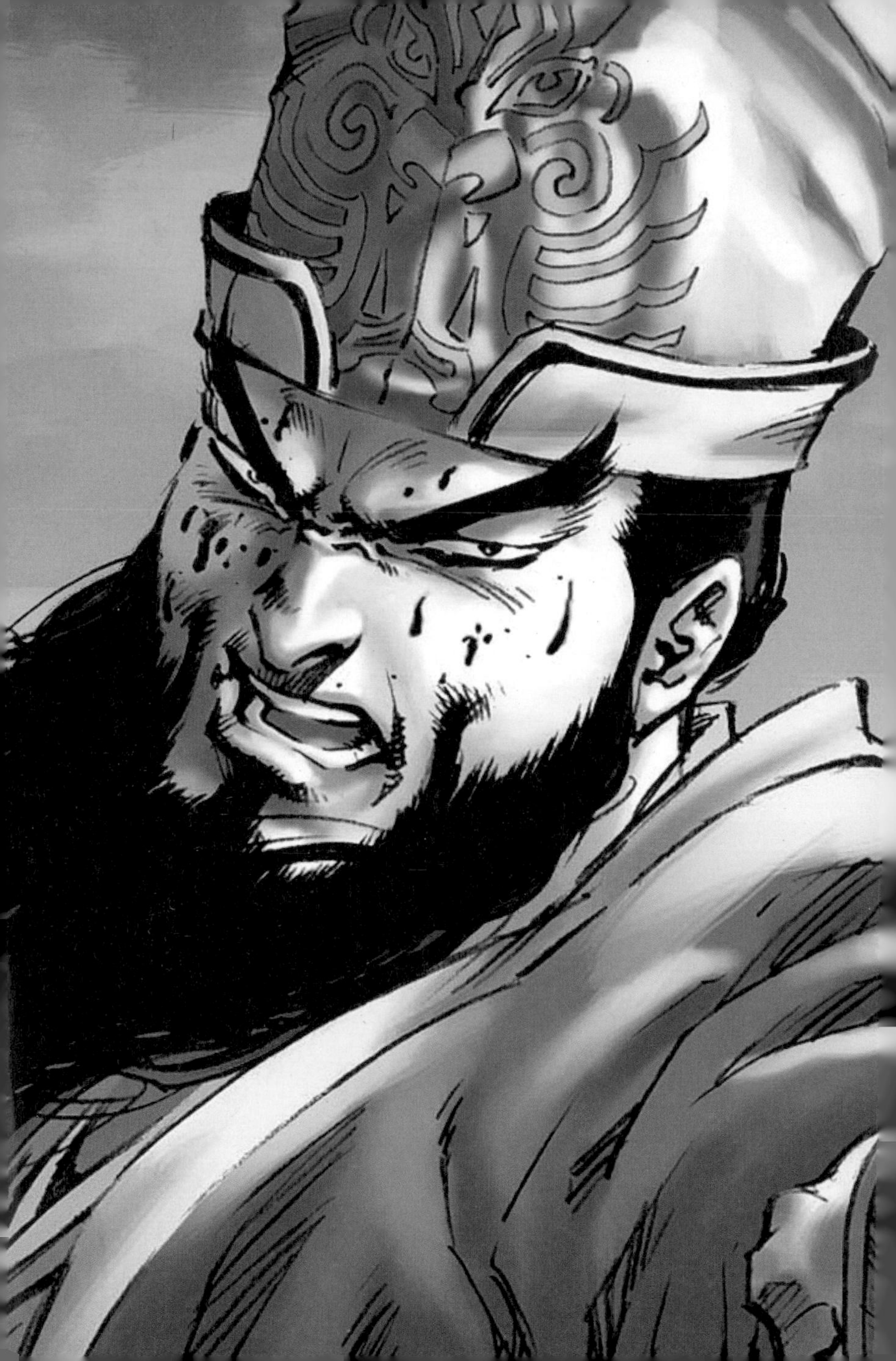

OUTLAWS of the MARSH

Vol. 05

Outlaws of the Marsh

Created by WEI DONG CHEN

Wei Dong Chen is a highly acclaimed artist and an influential leader
in the "New Chinese Cartoon" trend. He is the founder of Creator World,
the largest comics studio in China. His spirited and energetic work has attracted
many students to his tutelage. He has published more than 300 cartoons in
several countries and gained both recognition and admirers across Asia, Europe,
and the USA. Mr. Chen's work is serialized in several publications,
and he continues to explore new dimensions of the graphic medium.

Illustrated by XIAO LONG LIANG

Xiao Long Liang is considered one of Wei Dong Chen's greatest students.
One of the most highly regarded cartoonists in China today, Xiao Long's
fantastic technique and expression of Chinese culture have won him
the acclaim of cartoon lovers throughout China.

Original Story
"The Water Margin" by Shi, Nai An

Editing & Designing
Mybloomy, Jonathan Evans, KH Lee, YK Kim,
HJ Lee, JS Kim, Lampin, Qing Shao, Xiao Nan Li, Ke Hu

Characters

Volume 05

ZHI YANG

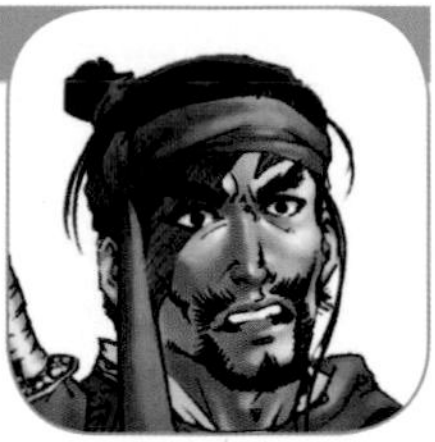

Zhi Yang, known as The Blue-Faced Beast, is a confessed murderer who was sentenced to exile for his crime, but nevertheless earned the trust of a local governor. That governor has tasked Zhi Yang with safely delivering precious treasures to a member of his family, a job Zhi Yang takes very seriously.

GAI CHAO

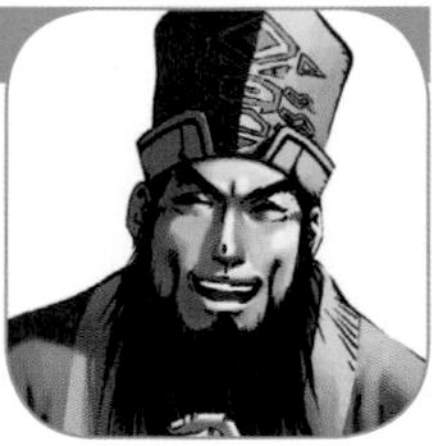

Gai Chao is a local official who is known for his generosity and good nature. But his good nature does not extend to sympathy for the government he serves, and when he learns of a caravan of precious cargo passing through his lands, he hatches a plan to take that precious cargo away from those he believes deserve it least.

ZHENG CAO

Zheng Cao is a tavern owner and one of Chong Lin's former disciples. When Zheng Cao confronts Zhi Yang over an unpaid bill, he learns that his former master has touched the lives of both men. Upon Zheng Cao's recommendation, Zhi Yang sets out for Mount ErLong.

ZHISHEN LU

ZhiShen Lu, also known as The Painted Monk, is a former major in a local military force who went by the name Da Lu. Known for his enormous strength and short temper, ZhiShen was driven into exile after killing a man on impulse. He has spent the time since wandering the countryside and looking for a place to call home. When he meets Zhi Yang, it is right after yet another place has cast him out.

Characters

Volume 05

TAO HE

Tao He is brought in by the Prefect of JiZhou to hunt down those who raided the governor's shipment of precious goods. When he arrives in YunCheng to investigate, the first person he questions is a local clerk by the name of Jiang Song. The conversation will not help his investigation one bit.

JIANG SONG

Jiang Song, who is known by many as "The Timely Rain," is a clerk in YunCheng who has a reputation for being a good public official who doesn't cause too much trouble. But Jiang Song's motives are dubious, and any effort made to catch Gai Chao and his partners will be made more difficult thanks to Jiang Song's efforts.

OUTLAWS of the MARSH

THE RUAN BROTHERS

The Ruan brothers are fishermen from the village of
ShiJie. They have been brought in on the plot to raid the
governor's caravan by Gai Chao, who instructs them to
act as fruit merchants in order to deceive Zhi Yang. But
when local officials learn that Gai Chao is behind the
theft and dispatch the royal military to bring him in, the
brothers' expert knowledge of fighting on water will
allow Gai Chao to escape to LiangShan Marsh.

Chapter 1

A Tale of Two Thefts

Summary

Zhi Yang has been entrusted with the delivery of precious cargo from Secretary Liang to his father-in-law. He takes the job very seriously, and drives his men to the point of exhaustion. While taking a rest, Zhi Yang encounters Gai Chao and his men, who claim to be fruit merchants, as well as a wine merchant who claims to be passing through. Zhi Yang's men beg for the chance to buy some wine. After first refusing, Zhi Yang takes pity on his men and lets them quench their thirst. But the wine has been drugged, and Gai Chao's men steal all the cargo while Zhi Yang and his men are unconscious.

When he wakes up, Zhi Yang realizes he is in serious trouble, and flees. He takes shelter with Zheng Cao, and then meets ZhiShen Lu. Together, they hatch a plan for turning their fortunes around.

DaiZhou
CangZhou
BOHAI SEA
Mt. WuTai
QingZhou
B
Mt. ErLong
BeiJing
Mt. TaoHua
A
HuangNi Hill
LiangShan Marsh
JiZhou
DongJing (KaiFung)
XiJing
Mt. XiaoHua
NanJing

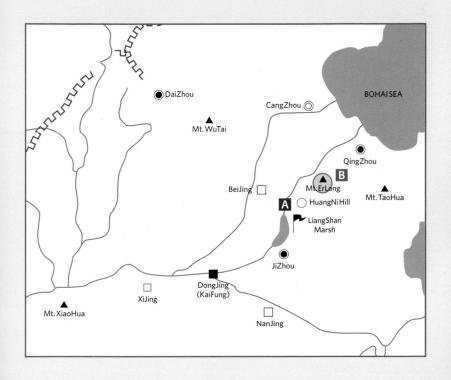

A Zhi Yang and his men encounter Gai Chao and his band of thieves, who conspire to steal Zhi Yang's cargo.

B Zhi Yang meets ZhiShen Lu and Zheng Cao, and together the three men take over Mount ErLong.

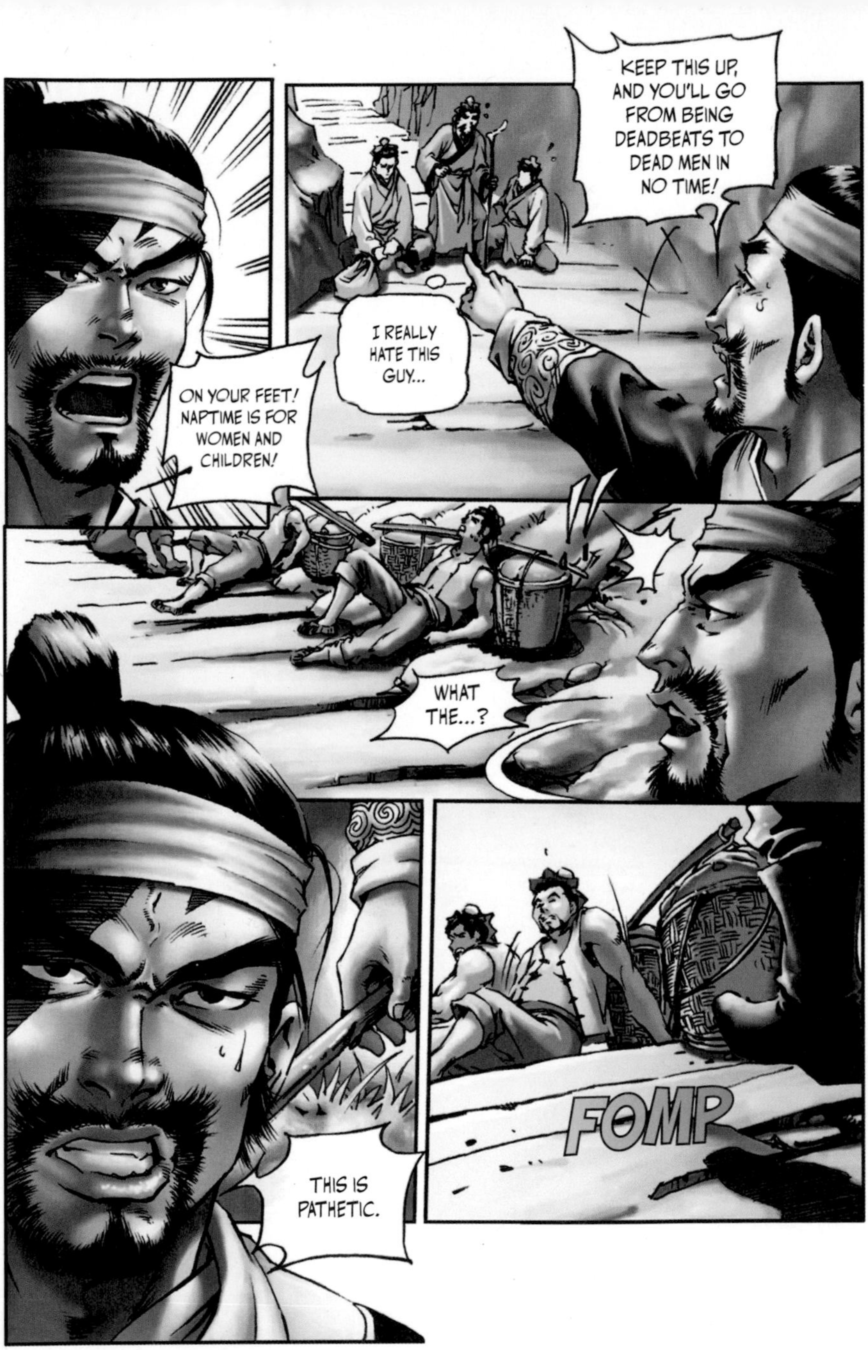
ON YOUR FEET! NAPTIME IS FOR WOMEN AND CHILDREN!
KEEP THIS UP, AND YOU'LL GO FROM BEING DEADBEATS TO DEAD MEN IN NO TIME!
I REALLY HATE THIS GUY...
WHAT THE...?
THIS IS PATHETIC.
FOMP

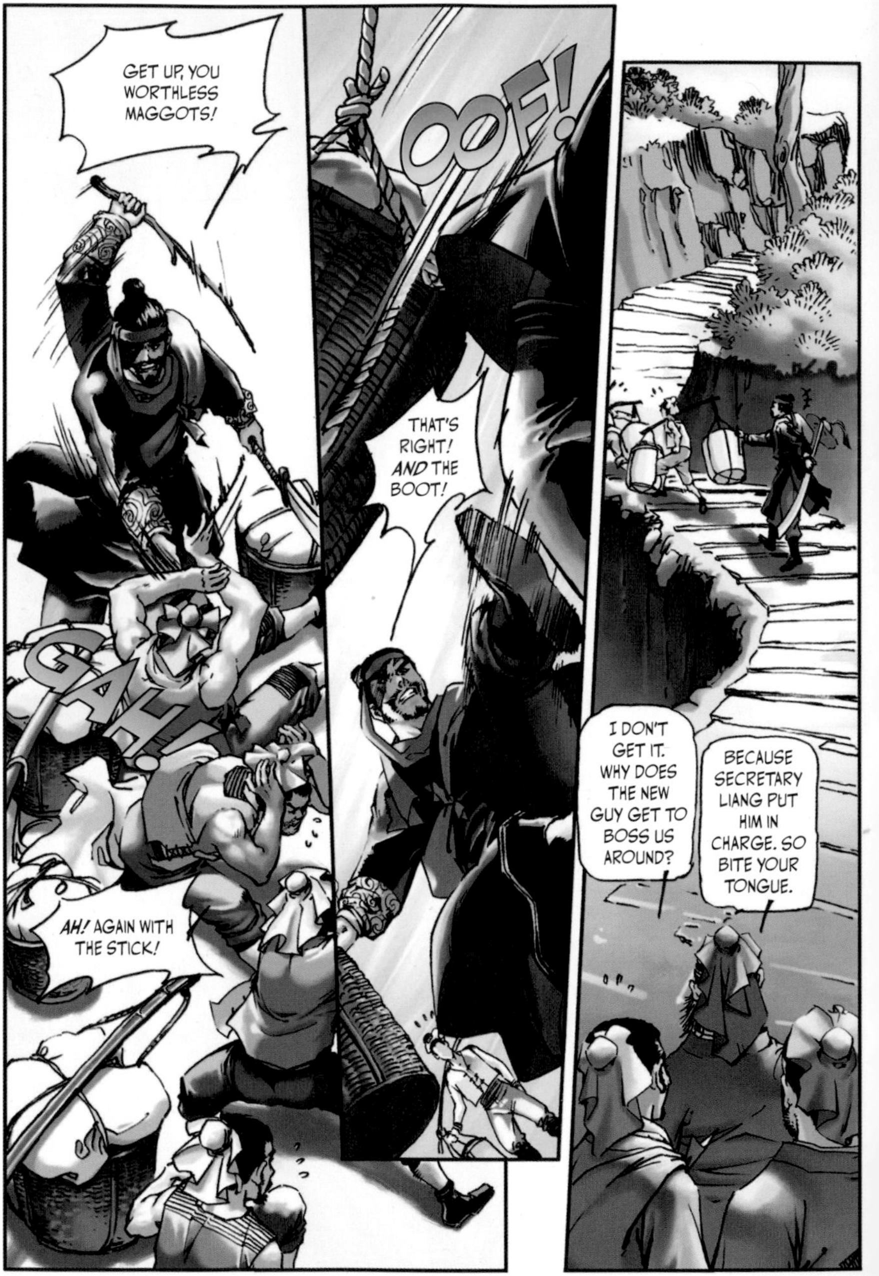
GET UP, YOU WORTHLESS MAGGOTS!
GAH!
AH! AGAIN WITH THE STICK!
OOF!
THAT'S RIGHT! AND THE BOOT!
I DON'T GET IT. WHY DOES THE NEW GUY GET TO BOSS US AROUND?
BECAUSE SECRETARY LIANG PUT HIM IN CHARGE. SO BITE YOUR TONGUE.

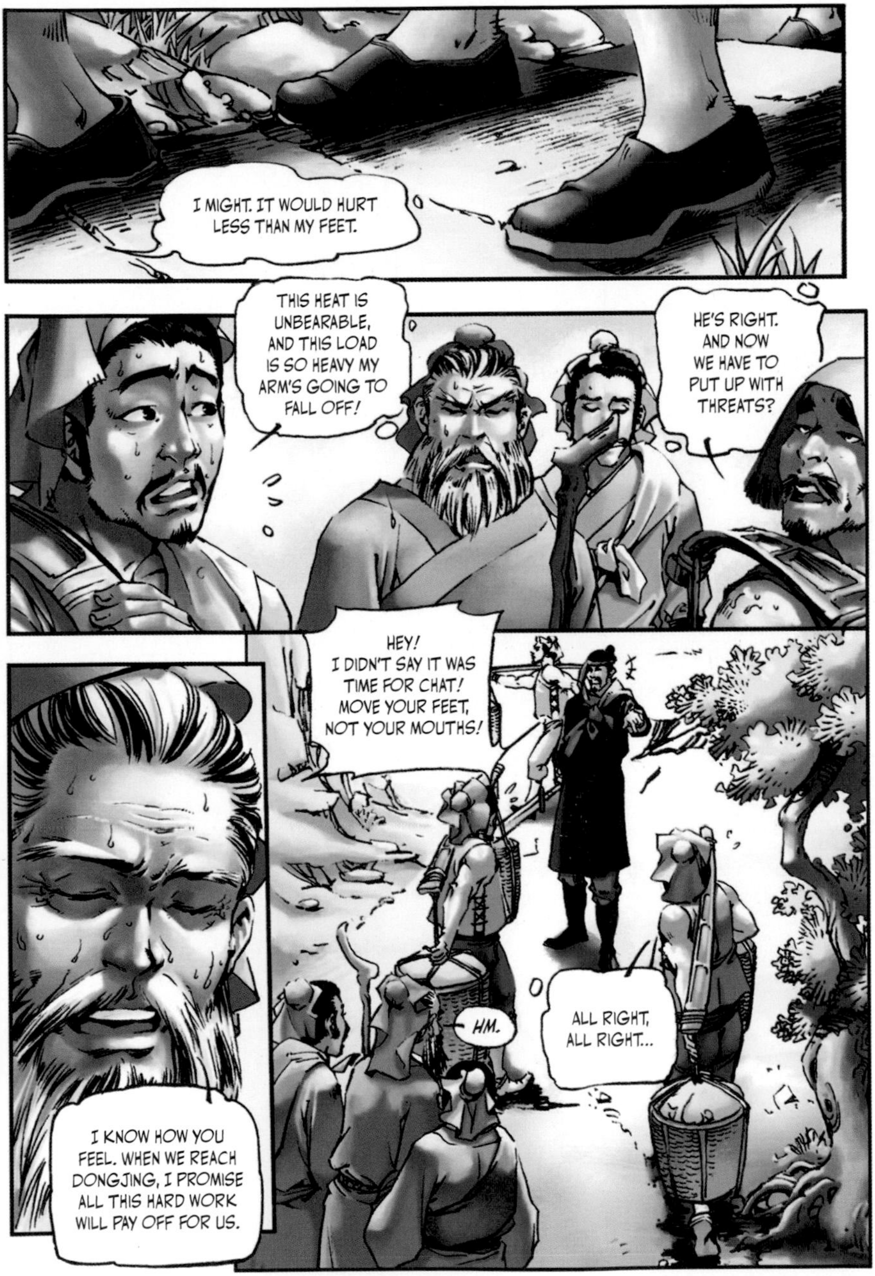
I MIGHT. IT WOULD HURT LESS THAN MY FEET.
THIS HEAT IS UNBEARABLE, AND THIS LOAD IS SO HEAVY MY ARM'S GOING TO FALL OFF!
HE'S RIGHT. AND NOW WE HAVE TO PUT UP WITH THREATS?
HEY! I DIDN'T SAY IT WAS TIME FOR CHAT! MOVE YOUR FEET, NOT YOUR MOUTHS!
HM.
ALL RIGHT, ALL RIGHT...
I KNOW HOW YOU FEEL. WHEN WE REACH DONGJING, I PROMISE ALL THIS HARD WORK WILL PAY OFF FOR US.

Zhi Yang had been appointed a major by Secretary Liang and put in charge of the caravan entrusted with the delivery of precious birthday gifts from Secretary Liang to his father-in-law. Major Yang owed the secretary his life, and took his job with the utmost seriousness. The men he travelled with did not share his passion.

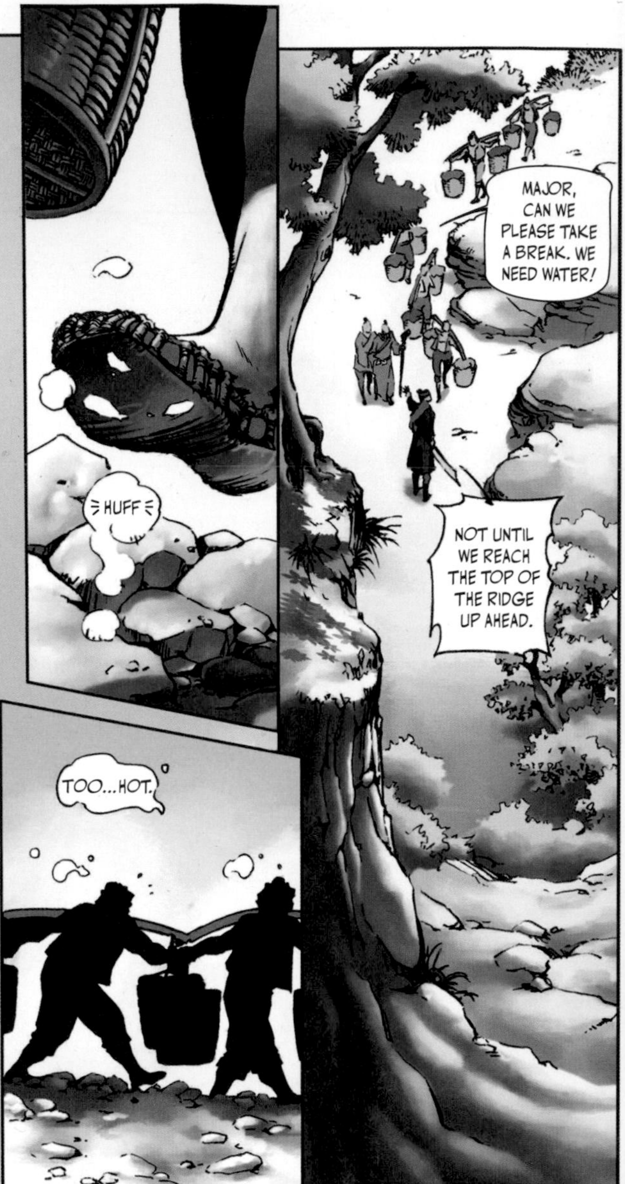
HUFF
TOO...HOT.
MAJOR, CAN WE PLEASE TAKE A BREAK. WE NEED WATER!
NOT UNTIL WE REACH THE TOP OF THE RIDGE UP AHEAD.

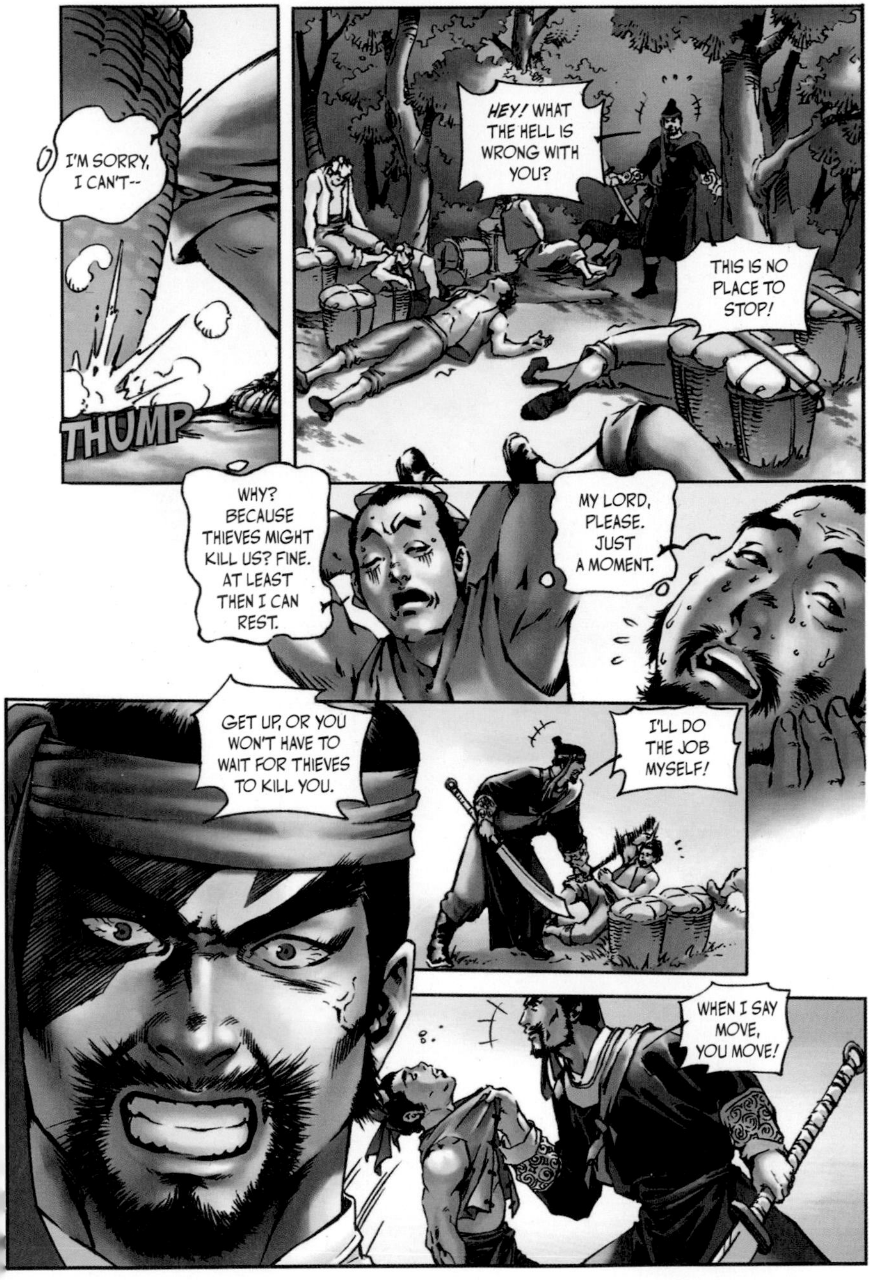
I'M SORRY, I CAN'T--
THUMP
HEY! WHAT THE HELL IS WRONG WITH YOU?
THIS IS NO PLACE TO STOP!
WHY? BECAUSE THIEVES MIGHT KILL US? FINE. AT LEAST THEN I CAN REST.
MY LORD, PLEASE. JUST A MOMENT.
GET UP, OR YOU WON'T HAVE TO WAIT FOR THIEVES TO KILL YOU.
I'LL DO THE JOB MYSELF!
WHEN I SAY MOVE, YOU MOVE!

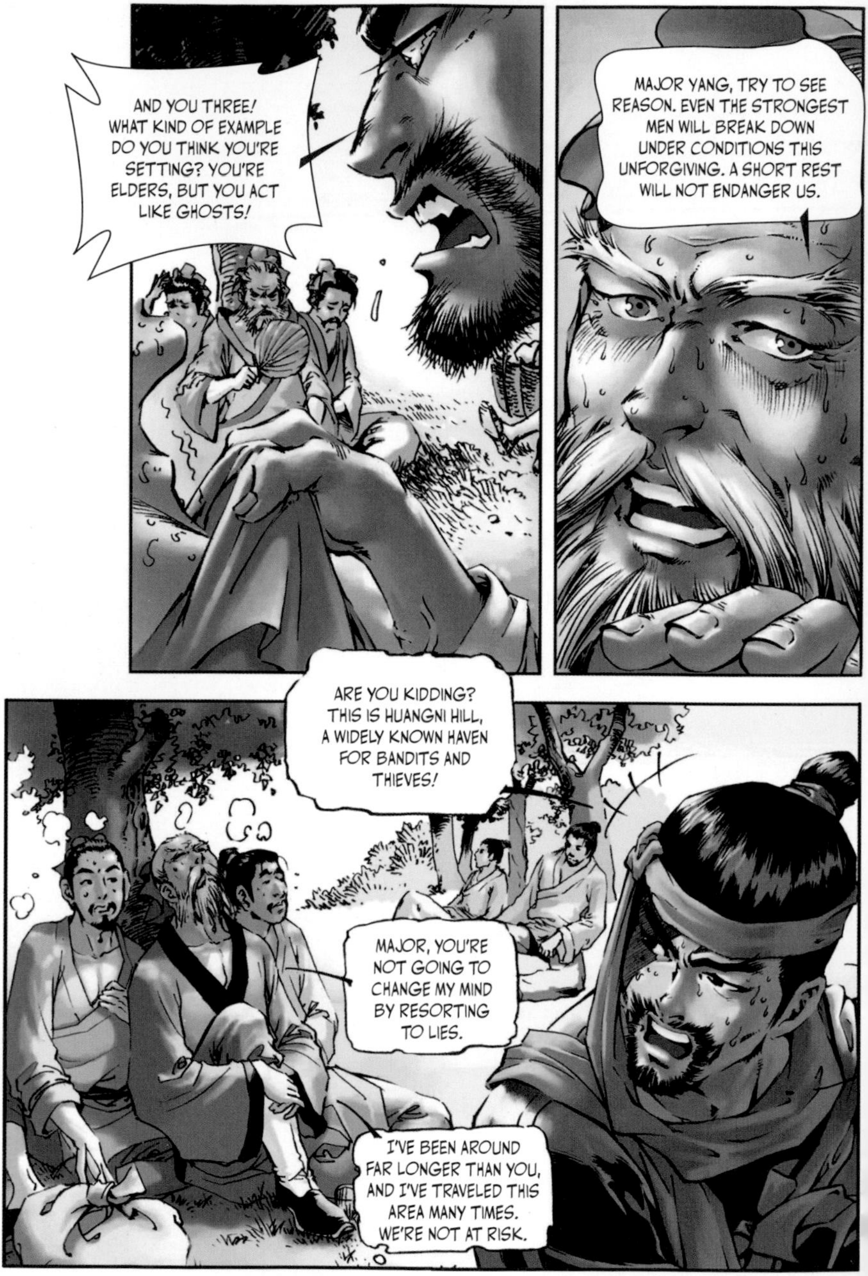
AND YOU THREE! WHAT KIND OF EXAMPLE DO YOU THINK YOU'RE SETTING? YOU'RE ELDERS, BUT YOU ACT LIKE GHOSTS!
MAJOR YANG, TRY TO SEE REASON. EVEN THE STRONGEST MEN WILL BREAK DOWN UNDER CONDITIONS THIS UNFORGIVING. A SHORT REST WILL NOT ENDANGER US.
ARE YOU KIDDING? THIS IS HUANGNI HILL, A WIDELY KNOWN HAVEN FOR BANDITS AND THIEVES!
MAJOR, YOU'RE NOT GOING TO CHANGE MY MIND BY RESORTING TO LIES.
I'VE BEEN AROUND FAR LONGER THAN YOU, AND I'VE TRAVELED THIS AREA MANY TIMES. WE'RE NOT AT RISK.

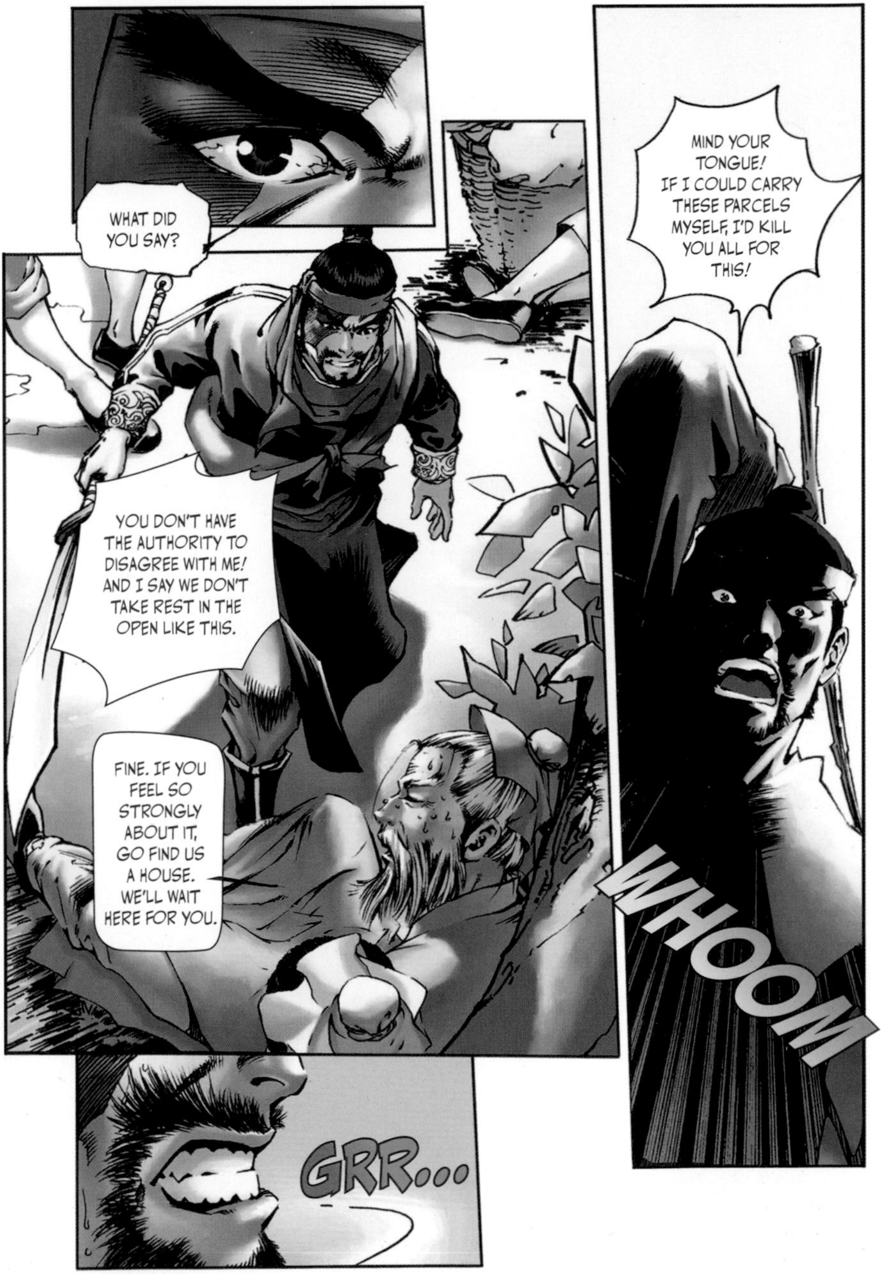
WHAT DID YOU SAY?
YOU DON'T HAVE THE AUTHORITY TO DISAGREE WITH ME! AND I SAY WE DON'T TAKE REST IN THE OPEN LIKE THIS.
FINE. IF YOU FEEL SO STRONGLY ABOUT IT, GO FIND US A HOUSE. WE'LL WAIT HERE FOR YOU.
GRR...
MIND YOUR TONGUE! IF I COULD CARRY THESE PARCELS MYSELF, I'D KILL YOU ALL FOR THIS!
WHOOM

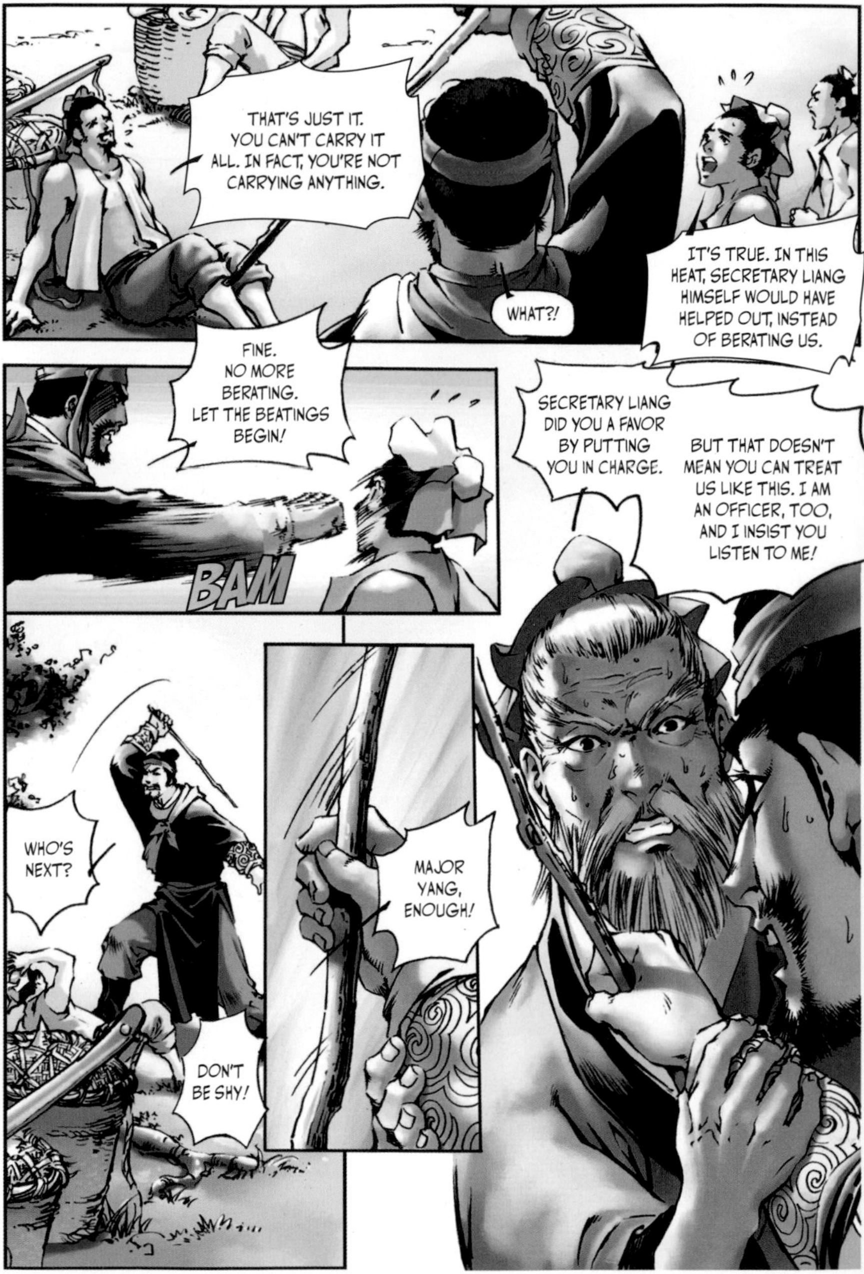
THAT'S JUST IT. YOU CAN'T CARRY IT ALL. IN FACT, YOU'RE NOT CARRYING ANYTHING.
WHAT?!
IT'S TRUE. IN THIS HEAT, SECRETARY LIANG HIMSELF WOULD HAVE HELPED OUT, INSTEAD OF BERATING US.
SECRETARY LIANG DID YOU A FAVOR BY PUTTING YOU IN CHARGE.
BUT THAT DOESN'T MEAN YOU CAN TREAT US LIKE THIS. I AM AN OFFICER, TOO, AND I INSIST YOU LISTEN TO ME!
FINE. NO MORE BERATING. LET THE BEATINGS BEGIN!
BAM
WHO'S NEXT?
DON'T BE SHY!
MAJOR YANG, ENOUGH!

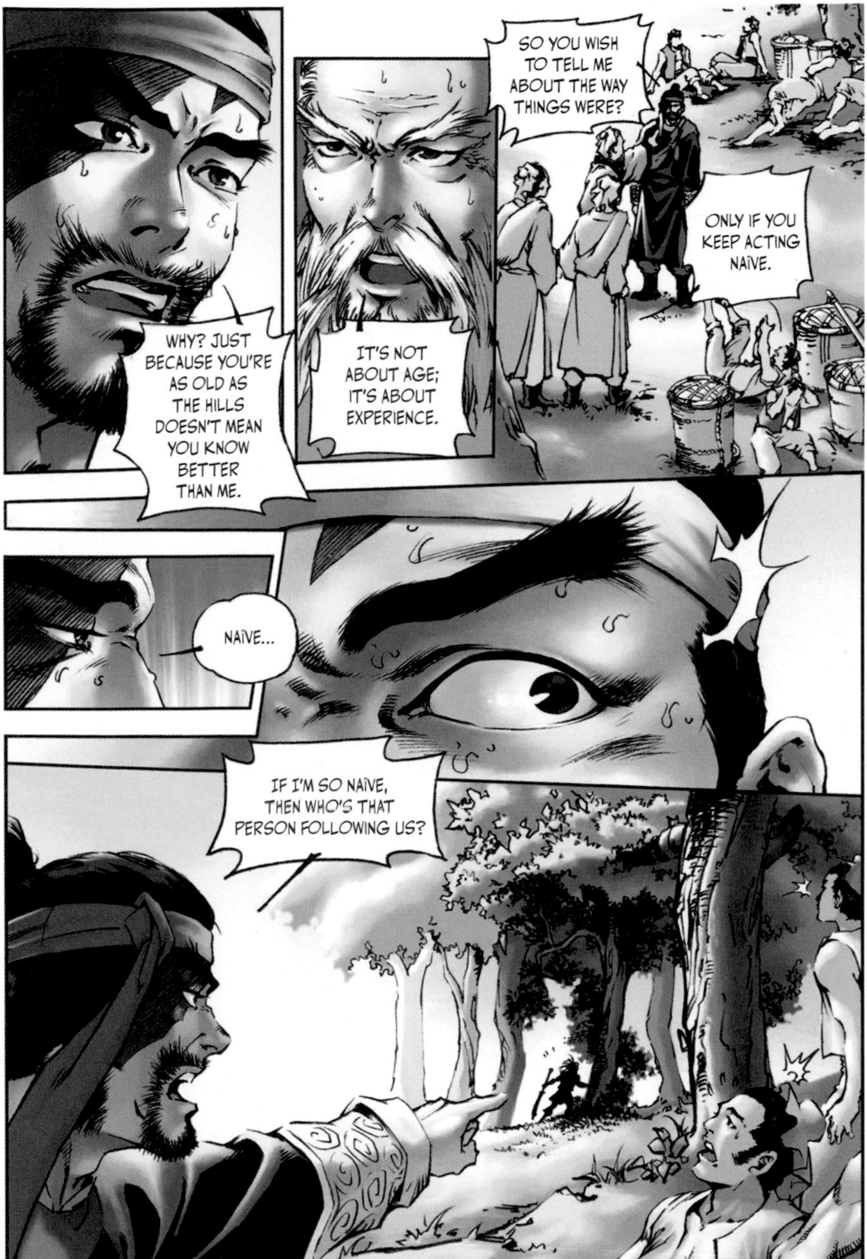
WHY? JUST BECAUSE YOU'RE AS OLD AS THE HILLS DOESN'T MEAN YOU KNOW BETTER THAN ME.
IT'S NOT ABOUT AGE; IT'S ABOUT EXPERIENCE.
SO YOU WISH TO TELL ME ABOUT THE WAY THINGS WERE?
ONLY IF YOU KEEP ACTING NAÏVE.
NAÏVE...
IF I'M SO NAÏVE, THEN WHO'S THAT PERSON FOLLOWING US?

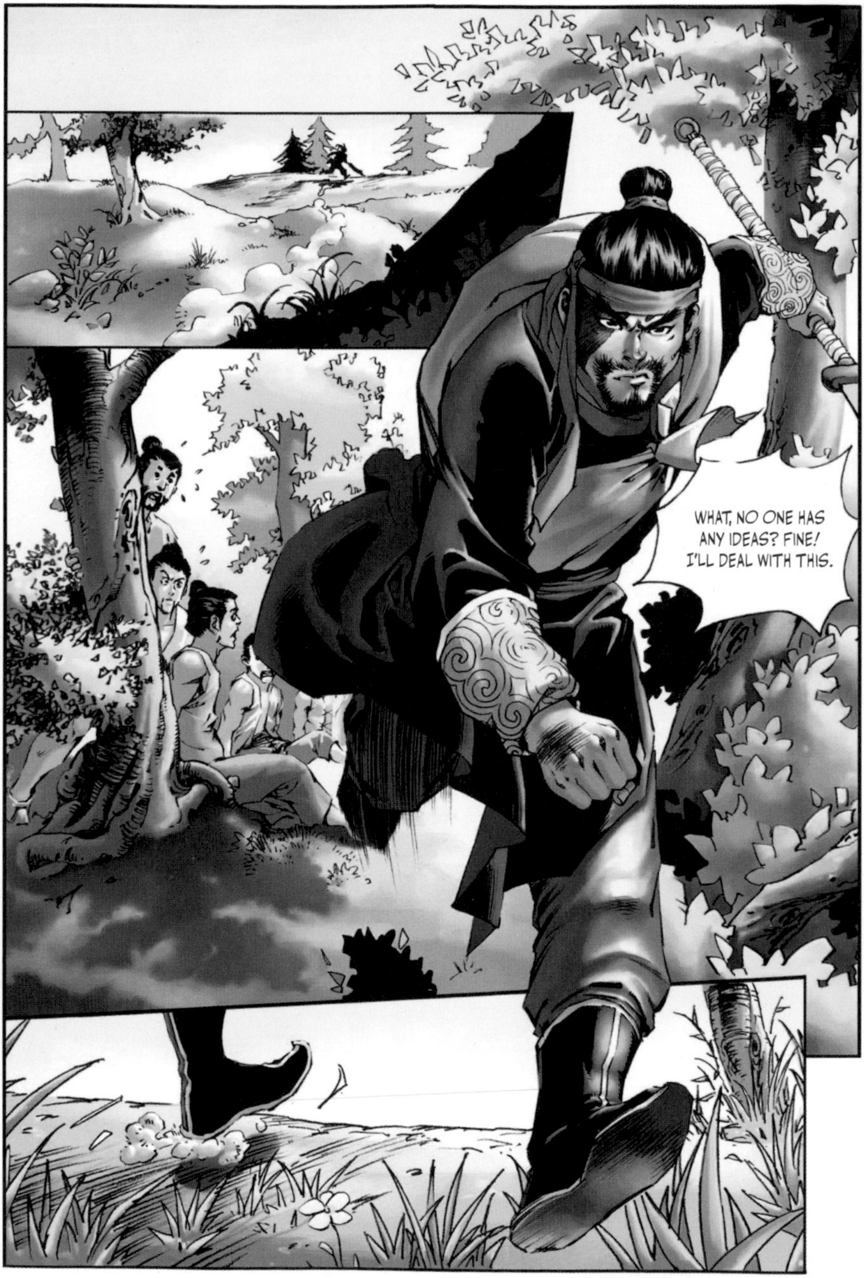
WHAT, NO ONE HAS
ANY IDEAS? FINE!
I'LL DEAL WITH THIS.

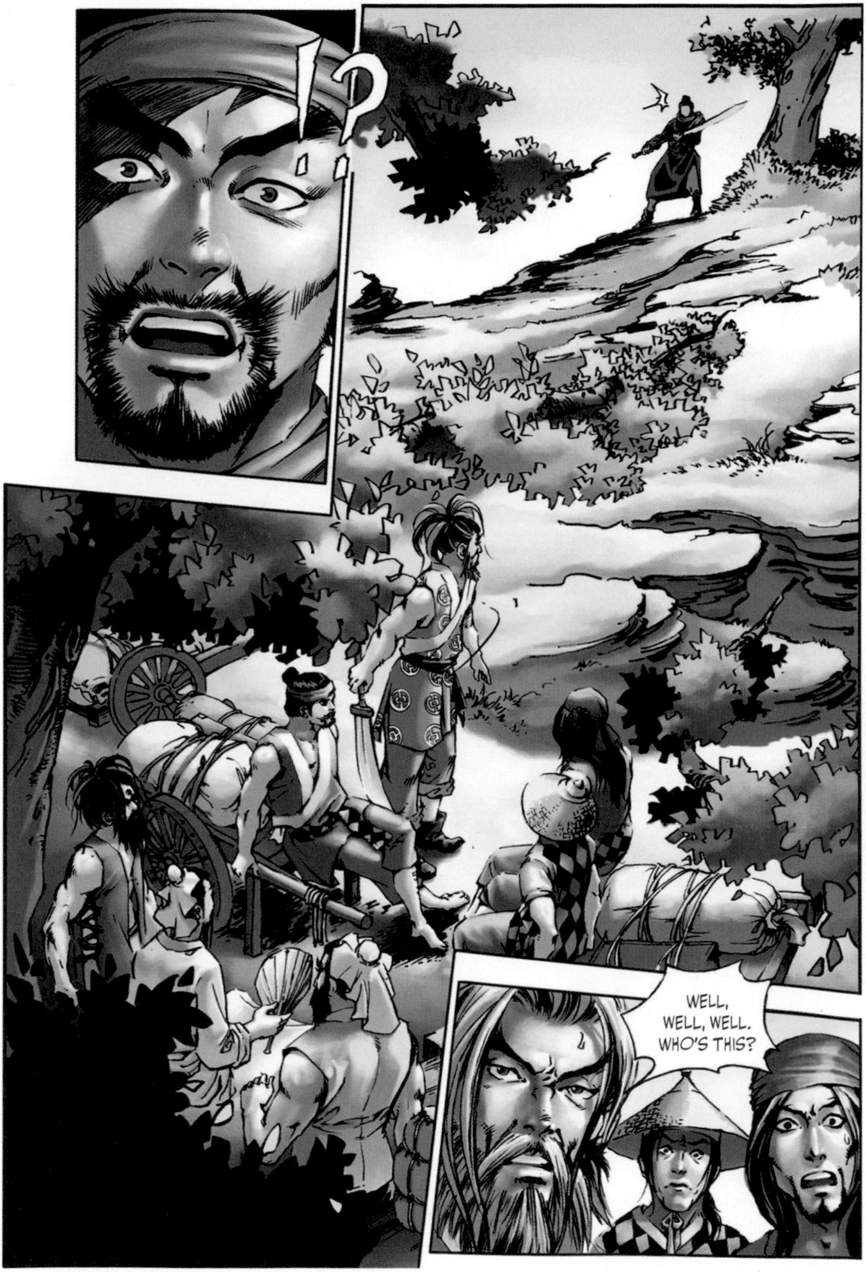
!?
WELL, WELL, WELL. WHO'S THIS?

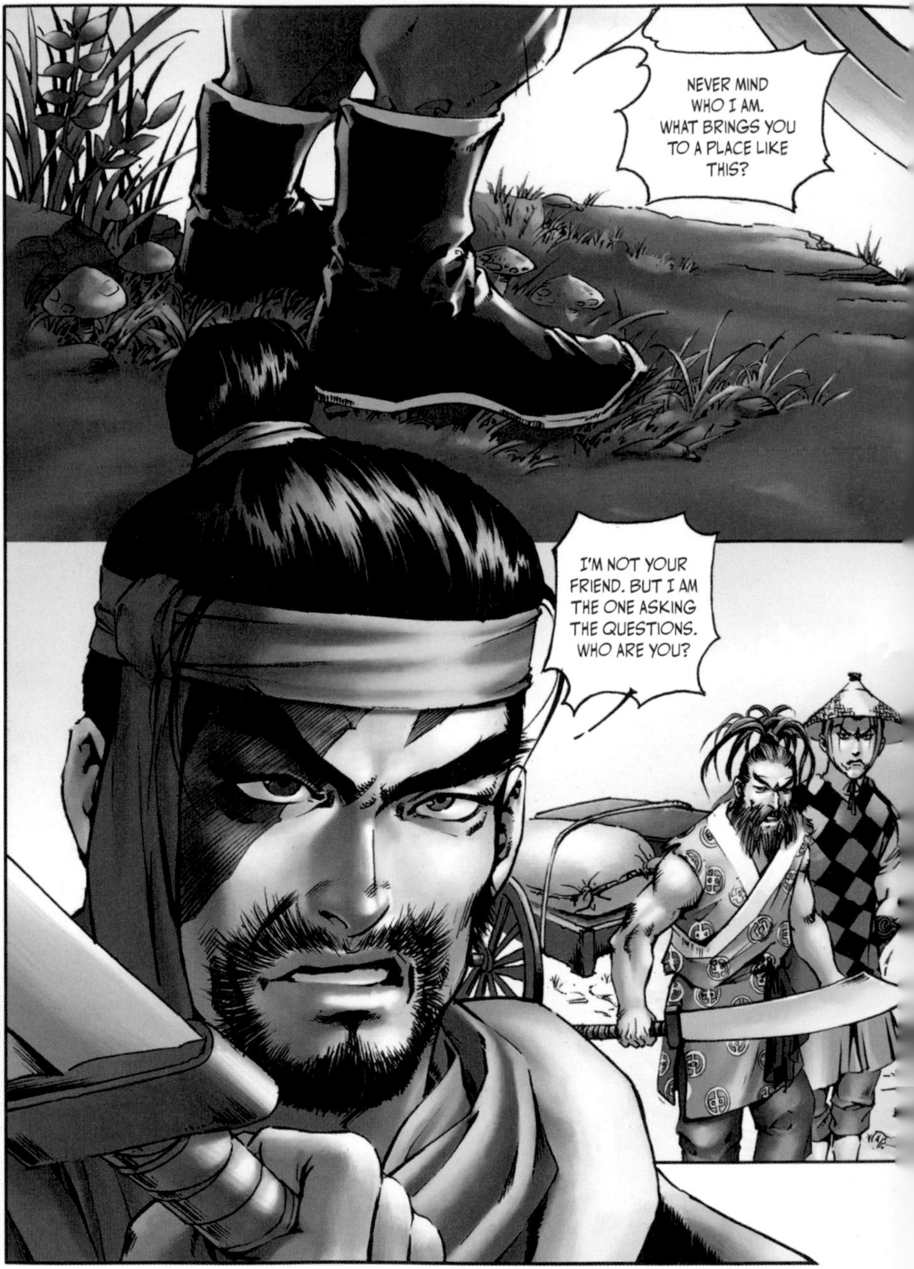
NEVER MIND WHO I AM. WHAT BRINGS YOU TO A PLACE LIKE THIS?
I'M NOT YOUR FRIEND. BUT I AM THE ONE ASKING THE QUESTIONS. WHO ARE YOU?

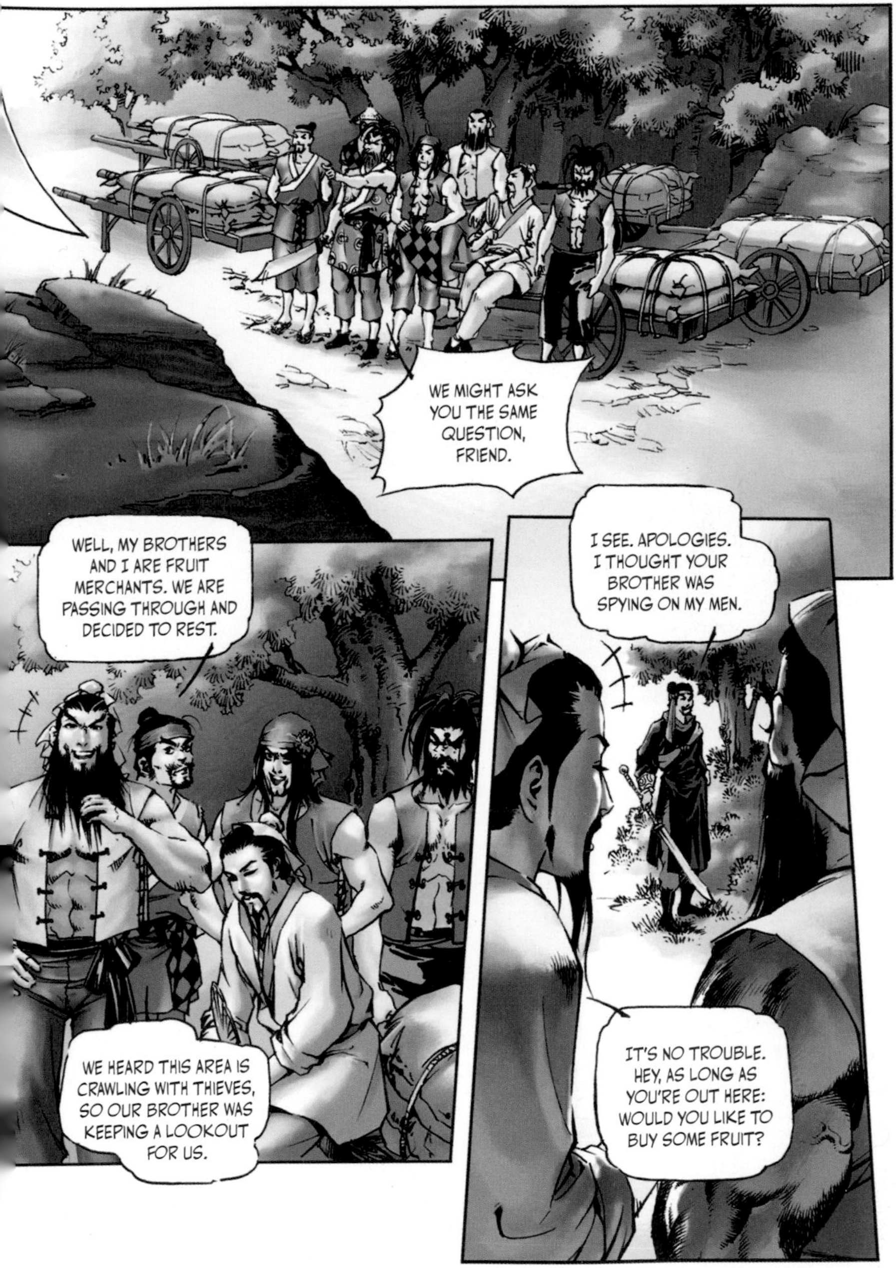
WE MIGHT ASK YOU THE SAME QUESTION, FRIEND.
WELL, MY BROTHERS AND I ARE FRUIT MERCHANTS. WE ARE PASSING THROUGH AND DECIDED TO REST.
WE HEARD THIS AREA IS CRAWLING WITH THIEVES, SO OUR BROTHER WAS KEEPING A LOOKOUT FOR US.
I SEE. APOLOGIES. I THOUGHT YOUR BROTHER WAS SPYING ON MY MEN.
IT'S NO TROUBLE. HEY, AS LONG AS YOU'RE OUT HERE: WOULD YOU LIKE TO BUY SOME FRUIT?

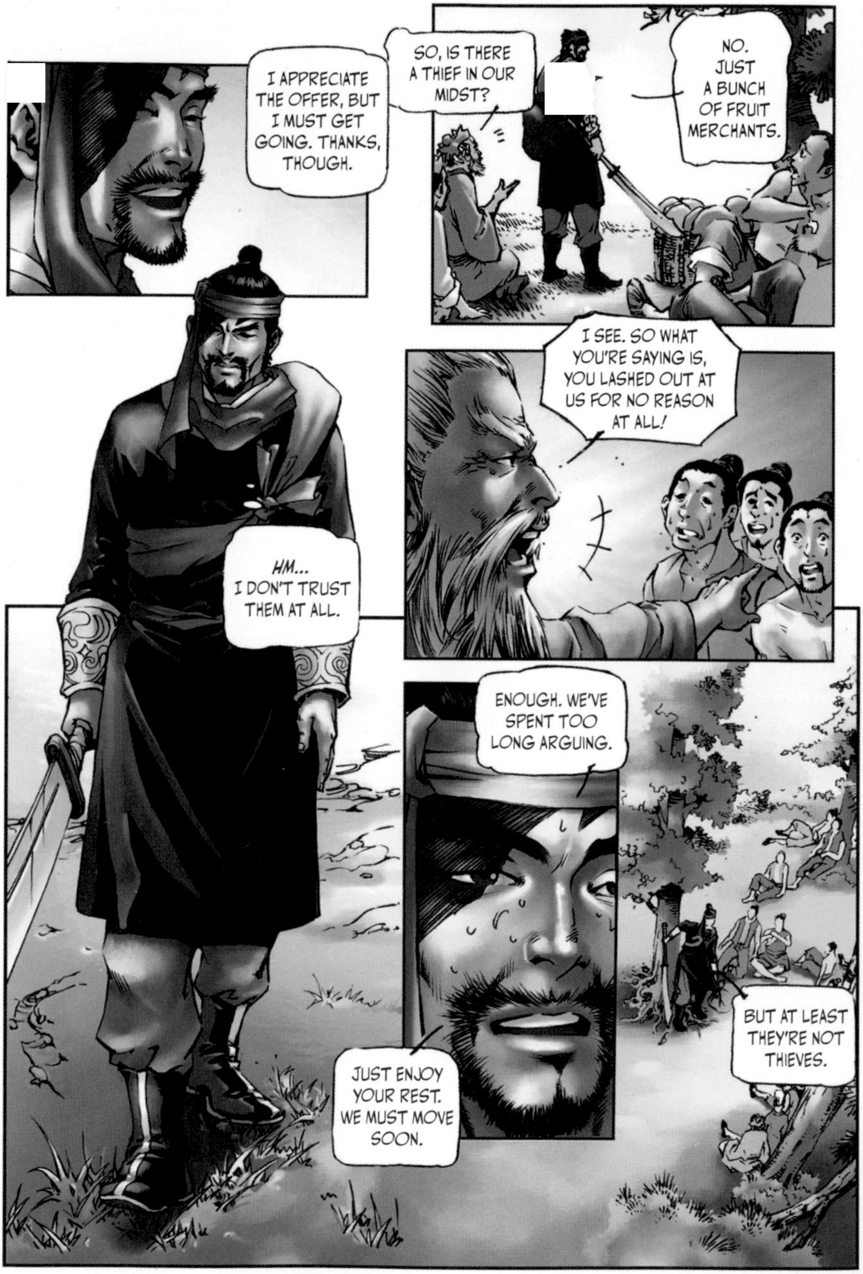
I APPRECIATE THE OFFER, BUT I MUST GET GOING. THANKS, THOUGH.
SO, IS THERE A THIEF IN OUR MIDST?
NO. JUST A BUNCH OF FRUIT MERCHANTS.
I SEE. SO WHAT YOU'RE SAYING IS, YOU LASHED OUT AT US FOR NO REASON AT ALL!
HM... I DON'T TRUST THEM AT ALL.
ENOUGH. WE'VE SPENT TOO LONG ARGUING.
JUST ENJOY YOUR REST. WE MUST MOVE SOON.
BUT AT LEAST THEY'RE NOT THIEVES.

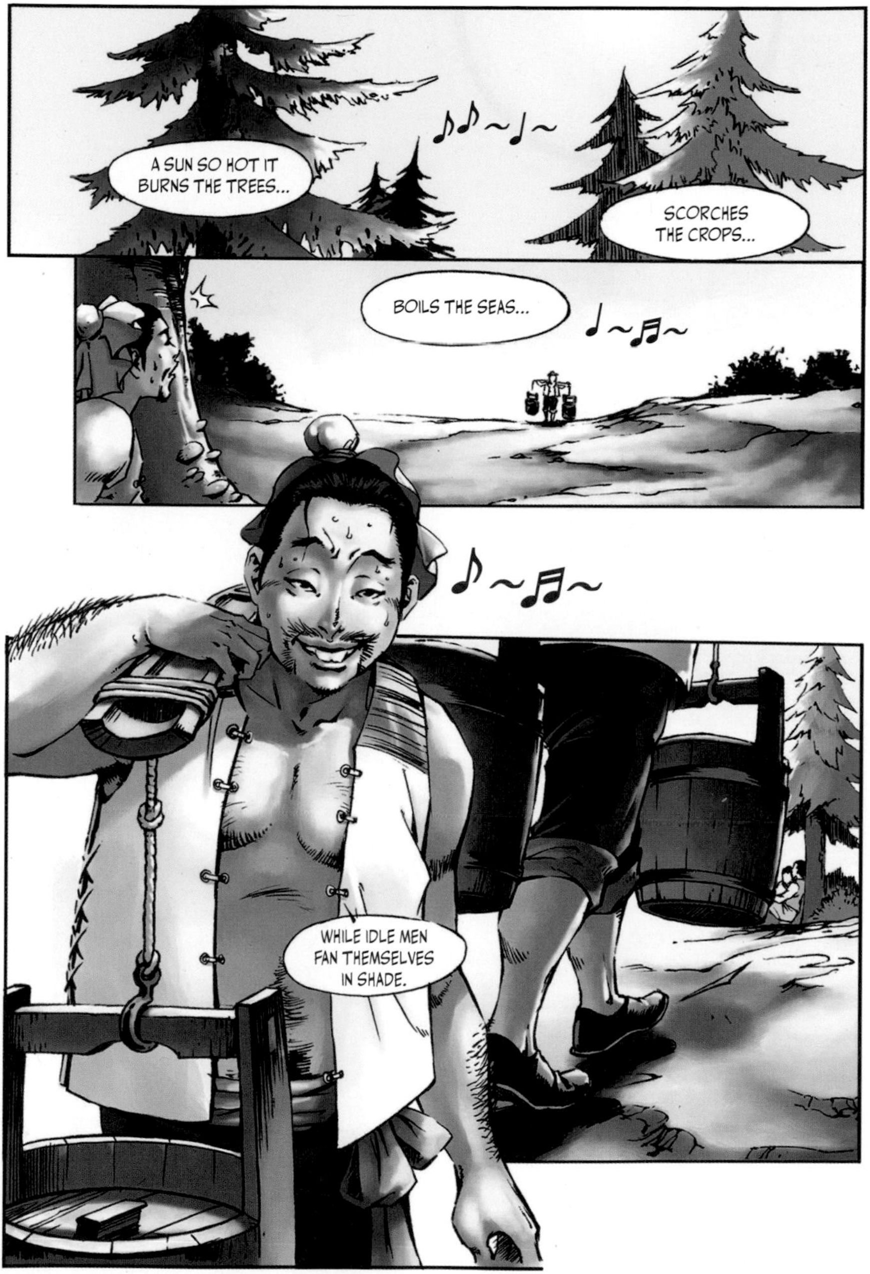
A SUN SO HOT IT BURNS THE TREES...
SCORCHES THE CROPS...
BOILS THE SEAS...
WHILE IDLE MEN FAN THEMSELVES IN SHADE.

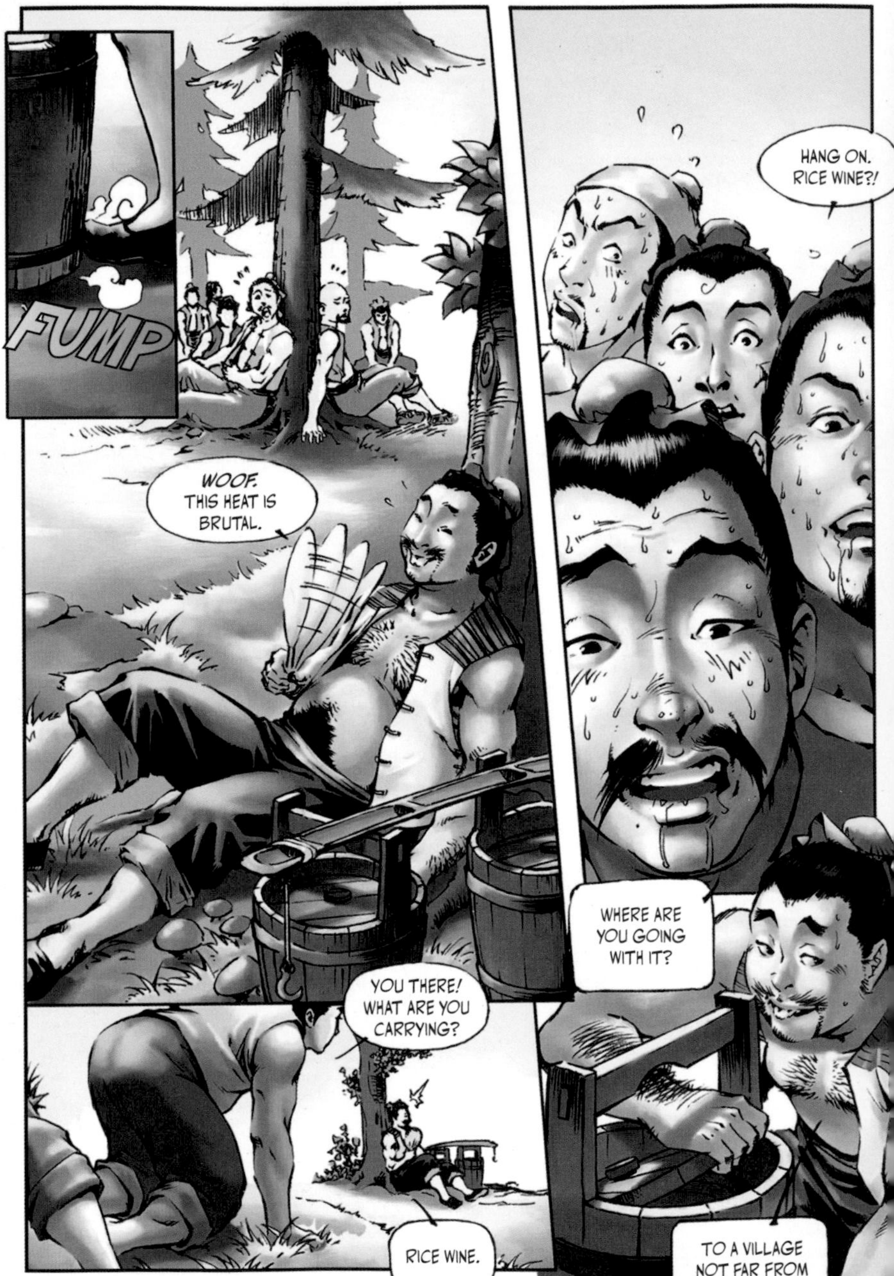
FUMP
WOOF. THIS HEAT IS BRUTAL.
YOU THERE! WHAT ARE YOU CARRYING?
RICE WINE.
HANG ON. RICE WINE?!
WHERE ARE YOU GOING WITH IT?
TO A VILLAGE NOT FAR FROM HERE. WHY?

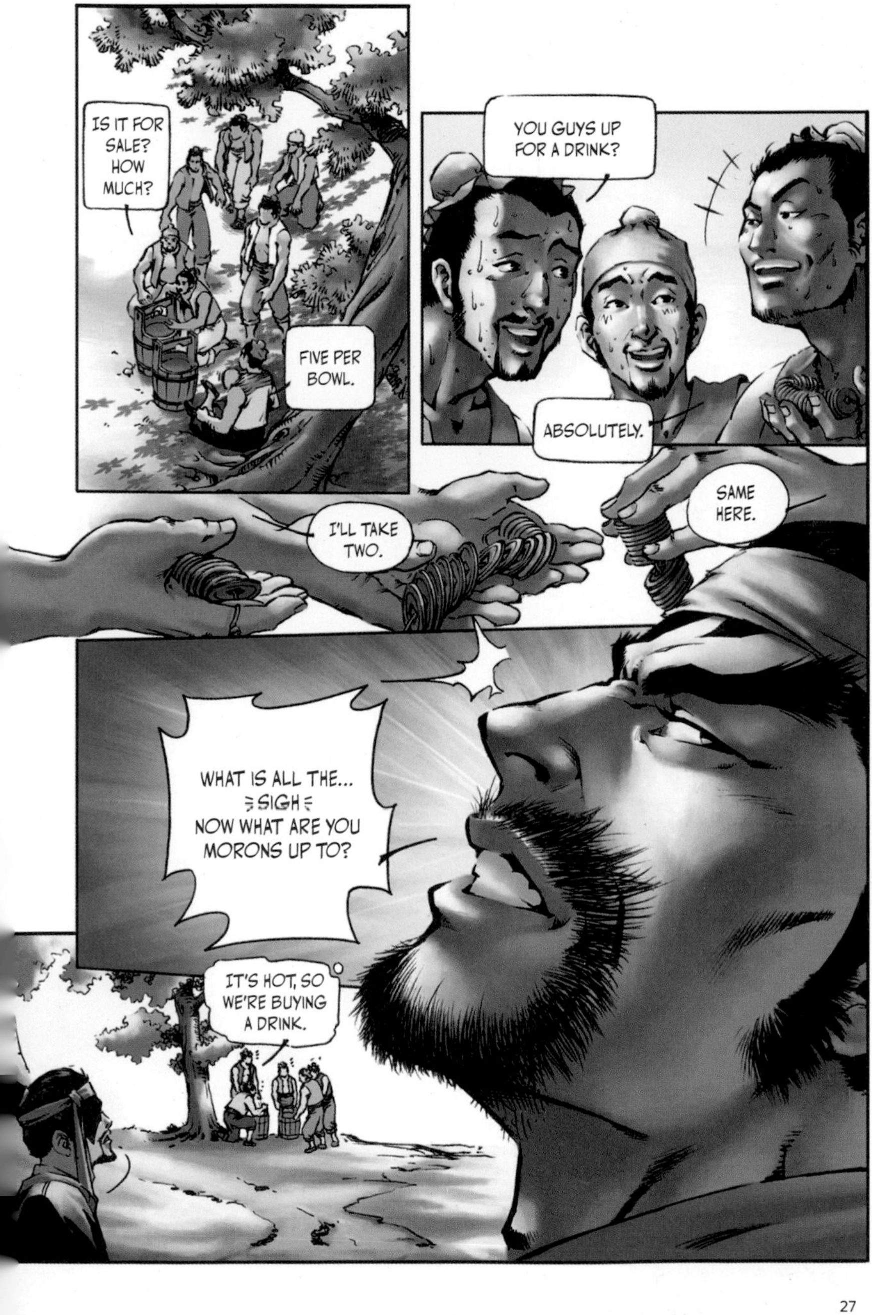
IS IT FOR SALE? HOW MUCH?
FIVE PER BOWL.
YOU GUYS UP FOR A DRINK?
ABSOLUTELY.
I'LL TAKE TWO.
SAME HERE.
WHAT IS ALL THE... ≡SIGH≡ NOW WHAT ARE YOU MORONS UP TO?
IT'S HOT, SO WE'RE BUYING A DRINK.

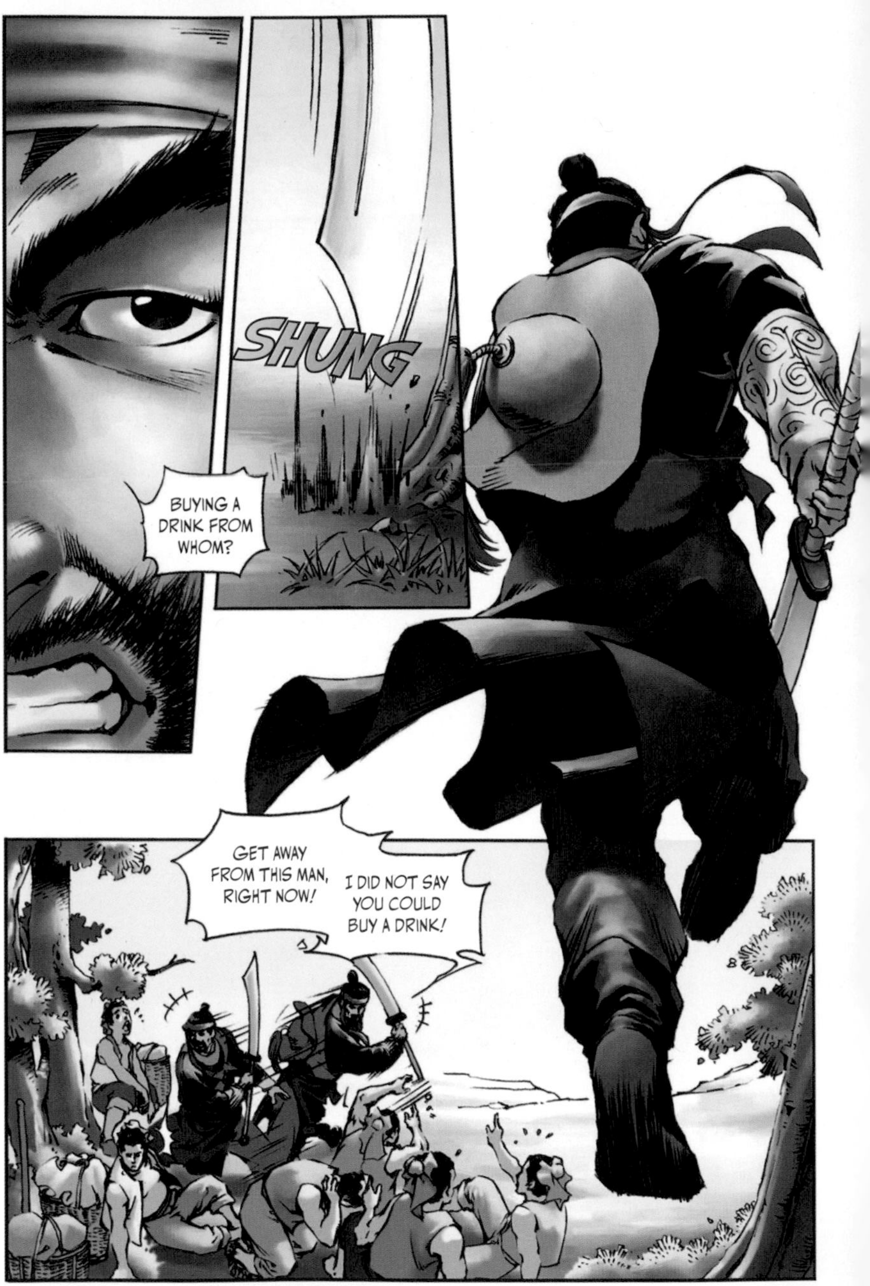
SHUNG
BUYING A DRINK FROM WHOM?
GET AWAY FROM THIS MAN, RIGHT NOW!
I DID NOT SAY YOU COULD BUY A DRINK!

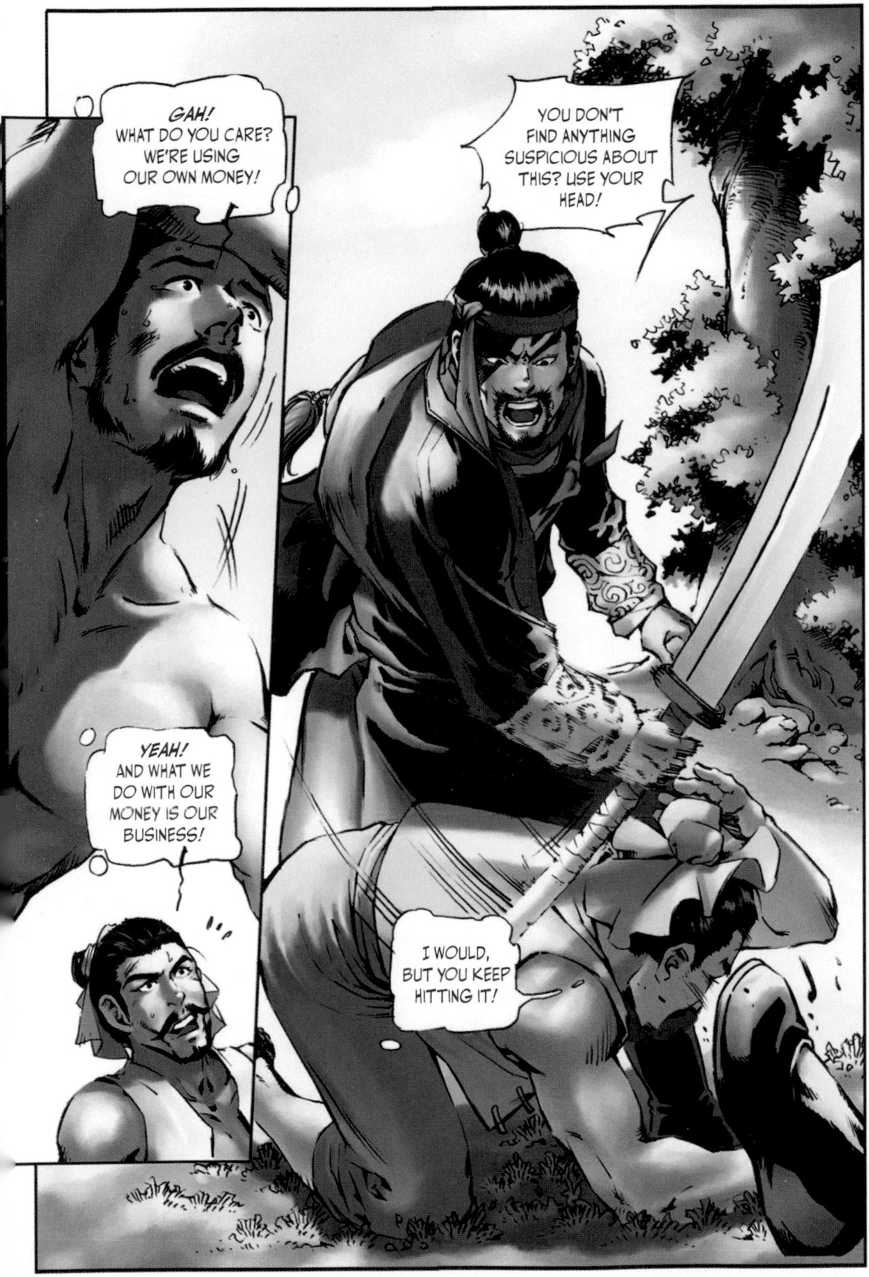
YOU DON'T FIND ANYTHING SUSPICIOUS ABOUT THIS? USE YOUR HEAD!
GAH! WHAT DO YOU CARE? WE'RE USING OUR OWN MONEY!
YEAH! AND WHAT WE DO WITH OUR MONEY IS OUR BUSINESS!
I WOULD, BUT YOU KEEP HITTING IT!

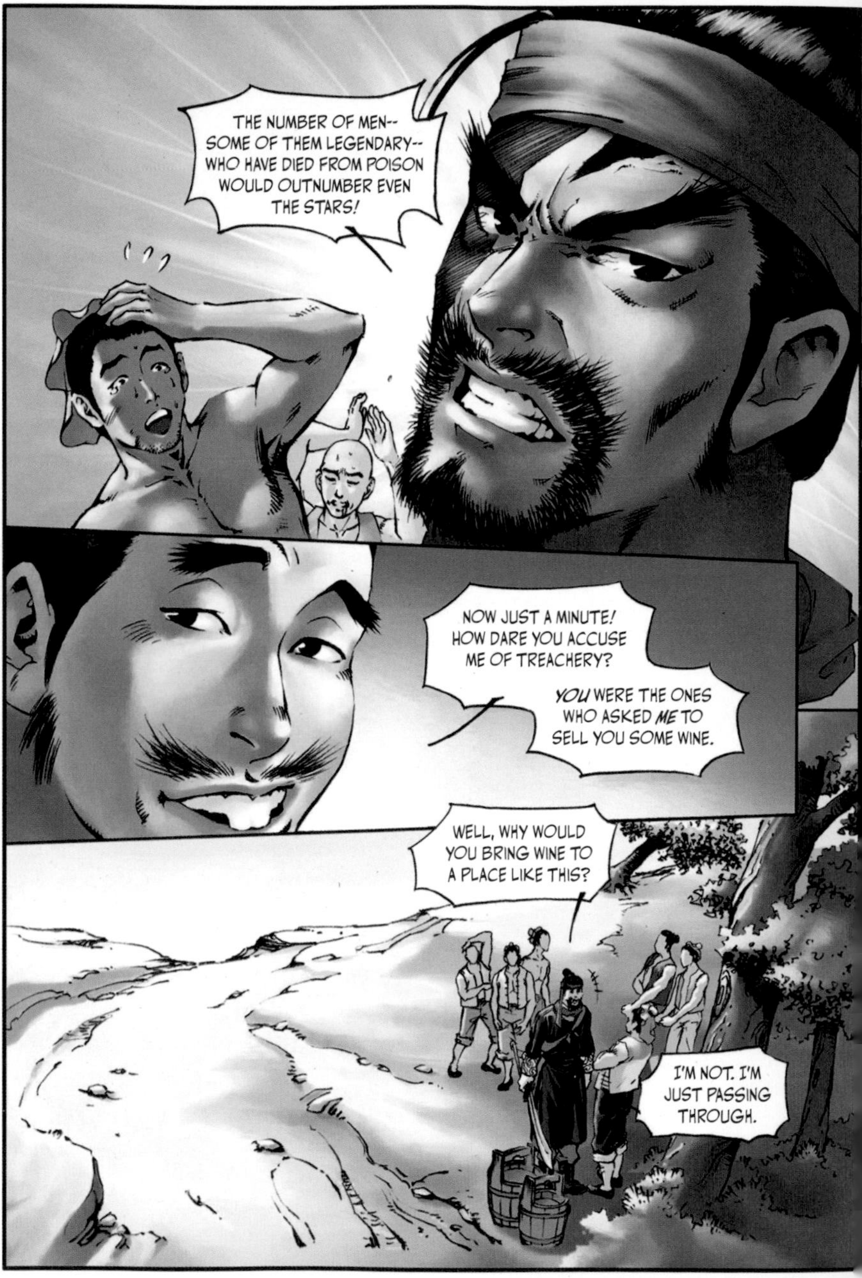
THE NUMBER OF MEN-- SOME OF THEM LEGENDARY-- WHO HAVE DIED FROM POISON WOULD OUTNUMBER EVEN THE STARS!
NOW JUST A MINUTE! HOW DARE YOU ACCUSE ME OF TREACHERY?
YOU WERE THE ONES WHO ASKED ME TO SELL YOU SOME WINE.
WELL, WHY WOULD YOU BRING WINE TO A PLACE LIKE THIS?
I'M NOT. I'M JUST PASSING THROUGH.

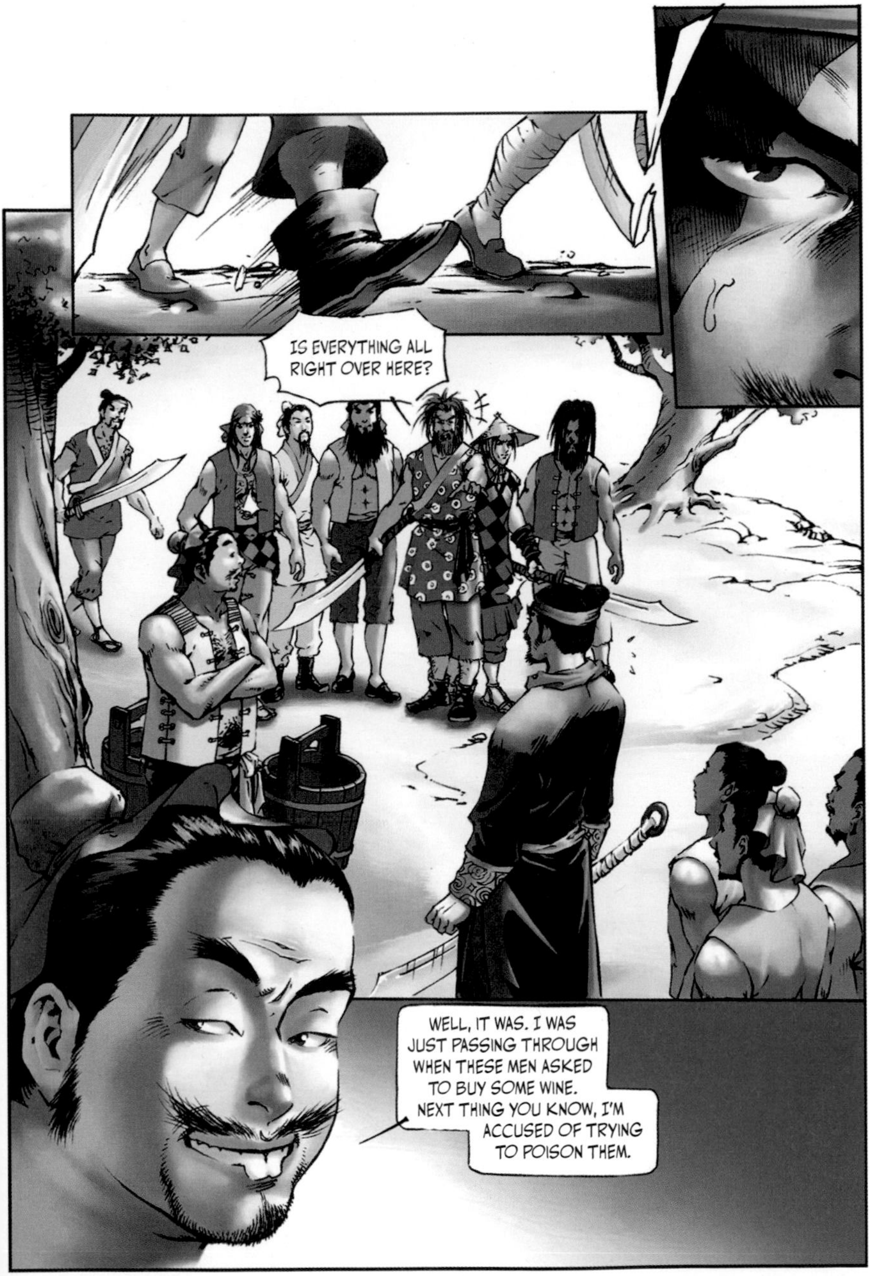
IS EVERYTHING ALL RIGHT OVER HERE?
WELL, IT WAS. I WAS JUST PASSING THROUGH WHEN THESE MEN ASKED TO BUY SOME WINE. NEXT THING YOU KNOW, I'M ACCUSED OF TRYING TO POISON THEM.

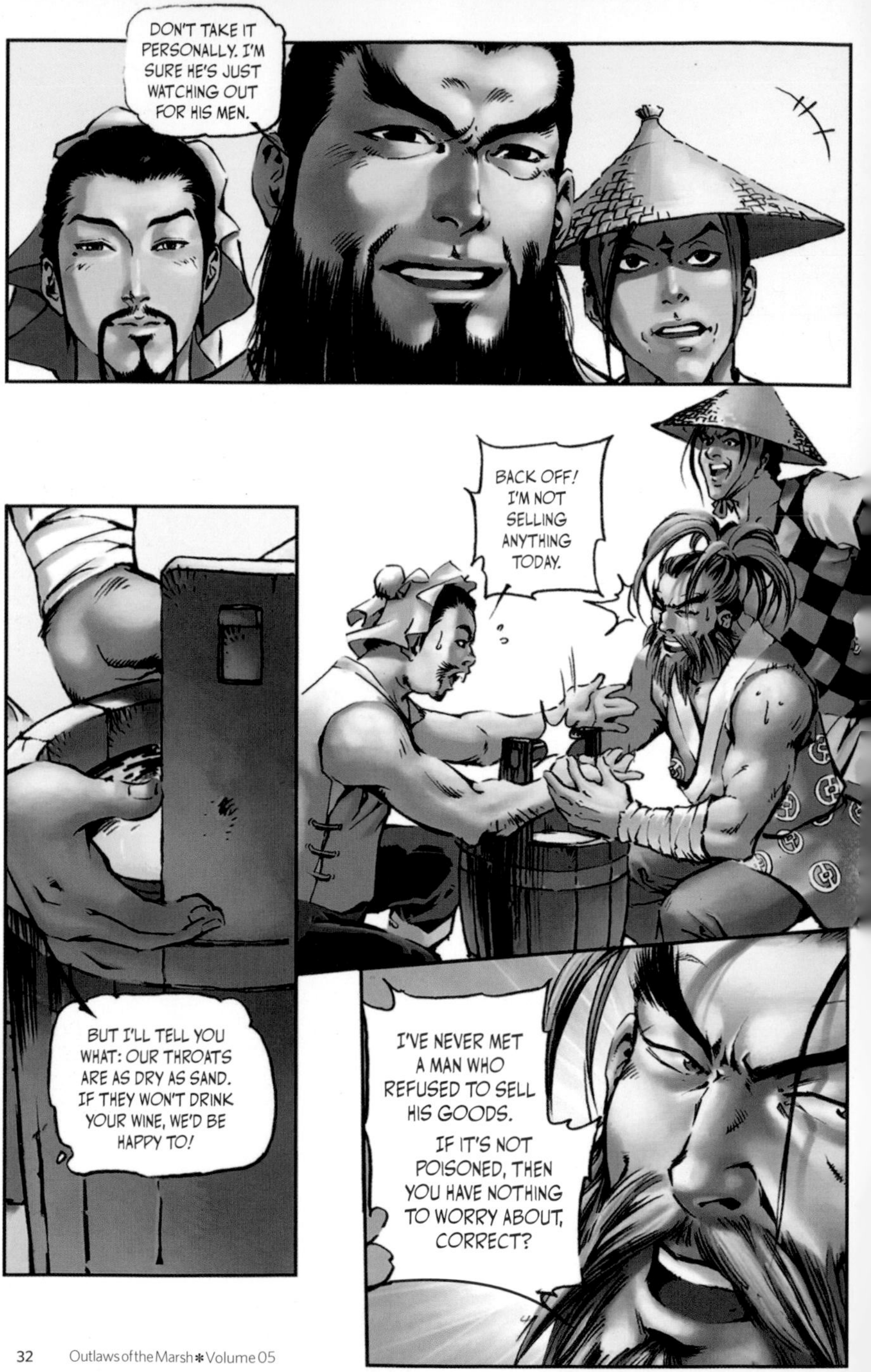
DON'T TAKE IT PERSONALLY. I'M SURE HE'S JUST WATCHING OUT FOR HIS MEN.
BACK OFF! I'M NOT SELLING ANYTHING TODAY.
BUT I'LL TELL YOU WHAT: OUR THROATS ARE AS DRY AS SAND. IF THEY WON'T DRINK YOUR WINE, WE'D BE HAPPY TO!
I'VE NEVER MET A MAN WHO REFUSED TO SELL HIS GOODS.
IF IT'S NOT POISONED, THEN YOU HAVE NOTHING TO WORRY ABOUT, CORRECT?

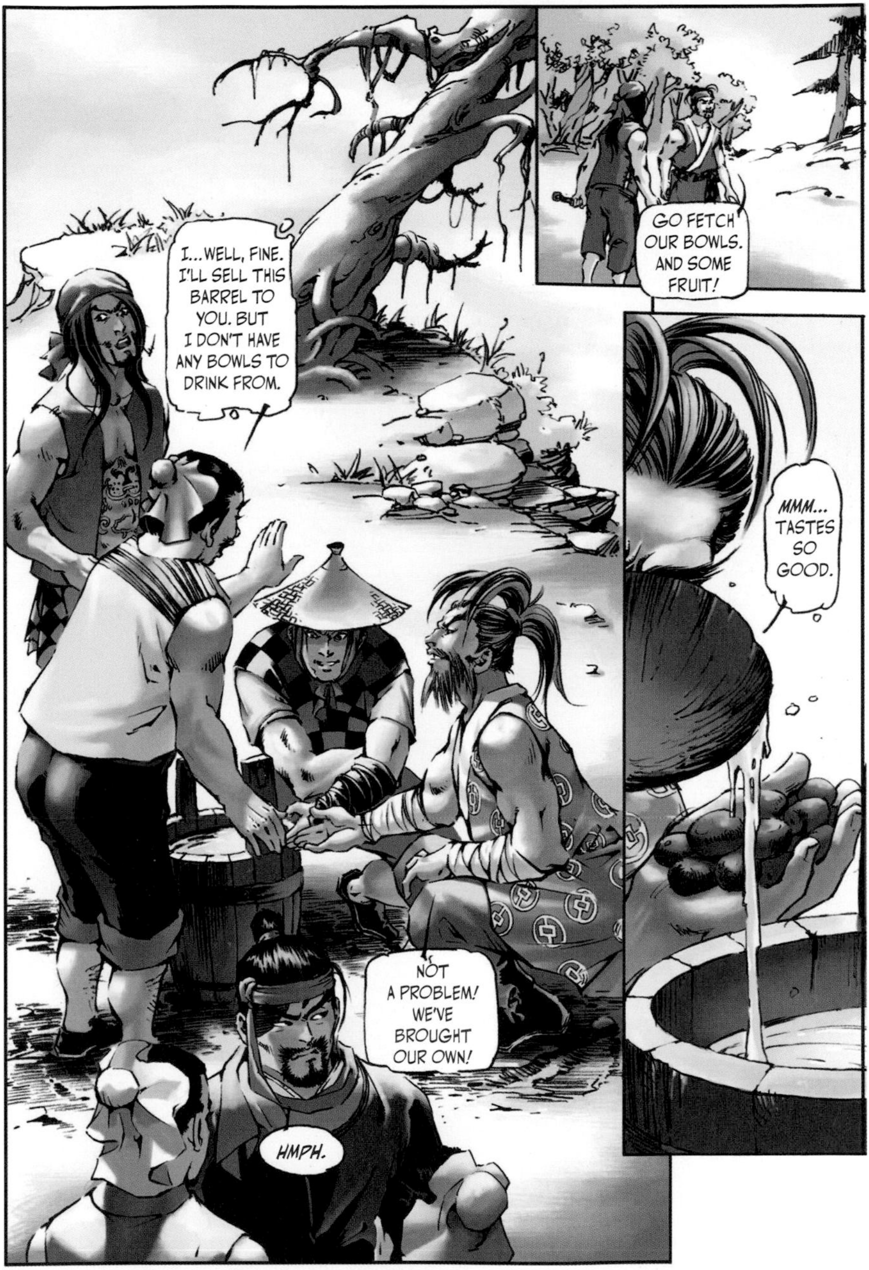
GO FETCH OUR BOWLS. AND SOME FRUIT!
I...WELL, FINE. I'LL SELL THIS BARREL TO YOU. BUT I DON'T HAVE ANY BOWLS TO DRINK FROM.
NOT A PROBLEM! WE'VE BROUGHT OUR OWN!
HMPH.
MMM... TASTES SO GOOD.

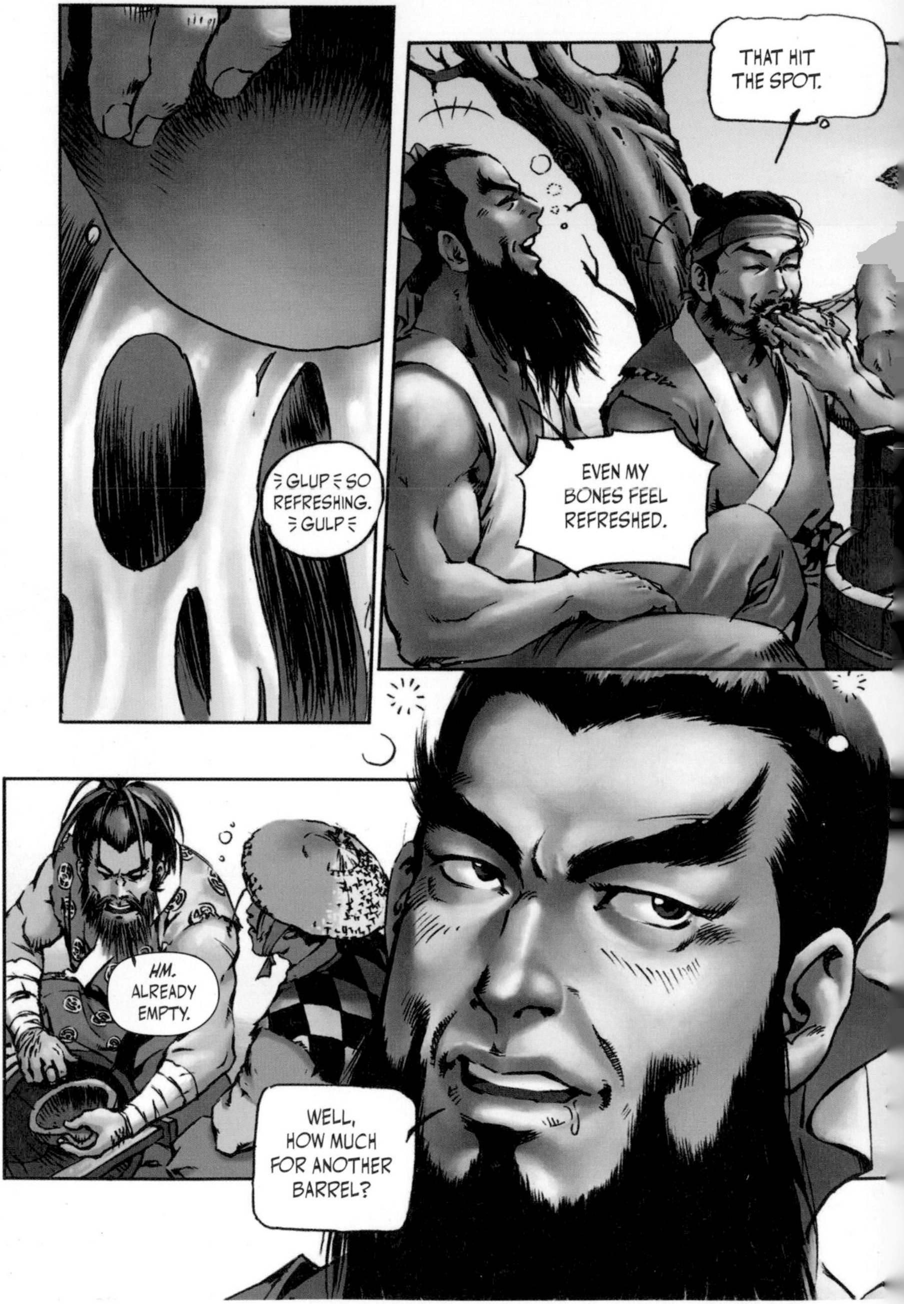
⁼GLUP⁼ SO REFRESHING. ⁼GLUP⁼
THAT HIT THE SPOT.
EVEN MY BONES FEEL REFRESHED.
HM. ALREADY EMPTY.
WELL, HOW MUCH FOR ANOTHER BARREL?

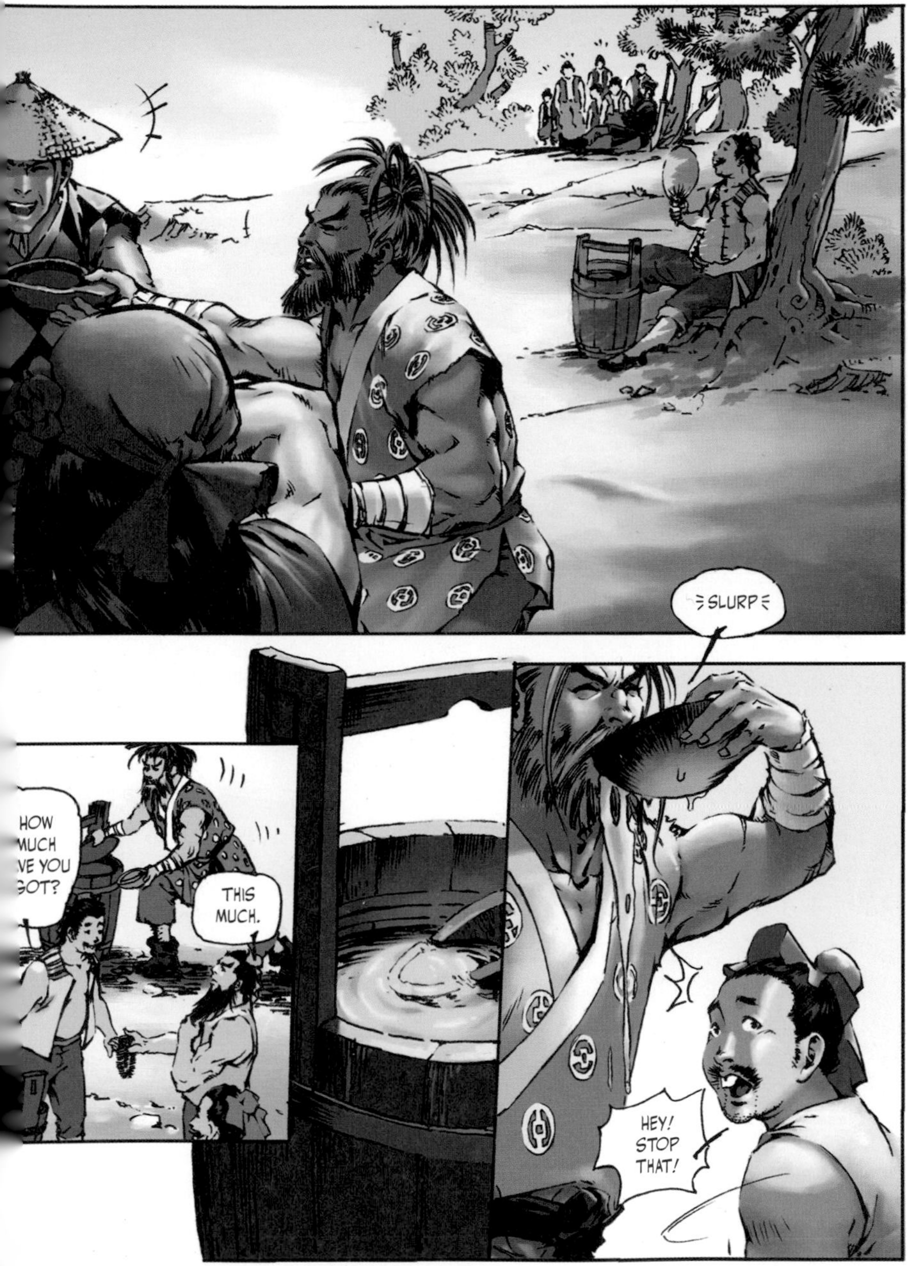
SLURP
HOW MUCH
VE YOU
GOT?
THIS MUCH.
HEY! STOP THAT!

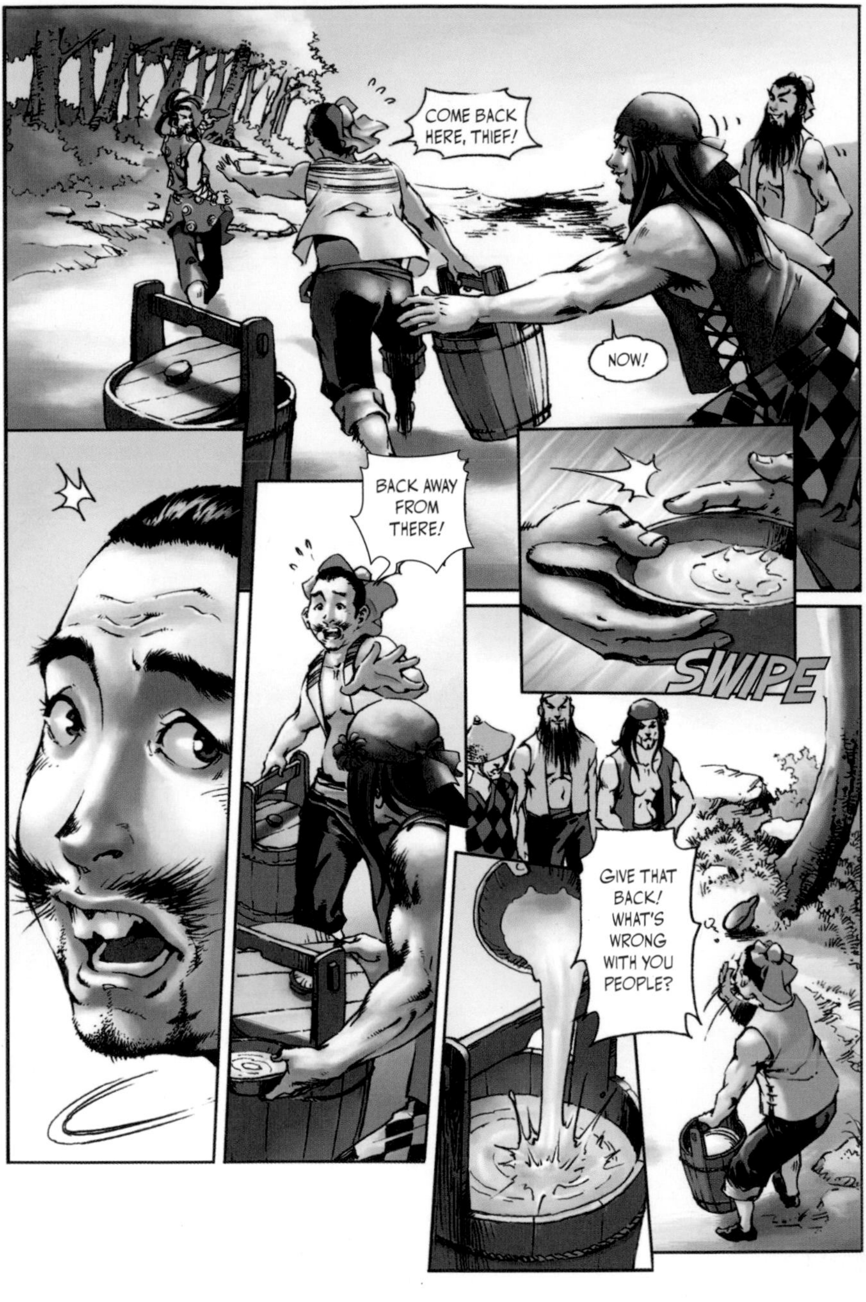
COME BACK HERE, THIEF!
NOW!
BACK AWAY FROM THERE!
SWIPE
GIVE THAT BACK! WHAT'S WRONG WITH YOU PEOPLE?

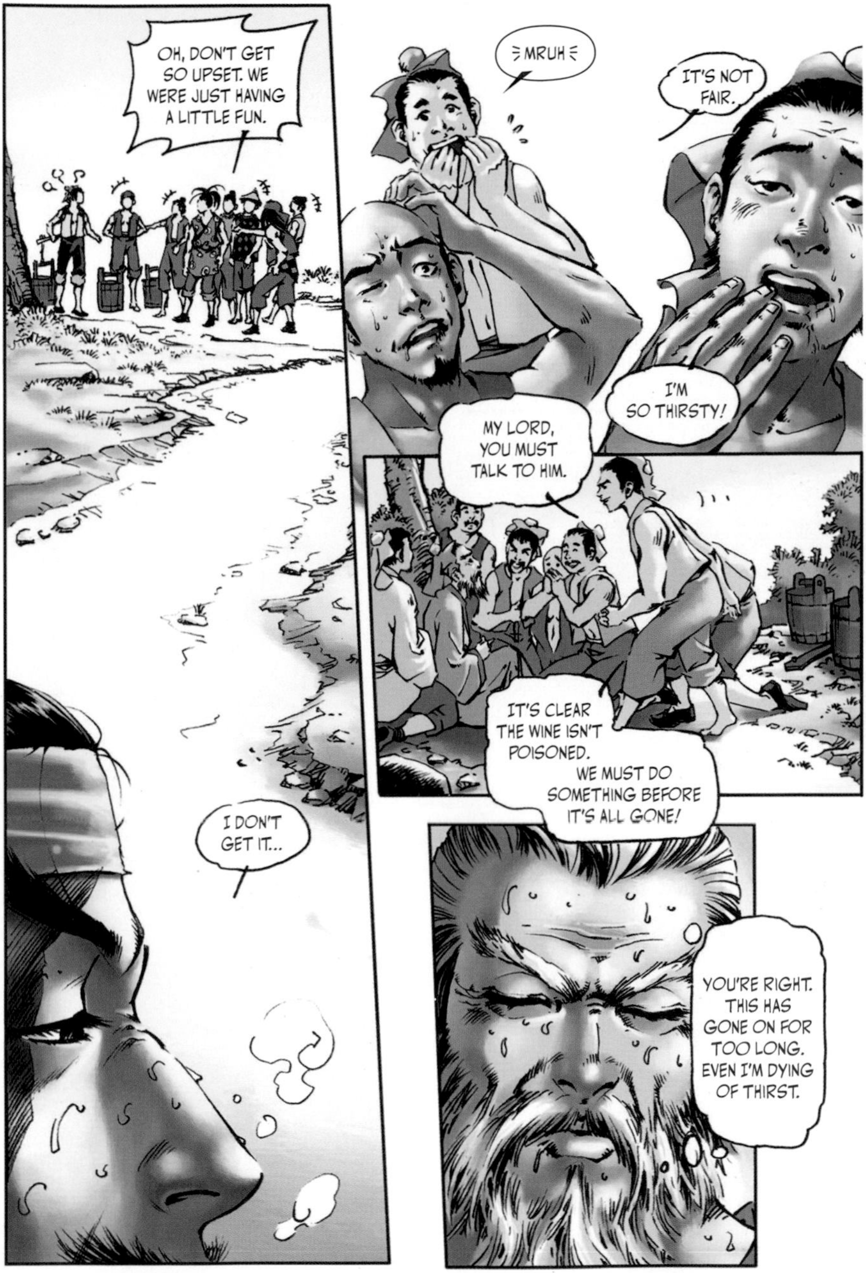
OH, DON'T GET SO UPSET. WE WERE JUST HAVING A LITTLE FUN.
I DON'T GET IT...
MRUH
IT'S NOT FAIR.
I'M SO THIRSTY!
MY LORD, YOU MUST TALK TO HIM.
IT'S CLEAR THE WINE ISN'T POISONED.
WE MUST DO SOMETHING BEFORE IT'S ALL GONE!
YOU'RE RIGHT. THIS HAS GONE ON FOR TOO LONG. EVEN I'M DYING OF THIRST.

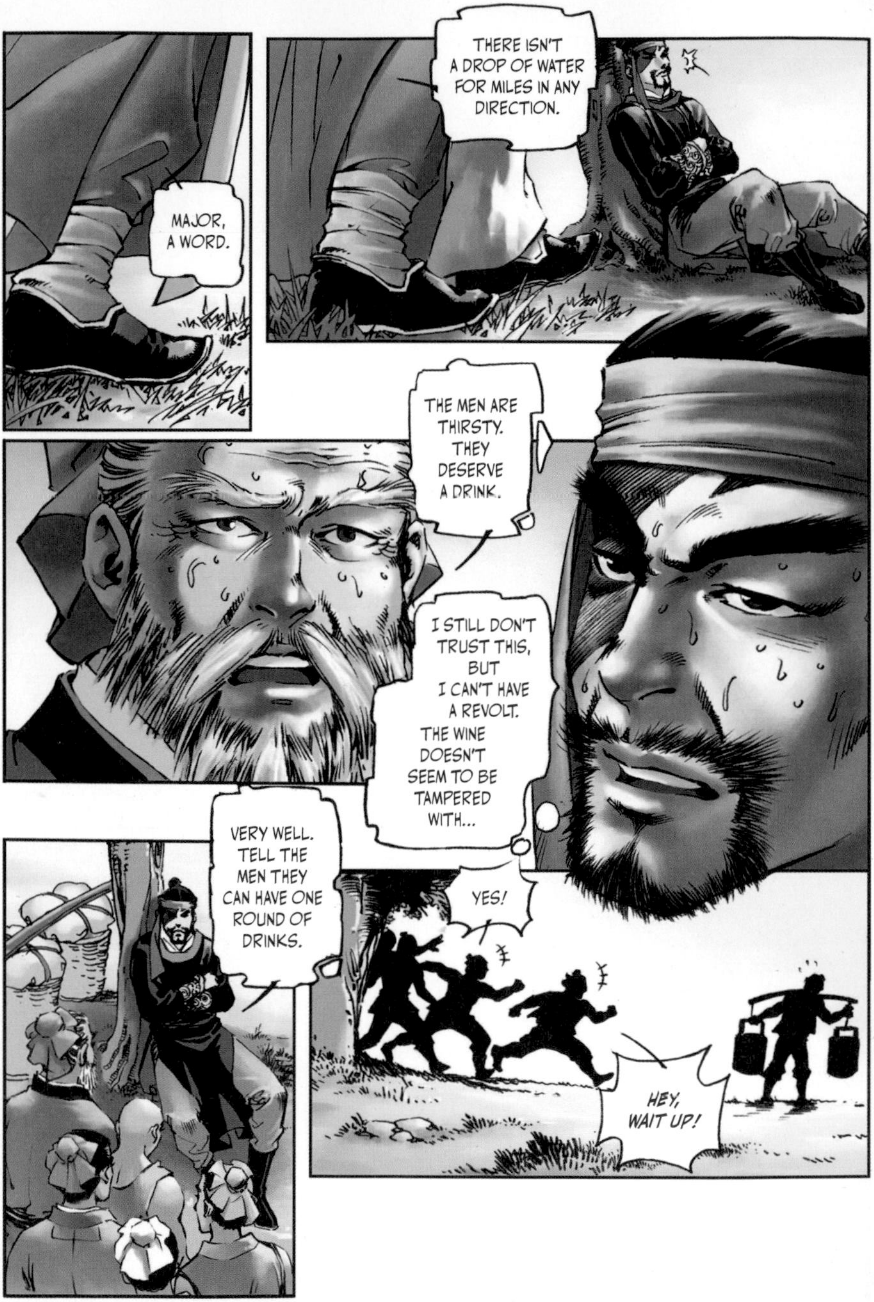
MAJOR, A WORD.
THERE ISN'T A DROP OF WATER FOR MILES IN ANY DIRECTION.
THE MEN ARE THIRSTY. THEY DESERVE A DRINK.
I STILL DON'T TRUST THIS, BUT I CAN'T HAVE A REVOLT. THE WINE DOESN'T SEEM TO BE TAMPERED WITH...
VERY WELL. TELL THE MEN THEY CAN HAVE ONE ROUND OF DRINKS.
YES!
HEY, WAIT UP!

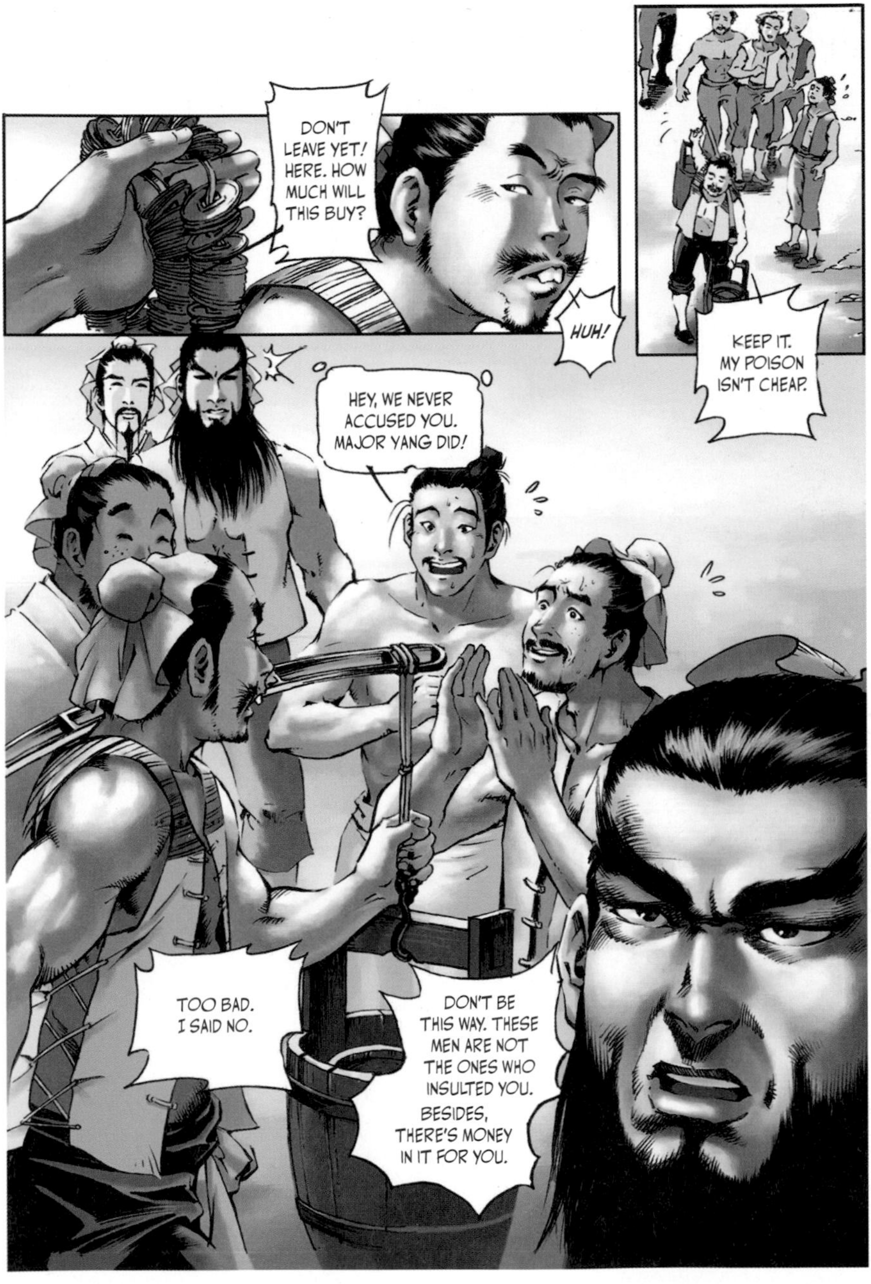
DON'T LEAVE YET! HERE. HOW MUCH WILL THIS BUY?
HUH!
KEEP IT. MY POISON ISN'T CHEAP.
HEY, WE NEVER ACCUSED YOU. MAJOR YANG DID!
TOO BAD. I SAID NO.
DON'T BE THIS WAY. THESE MEN ARE NOT THE ONES WHO INSULTED YOU.
BESIDES, THERE'S MONEY IN IT FOR YOU.

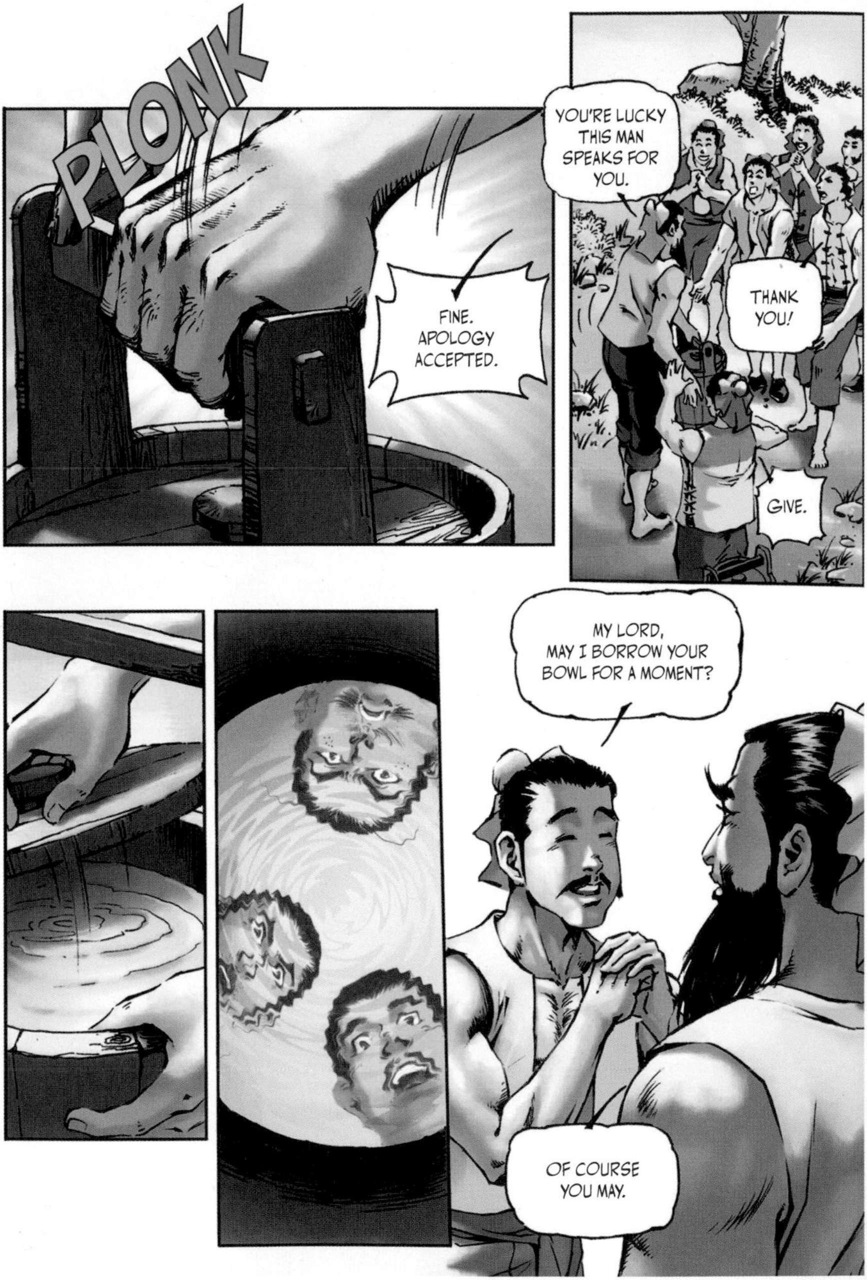
PLONK
FINE. APOLOGY ACCEPTED.
YOU'RE LUCKY THIS MAN SPEAKS FOR YOU.
THANK YOU!
GIVE.
MY LORD, MAY I BORROW YOUR BOWL FOR A MOMENT?
OF COURSE YOU MAY.

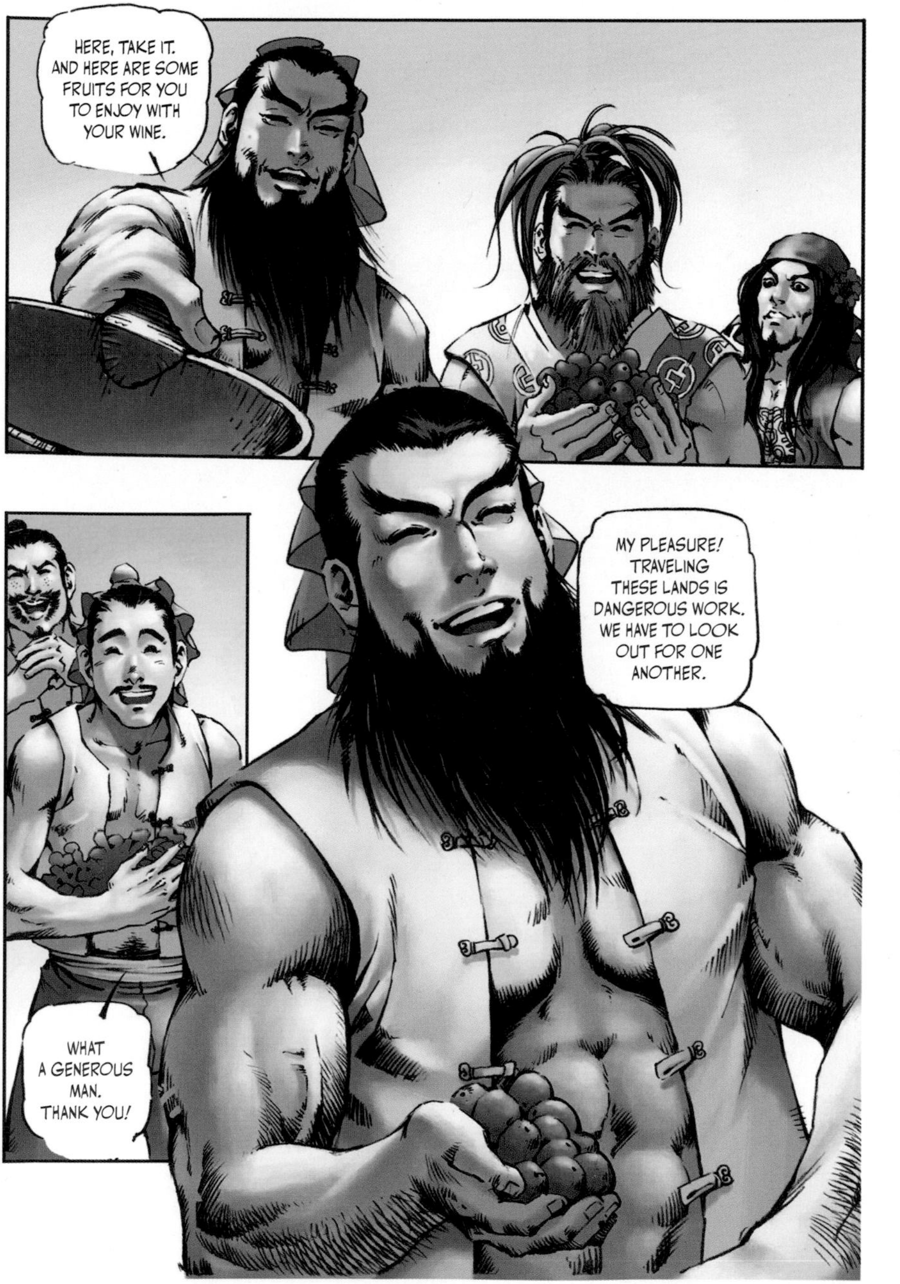
HERE, TAKE IT. AND HERE ARE SOME FRUITS FOR YOU TO ENJOY WITH YOUR WINE.
MY PLEASURE! TRAVELING THESE LANDS IS DANGEROUS WORK. WE HAVE TO LOOK OUT FOR ONE ANOTHER.
WHAT A GENEROUS MAN. THANK YOU!

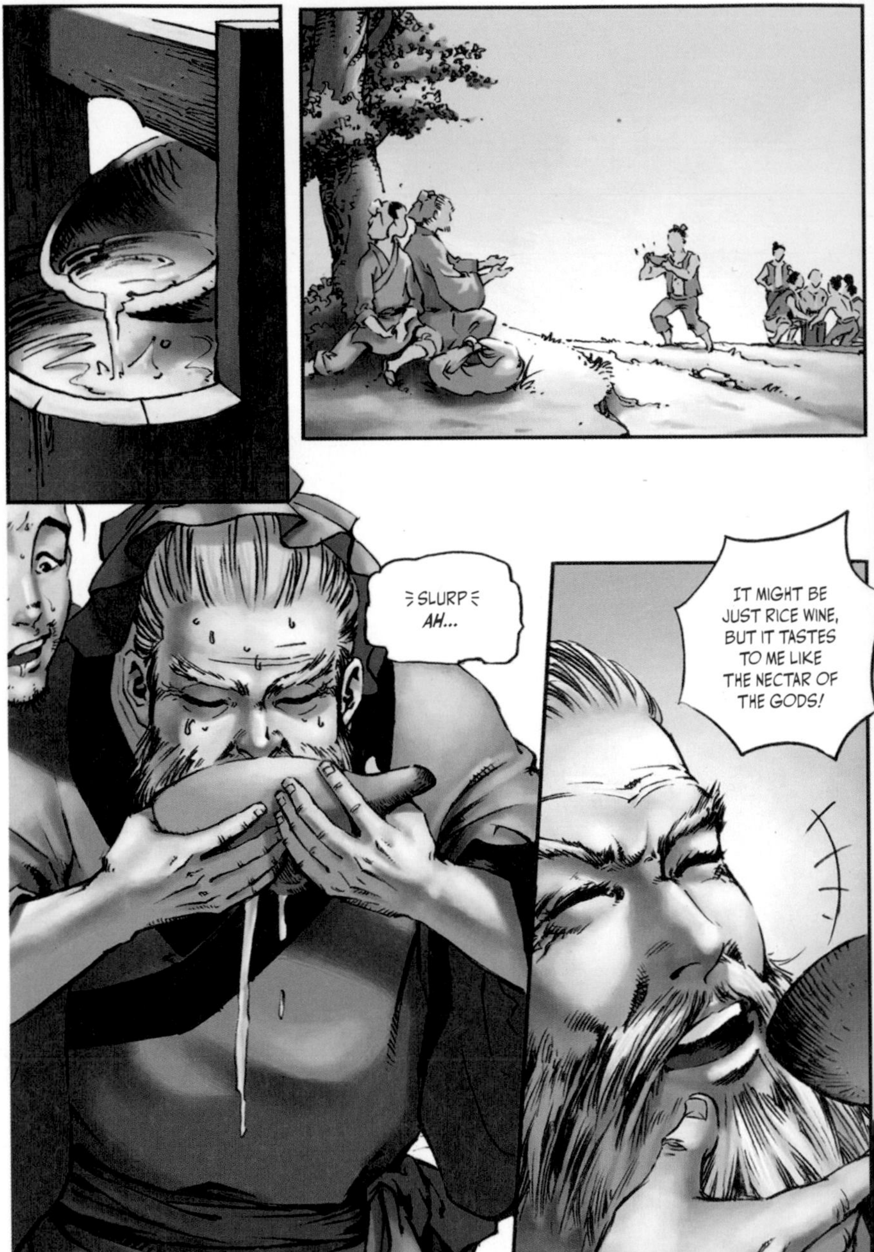

SLURP
AH...
IT MIGHT BE JUST RICE WINE, BUT IT TASTES TO ME LIKE THE NECTAR OF THE GODS!

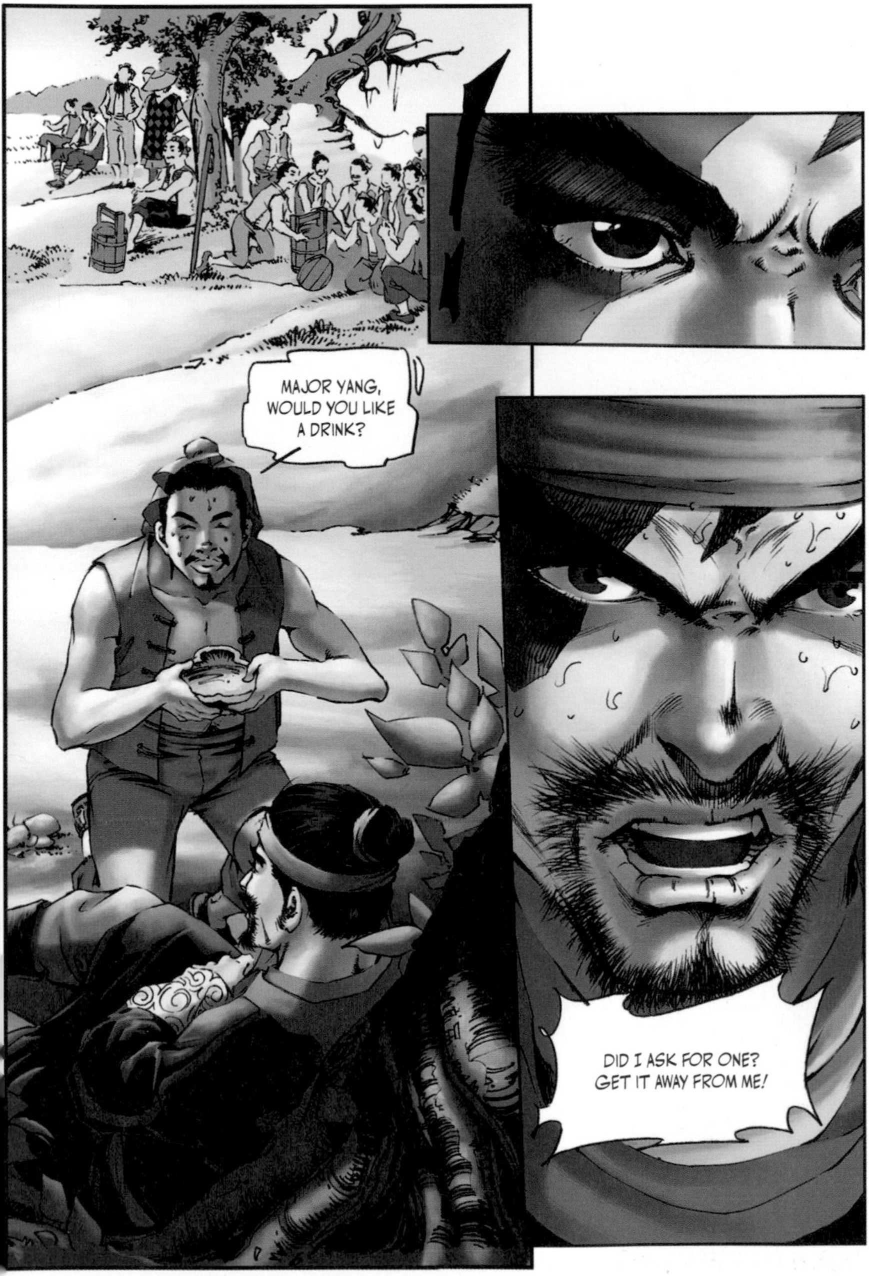
MAJOR YANG, WOULD YOU LIKE A DRINK?
DID I ASK FOR ONE? GET IT AWAY FROM ME!

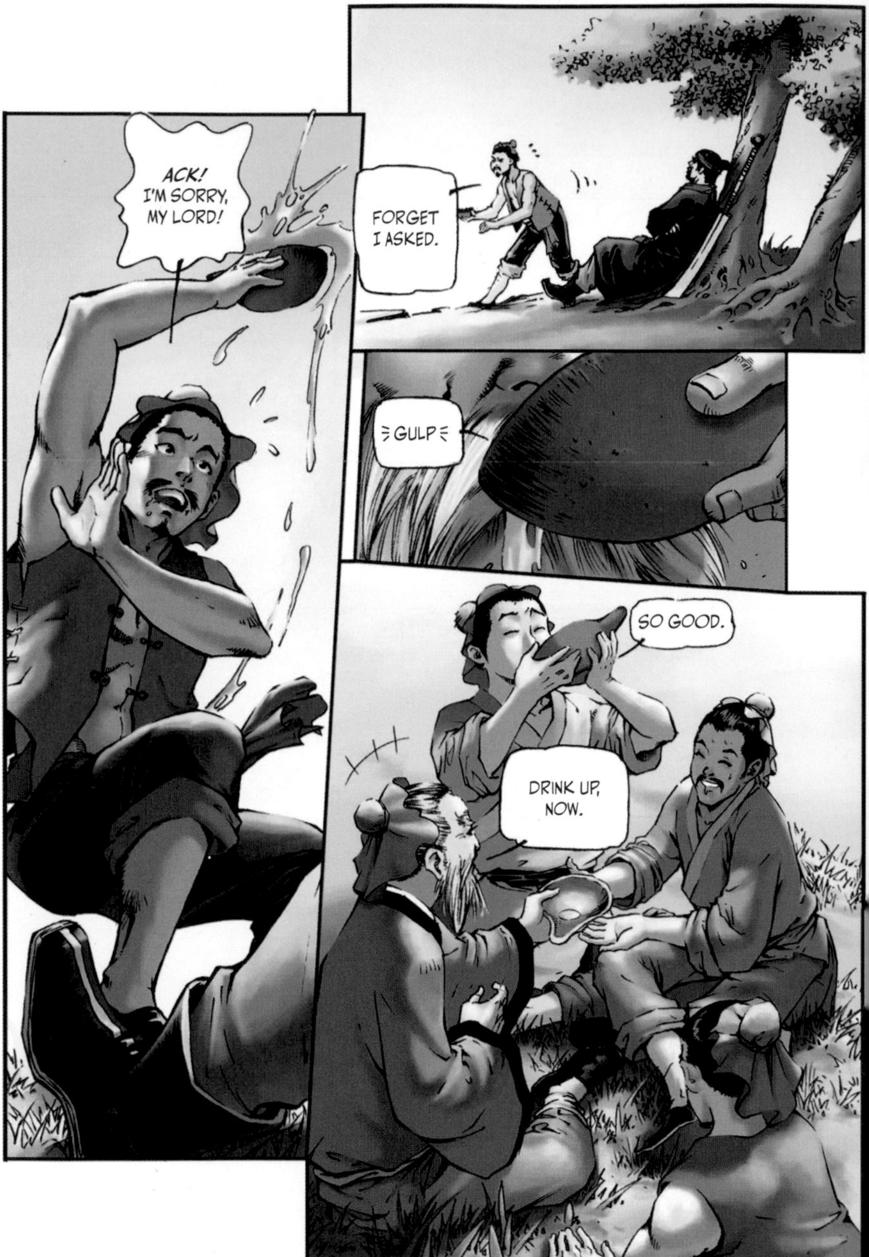
ACK! I'M SORRY, MY LORD!
FORGET I ASKED.
GULP
SO GOOD.
DRINK UP, NOW.

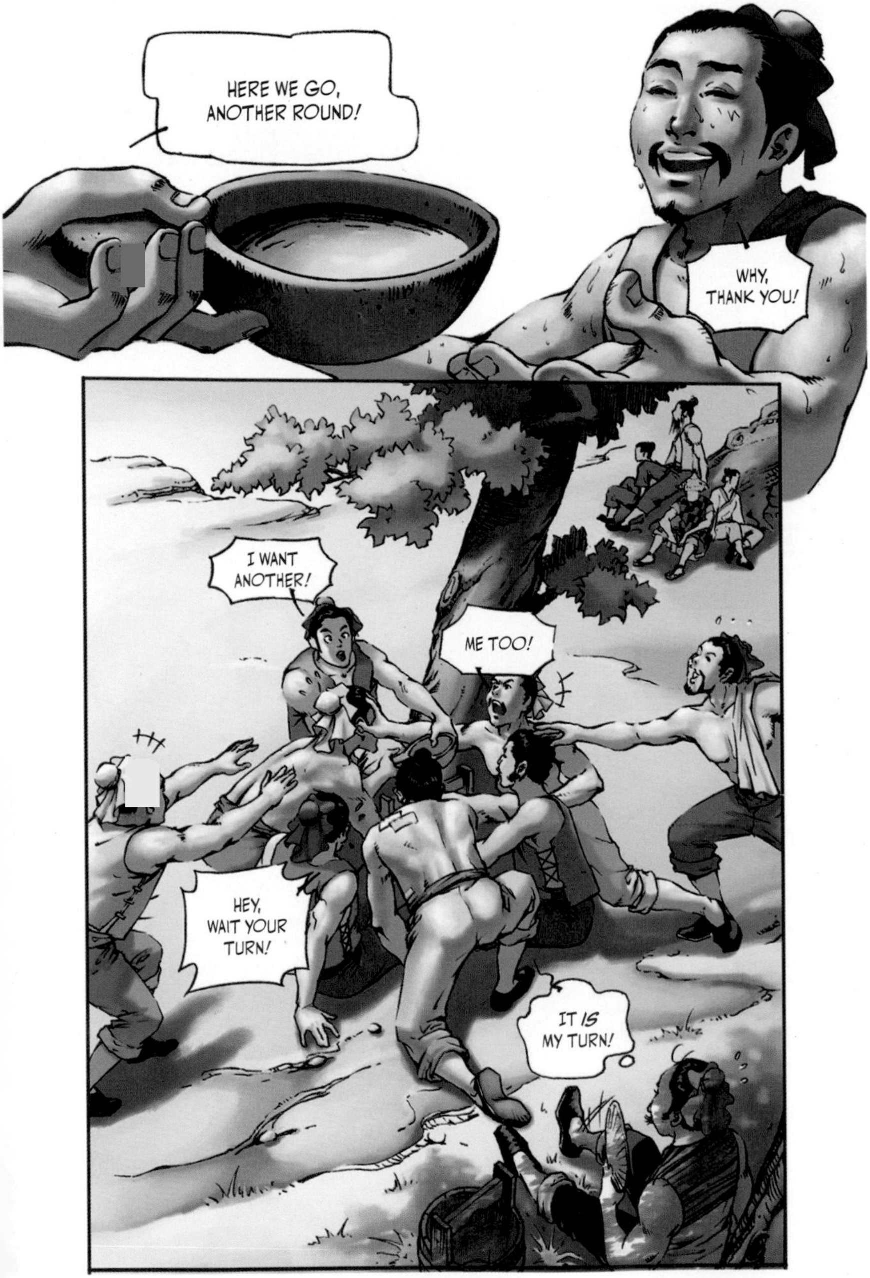

HERE WE GO, ANOTHER ROUND!
WHY, THANK YOU!
I WANT ANOTHER!
ME TOO!
HEY, WAIT YOUR TURN!
IT IS MY TURN!

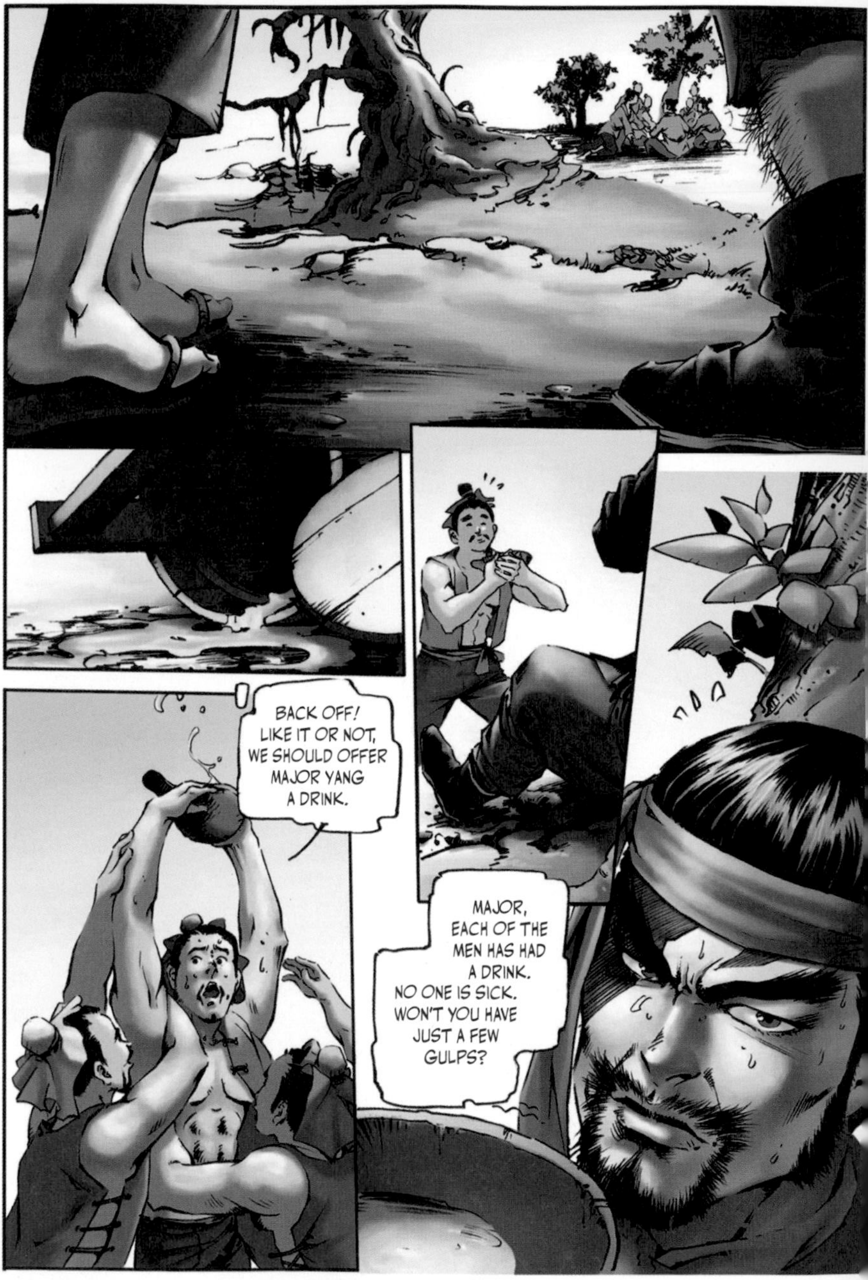
BACK OFF!
LIKE IT OR NOT, WE SHOULD OFFER MAJOR YANG A DRINK.
MAJOR, EACH OF THE MEN HAS HAD A DRINK. NO ONE IS SICK. WON'T YOU HAVE JUST A FEW GULPS?

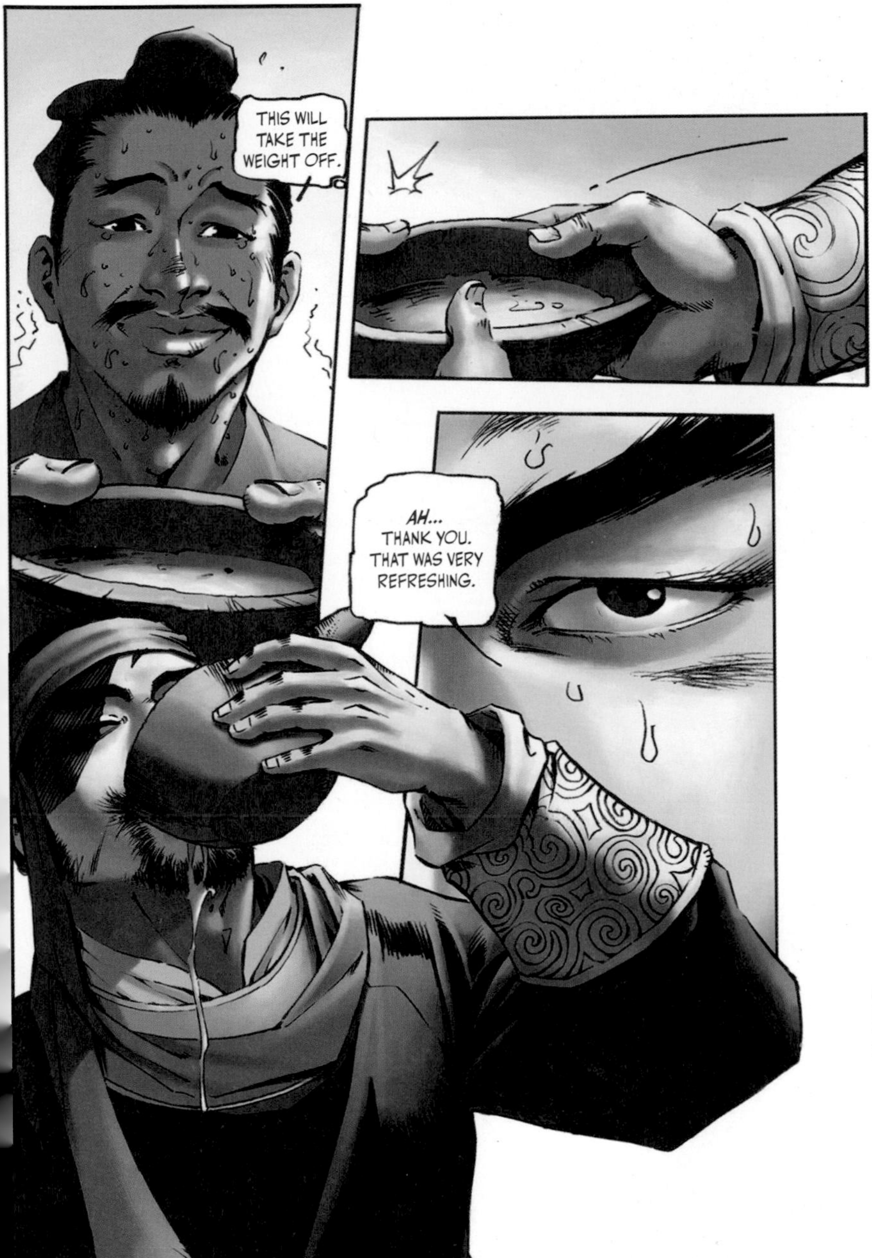
THIS WILL TAKE THE WEIGHT OFF.
AH... THANK YOU. THAT WAS VERY REFRESHING.

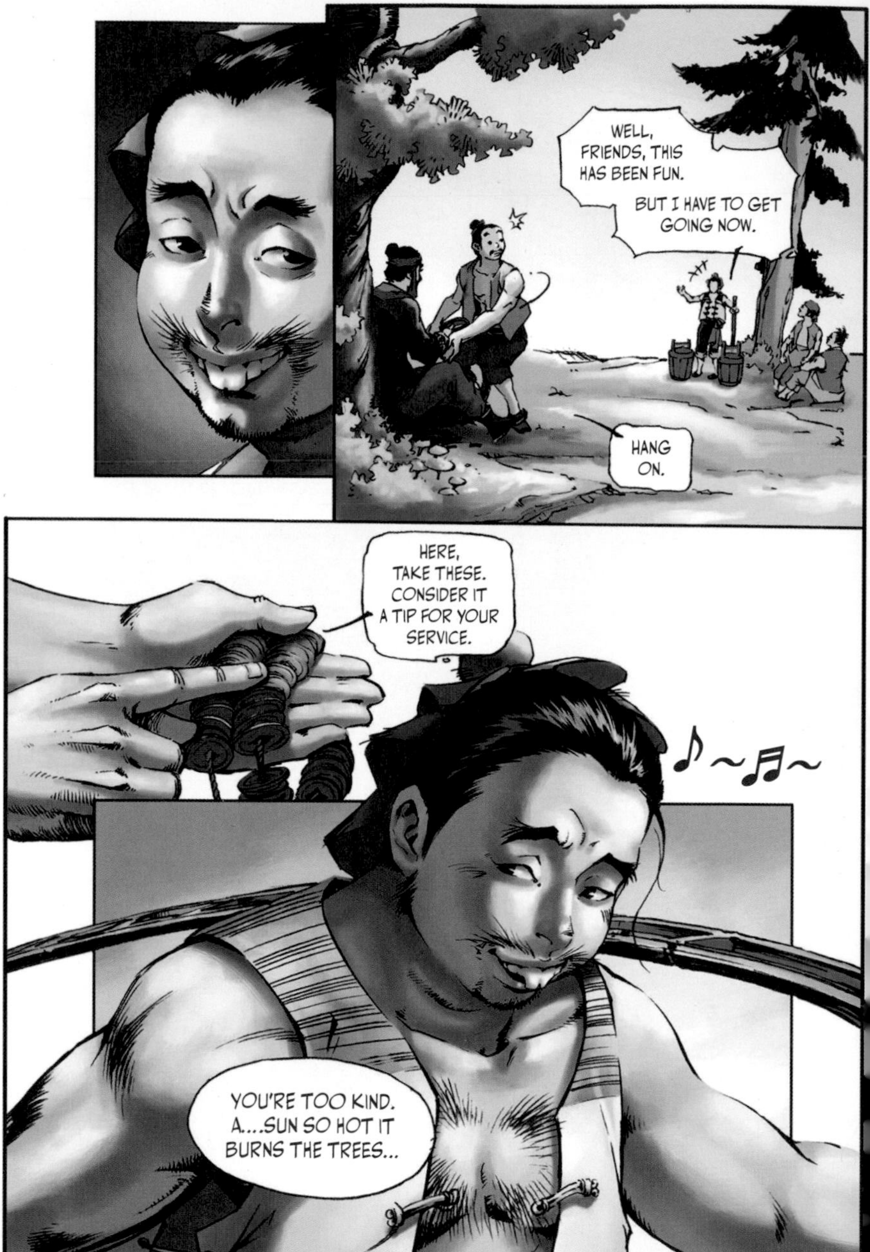
WELL, FRIENDS, THIS HAS BEEN FUN.
BUT I HAVE TO GET GOING NOW.
HANG ON.
HERE, TAKE THESE. CONSIDER IT A TIP FOR YOUR SERVICE.
♪~♬~
YOU'RE TOO KIND. A....SUN SO HOT IT BURNS THE TREES...

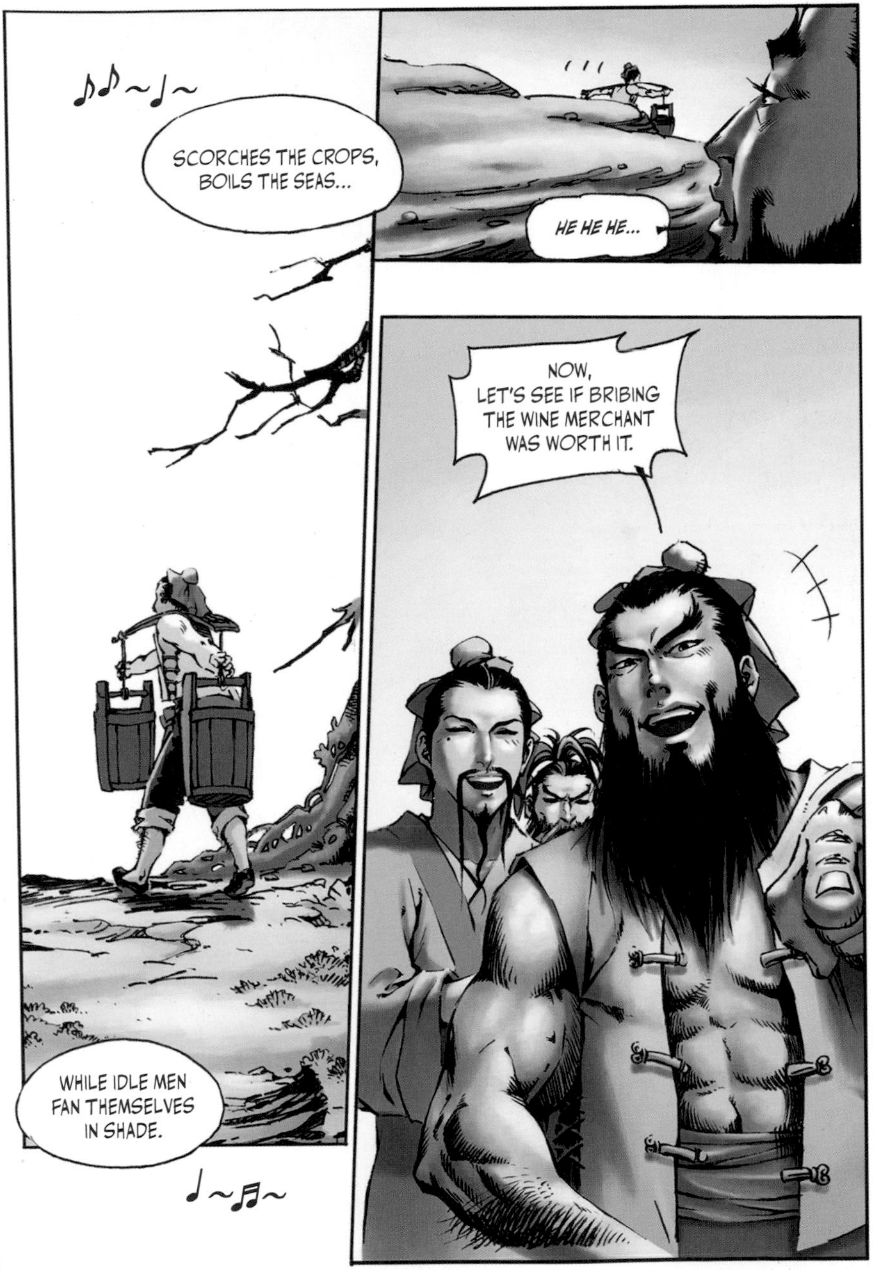
♪♪~♩~
SCORCHES THE CROPS, BOILS THE SEAS...
HE HE HE...
WHILE IDLE MEN FAN THEMSELVES IN SHADE.
♩~♬~
NOW, LET'S SEE IF BRIBING THE WINE MERCHANT WAS WORTH IT.

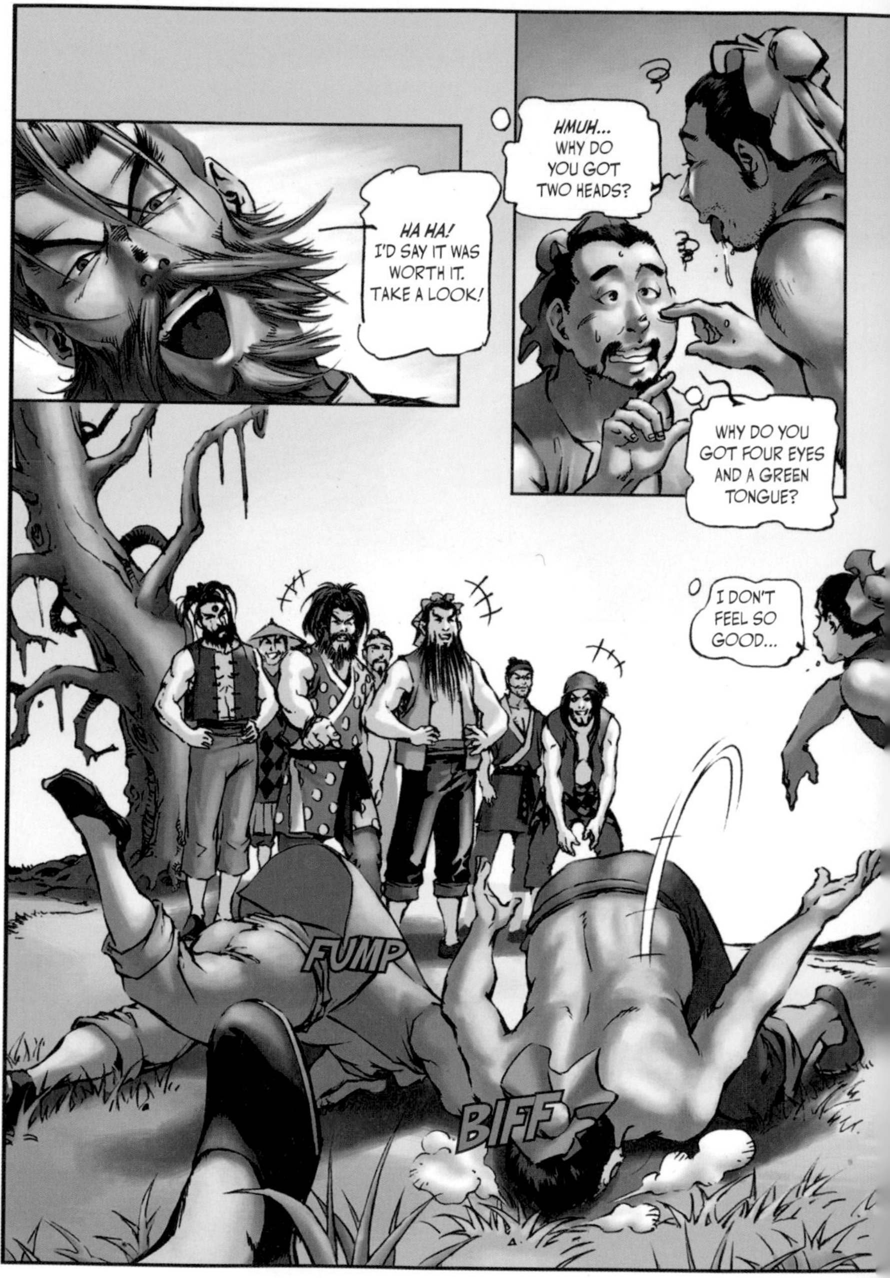
HA HA!
I'D SAY IT WAS WORTH IT. TAKE A LOOK!
HMUH... WHY DO YOU GOT TWO HEADS?
WHY DO YOU GOT FOUR EYES AND A GREEN TONGUE?
I DON'T FEEL SO GOOD...
FUMP
BIFF

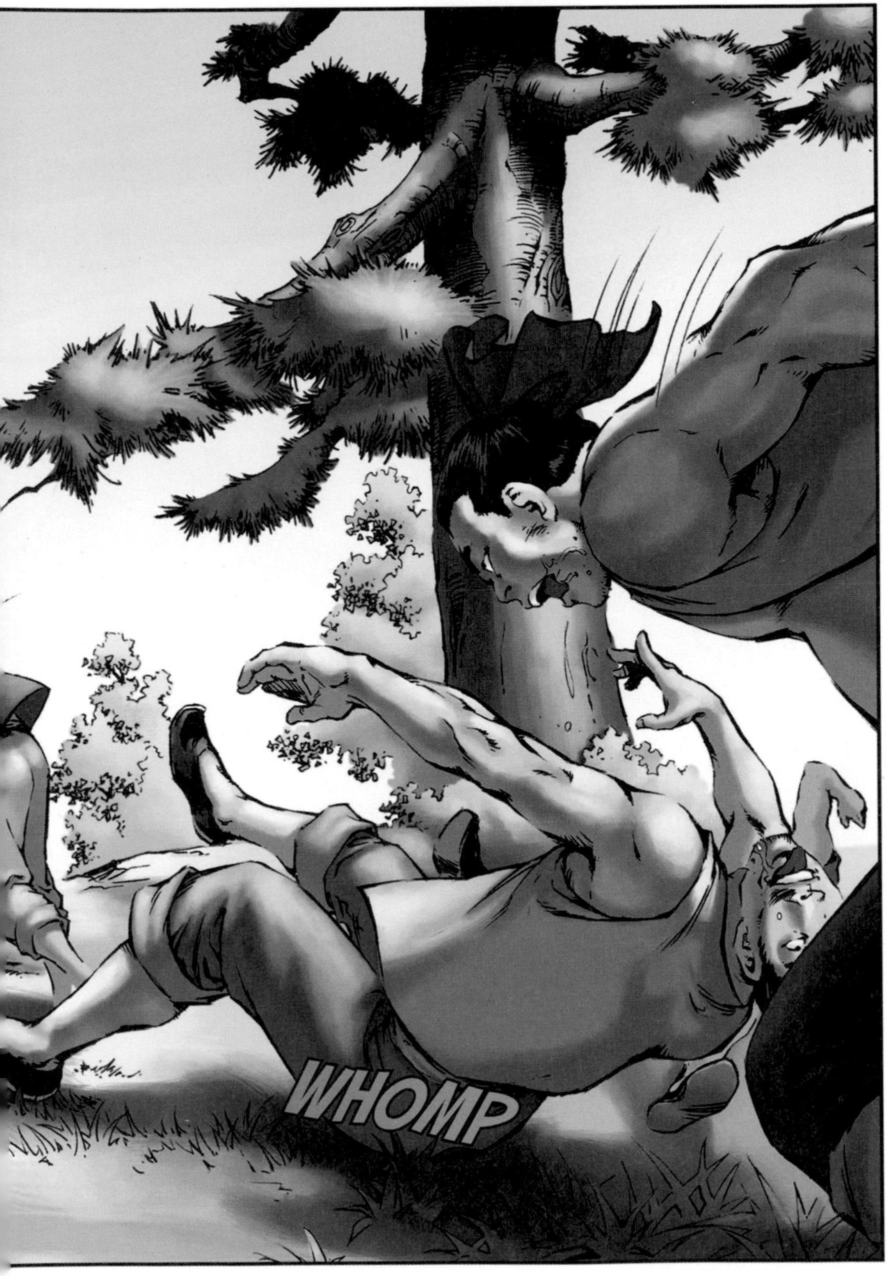
WHOMP

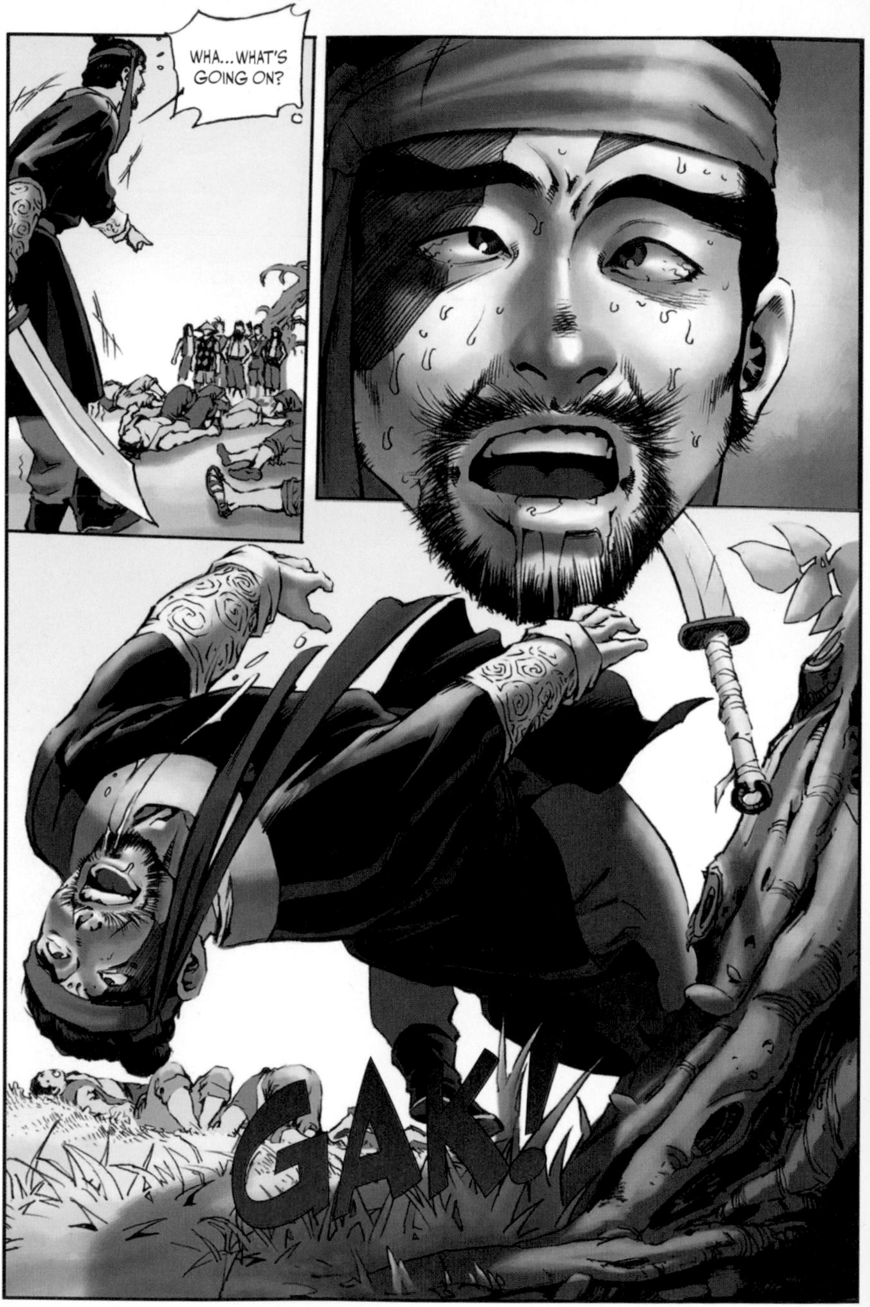
WHA...WHAT'S GOING ON?
GAK!!

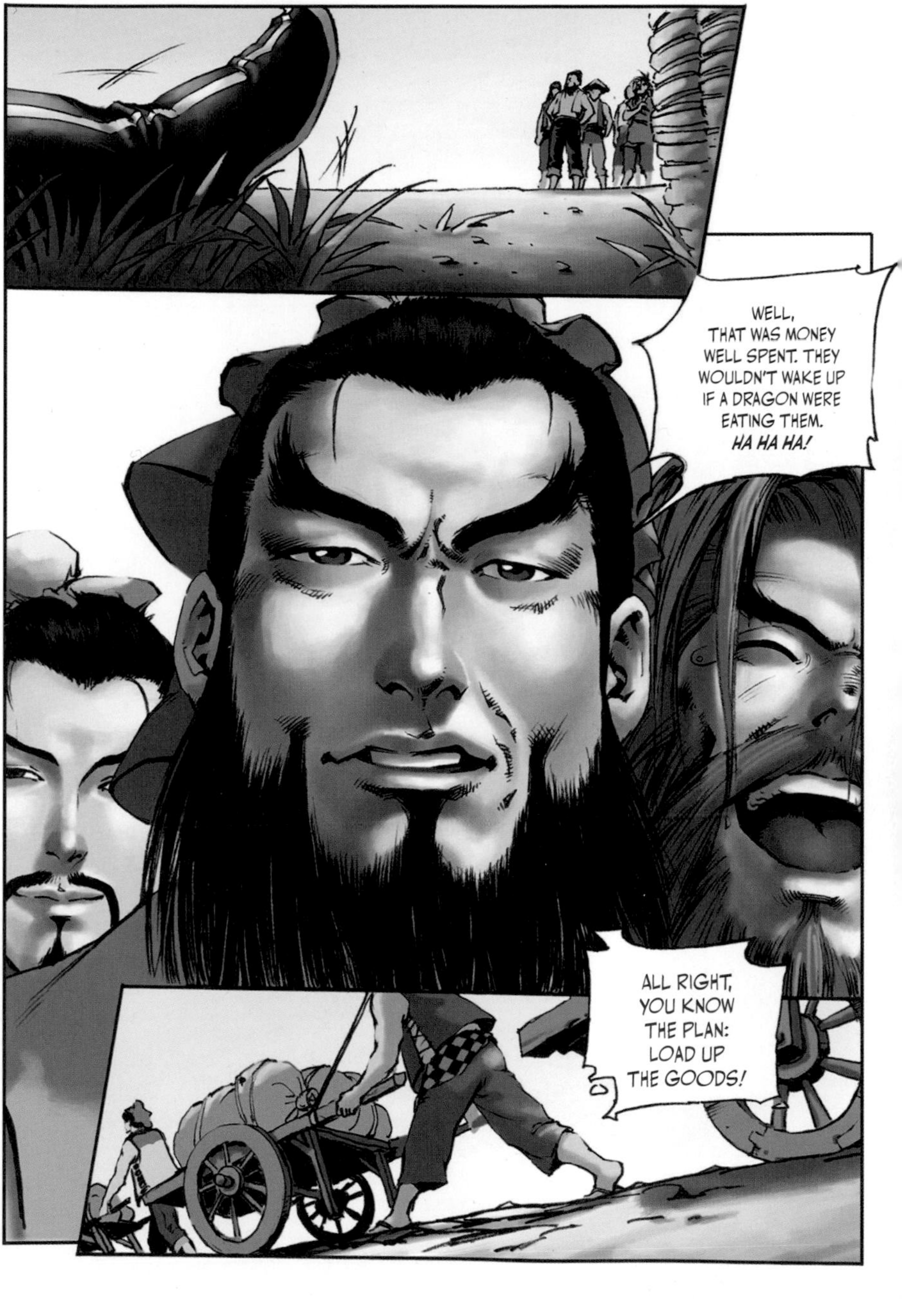
WELL, THAT WAS MONEY WELL SPENT. THEY WOULDN'T WAKE UP IF A DRAGON WERE EATING THEM. *HA HA HA!*
ALL RIGHT, YOU KNOW THE PLAN: LOAD UP THE GOODS!

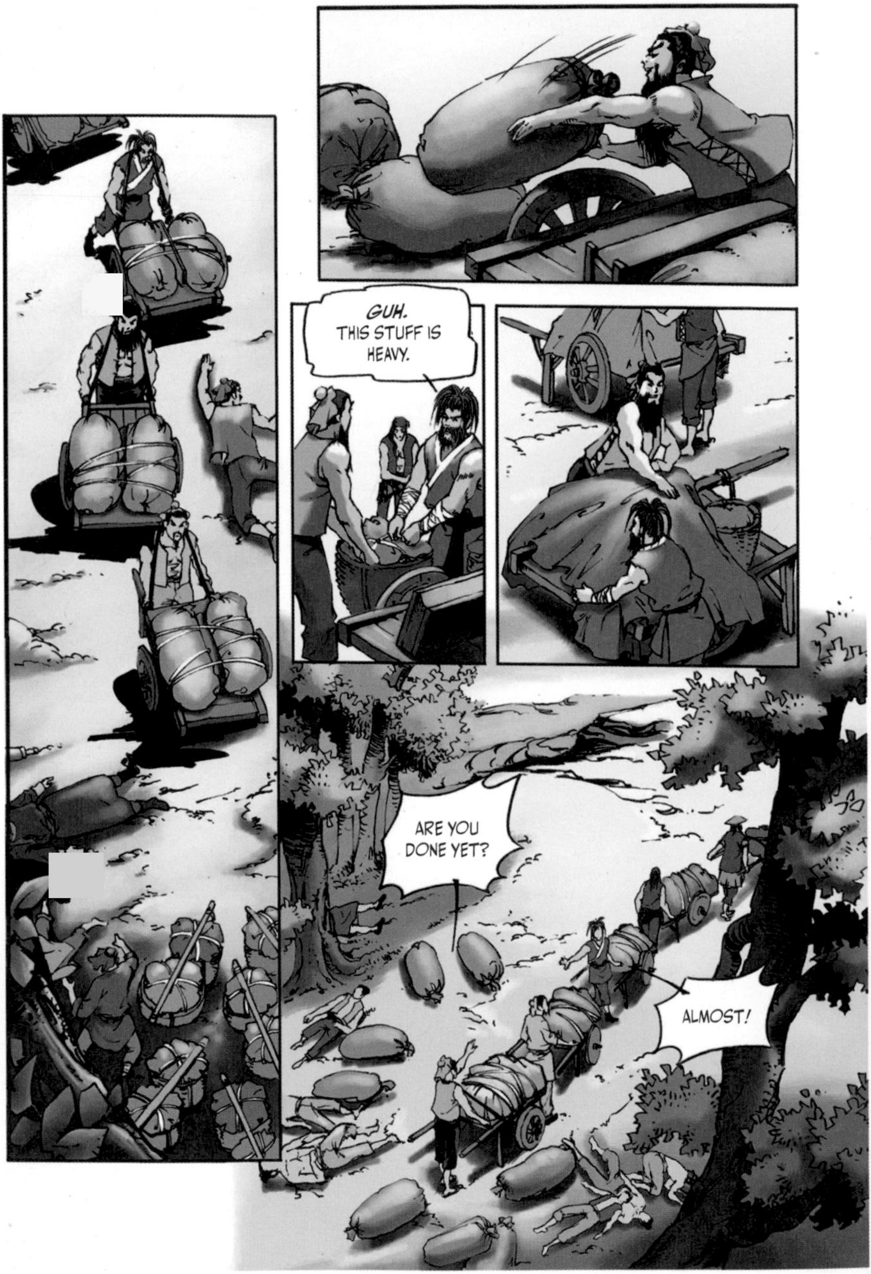
GUH. THIS STUFF IS HEAVY.
ARE YOU DONE YET?
ALMOST!

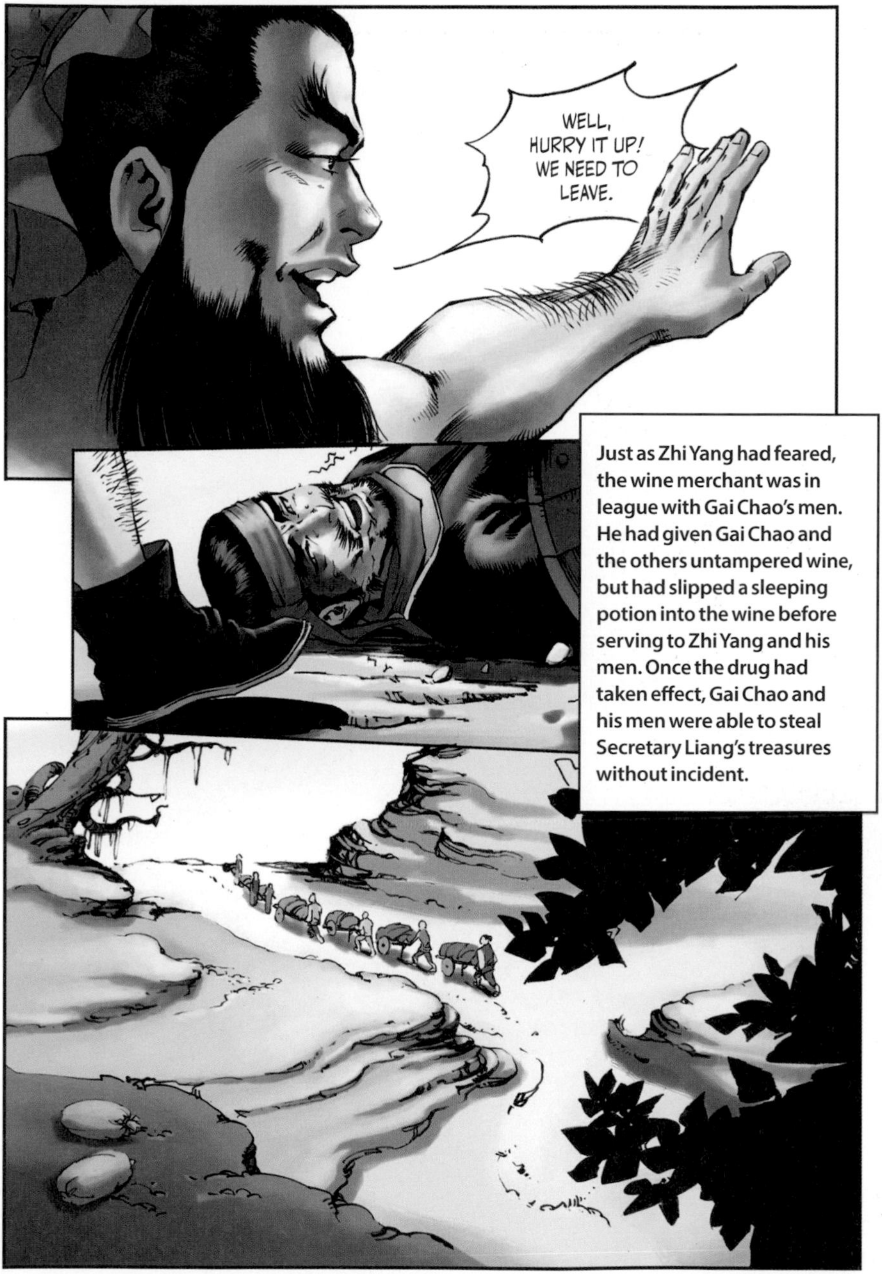
WELL, HURRY IT UP! WE NEED TO LEAVE.
Just as Zhi Yang had feared, the wine merchant was in league with Gai Chao's men. He had given Gai Chao and the others untampered wine, but had slipped a sleeping potion into the wine before serving to Zhi Yang and his men. Once the drug had taken effect, Gai Chao and his men were able to steal Secretary Liang's treasures without incident.

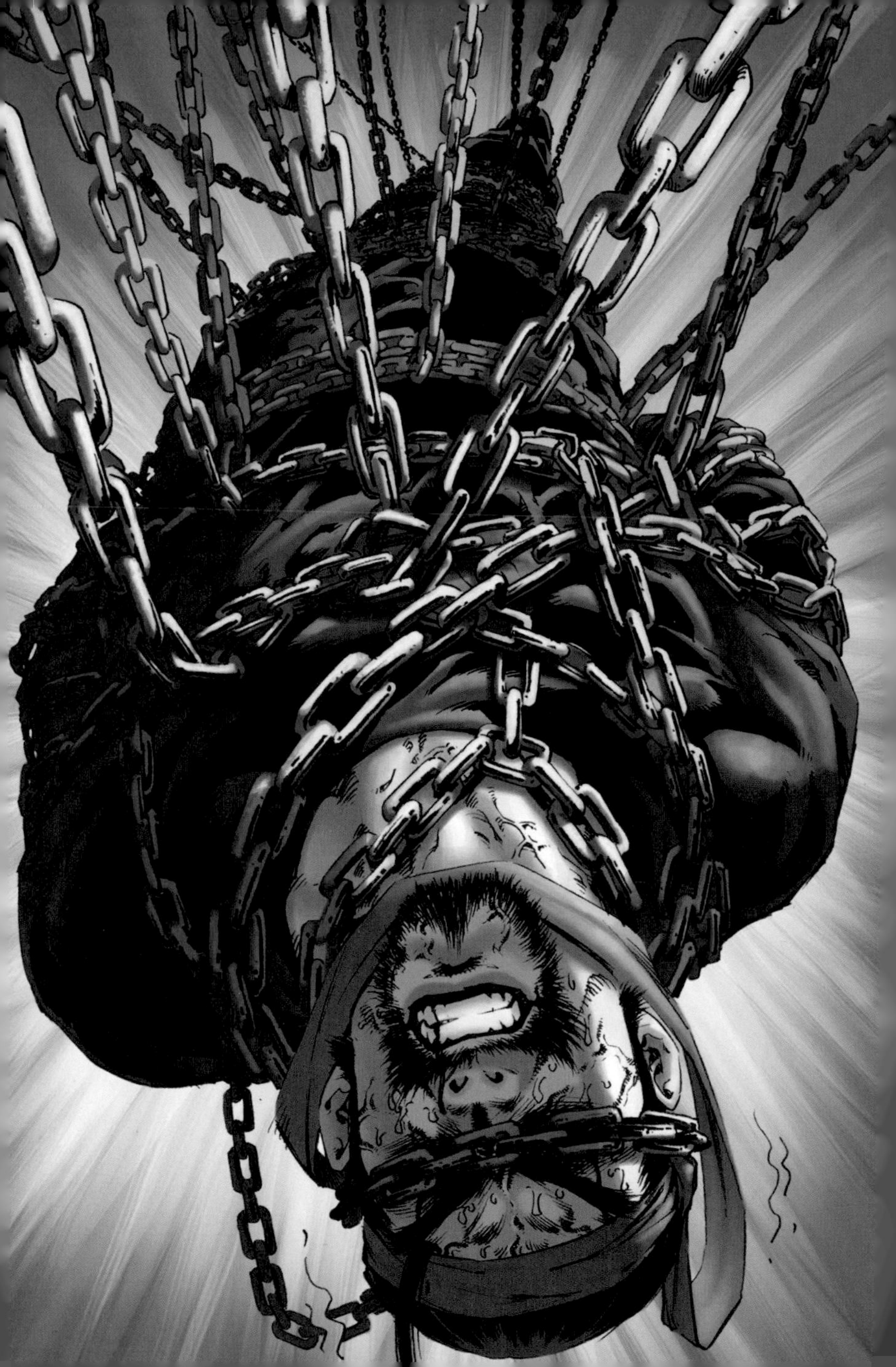

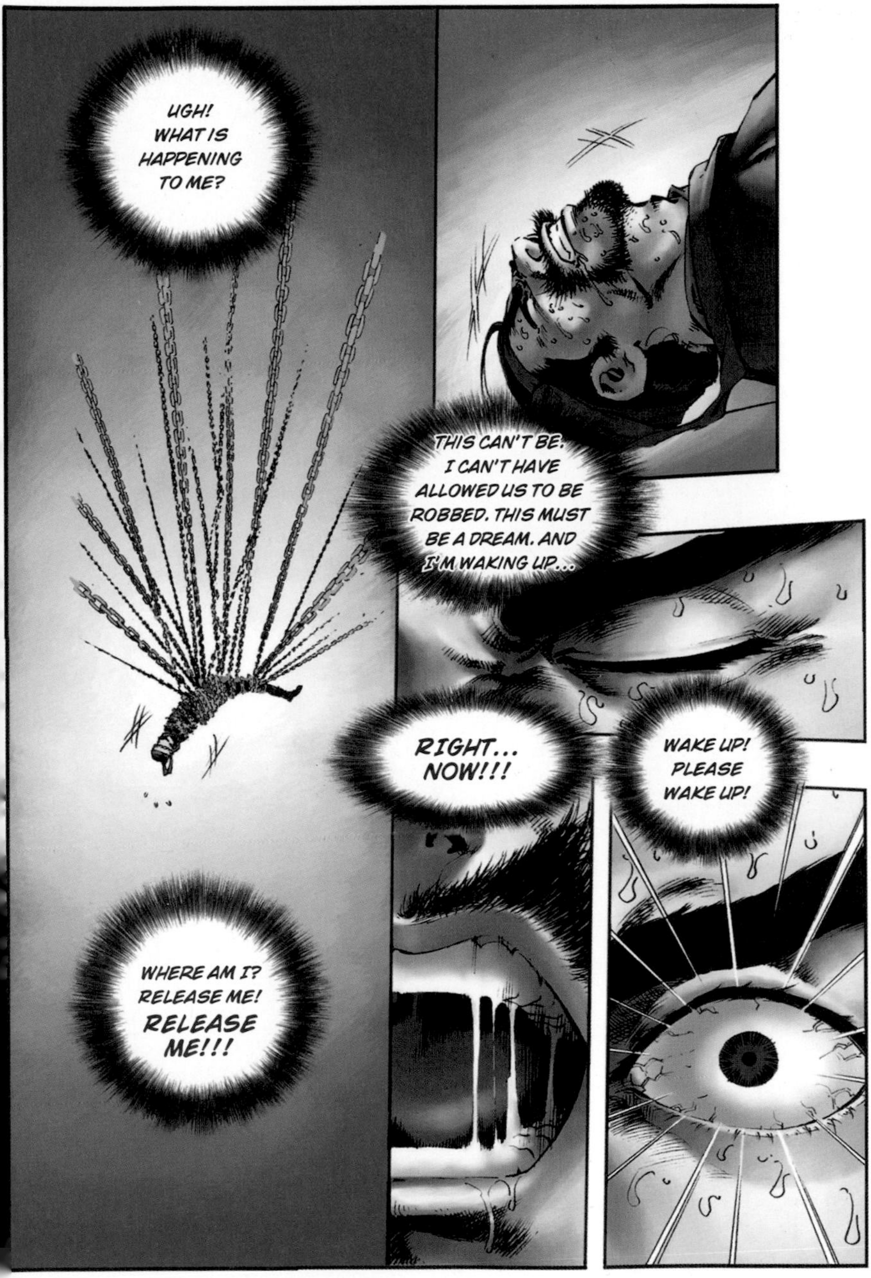
UGH! WHAT IS HAPPENING TO ME?
THIS CAN'T BE. I CAN'T HAVE ALLOWED US TO BE ROBBED. THIS MUST BE A DREAM. AND I'M WAKING UP...
RIGHT... NOW!!!
WAKE UP! PLEASE WAKE UP!
WHERE AM I? RELEASE ME! RELEASE ME!!!

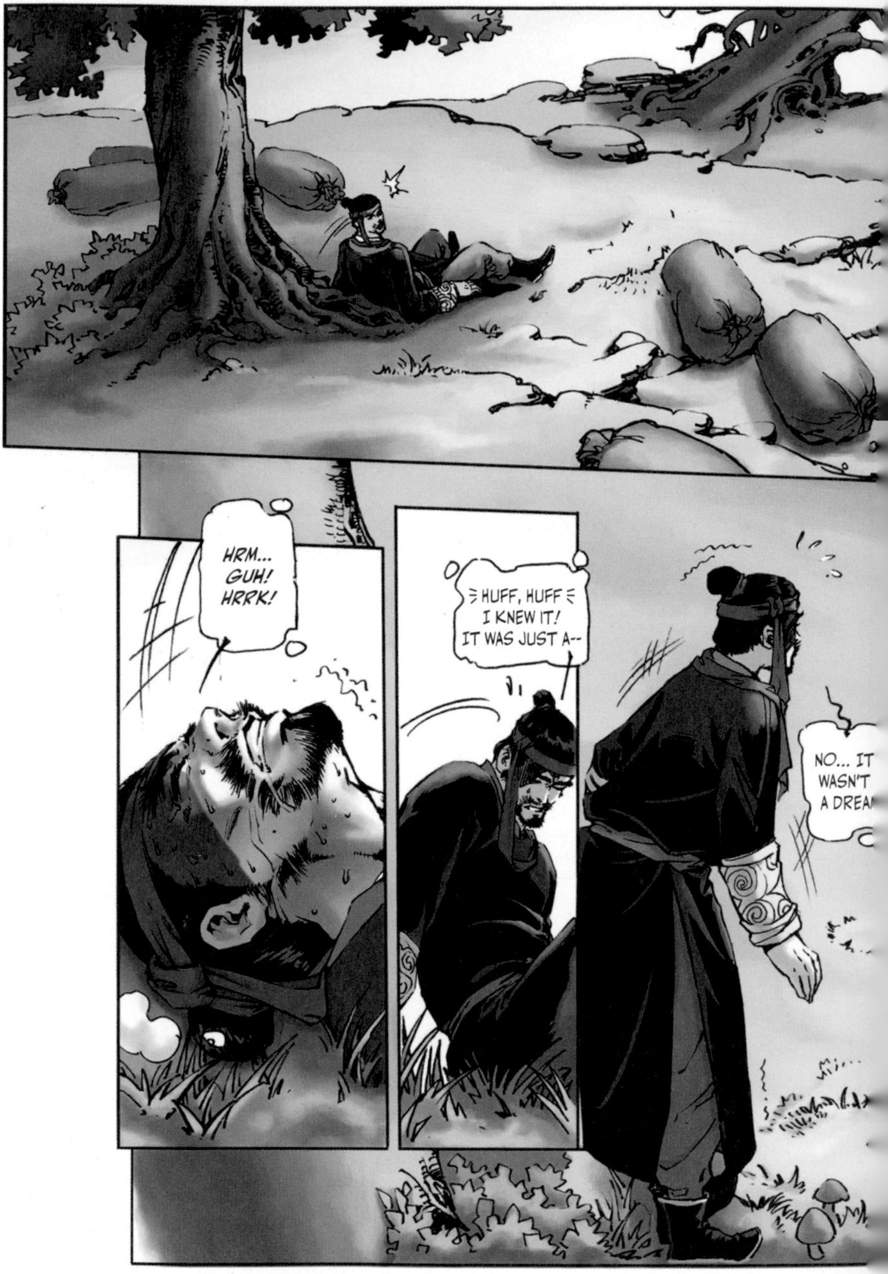
HRM... GUH! HRRK!
≡ HUFF, HUFF ≡ I KNEW IT! IT WAS JUST A--
NO... IT WASN'T A DREAM

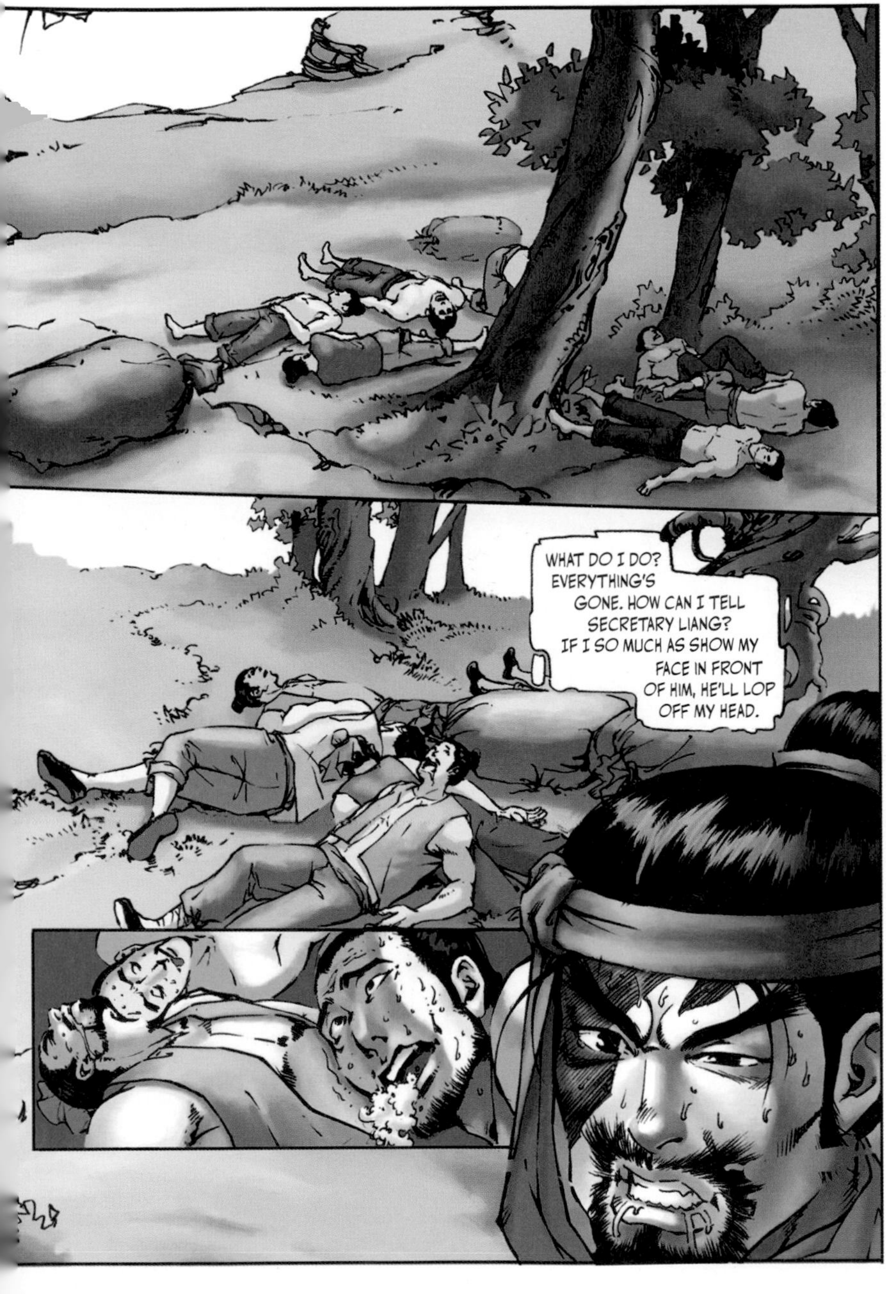
WHAT DO I DO? EVERYTHING'S GONE. HOW CAN I TELL SECRETARY LIANG? IF I SO MUCH AS SHOW MY FACE IN FRONT OF HIM, HE'LL LOP OFF MY HEAD.

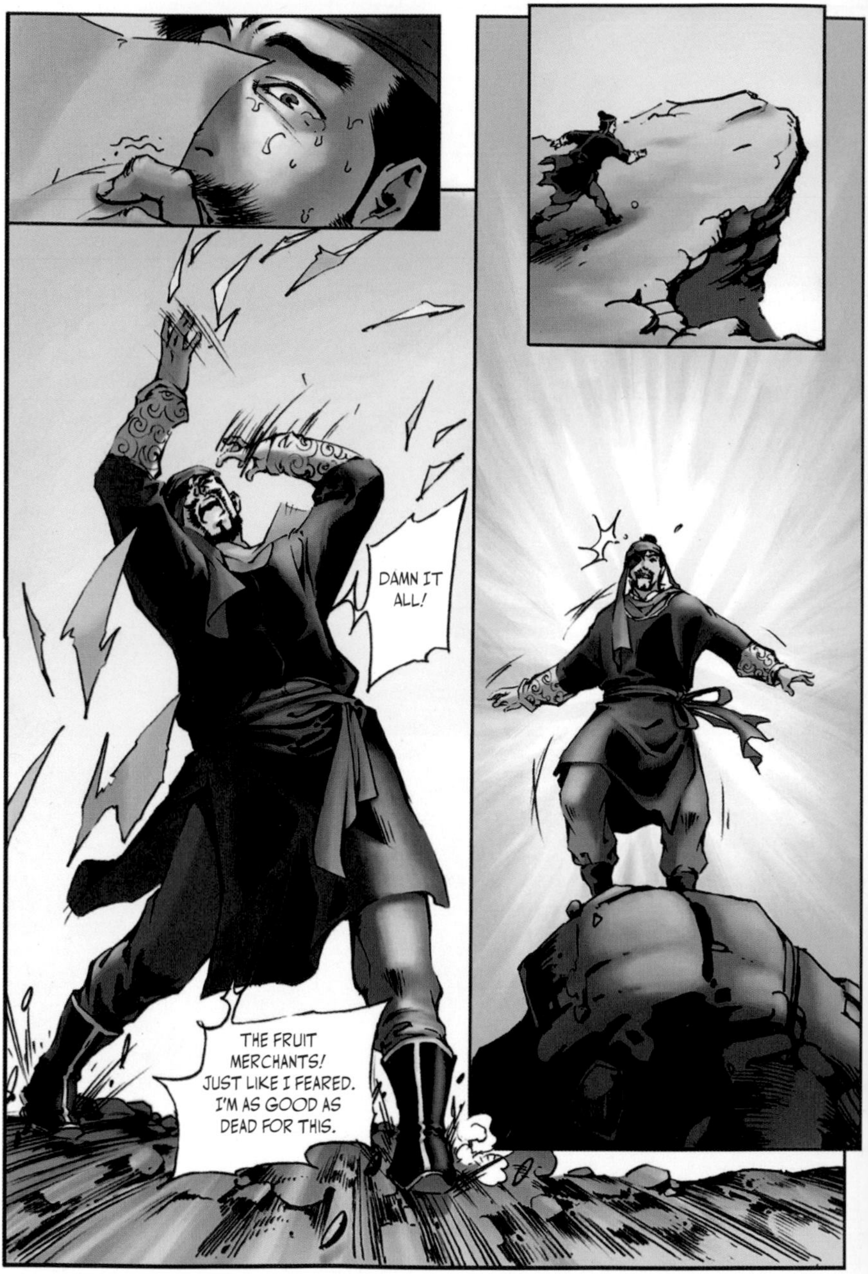
DAMN IT ALL!
THE FRUIT MERCHANTS! JUST LIKE I FEARED. I'M AS GOOD AS DEAD FOR THIS.

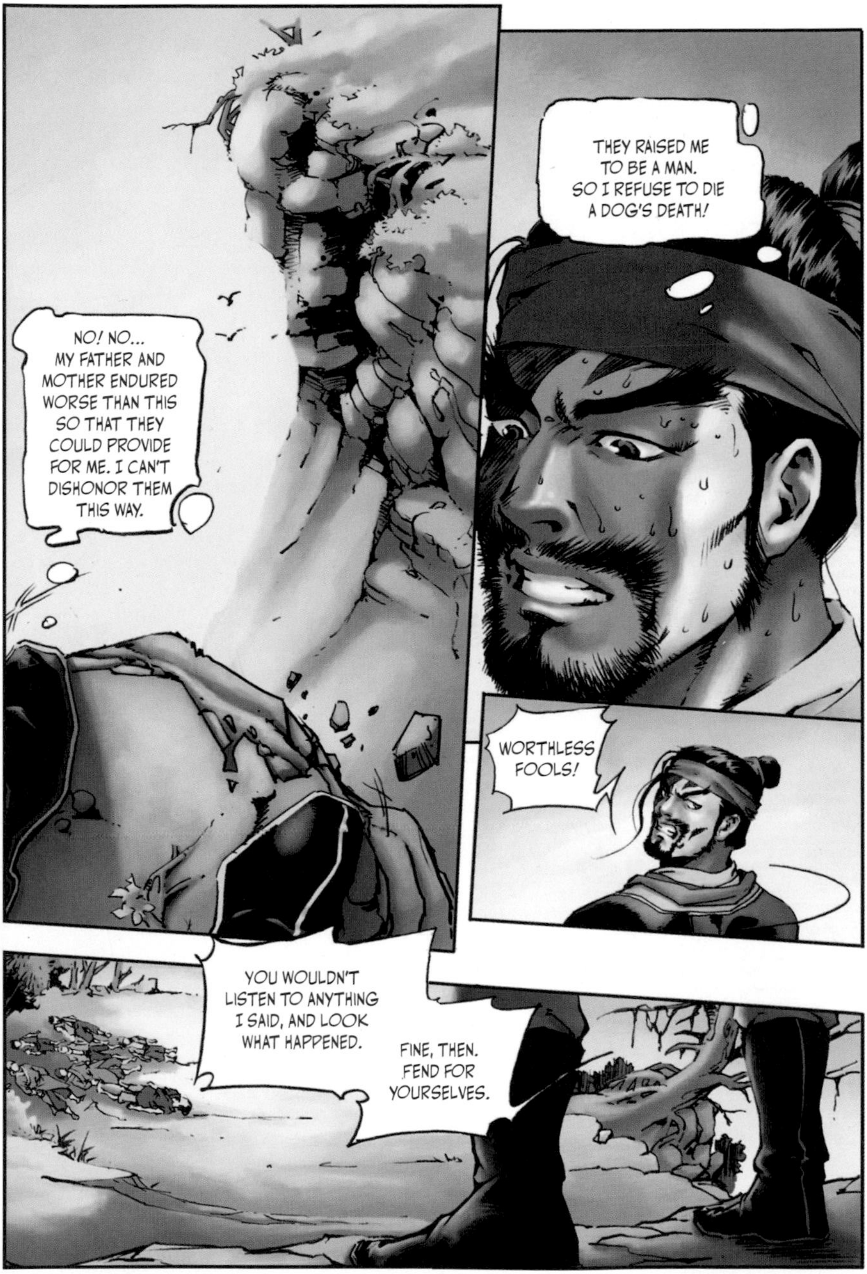

THEY RAISED ME TO BE A MAN. SO I REFUSE TO DIE A DOG'S DEATH!
NO! NO... MY FATHER AND MOTHER ENDURED WORSE THAN THIS SO THAT THEY COULD PROVIDE FOR ME. I CAN'T DISHONOR THEM THIS WAY.
WORTHLESS FOOLS!
YOU WOULDN'T LISTEN TO ANYTHING I SAID, AND LOOK WHAT HAPPENED.
FINE, THEN. FEND FOR YOURSELVES.

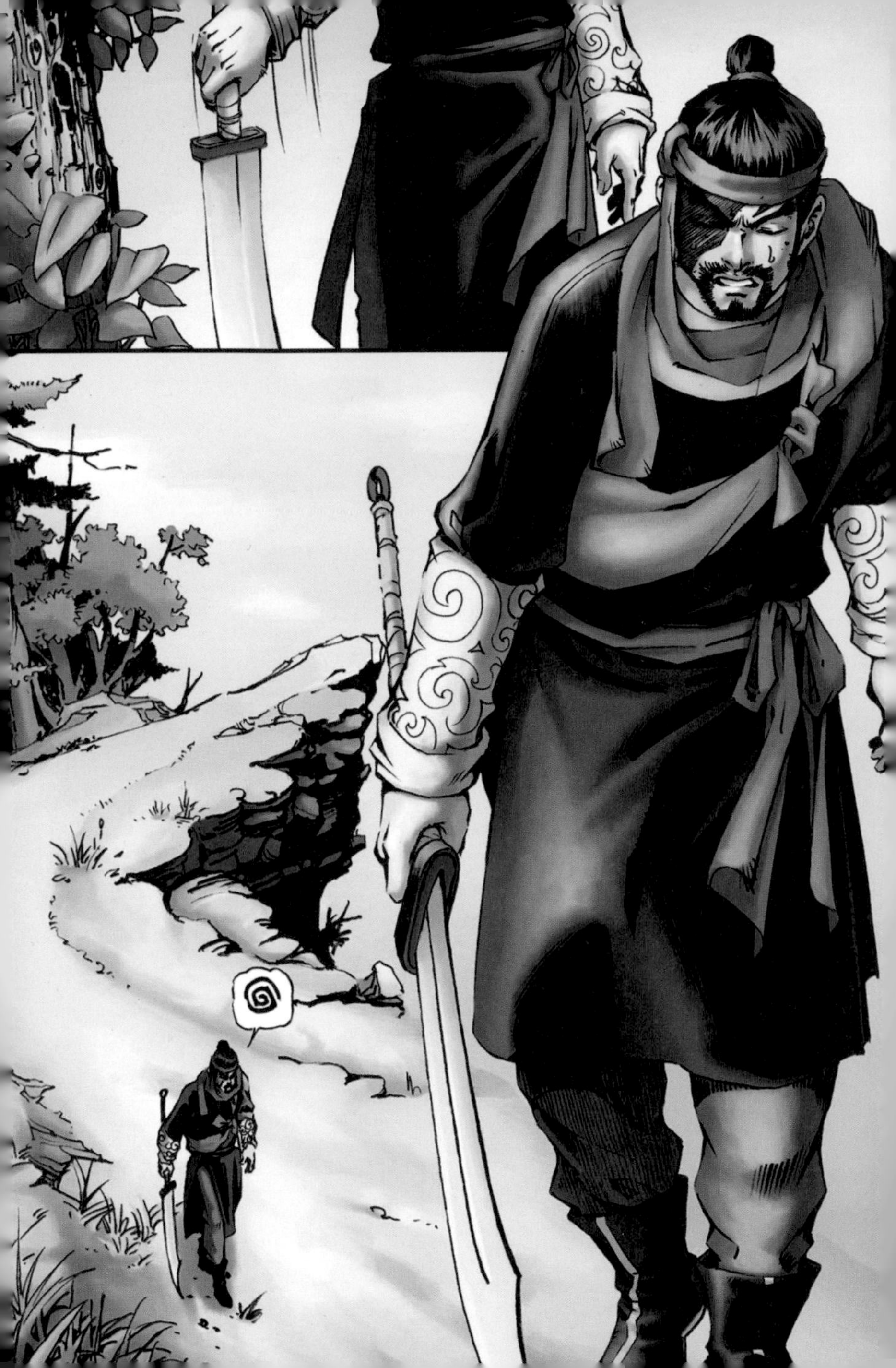

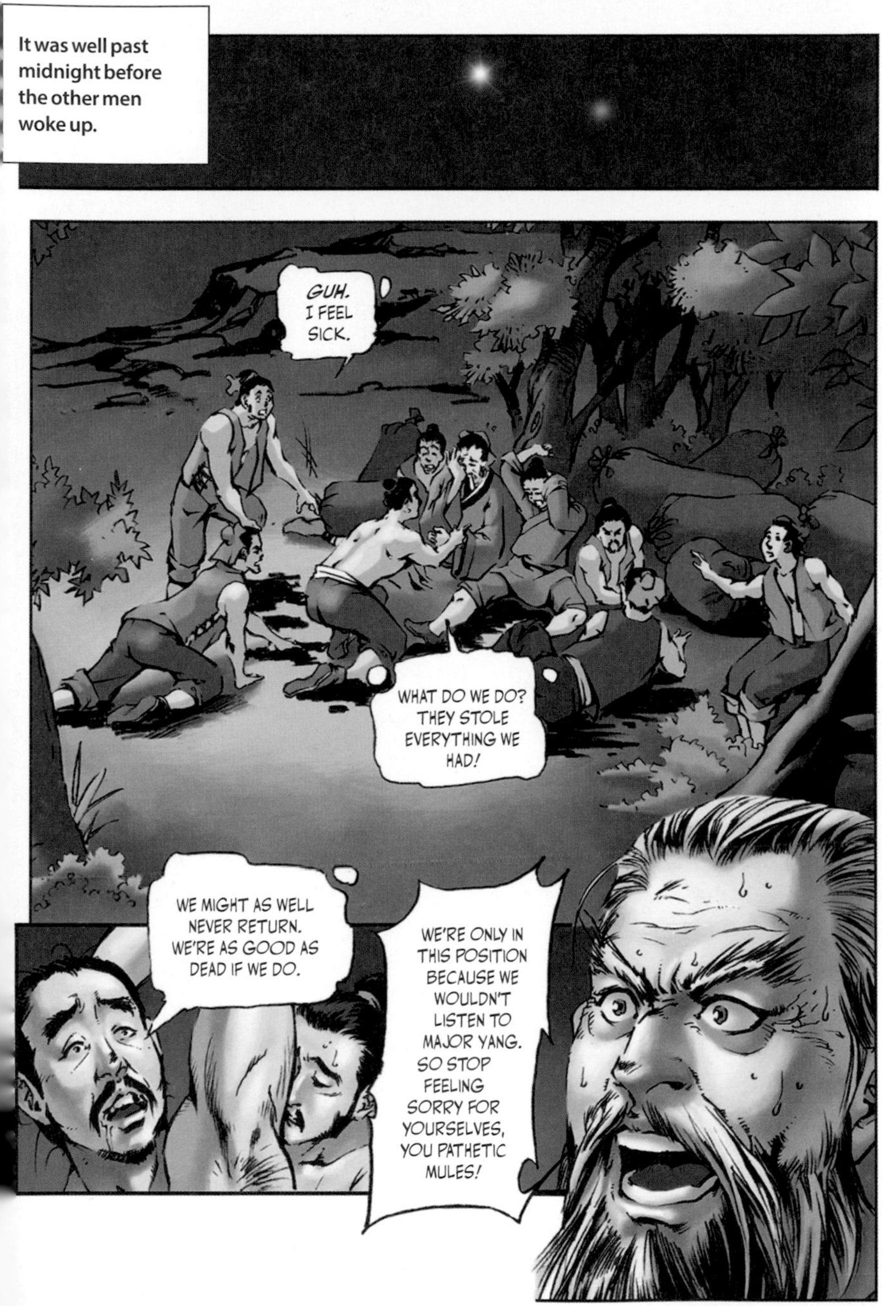
It was well past midnight before the other men woke up.
GUH. I FEEL SICK.
WHAT DO WE DO? THEY STOLE EVERYTHING WE HAD!
WE MIGHT AS WELL NEVER RETURN. WE'RE AS GOOD AS DEAD IF WE DO.
WE'RE ONLY IN THIS POSITION BECAUSE WE WOULDN'T LISTEN TO MAJOR YANG. SO STOP FEELING SORRY FOR YOURSELVES, YOU PATHETIC MULES!

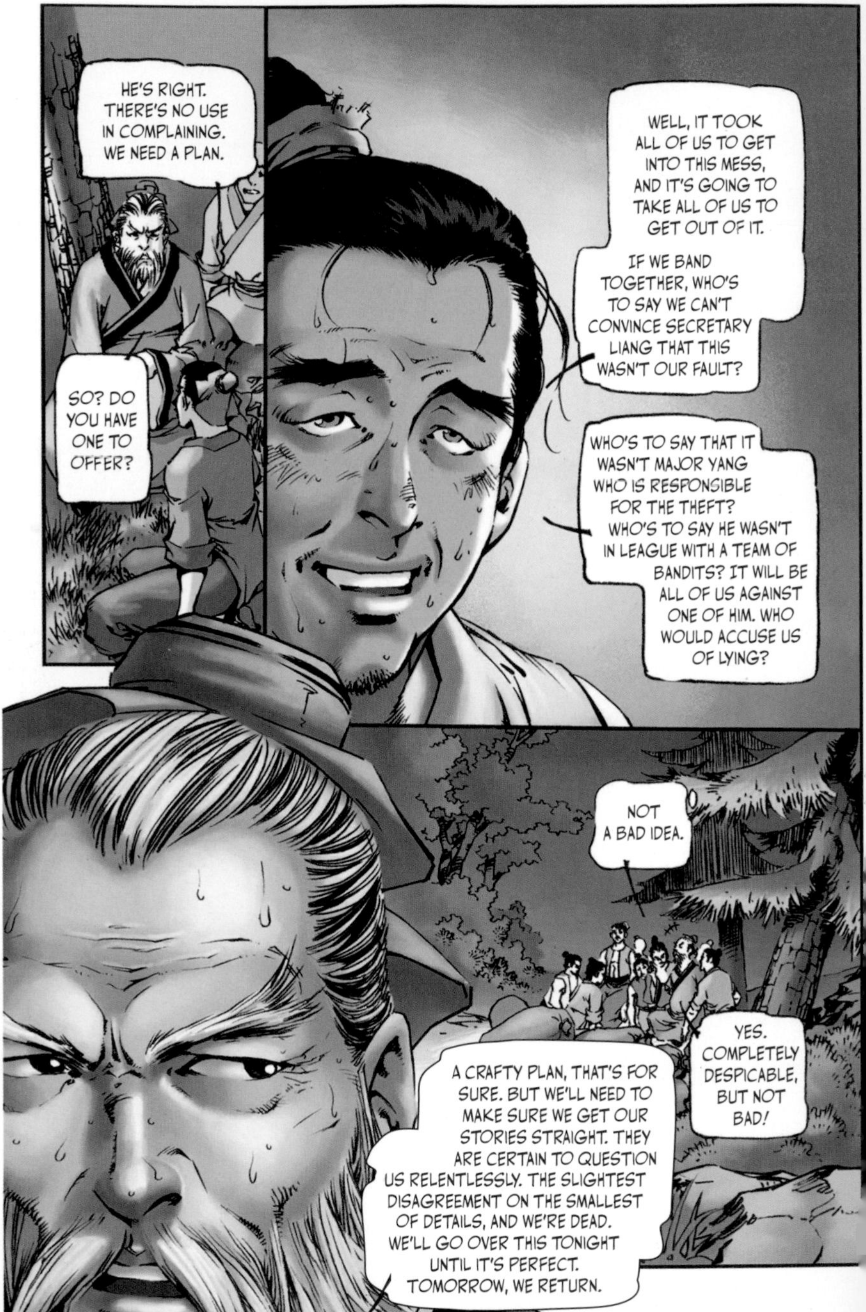
HE'S RIGHT. THERE'S NO USE IN COMPLAINING. WE NEED A PLAN.
SO? DO YOU HAVE ONE TO OFFER?
WELL, IT TOOK ALL OF US TO GET INTO THIS MESS, AND IT'S GOING TO TAKE ALL OF US TO GET OUT OF IT.
IF WE BAND TOGETHER, WHO'S TO SAY WE CAN'T CONVINCE SECRETARY LIANG THAT THIS WASN'T OUR FAULT?
WHO'S TO SAY THAT IT WASN'T MAJOR YANG WHO IS RESPONSIBLE FOR THE THEFT? WHO'S TO SAY HE WASN'T IN LEAGUE WITH A TEAM OF BANDITS? IT WILL BE ALL OF US AGAINST ONE OF HIM. WHO WOULD ACCUSE US OF LYING?
NOT A BAD IDEA.
YES. COMPLETELY DESPICABLE, BUT NOT BAD!
A CRAFTY PLAN, THAT'S FOR SURE. BUT WE'LL NEED TO MAKE SURE WE GET OUR STORIES STRAIGHT. THEY ARE CERTAIN TO QUESTION US RELENTLESSLY. THE SLIGHTEST DISAGREEMENT ON THE SMALLEST OF DETAILS, AND WE'RE DEAD. WE'LL GO OVER THIS TONIGHT UNTIL IT'S PERFECT. TOMORROW, WE RETURN.

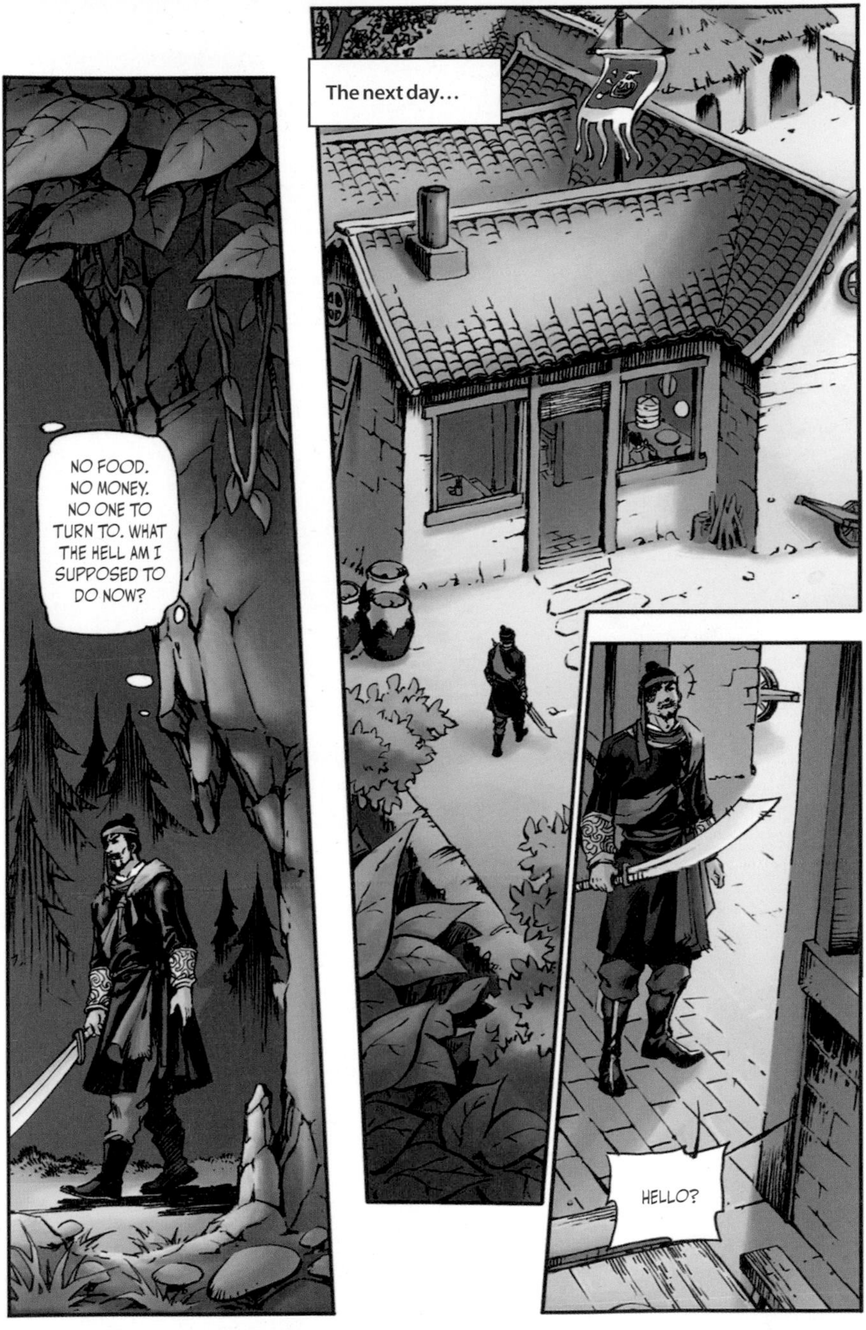
NO FOOD. NO MONEY. NO ONE TO TURN TO. WHAT THE HELL AM I SUPPOSED TO DO NOW?
The next day…
HELLO?

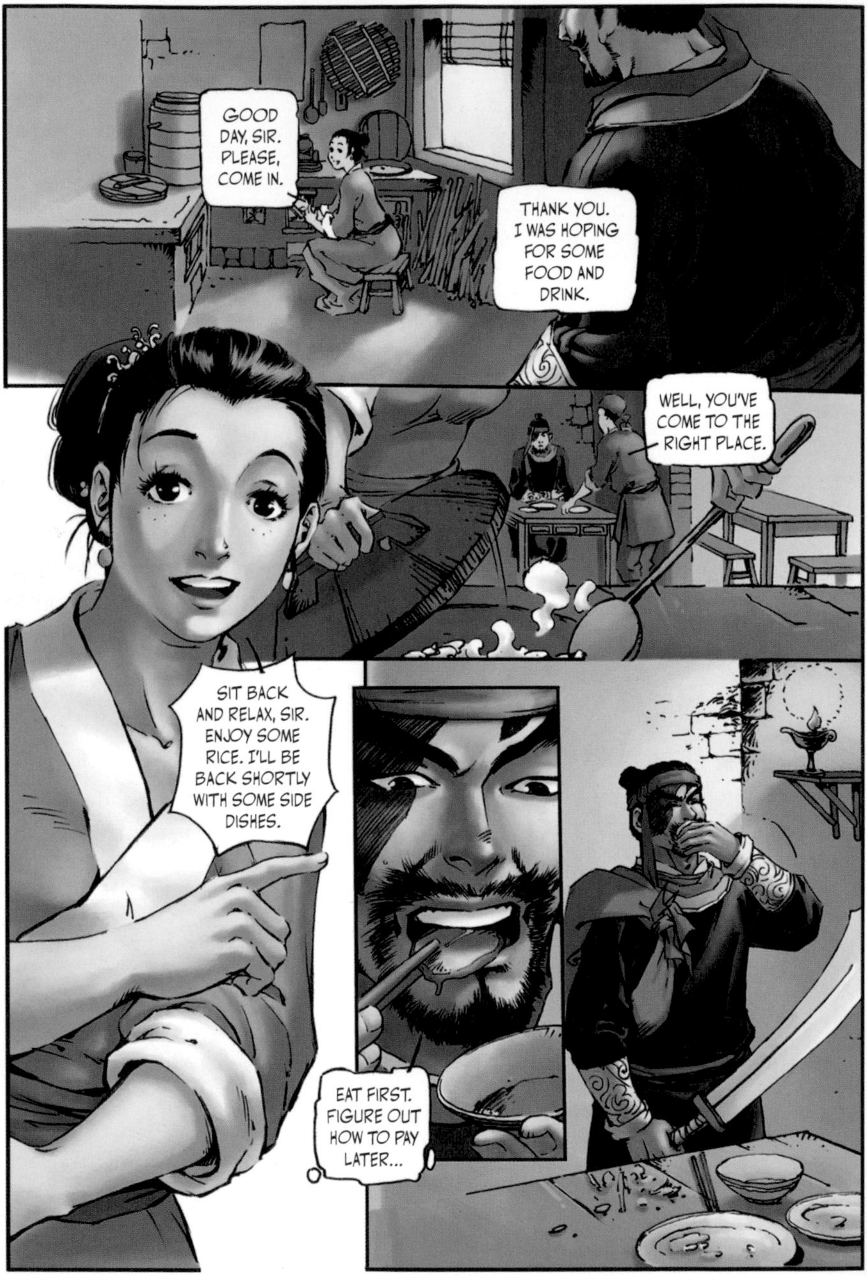
GOOD DAY, SIR. PLEASE, COME IN.
THANK YOU. I WAS HOPING FOR SOME FOOD AND DRINK.
WELL, YOU'VE COME TO THE RIGHT PLACE.
SIT BACK AND RELAX, SIR. ENJOY SOME RICE. I'LL BE BACK SHORTLY WITH SOME SIDE DISHES.
EAT FIRST. FIGURE OUT HOW TO PAY LATER...

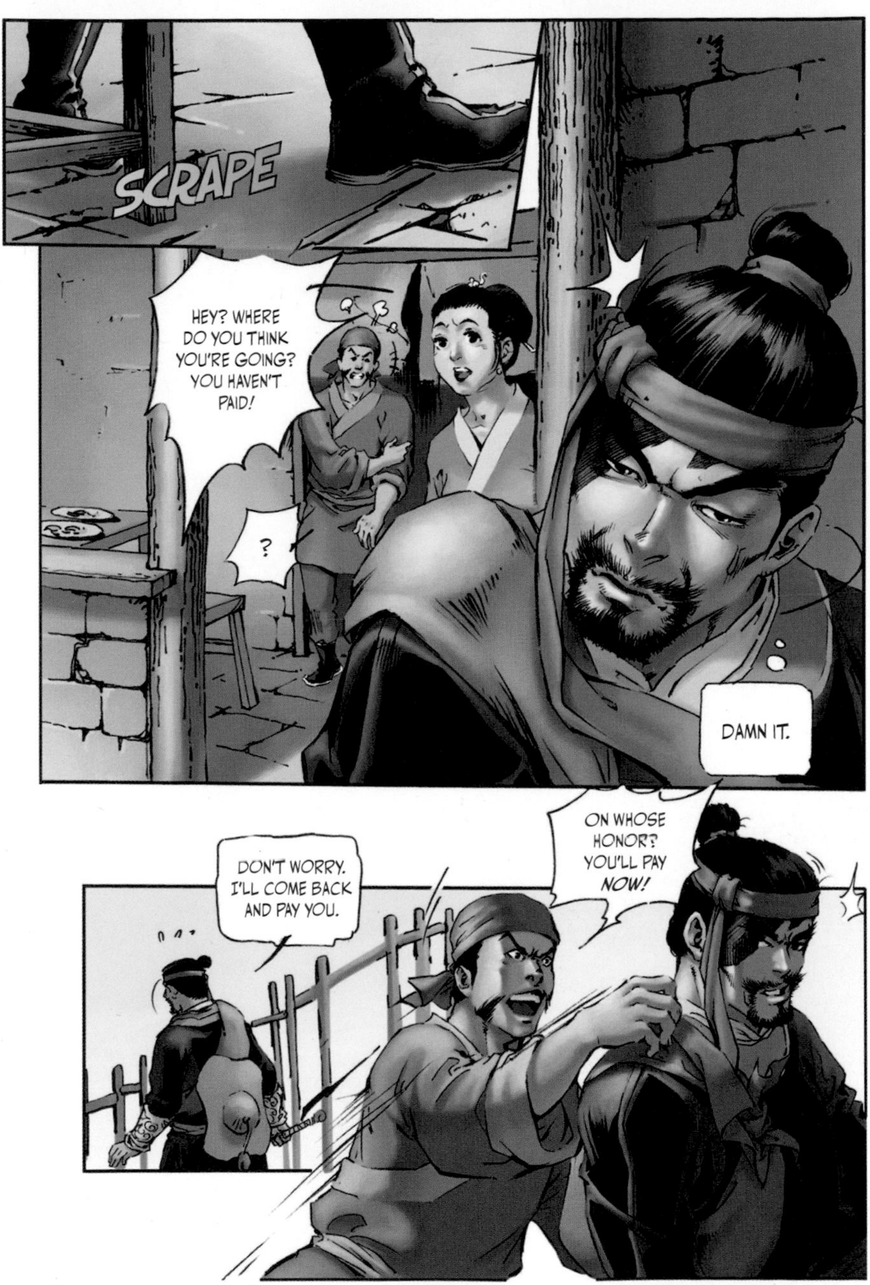
SCRAPE
HEY? WHERE DO YOU THINK YOU'RE GOING? YOU HAVEN'T PAID!
?
DAMN IT.
DON'T WORRY. I'LL COME BACK AND PAY YOU.
ON WHOSE HONOR? YOU'LL PAY NOW!

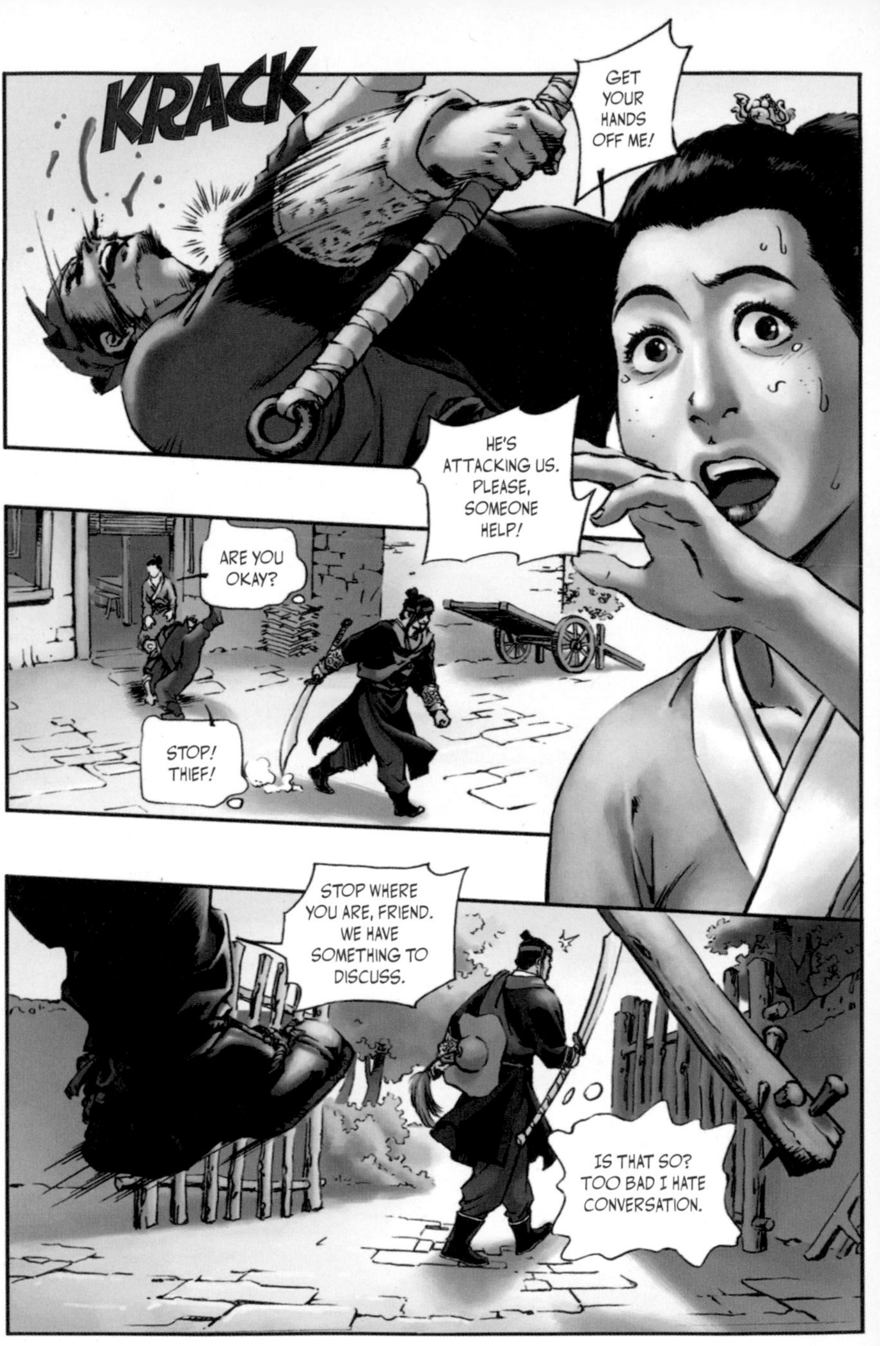
KRACK
GET YOUR HANDS OFF ME!
HE'S ATTACKING US. PLEASE, SOMEONE HELP!
ARE YOU OKAY?
STOP! THIEF!
STOP WHERE YOU ARE, FRIEND. WE HAVE SOMETHING TO DISCUSS.
IS THAT SO? TOO BAD I HATE CONVERSATION.

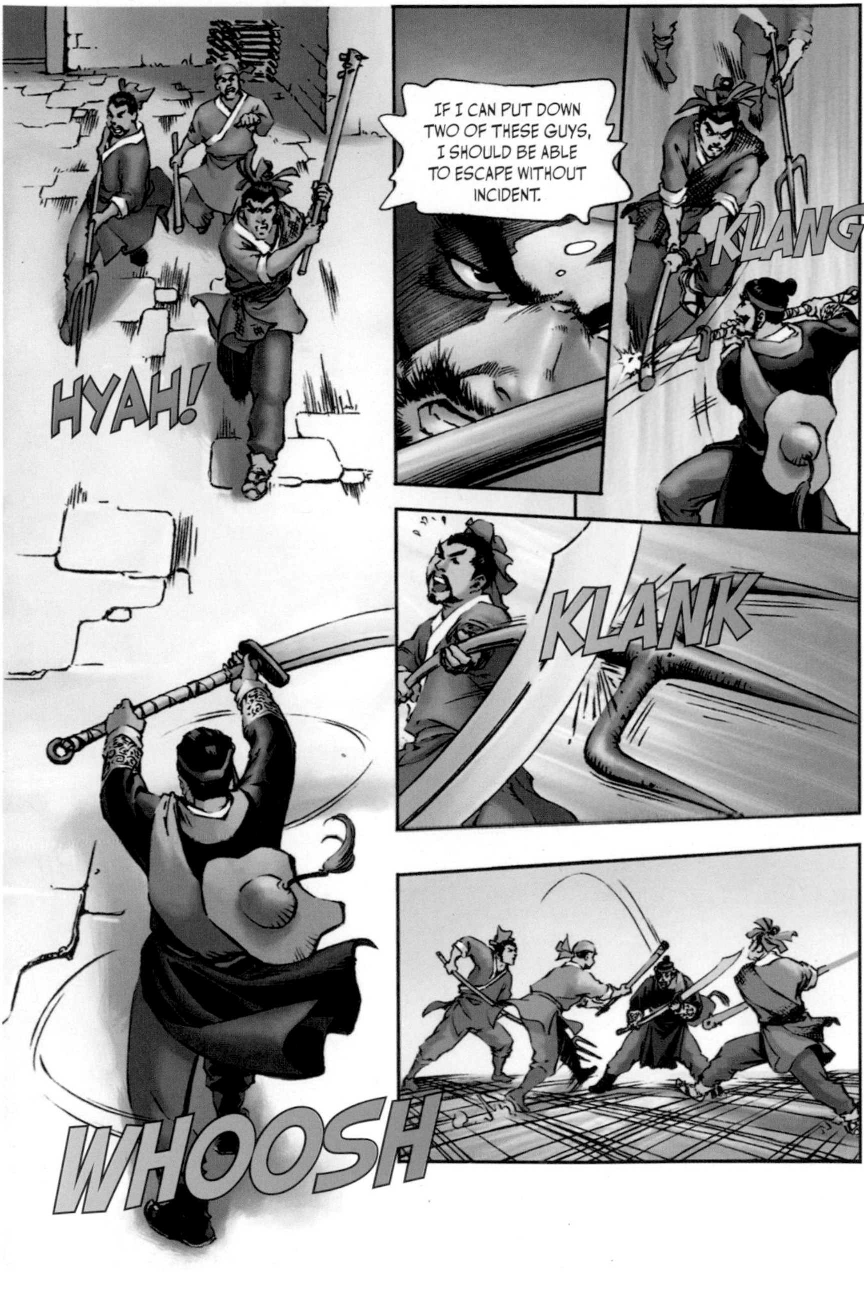
HYAH!
IF I CAN PUT DOWN TWO OF THESE GUYS, I SHOULD BE ABLE TO ESCAPE WITHOUT INCIDENT.
KLANG
WHOOSH
KLANK

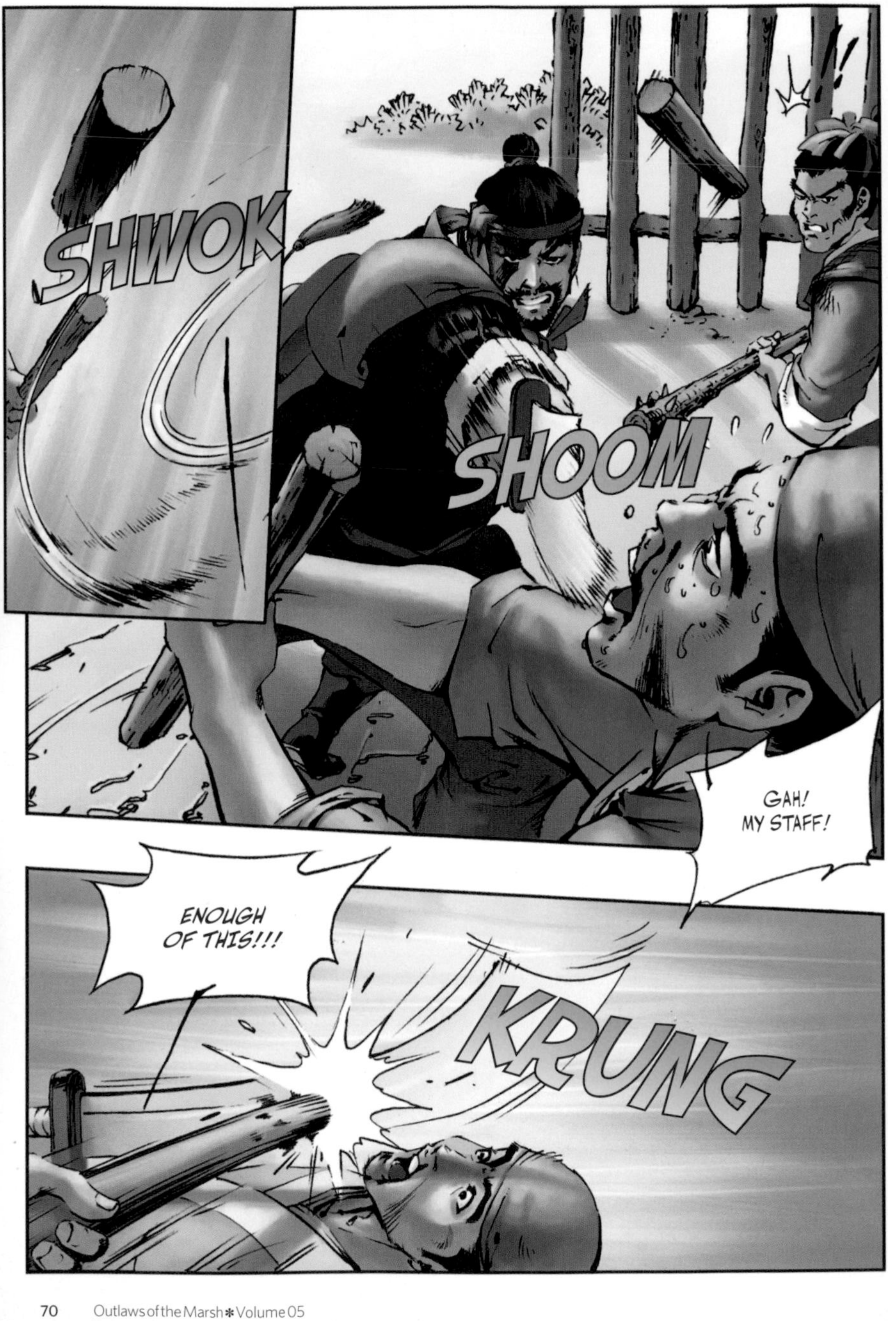
SHWOK
SHOOM
GAH! MY STAFF!
ENOUGH OF THIS!!!
KRUNG

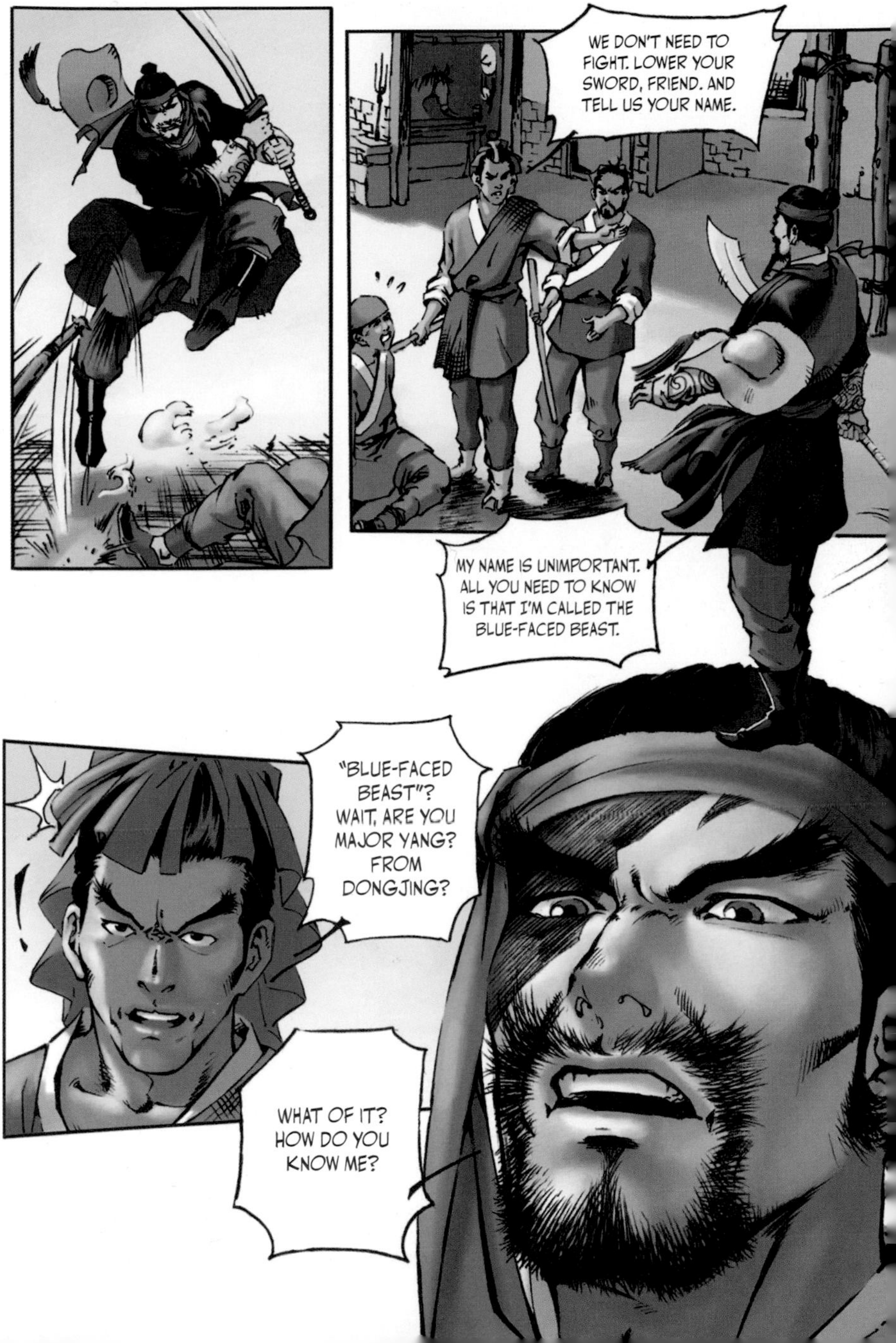
WE DON'T NEED TO FIGHT. LOWER YOUR SWORD, FRIEND. AND TELL US YOUR NAME.
MY NAME IS UNIMPORTANT. ALL YOU NEED TO KNOW IS THAT I'M CALLED THE BLUE-FACED BEAST.
"BLUE-FACED BEAST"? WAIT, ARE YOU MAJOR YANG? FROM DONGJING?
WHAT OF IT? HOW DO YOU KNOW ME?

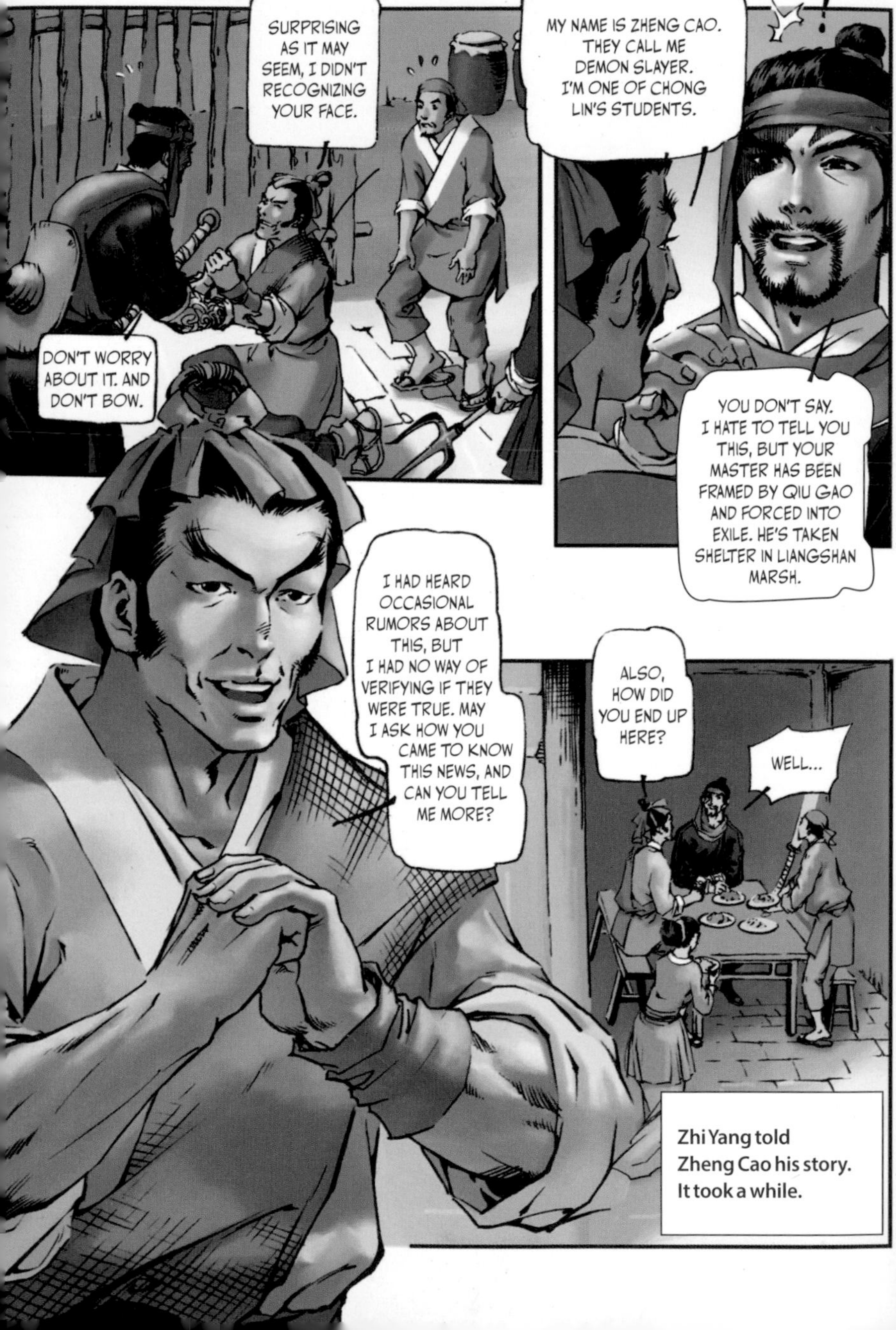
SURPRISING AS IT MAY SEEM, I DIDN'T RECOGNIZING YOUR FACE.
DON'T WORRY ABOUT IT. AND DON'T BOW.
MY NAME IS ZHENG CAO. THEY CALL ME DEMON SLAYER. I'M ONE OF CHONG LIN'S STUDENTS.
!
YOU DON'T SAY. I HATE TO TELL YOU THIS, BUT YOUR MASTER HAS BEEN FRAMED BY QIU GAO AND FORCED INTO EXILE. HE'S TAKEN SHELTER IN LIANGSHAN MARSH.
I HAD HEARD OCCASIONAL RUMORS ABOUT THIS, BUT I HAD NO WAY OF VERIFYING IF THEY WERE TRUE. MAY I ASK HOW YOU CAME TO KNOW THIS NEWS, AND CAN YOU TELL ME MORE?
ALSO, HOW DID YOU END UP HERE?
WELL...
Zhi Yang told Zheng Cao his story. It took a while.

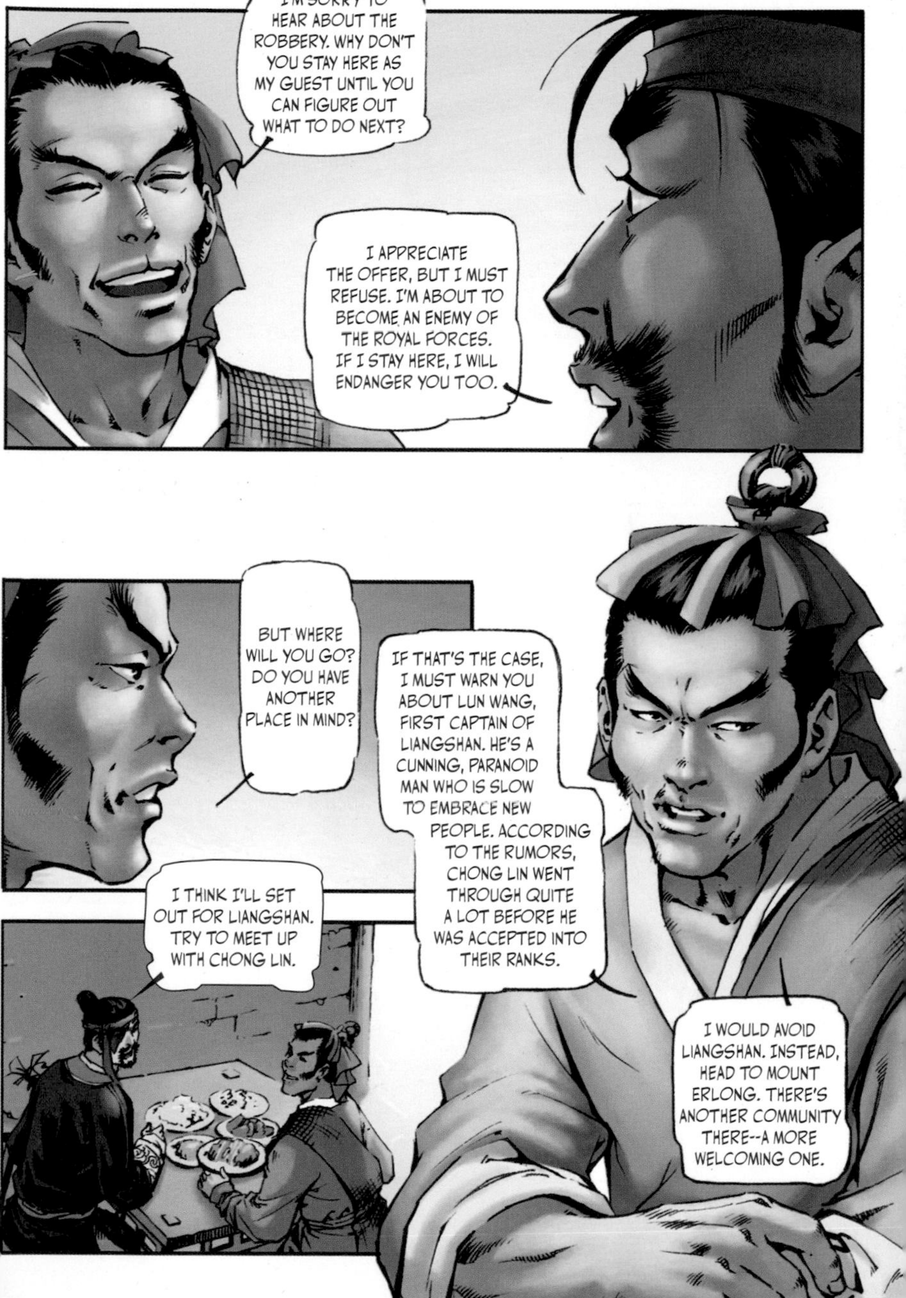
I'M SORRY TO HEAR ABOUT THE ROBBERY. WHY DON'T YOU STAY HERE AS MY GUEST UNTIL YOU CAN FIGURE OUT WHAT TO DO NEXT?
I APPRECIATE THE OFFER, BUT I MUST REFUSE. I'M ABOUT TO BECOME AN ENEMY OF THE ROYAL FORCES. IF I STAY HERE, I WILL ENDANGER YOU TOO.
BUT WHERE WILL YOU GO? DO YOU HAVE ANOTHER PLACE IN MIND?
I THINK I'LL SET OUT FOR LIANGSHAN. TRY TO MEET UP WITH CHONG LIN.
IF THAT'S THE CASE, I MUST WARN YOU ABOUT LUN WANG, FIRST CAPTAIN OF LIANGSHAN. HE'S A CUNNING, PARANOID MAN WHO IS SLOW TO EMBRACE NEW PEOPLE. ACCORDING TO THE RUMORS, CHONG LIN WENT THROUGH QUITE A LOT BEFORE HE WAS ACCEPTED INTO THEIR RANKS.
I WOULD AVOID LIANGSHAN. INSTEAD, HEAD TO MOUNT ERLONG. THERE'S ANOTHER COMMUNITY THERE--A MORE WELCOMING ONE.

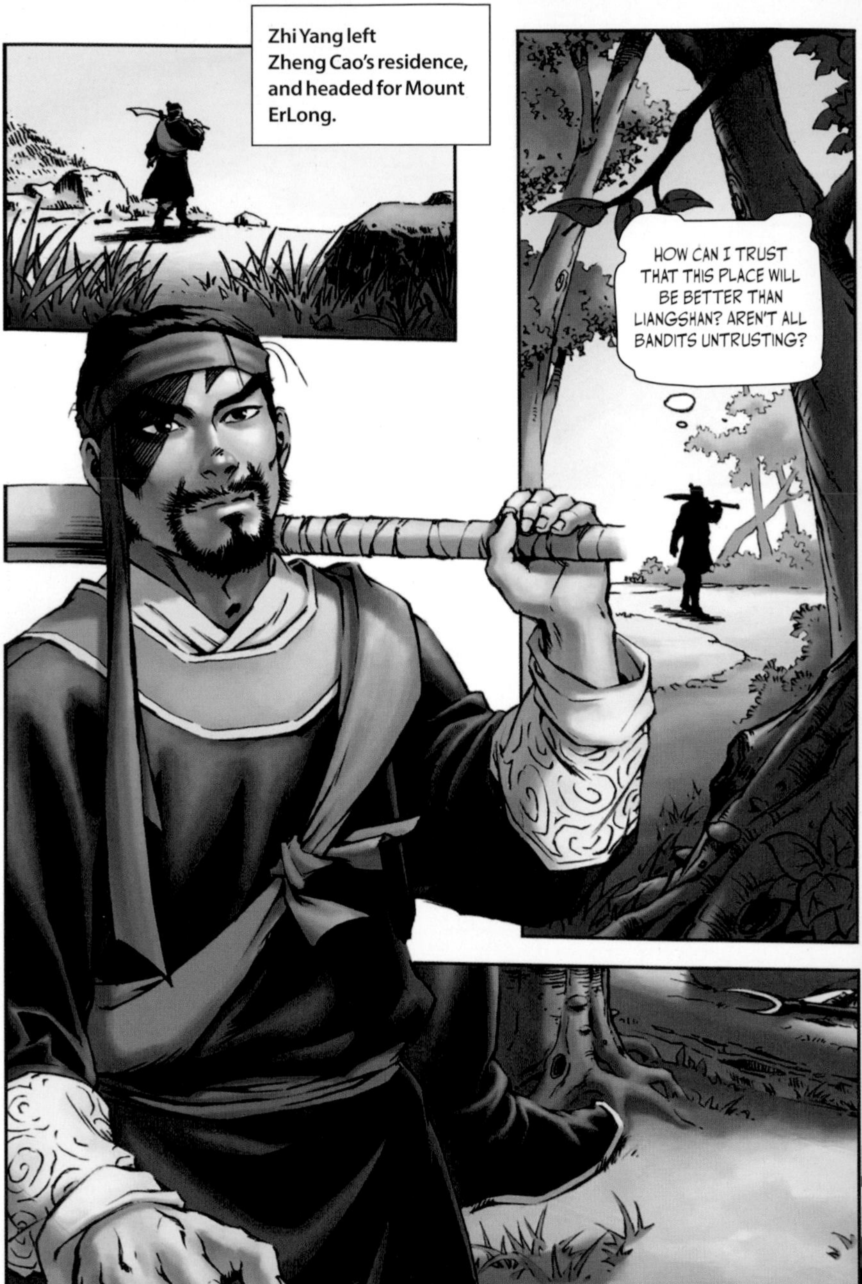
Zhi Yang left Zheng Cao's residence, and headed for Mount ErLong.
HOW CAN I TRUST THAT THIS PLACE WILL BE BETTER THAN LIANGSHAN? AREN'T ALL BANDITS UNTRUSTING?

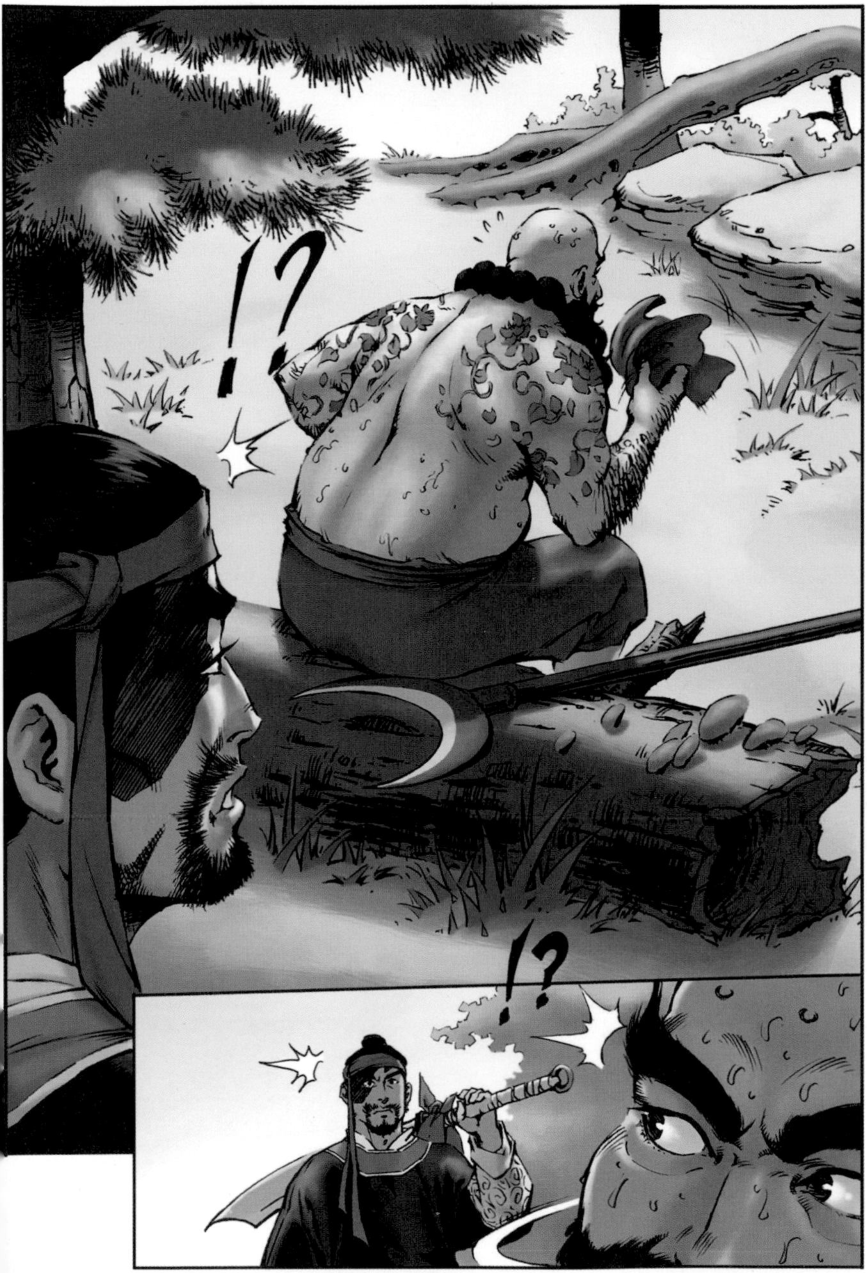
!?
!?

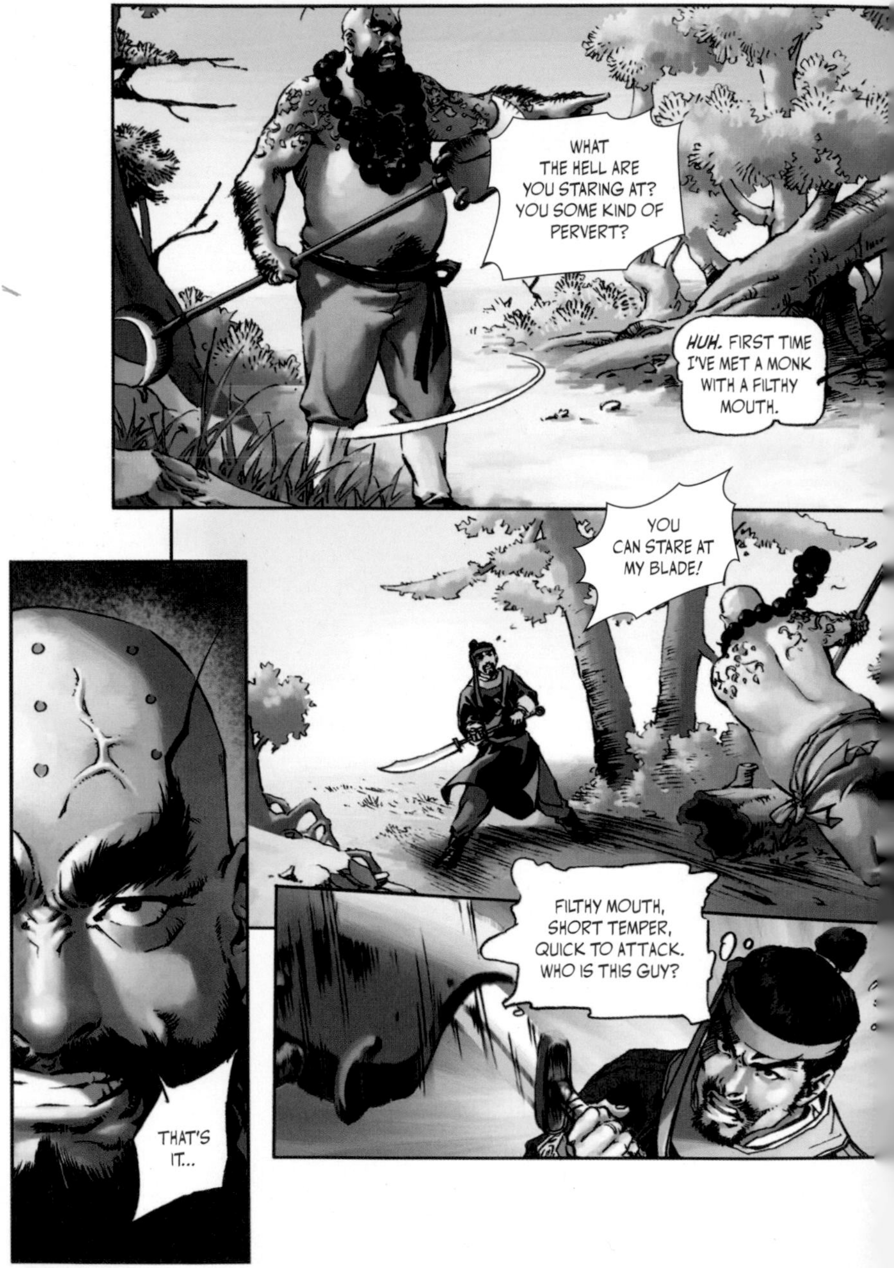
WHAT THE HELL ARE YOU STARING AT? YOU SOME KIND OF PERVERT?
HUH. FIRST TIME I'VE MET A MONK WITH A FILTHY MOUTH.
YOU CAN STARE AT MY BLADE!
THAT'S IT...
FILTHY MOUTH, SHORT TEMPER, QUICK TO ATTACK. WHO IS THIS GUY?

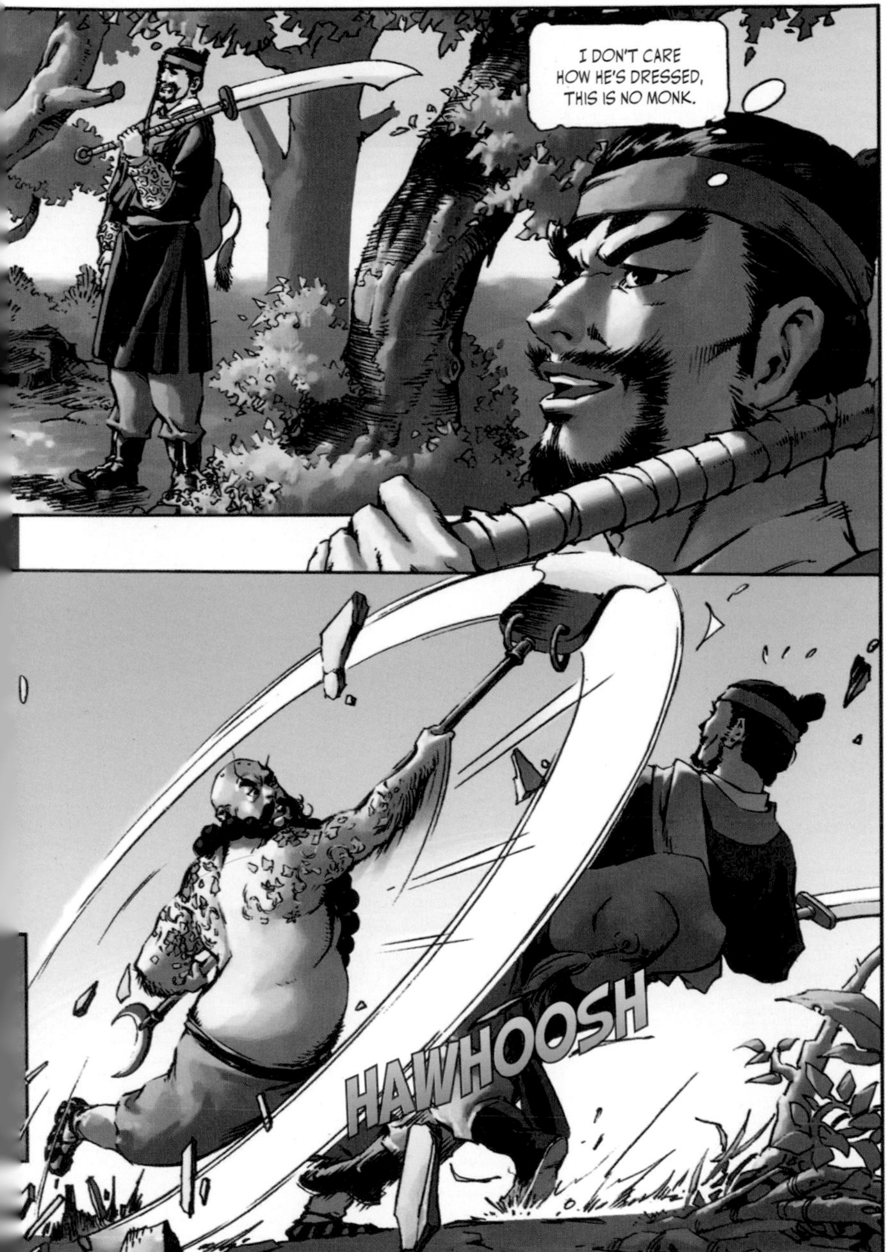
I DON'T CARE HOW HE'S DRESSED, THIS IS NO MONK.
HAWHOOSH

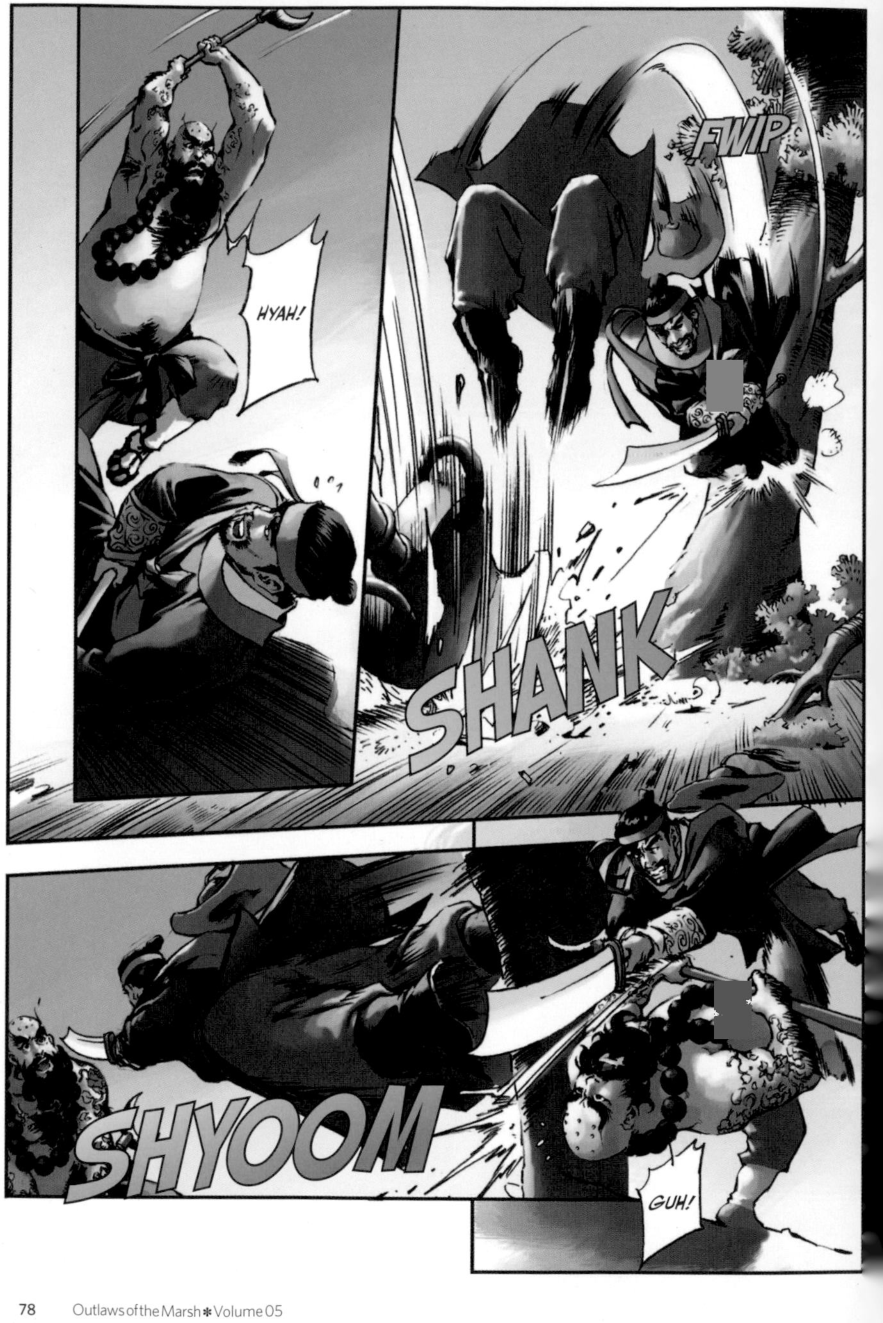
HYAH!
FWIP
SHANK
SHYOOM
GUH!

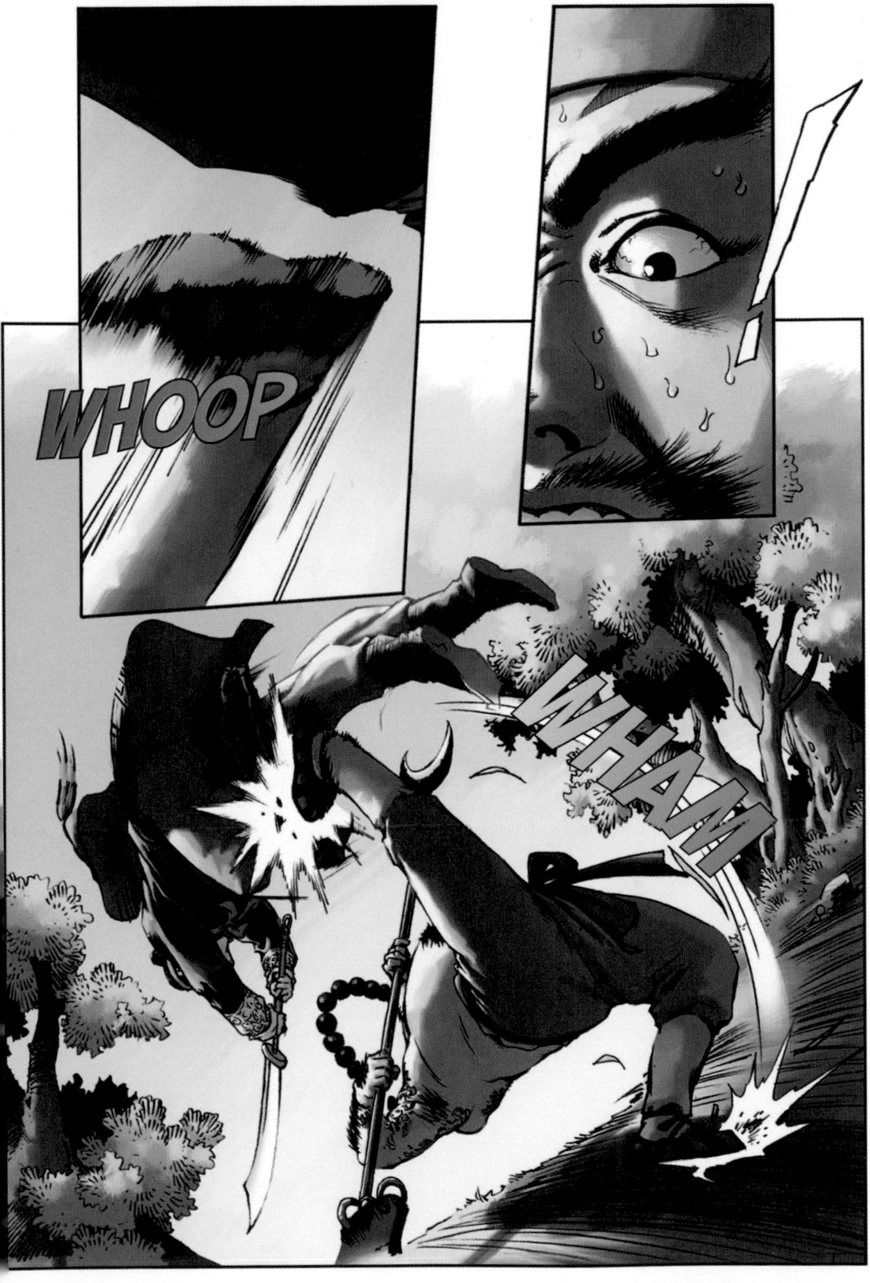
WHOOP
!
WHAM

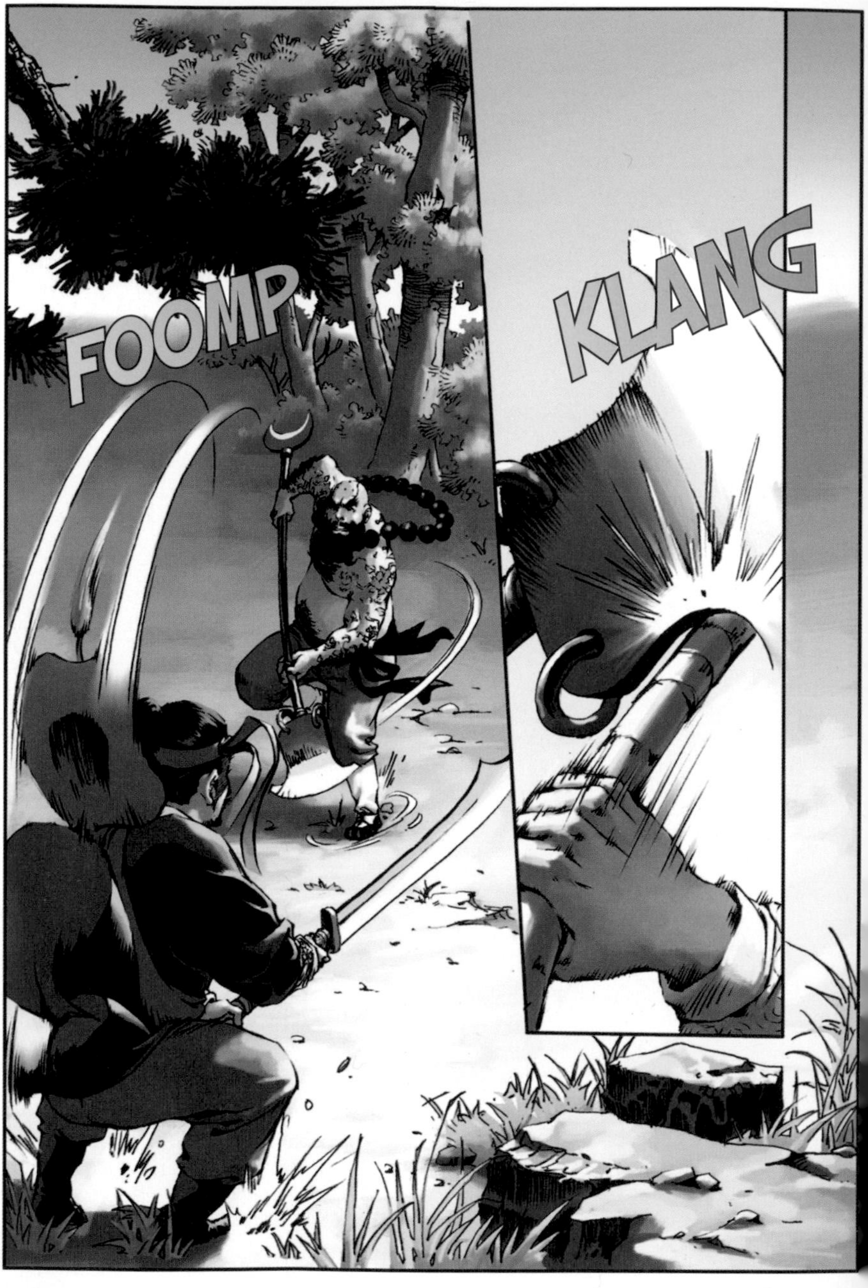
FOOMP
KLANG

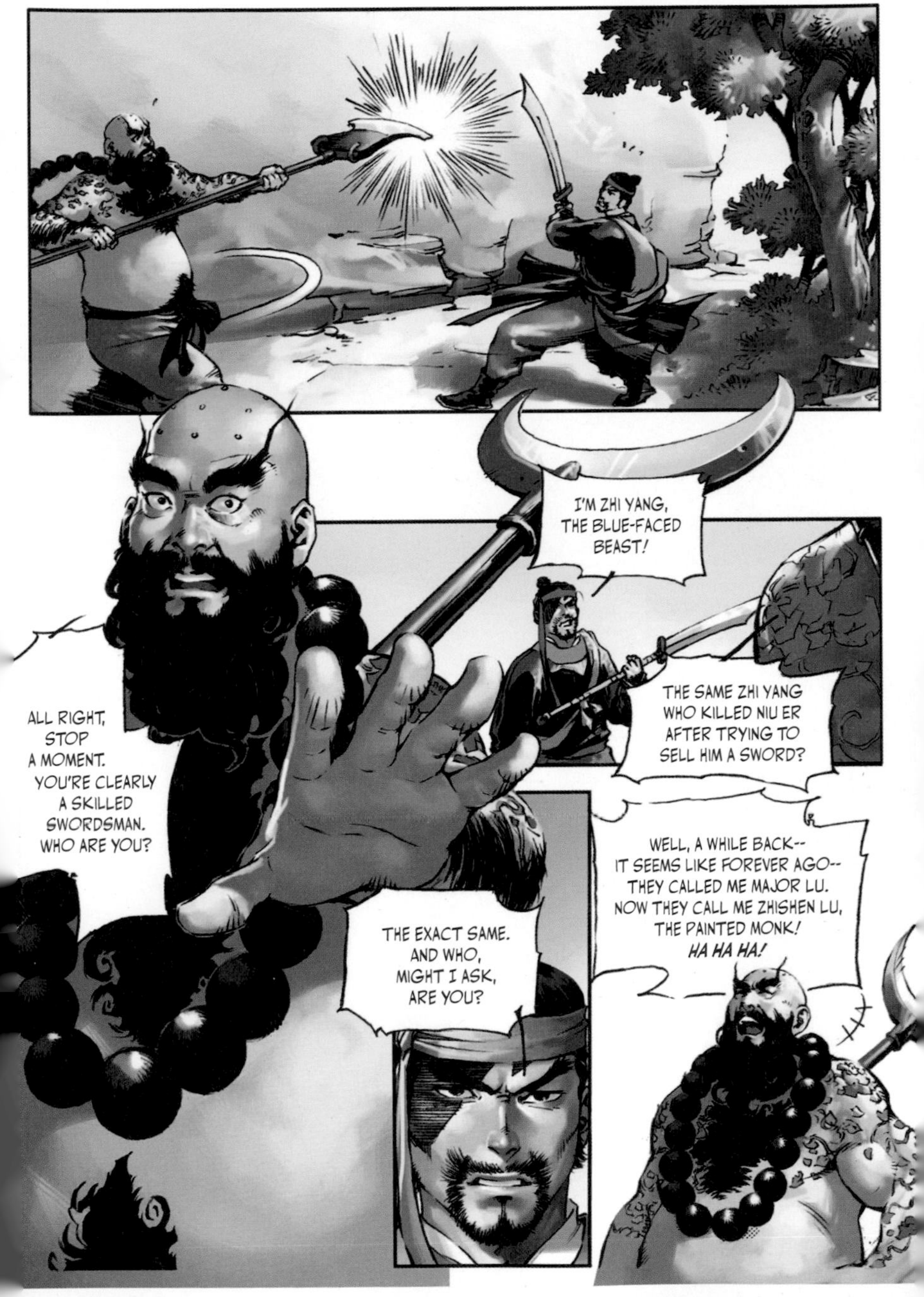
I'M ZHI YANG, THE BLUE-FACED BEAST!
ALL RIGHT, STOP A MOMENT. YOU'RE CLEARLY A SKILLED SWORDSMAN. WHO ARE YOU?
THE SAME ZHI YANG WHO KILLED NIU ER AFTER TRYING TO SELL HIM A SWORD?
THE EXACT SAME. AND WHO, MIGHT I ASK, ARE YOU?
WELL, A WHILE BACK-- IT SEEMS LIKE FOREVER AGO-- THEY CALLED ME MAJOR LU. NOW THEY CALL ME ZHISHEN LU, THE PAINTED MONK! HA HA HA!

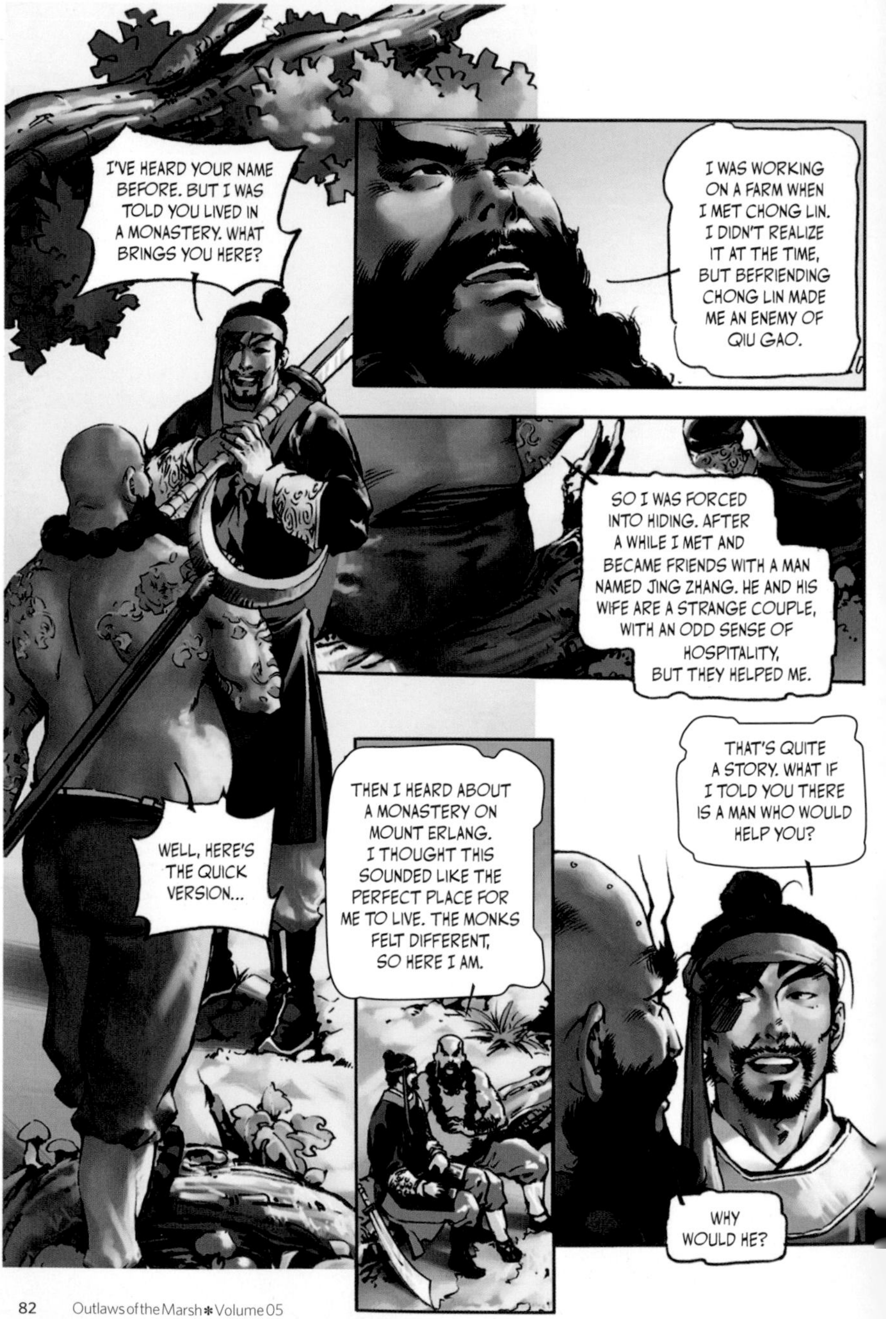
I'VE HEARD YOUR NAME BEFORE. BUT I WAS TOLD YOU LIVED IN A MONASTERY. WHAT BRINGS YOU HERE?
I WAS WORKING ON A FARM WHEN I MET CHONG LIN. I DIDN'T REALIZE IT AT THE TIME, BUT BEFRIENDING CHONG LIN MADE ME AN ENEMY OF QIU GAO.
SO I WAS FORCED INTO HIDING. AFTER A WHILE I MET AND BECAME FRIENDS WITH A MAN NAMED JING ZHANG. HE AND HIS WIFE ARE A STRANGE COUPLE, WITH AN ODD SENSE OF HOSPITALITY, BUT THEY HELPED ME.
WELL, HERE'S THE QUICK VERSION...
THEN I HEARD ABOUT A MONASTERY ON MOUNT ERLANG. I THOUGHT THIS SOUNDED LIKE THE PERFECT PLACE FOR ME TO LIVE. THE MONKS FELT DIFFERENT, SO HERE I AM.
THAT'S QUITE A STORY. WHAT IF I TOLD YOU THERE IS A MAN WHO WOULD HELP YOU?
WHY WOULD HE?

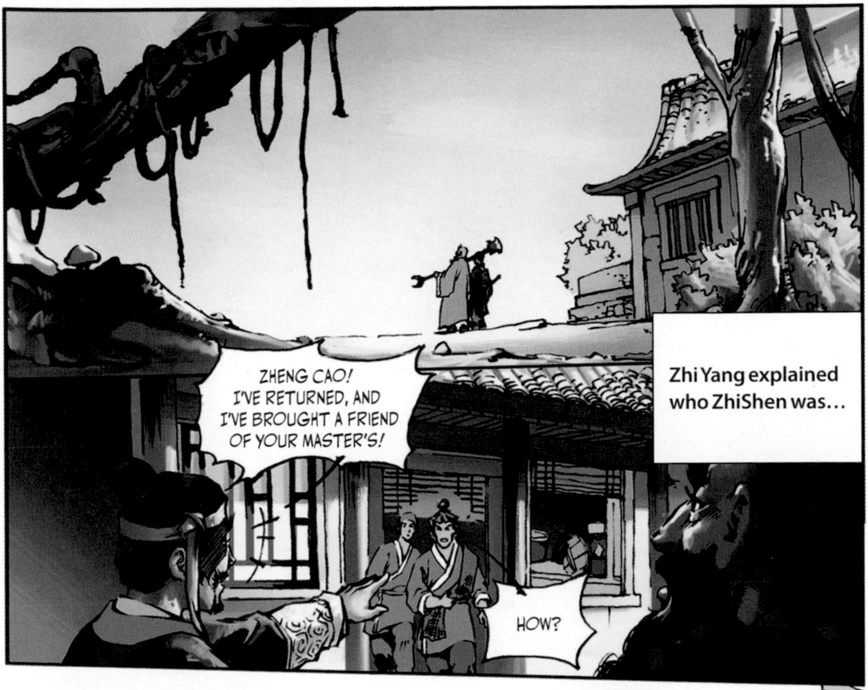

Zhi Yang explained who ZhiShen was…
ZHENG CAO! I'VE RETURNED, AND I'VE BROUGHT A FRIEND OF YOUR MASTER'S!
HOW?

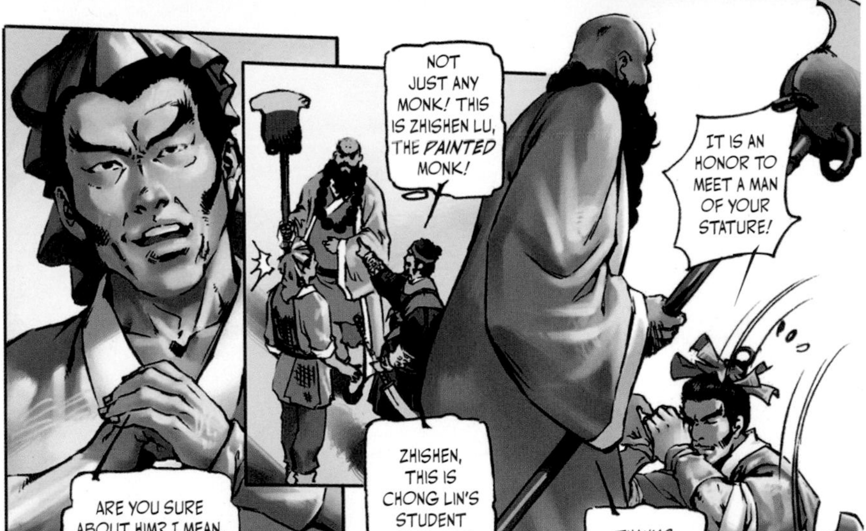

ARE YOU SURE ABOUT HIM? I MEAN, HE'S JUST A MONK.
NOT JUST ANY MONK! THIS IS ZHISHEN LU, THE PAINTED MONK!
ZHISHEN, THIS IS CHONG LIN'S STUDENT ZHENG CAO.
IT IS AN HONOR TO MEET A MAN OF YOUR STATURE!
THANKS. GET UP, THOUGH.

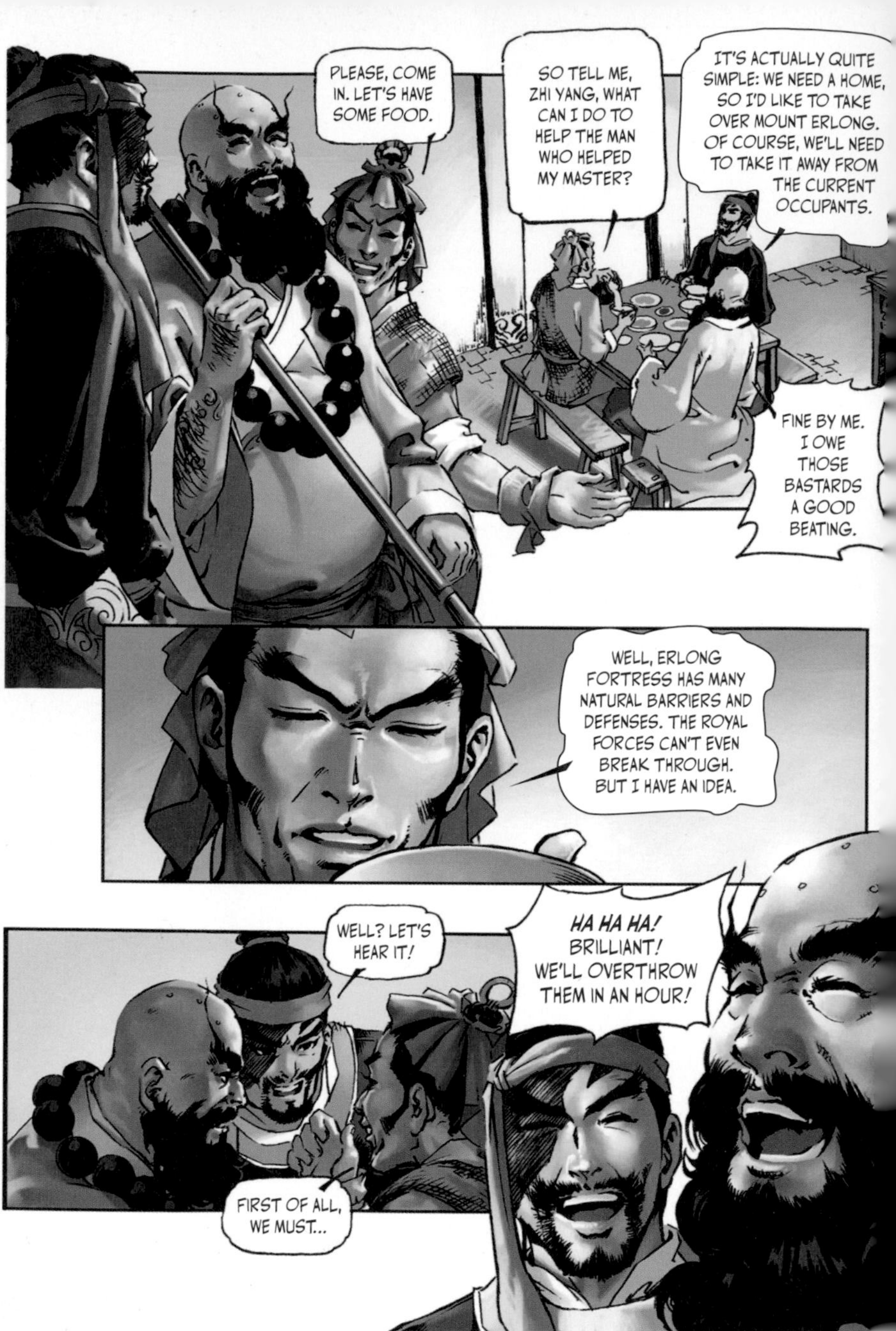
PLEASE, COME IN. LET'S HAVE SOME FOOD.
SO TELL ME, ZHI YANG, WHAT CAN I DO TO HELP THE MAN WHO HELPED MY MASTER?
IT'S ACTUALLY QUITE SIMPLE: WE NEED A HOME, SO I'D LIKE TO TAKE OVER MOUNT ERLONG. OF COURSE, WE'LL NEED TO TAKE IT AWAY FROM THE CURRENT OCCUPANTS.
FINE BY ME. I OWE THOSE BASTARDS A GOOD BEATING.
WELL, ERLONG FORTRESS HAS MANY NATURAL BARRIERS AND DEFENSES. THE ROYAL FORCES CAN'T EVEN BREAK THROUGH. BUT I HAVE AN IDEA.
WELL? LET'S HEAR IT!
FIRST OF ALL, WE MUST...
HA HA HA! BRILLIANT! WE'LL OVERTHROW THEM IN AN HOUR!

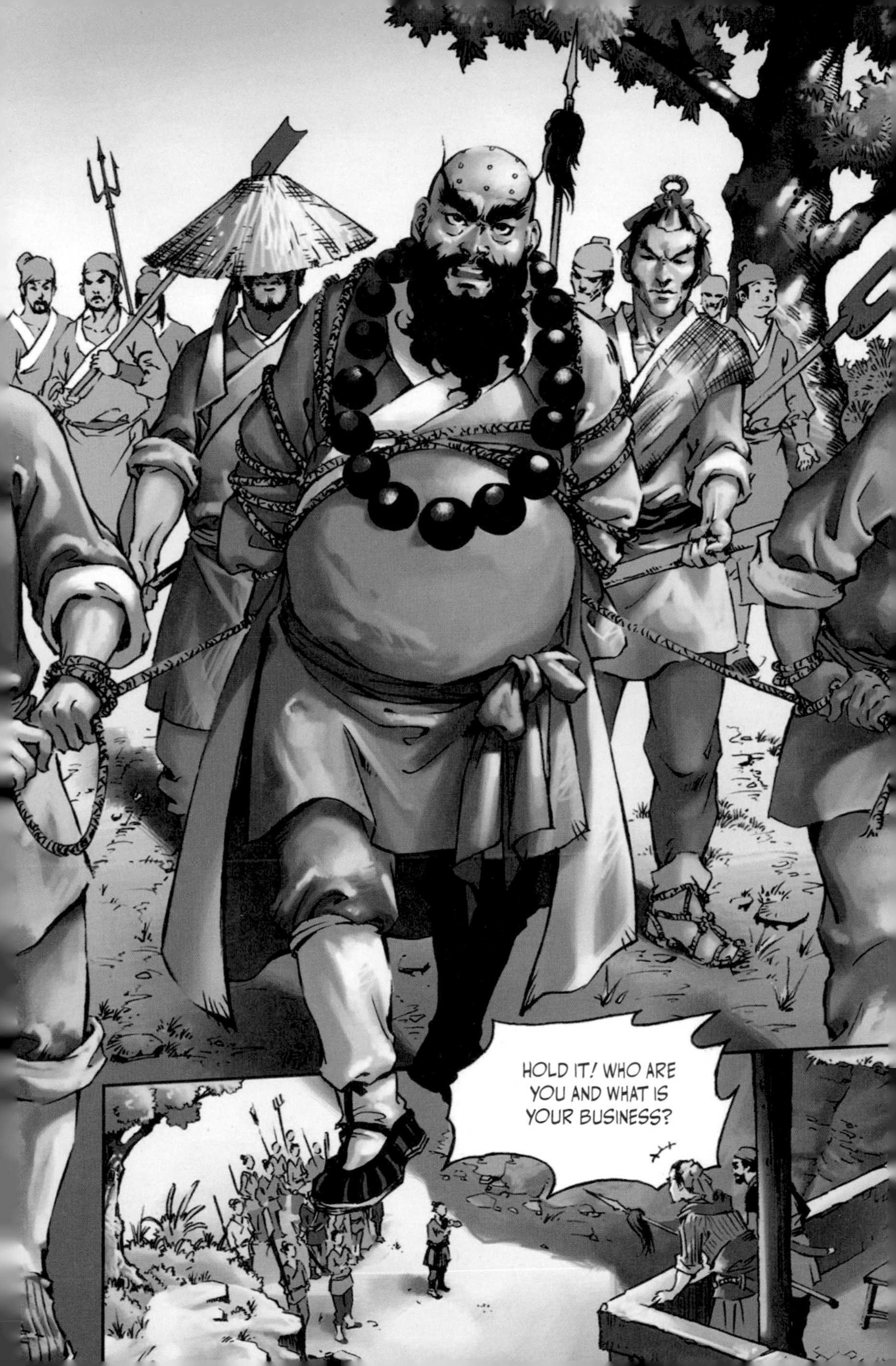
HOLD IT! WHO ARE
YOU AND WHAT IS
YOUR BUSINESS?

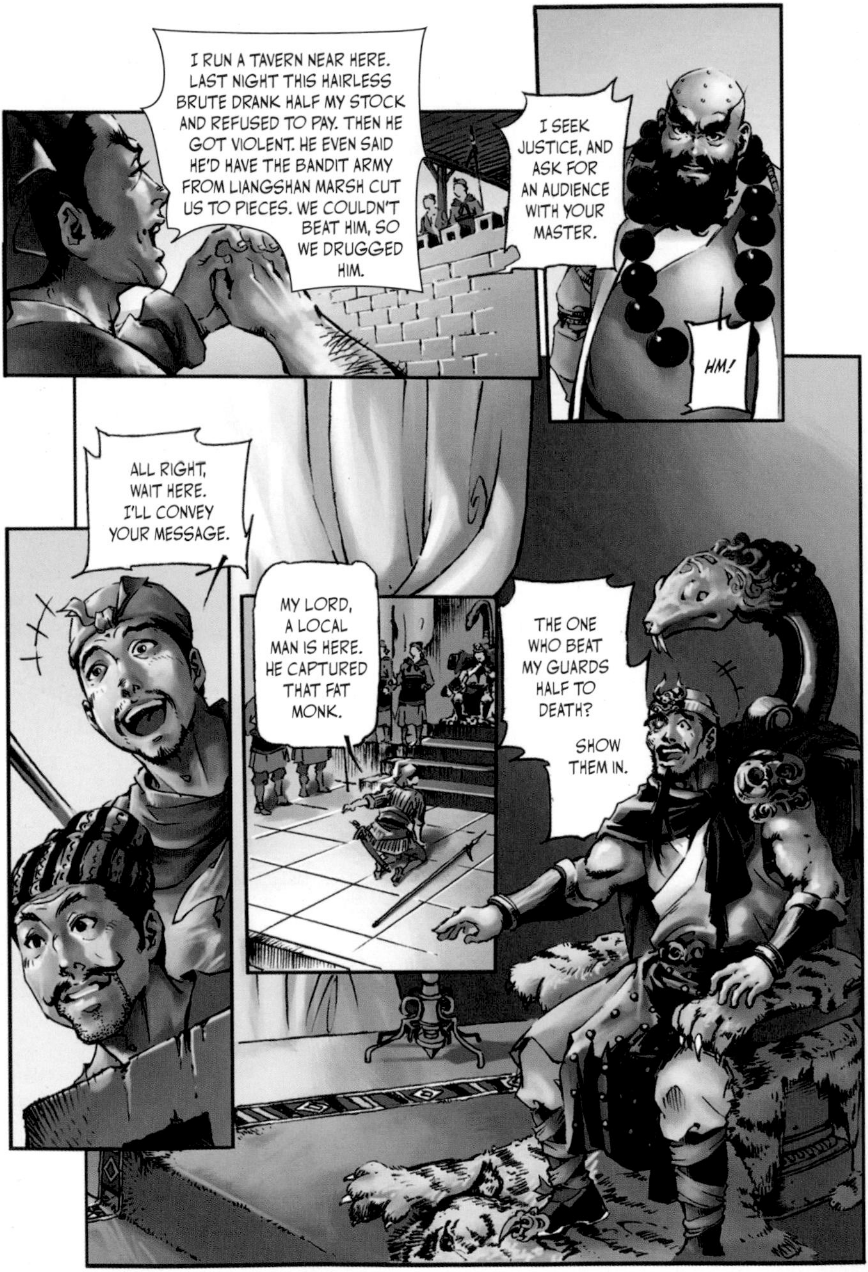
I RUN A TAVERN NEAR HERE. LAST NIGHT THIS HAIRLESS BRUTE DRANK HALF MY STOCK AND REFUSED TO PAY. THEN HE GOT VIOLENT. HE EVEN SAID HE'D HAVE THE BANDIT ARMY FROM LIANGSHAN MARSH CUT US TO PIECES. WE COULDN'T BEAT HIM, SO WE DRUGGED HIM.
I SEEK JUSTICE, AND ASK FOR AN AUDIENCE WITH YOUR MASTER.
HM!
ALL RIGHT, WAIT HERE. I'LL CONVEY YOUR MESSAGE.
MY LORD, A LOCAL MAN IS HERE. HE CAPTURED THAT FAT MONK.
THE ONE WHO BEAT MY GUARDS HALF TO DEATH?
SHOW THEM IN.

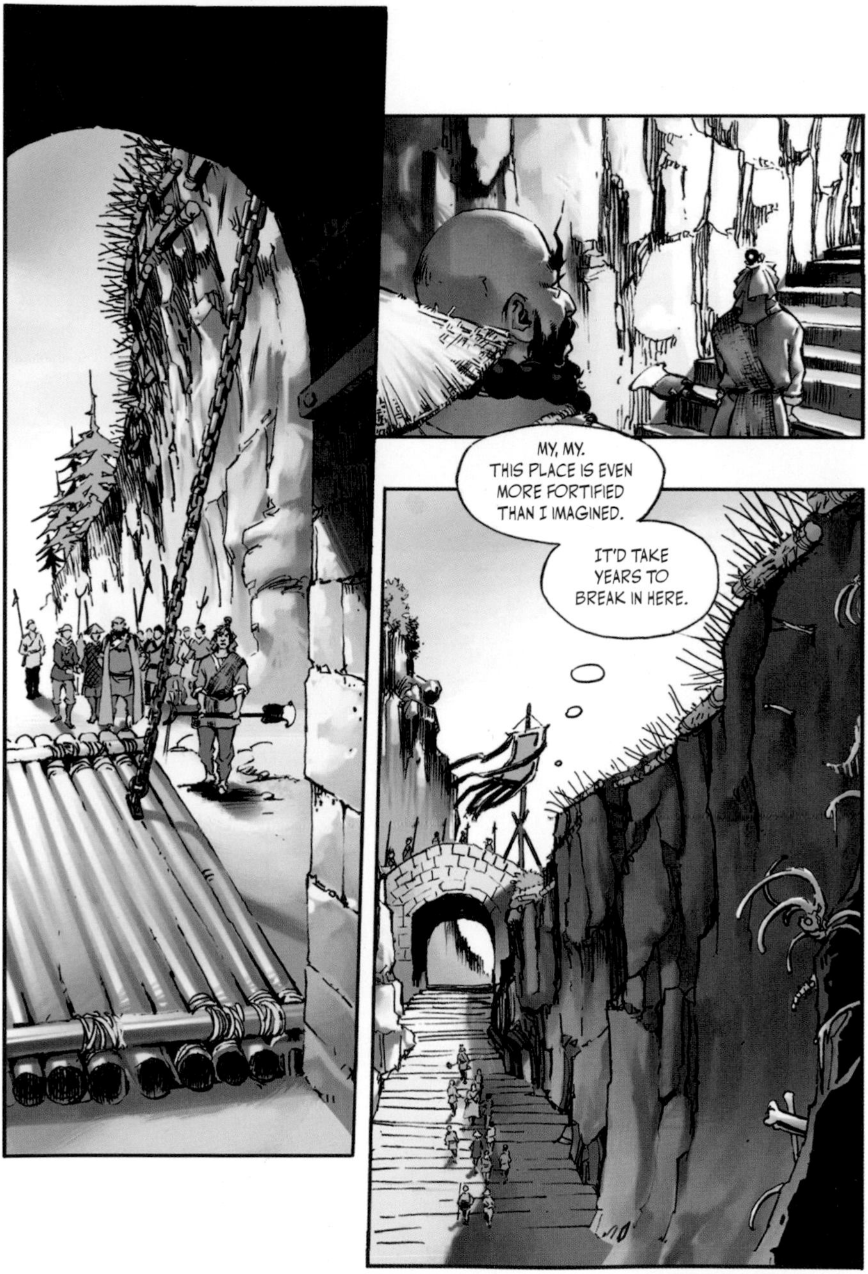
MY, MY.
THIS PLACE IS EVEN MORE FORTIFIED THAN I IMAGINED.
IT'D TAKE YEARS TO BREAK IN HERE.

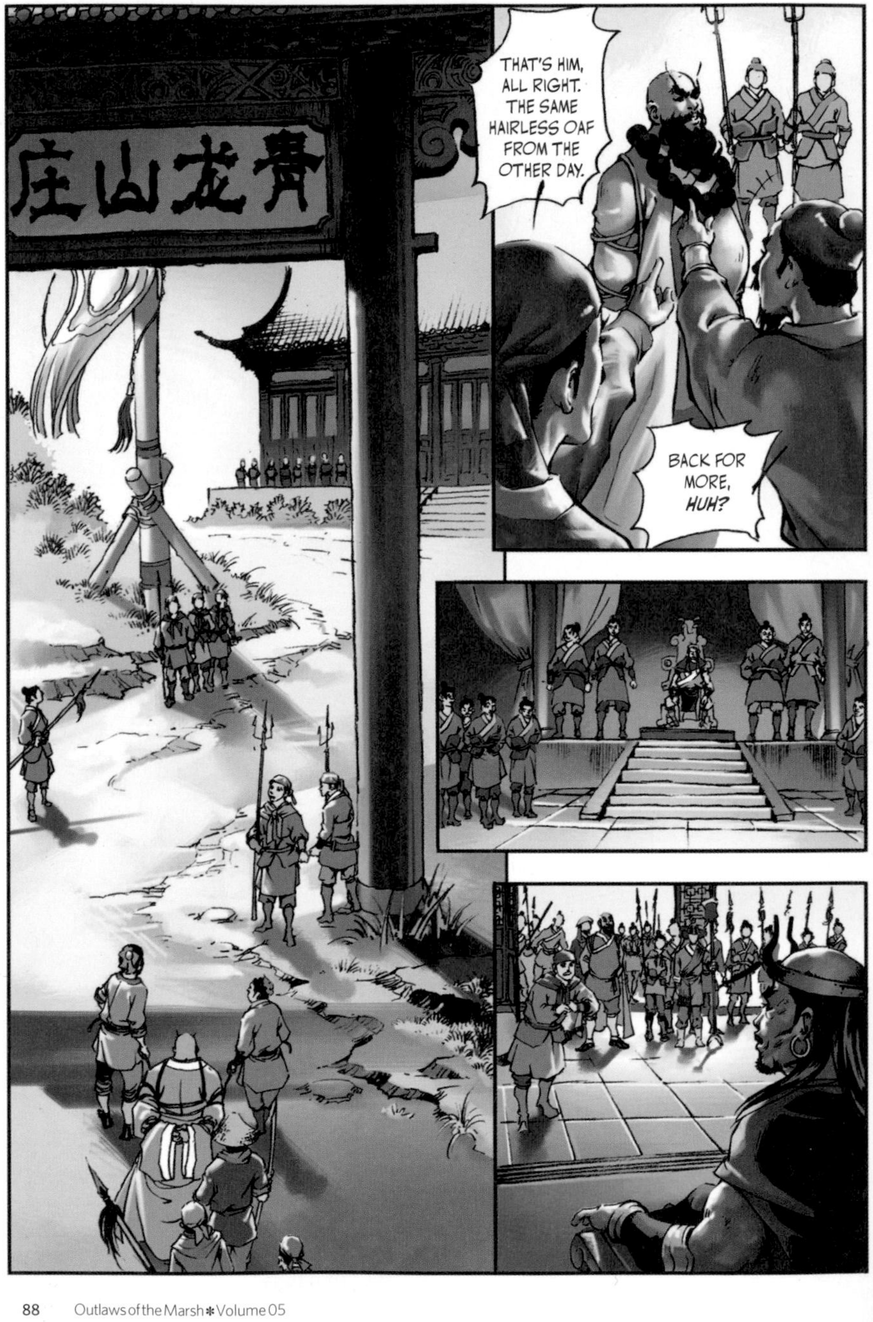
青龙山庄
THAT'S HIM, ALL RIGHT. THE SAME HAIRLESS OAF FROM THE OTHER DAY.
BACK FOR MORE, *HUH?*

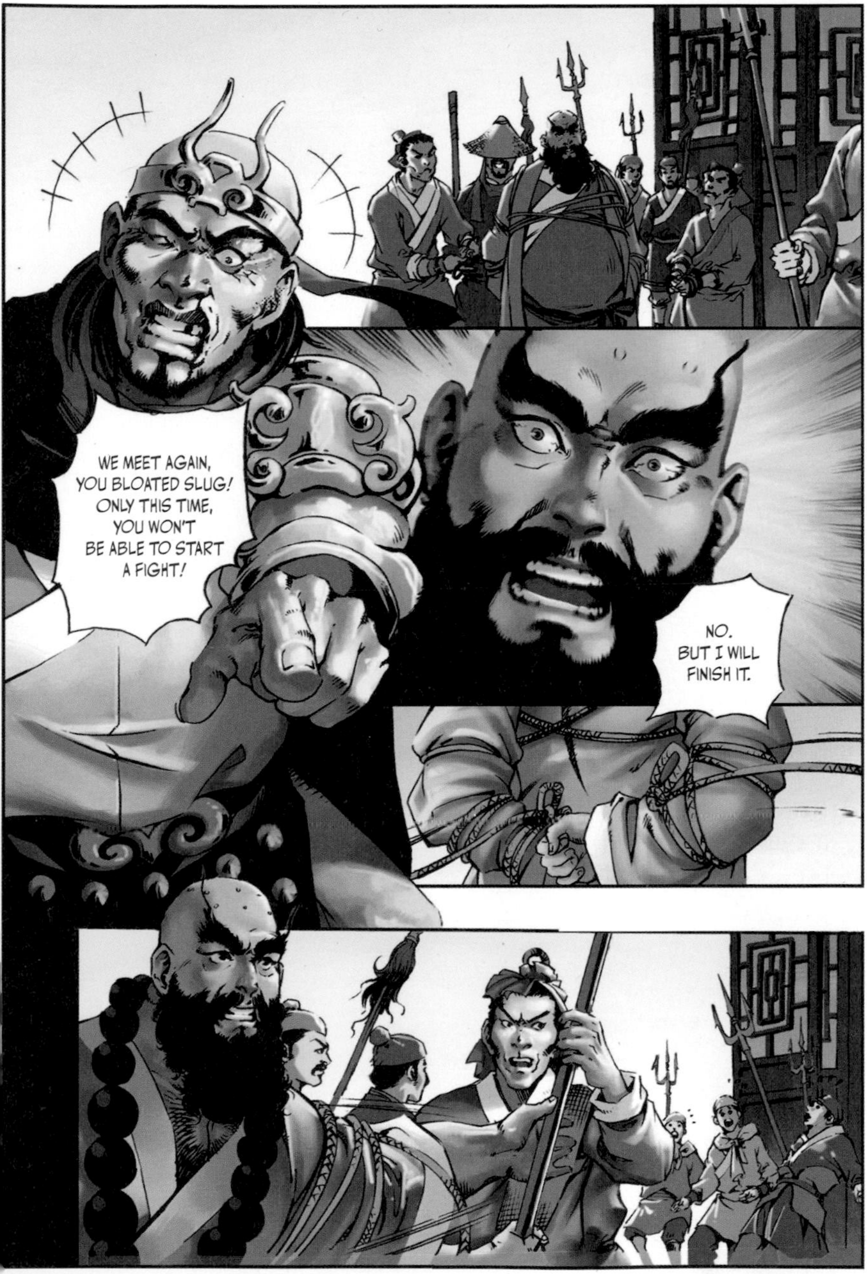
WE MEET AGAIN, YOU BLOATED SLUG! ONLY THIS TIME, YOU WON'T BE ABLE TO START A FIGHT!
NO. BUT I WILL FINISH IT.

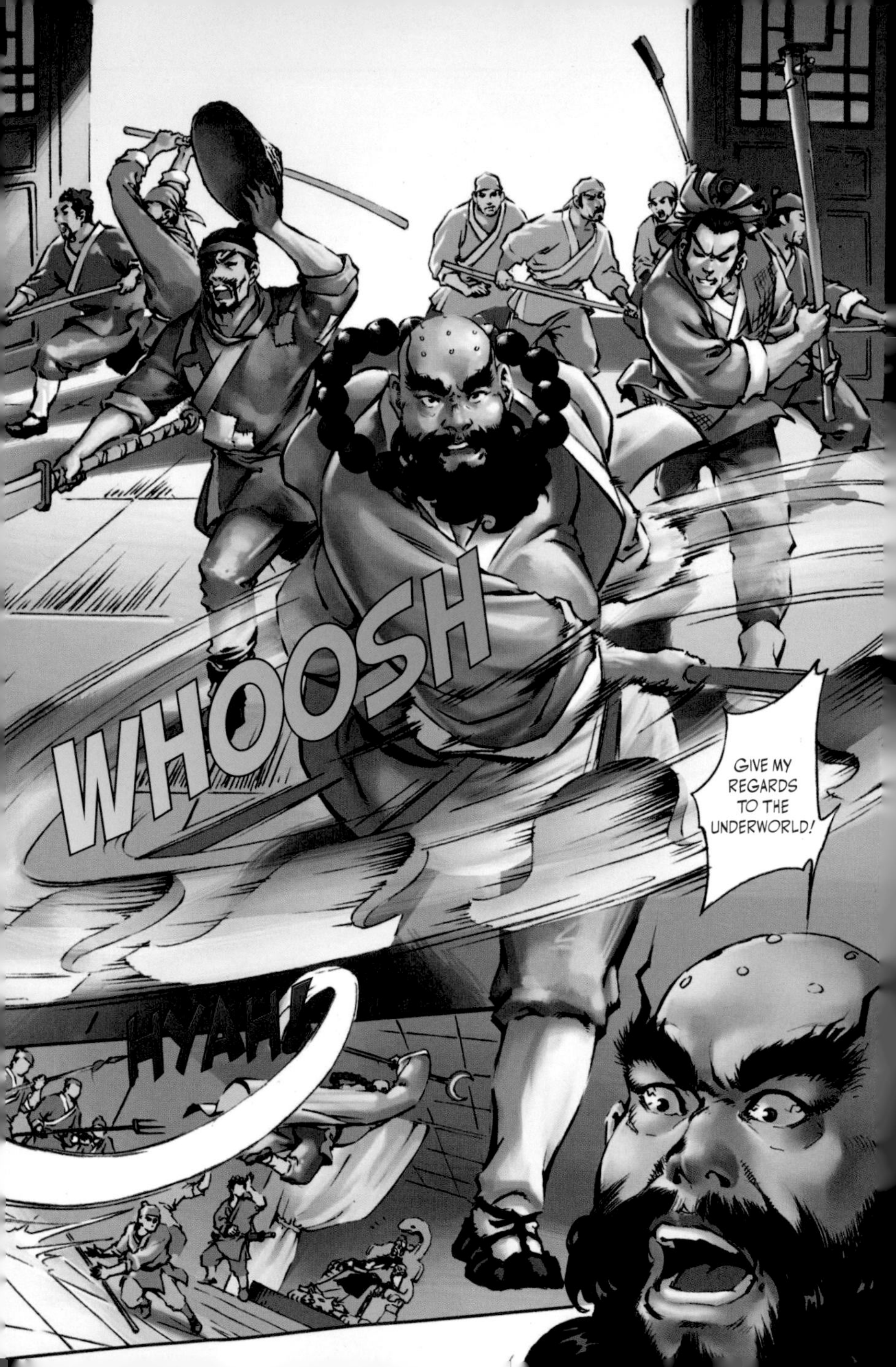
WHOOSH
GIVE MY REGARDS TO THE UNDERWORLD!
HYAH!

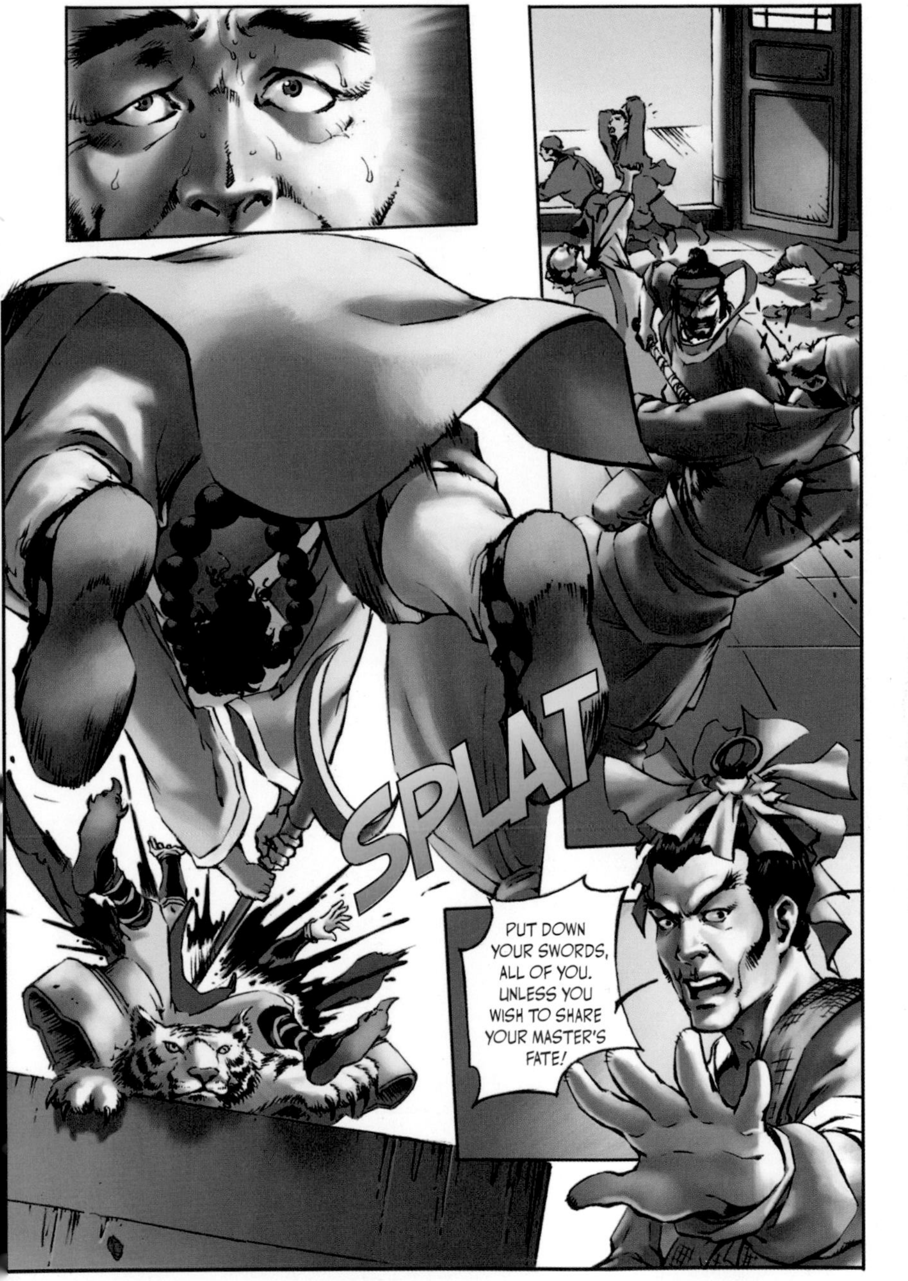
SPLAT
PUT DOWN YOUR SWORDS, ALL OF YOU. UNLESS YOU WISH TO SHARE YOUR MASTER'S FATE!

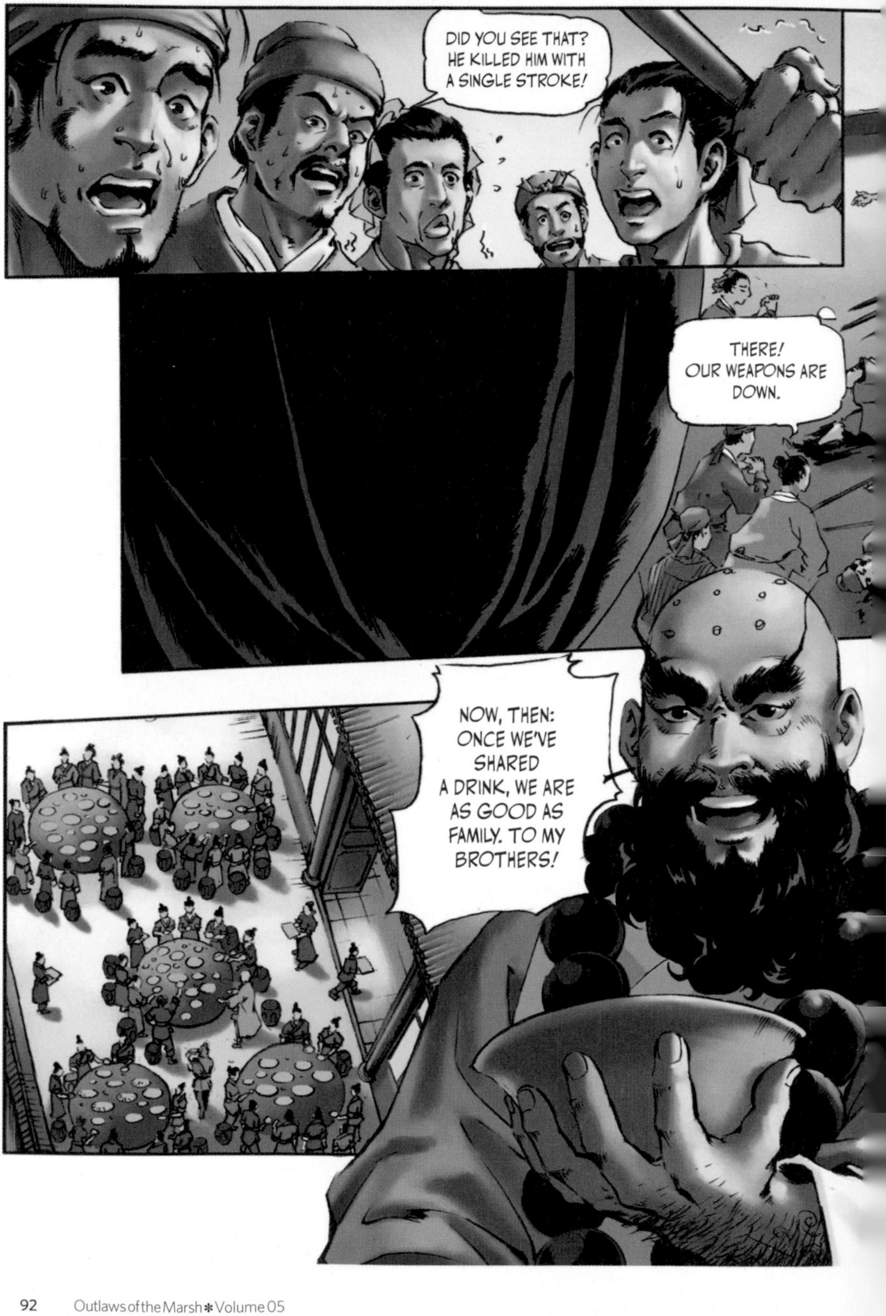
DID YOU SEE THAT? HE KILLED HIM WITH A SINGLE STROKE!
THERE! OUR WEAPONS ARE DOWN.
NOW, THEN: ONCE WE'VE SHARED A DRINK, WE ARE AS GOOD AS FAMILY. TO MY BROTHERS!

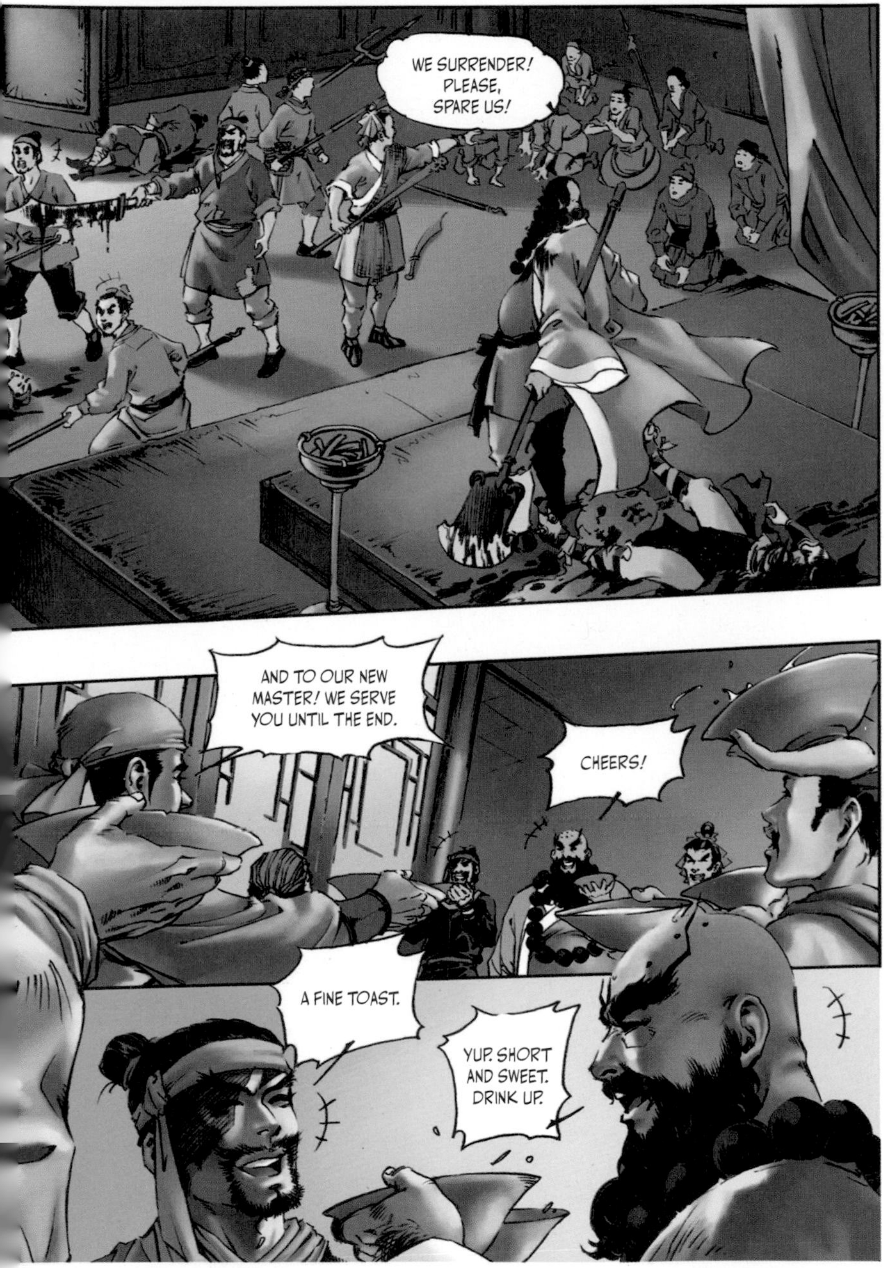
WE SURRENDER! PLEASE, SPARE US!
AND TO OUR NEW MASTER! WE SERVE YOU UNTIL THE END.
CHEERS!
A FINE TOAST.
YUP. SHORT AND SWEET. DRINK UP.

Chapter 2

Outlaws of the Marsh

Summary

When Governor Jing Cai discovers that once again his son-in-law has had priceless gifts stolen en route to the governor, he orders a local prefect to hunt the thieves down immediately. Tao He, an inspector known for tracking and capturing bandits, embarks for YunCheng Province after an accomplice admits that Gai Chao was responsible for the theft.

When Tao He reaches YunCheng, he speaks with a local official named Jiang Song, who pledges to help him with the search but is secretly helping Gai Chao. When local forces attempt to capture Gai Chao, he flees his manor with the help of some trusted friends. Tao He tracks Gai Chao to the village of ShiJie, where he is being sheltered by the Ruan brothers. Tao He launches an attack by boat, but quickly learns that Gai Chao's most dangerous allies are the marshes.

DaiZhou
CangZhou
BOHAI SEA
Mt. WuTai
QingZhou
Mt. ErLong
BeiJing
B
HuangNi Hill
Mt. TaoHua
A
ShiJie
LiangShan
Marsh
YunCheng
JiZhou
DongJing
(KaiFung)
XiJing
Mt. XiaoHua
NanJing

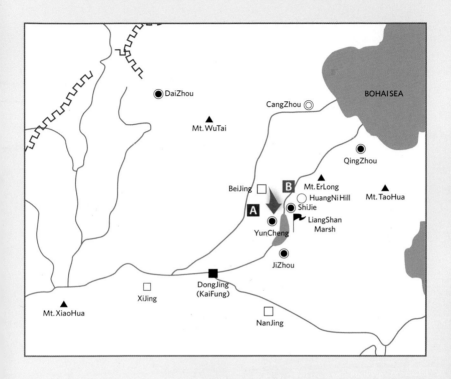

A Tao He leads a regiment of royal troops to YunCheng Province, where he's hunting down Gai Chao. There he meets Jiang Song.

B The royal forces confront the Ruan brothers in ShiJie Village.

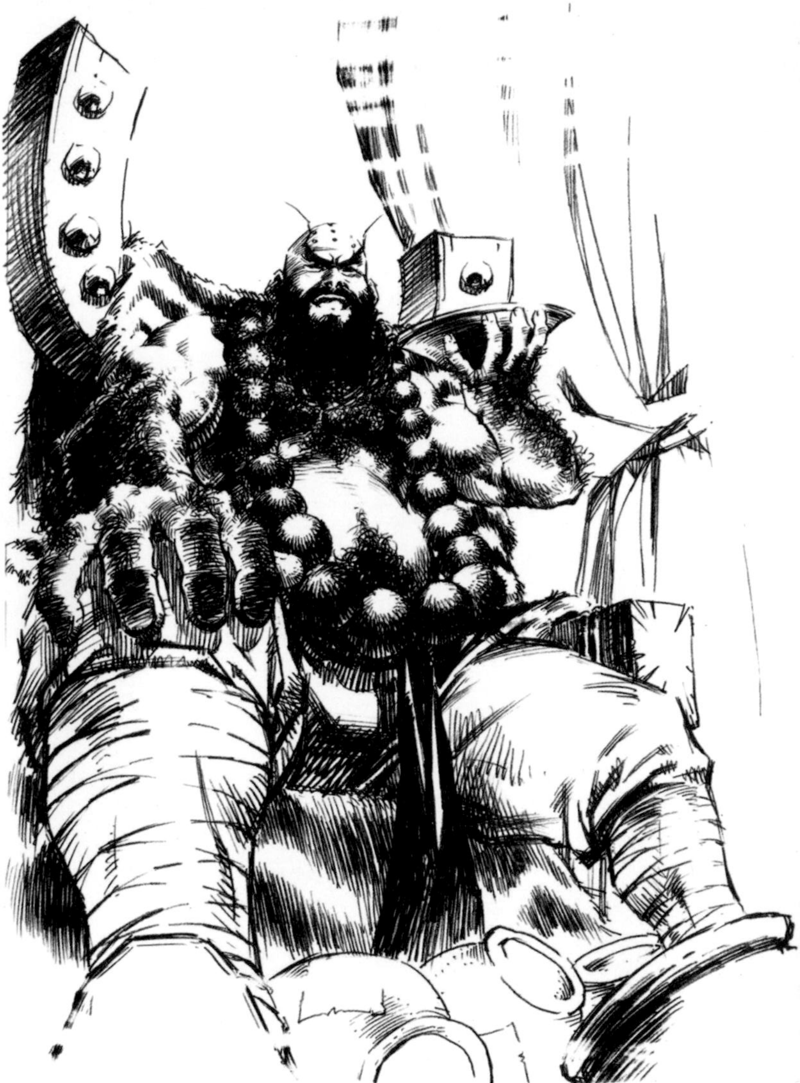

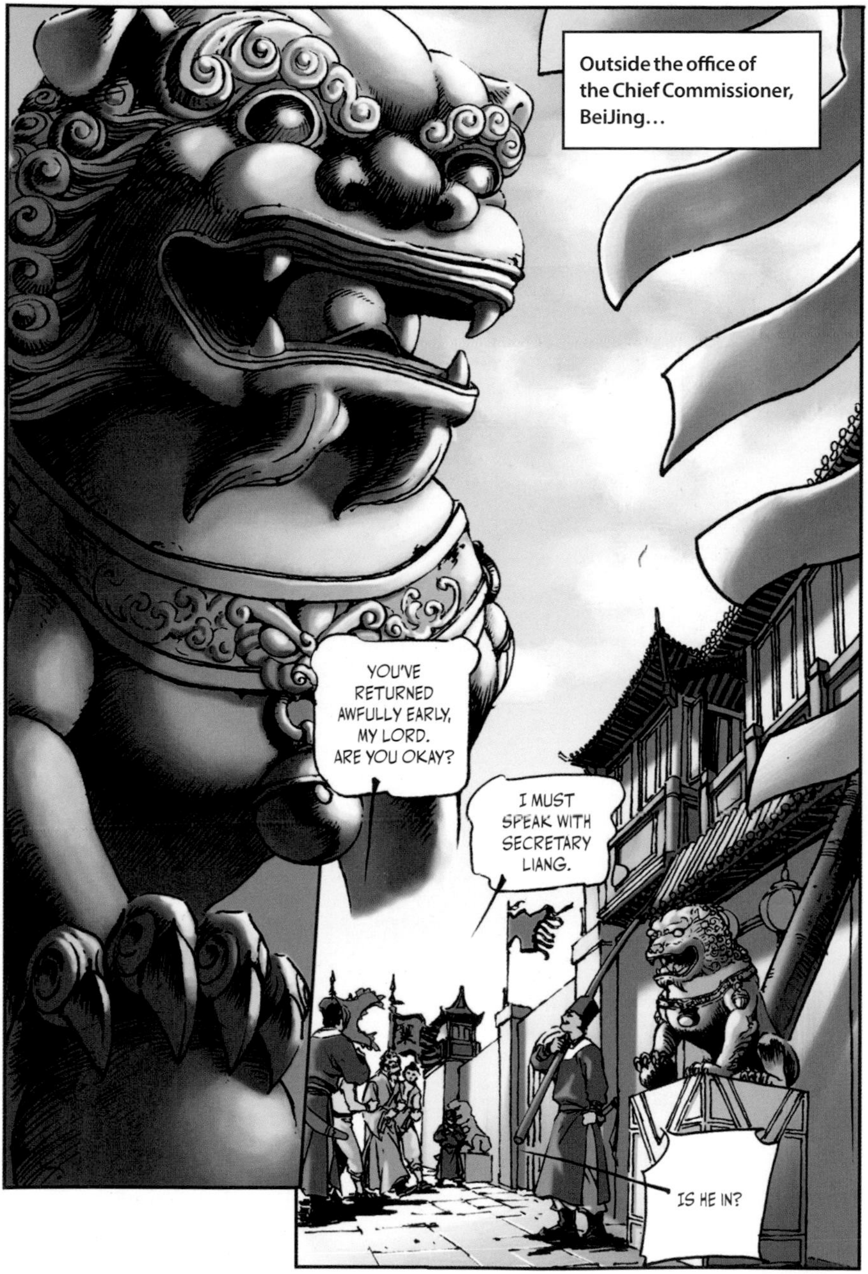
Outside the office of the Chief Commissioner, BeiJing…
YOU'VE RETURNED AWFULLY EARLY, MY LORD. ARE YOU OKAY?
I MUST SPEAK WITH SECRETARY LIANG.
IS HE IN?

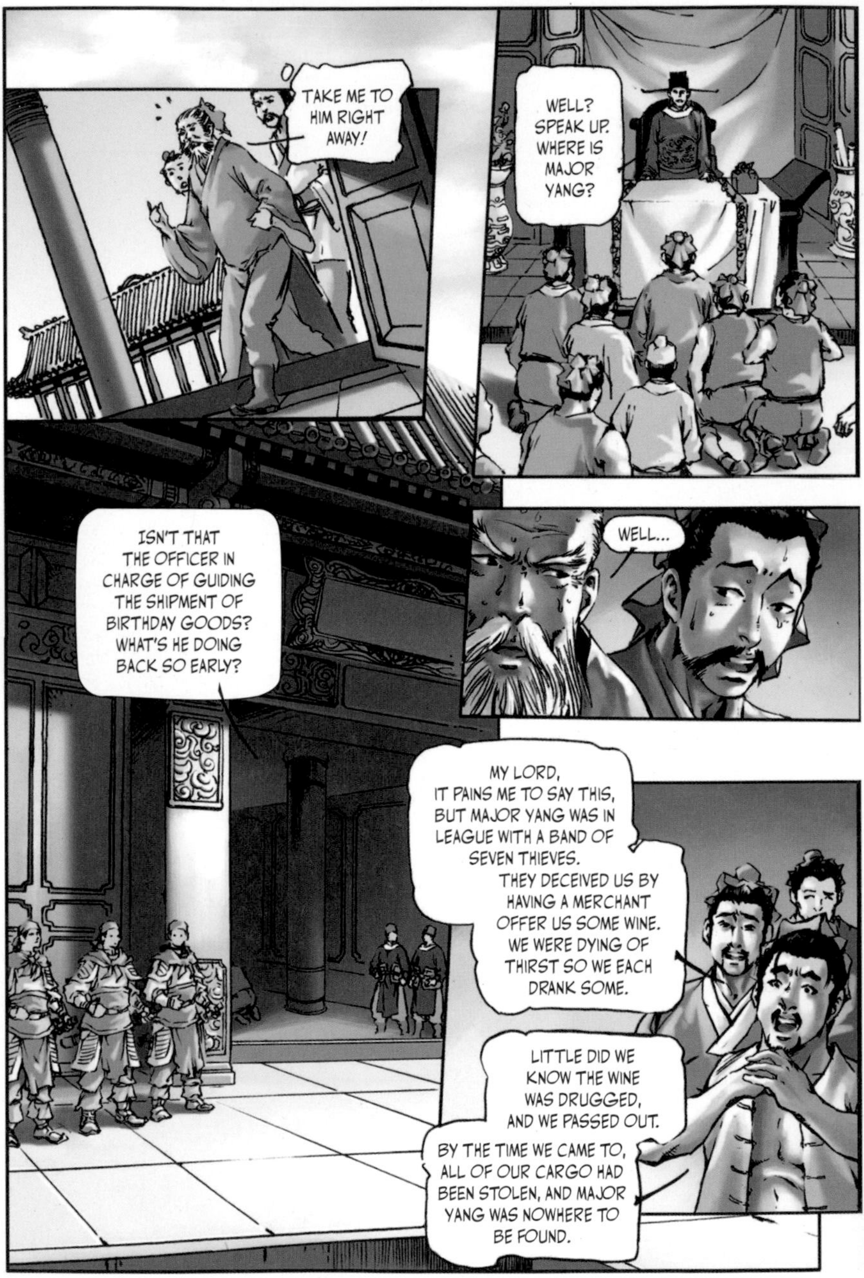

TAKE ME TO HIM RIGHT AWAY!
WELL? SPEAK UP. WHERE IS MAJOR YANG?
ISN'T THAT THE OFFICER IN CHARGE OF GUIDING THE SHIPMENT OF BIRTHDAY GOODS? WHAT'S HE DOING BACK SO EARLY?
WELL...
MY LORD, IT PAINS ME TO SAY THIS, BUT MAJOR YANG WAS IN LEAGUE WITH A BAND OF SEVEN THIEVES.
THEY DECEIVED US BY HAVING A MERCHANT OFFER US SOME WINE. WE WERE DYING OF THIRST SO WE EACH DRANK SOME.
LITTLE DID WE KNOW THE WINE WAS DRUGGED, AND WE PASSED OUT.
BY THE TIME WE CAME TO, ALL OF OUR CARGO HAD BEEN STOLEN, AND MAJOR YANG WAS NOWHERE TO BE FOUND.

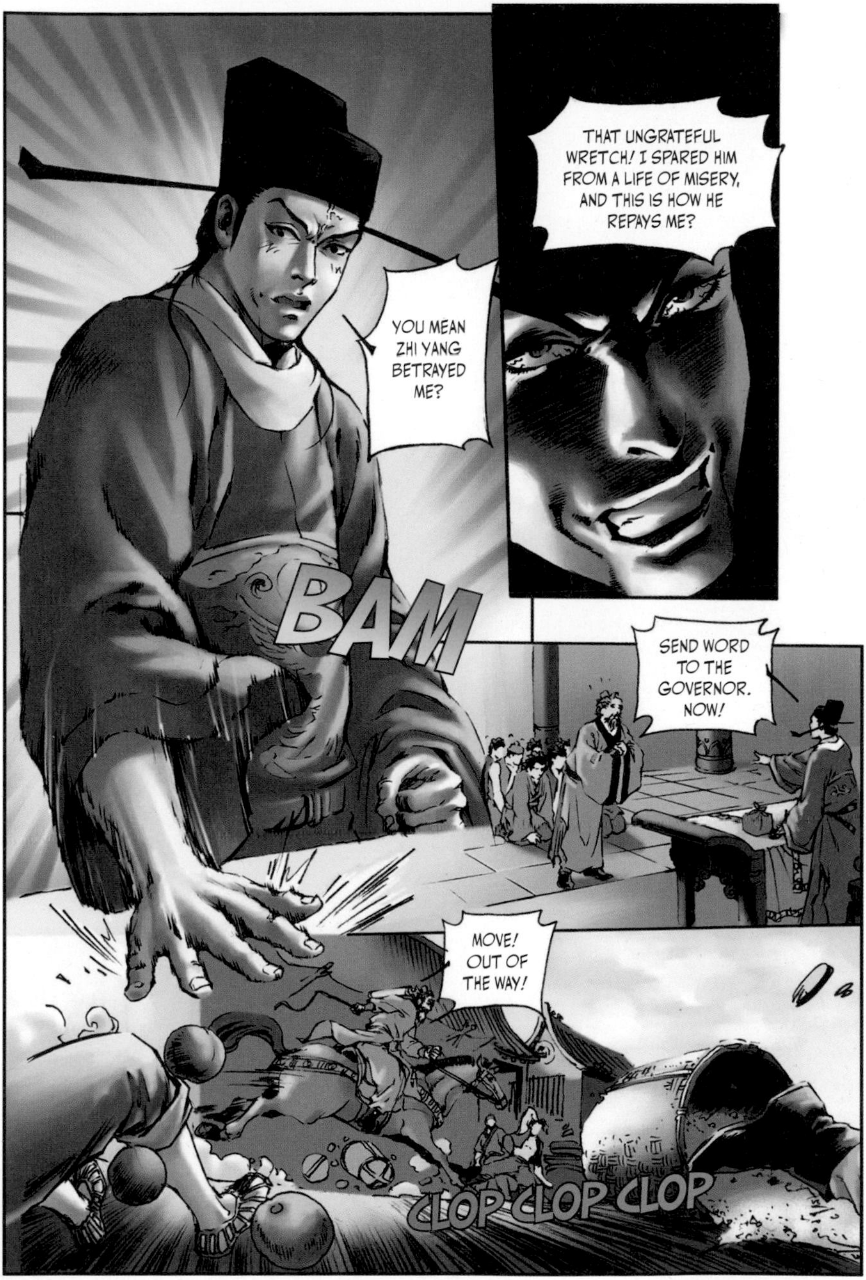
YOU MEAN ZHI YANG BETRAYED ME?
THAT UNGRATEFUL WRETCH! I SPARED HIM FROM A LIFE OF MISERY, AND THIS IS HOW HE REPAYS ME?
BAM
SEND WORD TO THE GOVERNOR. NOW!
MOVE! OUT OF THE WAY!
CLOP CLOP CLOP

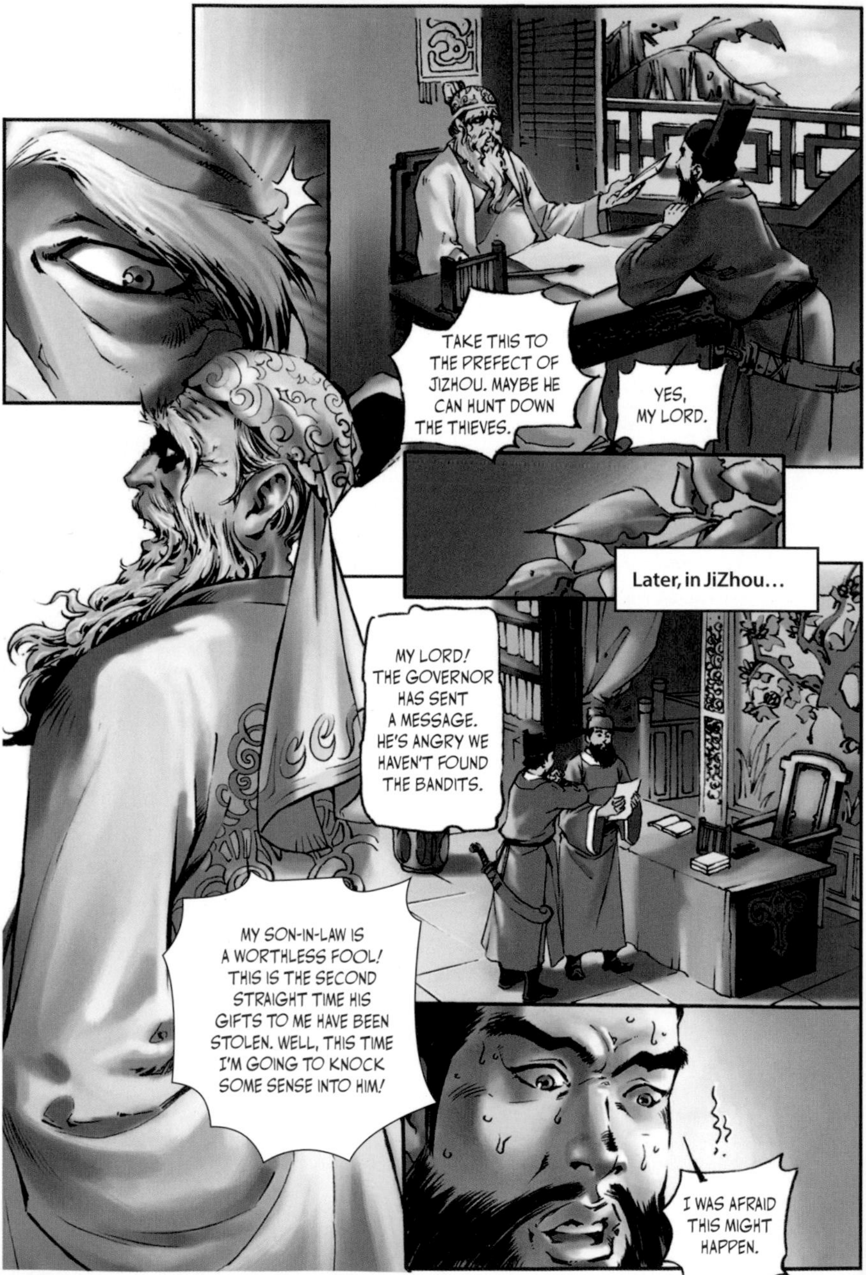
TAKE THIS TO THE PREFECT OF JIZHOU. MAYBE HE CAN HUNT DOWN THE THIEVES.
YES, MY LORD.
Later, in JiZhou...
MY LORD! THE GOVERNOR HAS SENT A MESSAGE. HE'S ANGRY WE HAVEN'T FOUND THE BANDITS.
MY SON-IN-LAW IS A WORTHLESS FOOL! THIS IS THE SECOND STRAIGHT TIME HIS GIFTS TO ME HAVE BEEN STOLEN. WELL, THIS TIME I'M GOING TO KNOCK SOME SENSE INTO HIM!
I WAS AFRAID THIS MIGHT HAPPEN.

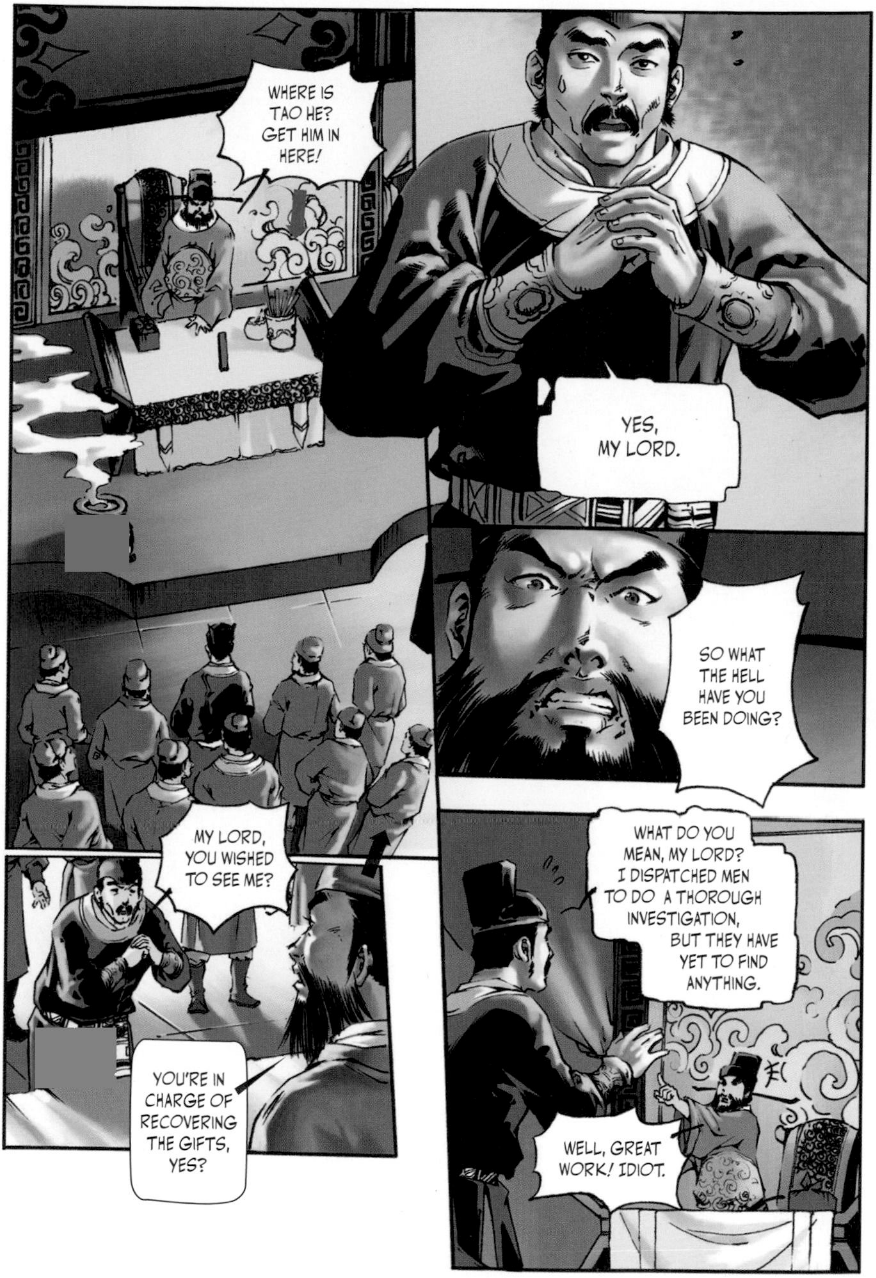
WHERE IS TAO HE? GET HIM IN HERE!
YES, MY LORD.
MY LORD, YOU WISHED TO SEE ME?
YOU'RE IN CHARGE OF RECOVERING THE GIFTS, YES?
SO WHAT THE HELL HAVE YOU BEEN DOING?
WHAT DO YOU MEAN, MY LORD? I DISPATCHED MEN TO DO A THOROUGH INVESTIGATION, BUT THEY HAVE YET TO FIND ANYTHING.
WELL, GREAT WORK! IDIOT.

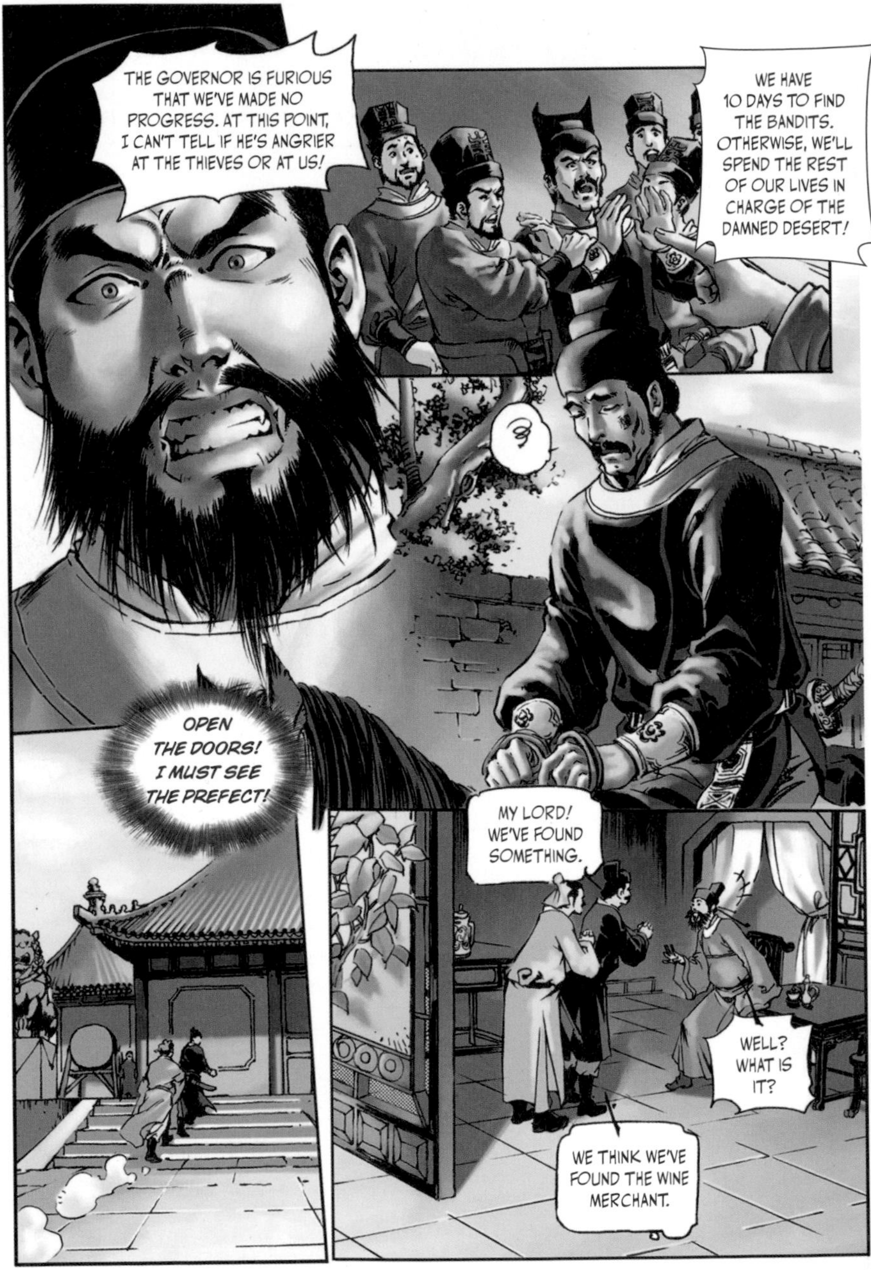
THE GOVERNOR IS FURIOUS THAT WE'VE MADE NO PROGRESS. AT THIS POINT, I CAN'T TELL IF HE'S ANGRIER AT THE THIEVES OR AT US!
WE HAVE 10 DAYS TO FIND THE BANDITS. OTHERWISE, WE'LL SPEND THE REST OF OUR LIVES IN CHARGE OF THE DAMNED DESERT!
OPEN THE DOORS! I MUST SEE THE PREFECT!
MY LORD! WE'VE FOUND SOMETHING.
WELL? WHAT IS IT?
WE THINK WE'VE FOUND THE WINE MERCHANT.

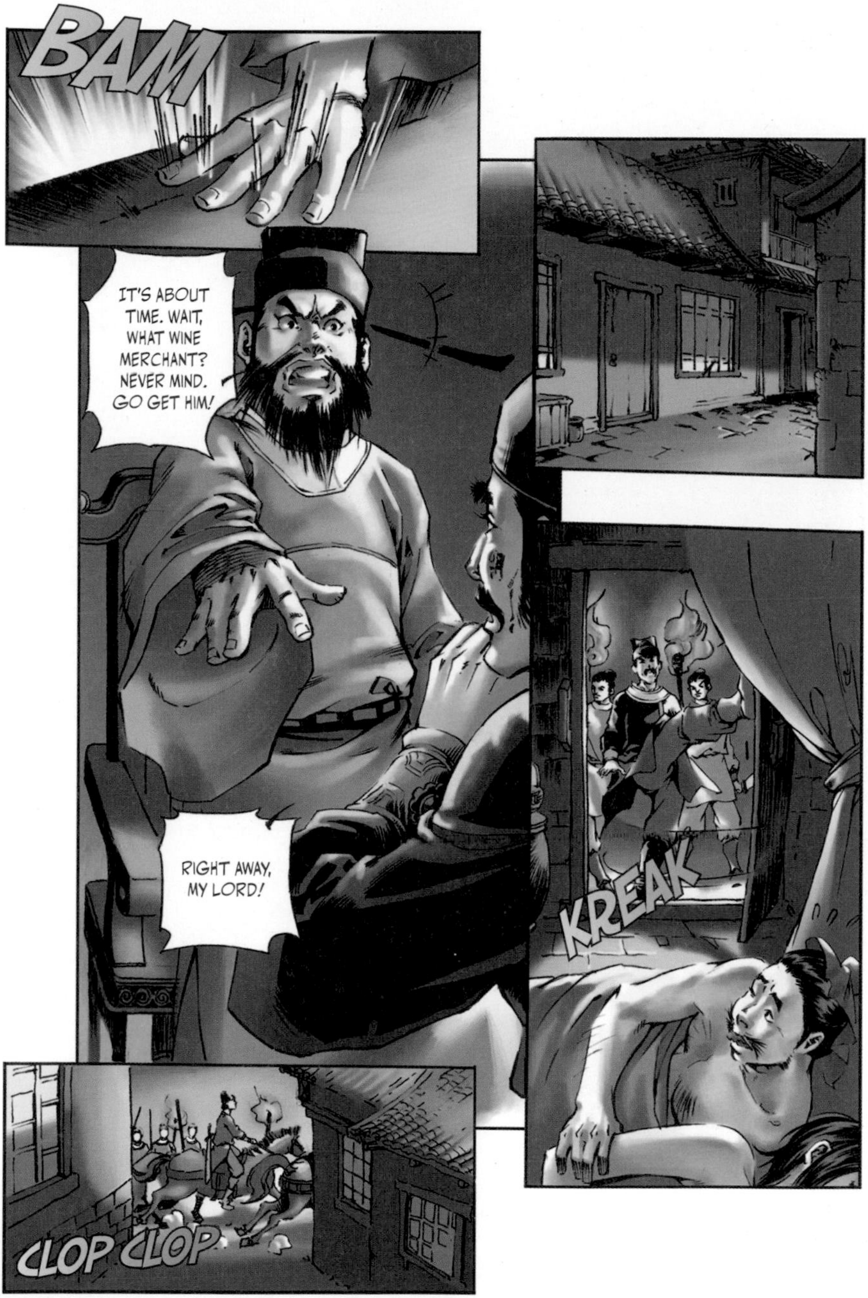
BAM
IT'S ABOUT TIME. WAIT, WHAT WINE MERCHANT? NEVER MIND. GO GET HIM!
RIGHT AWAY, MY LORD!
KREAK
CLOP CLOP

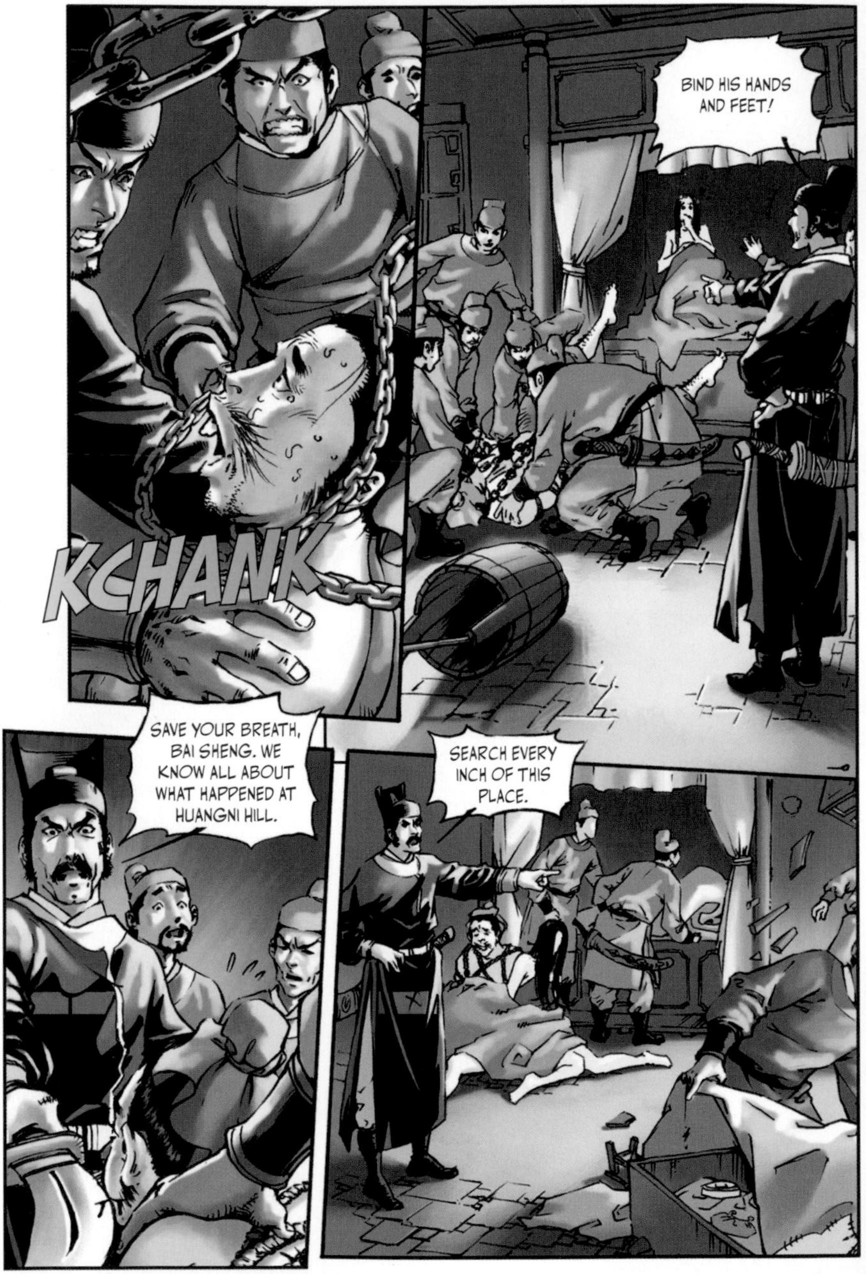
KCHANK
BIND HIS HANDS AND FEET!
SAVE YOUR BREATH, BAI SHENG. WE KNOW ALL ABOUT WHAT HAPPENED AT HUANGNI HILL.
SEARCH EVERY INCH OF THIS PLACE.

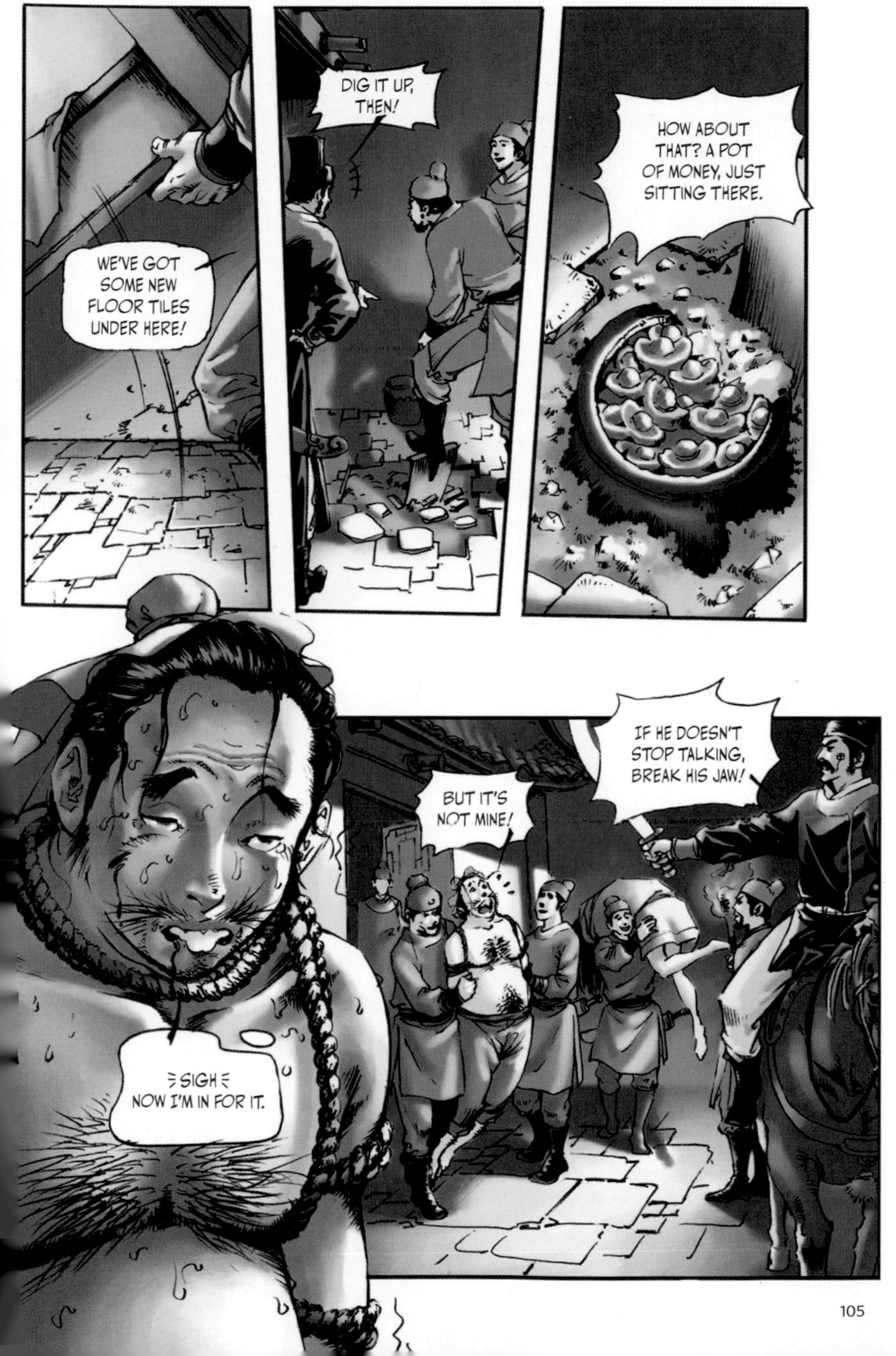
WE'VE GOT SOME NEW FLOOR TILES UNDER HERE!
DIG IT UP, THEN!
HOW ABOUT THAT? A POT OF MONEY, JUST SITTING THERE.
≡SIGH≡ NOW I'M IN FOR IT.
IF HE DOESN'T STOP TALKING, BREAK HIS JAW!
BUT IT'S NOT MINE!

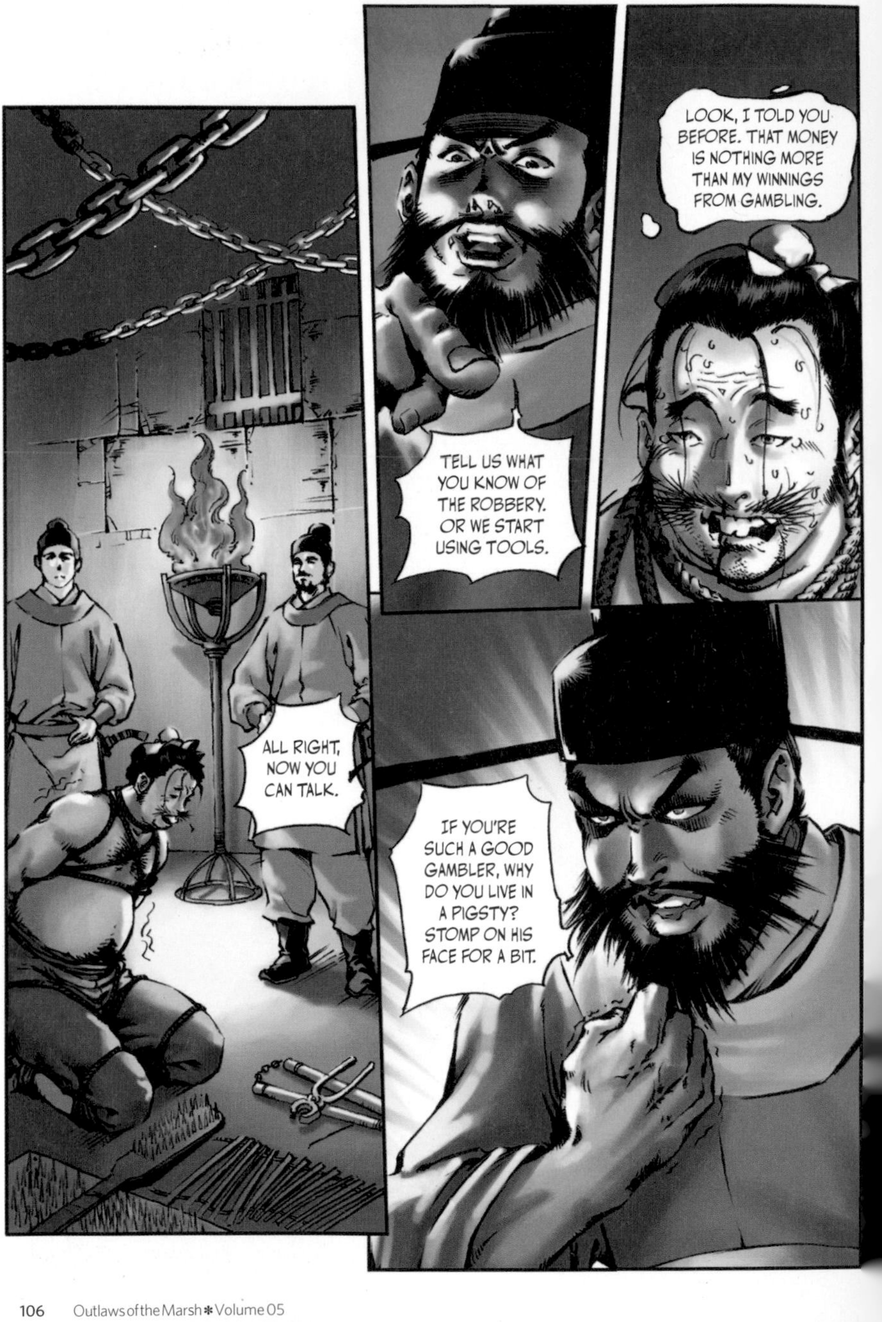
ALL RIGHT, NOW YOU CAN TALK.
TELL US WHAT YOU KNOW OF THE ROBBERY. OR WE START USING TOOLS.
LOOK, I TOLD YOU BEFORE. THAT MONEY IS NOTHING MORE THAN MY WINNINGS FROM GAMBLING.
IF YOU'RE SUCH A GOOD GAMBLER, WHY DO YOU LIVE IN A PIGSTY? STOMP ON HIS FACE FOR A BIT.

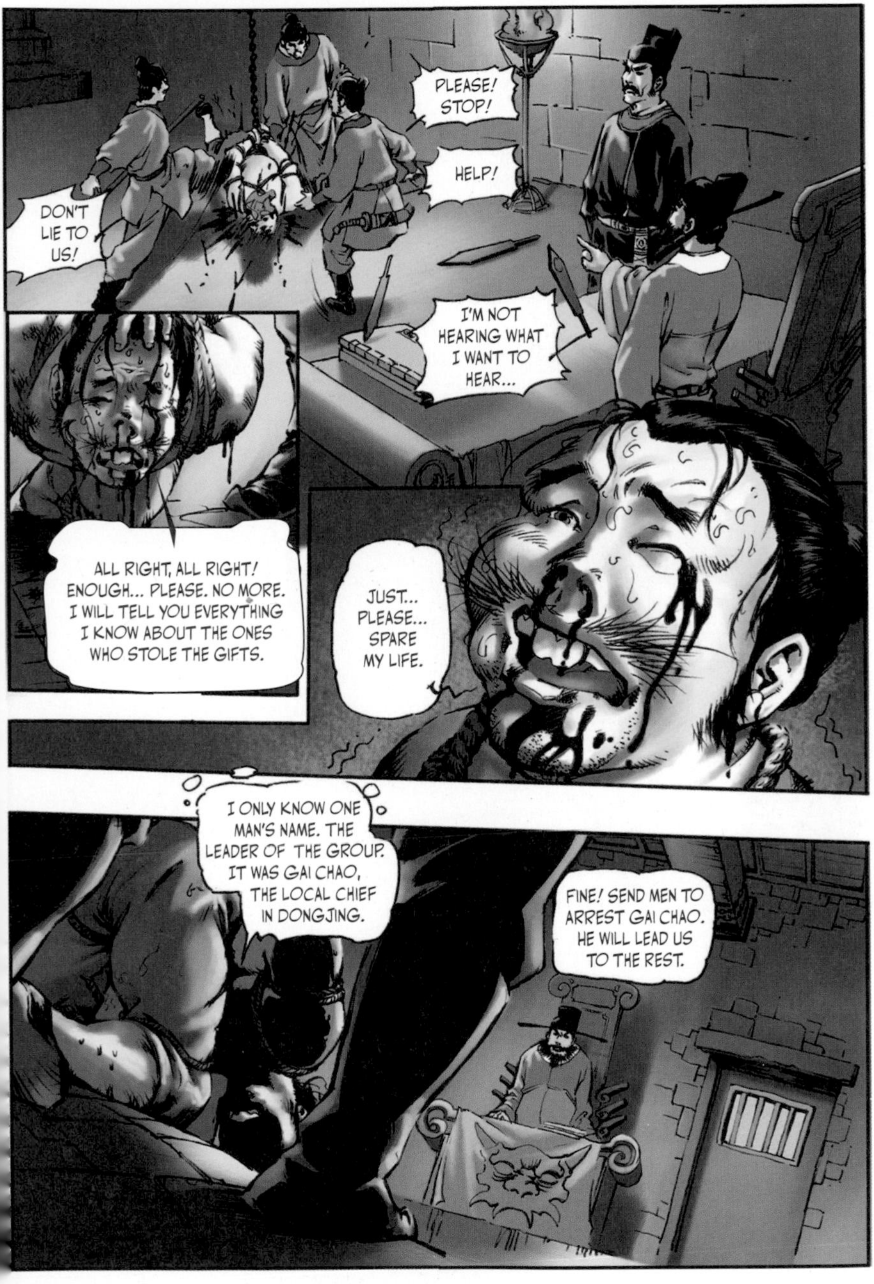
PLEASE! STOP!
HELP!
DON'T LIE TO US!
I'M NOT HEARING WHAT I WANT TO HEAR...
ALL RIGHT, ALL RIGHT! ENOUGH... PLEASE. NO MORE. I WILL TELL YOU EVERYTHING I KNOW ABOUT THE ONES WHO STOLE THE GIFTS.
JUST... PLEASE... SPARE MY LIFE.
I ONLY KNOW ONE MAN'S NAME. THE LEADER OF THE GROUP. IT WAS GAI CHAO, THE LOCAL CHIEF IN DONGJING.
FINE! SEND MEN TO ARREST GAI CHAO. HE WILL LEAD US TO THE REST.

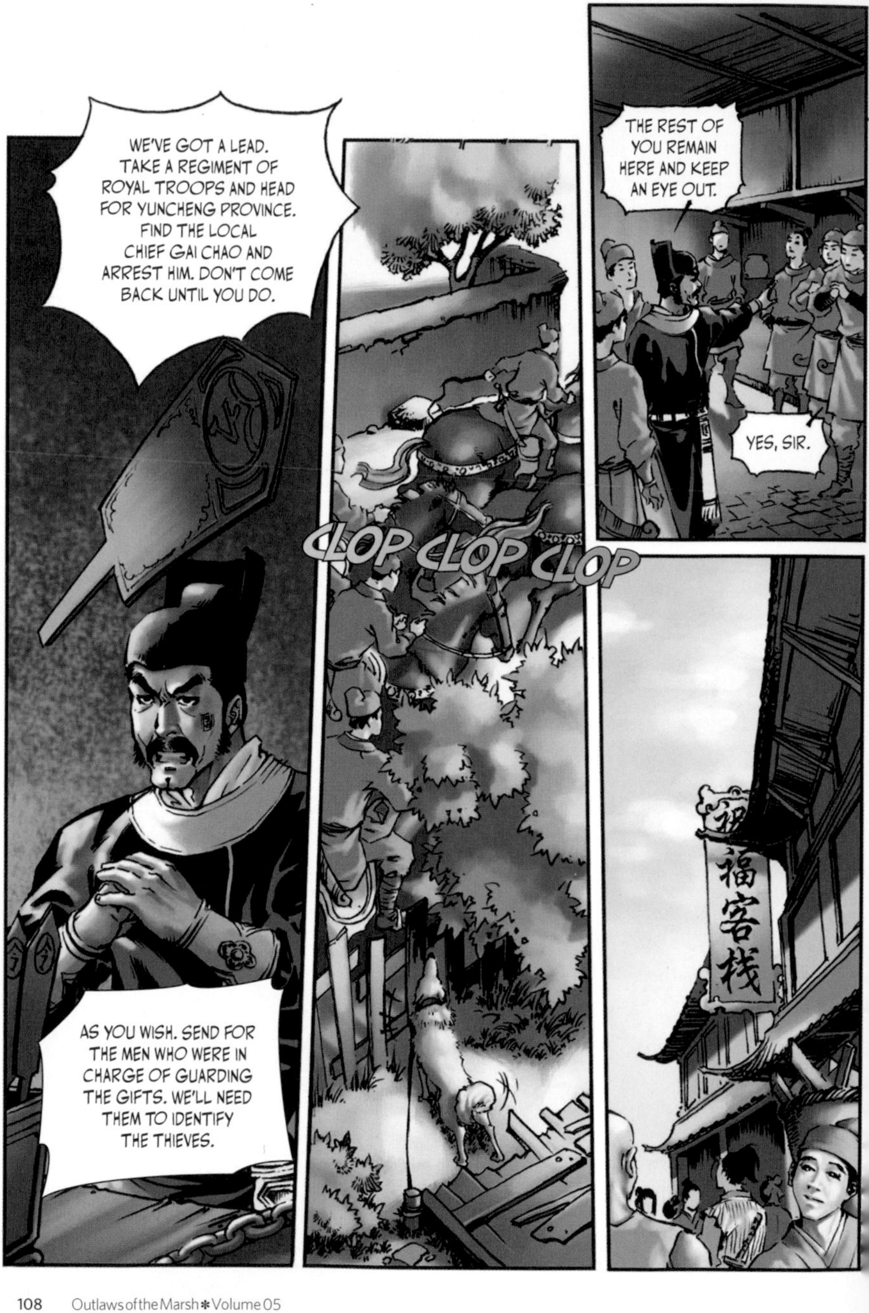
WE'VE GOT A LEAD. TAKE A REGIMENT OF ROYAL TROOPS AND HEAD FOR YUNCHENG PROVINCE. FIND THE LOCAL CHIEF GAI CHAO AND ARREST HIM. DON'T COME BACK UNTIL YOU DO.
AS YOU WISH. SEND FOR THE MEN WHO WERE IN CHARGE OF GUARDING THE GIFTS. WE'LL NEED THEM TO IDENTIFY THE THIEVES.
CLOP CLOP CLOP
THE REST OF YOU REMAIN HERE AND KEEP AN EYE OUT.
YES, SIR.
福客栈

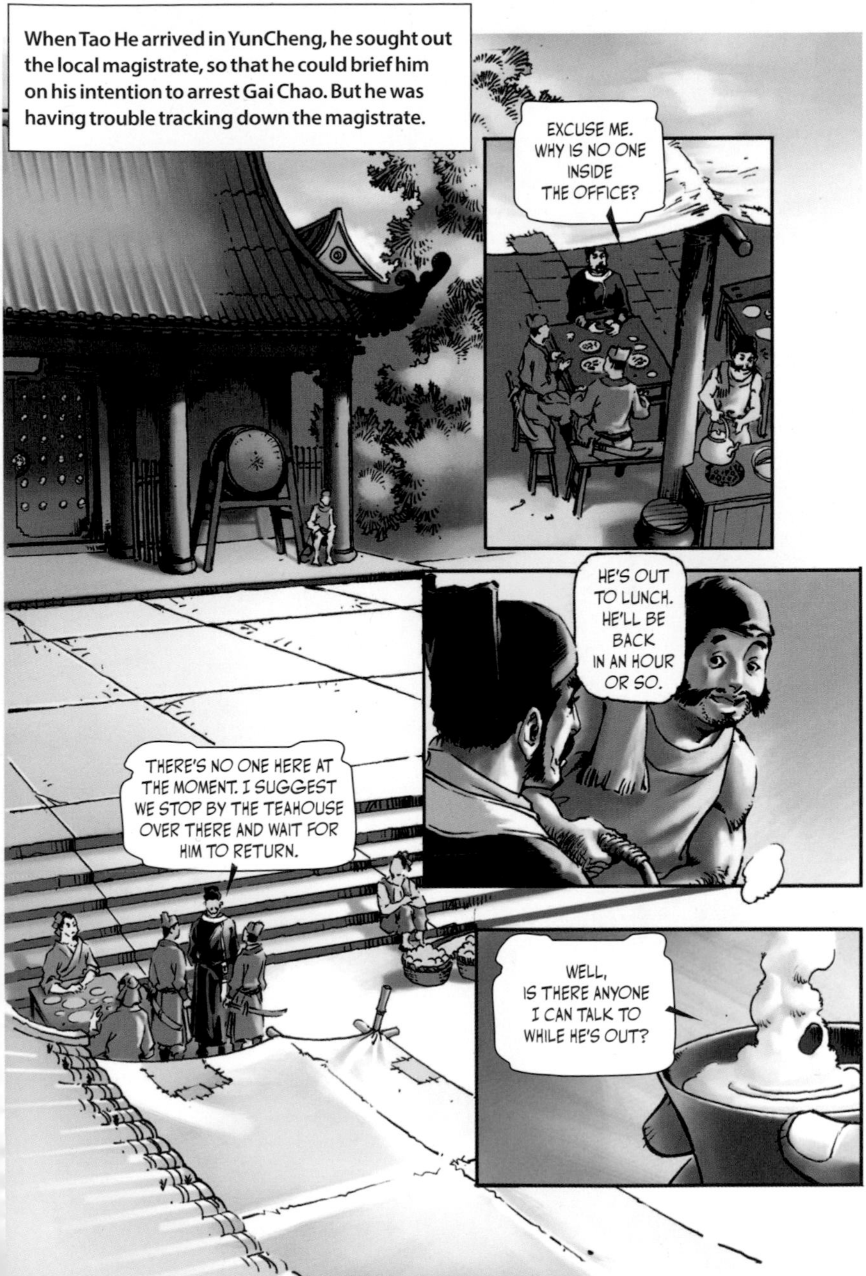
When Tao He arrived in YunCheng, he sought out the local magistrate, so that he could brief him on his intention to arrest Gai Chao. But he was having trouble tracking down the magistrate.
EXCUSE ME. WHY IS NO ONE INSIDE THE OFFICE?
HE'S OUT TO LUNCH. HE'LL BE BACK IN AN HOUR OR SO.
WELL, IS THERE ANYONE I CAN TALK TO WHILE HE'S OUT?
THERE'S NO ONE HERE AT THE MOMENT. I SUGGEST WE STOP BY THE TEAHOUSE OVER THERE AND WAIT FOR HIM TO RETURN.

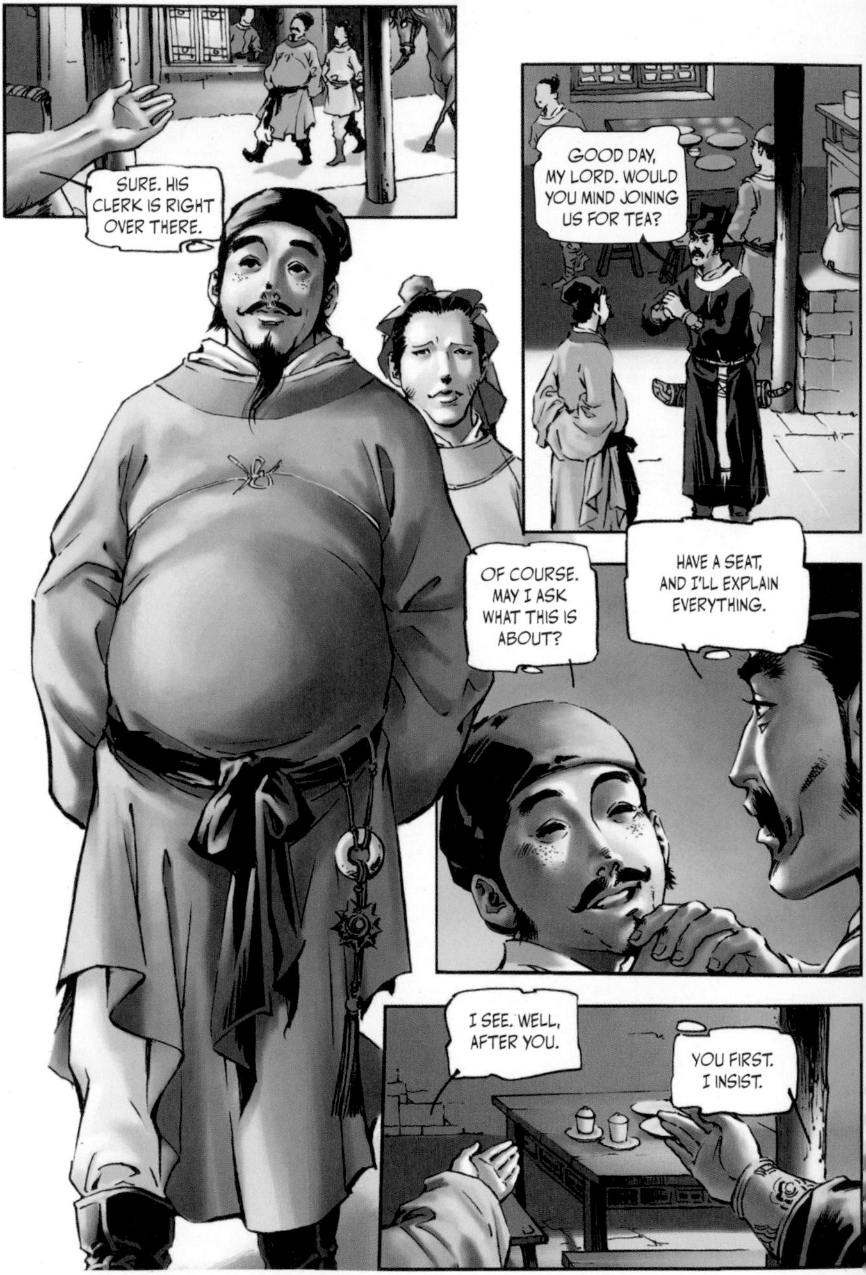
SURE. HIS CLERK IS RIGHT OVER THERE.
GOOD DAY, MY LORD. WOULD YOU MIND JOINING US FOR TEA?
OF COURSE. MAY I ASK WHAT THIS IS ABOUT?
HAVE A SEAT, AND I'LL EXPLAIN EVERYTHING.
I SEE. WELL, AFTER YOU.
YOU FIRST. I INSIST.

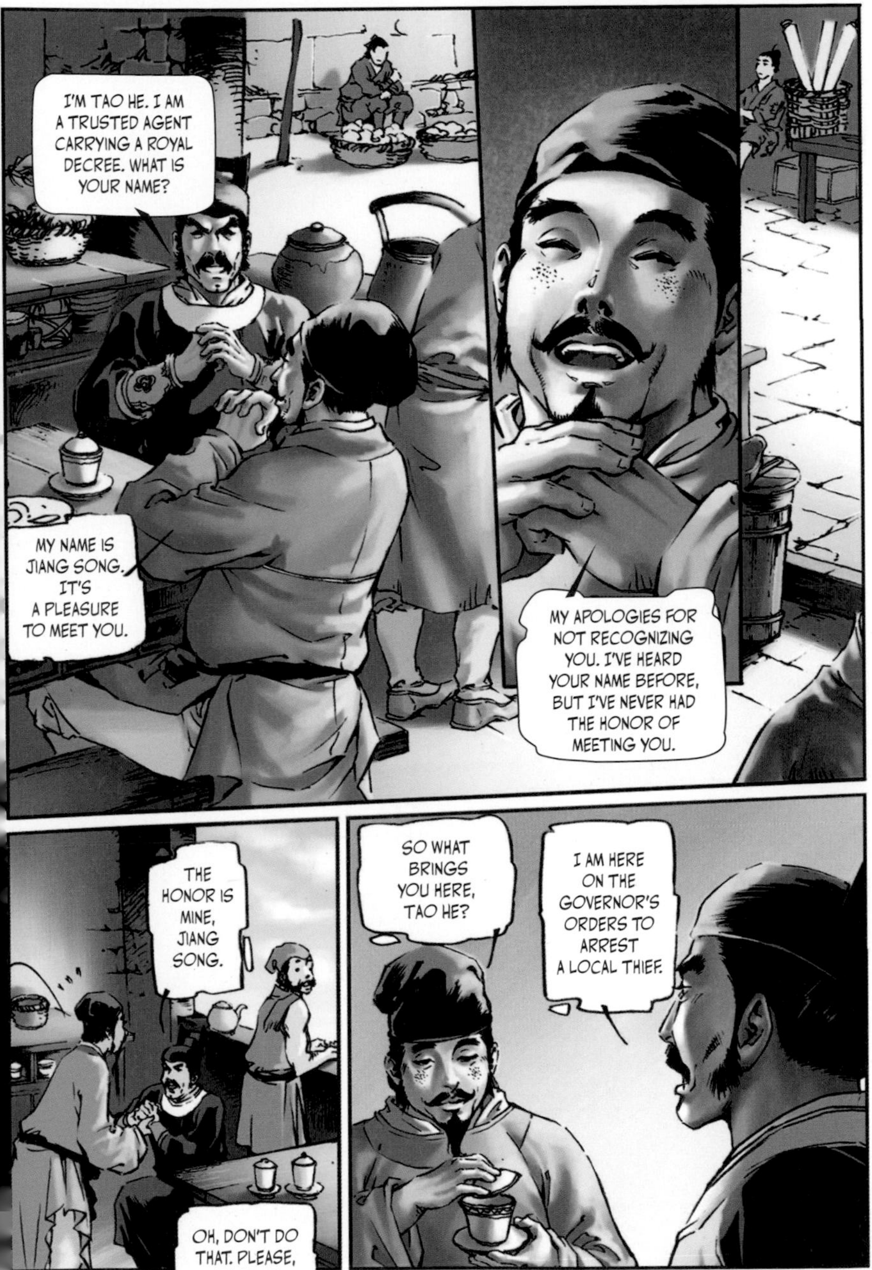
I'M TAO HE. I AM A TRUSTED AGENT CARRYING A ROYAL DECREE. WHAT IS YOUR NAME?
MY NAME IS JIANG SONG. IT'S A PLEASURE TO MEET YOU.
MY APOLOGIES FOR NOT RECOGNIZING YOU. I'VE HEARD YOUR NAME BEFORE, BUT I'VE NEVER HAD THE HONOR OF MEETING YOU.
THE HONOR IS MINE, JIANG SONG.
OH, DON'T DO THAT. PLEASE, STAND UP.
SO WHAT BRINGS YOU HERE, TAO HE?
I AM HERE ON THE GOVERNOR'S ORDERS TO ARREST A LOCAL THIEF.

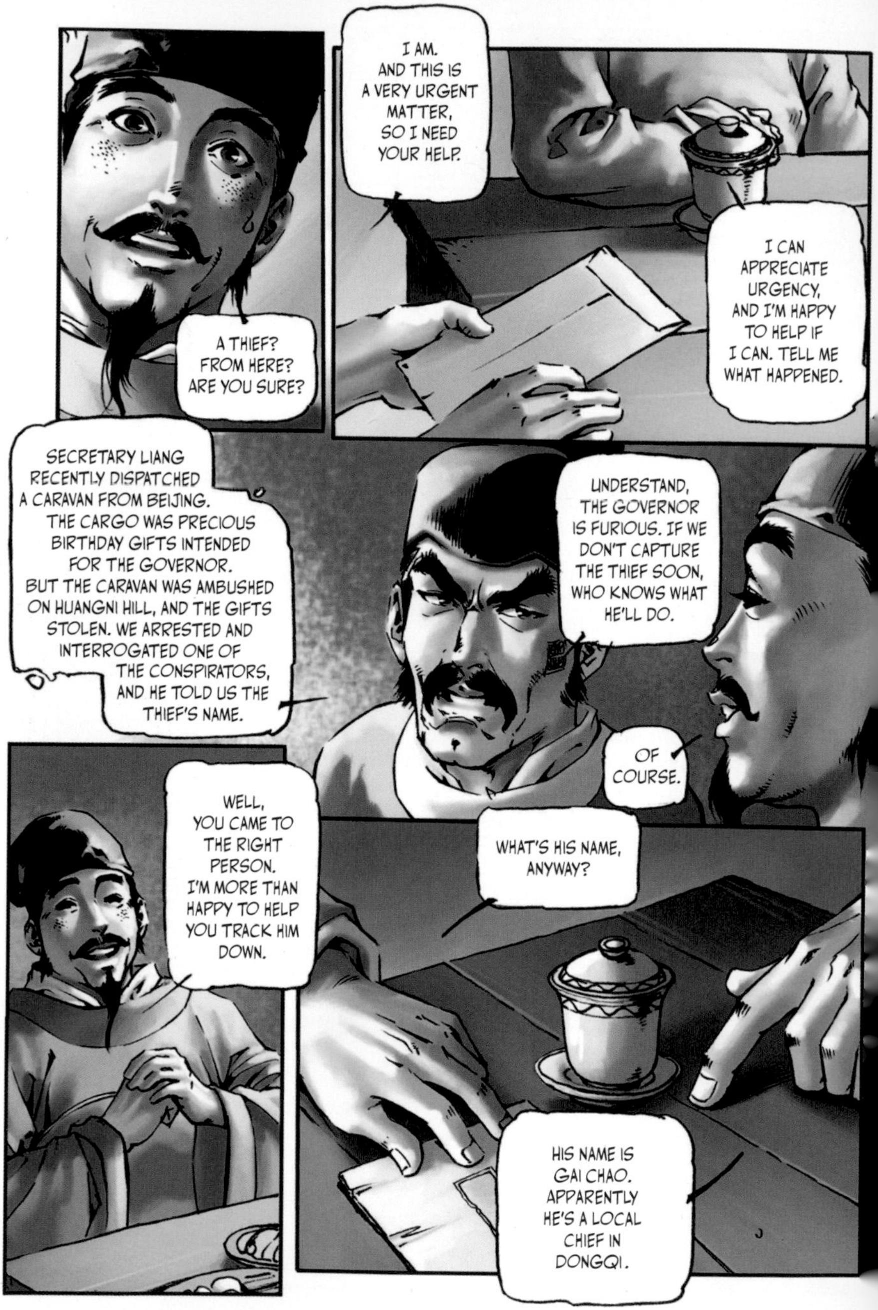
I AM. AND THIS IS A VERY URGENT MATTER, SO I NEED YOUR HELP.
A THIEF? FROM HERE? ARE YOU SURE?
I CAN APPRECIATE URGENCY, AND I'M HAPPY TO HELP IF I CAN. TELL ME WHAT HAPPENED.
SECRETARY LIANG RECENTLY DISPATCHED A CARAVAN FROM BEIJING. THE CARGO WAS PRECIOUS BIRTHDAY GIFTS INTENDED FOR THE GOVERNOR. BUT THE CARAVAN WAS AMBUSHED ON HUANGNI HILL, AND THE GIFTS STOLEN. WE ARRESTED AND INTERROGATED ONE OF THE CONSPIRATORS, AND HE TOLD US THE THIEF'S NAME.
UNDERSTAND, THE GOVERNOR IS FURIOUS. IF WE DON'T CAPTURE THE THIEF SOON, WHO KNOWS WHAT HE'LL DO.
OF COURSE.
WELL, YOU CAME TO THE RIGHT PERSON. I'M MORE THAN HAPPY TO HELP YOU TRACK HIM DOWN.
WHAT'S HIS NAME, ANYWAY?
HIS NAME IS GAI CHAO. APPARENTLY HE'S A LOCAL CHIEF IN DONGQI.

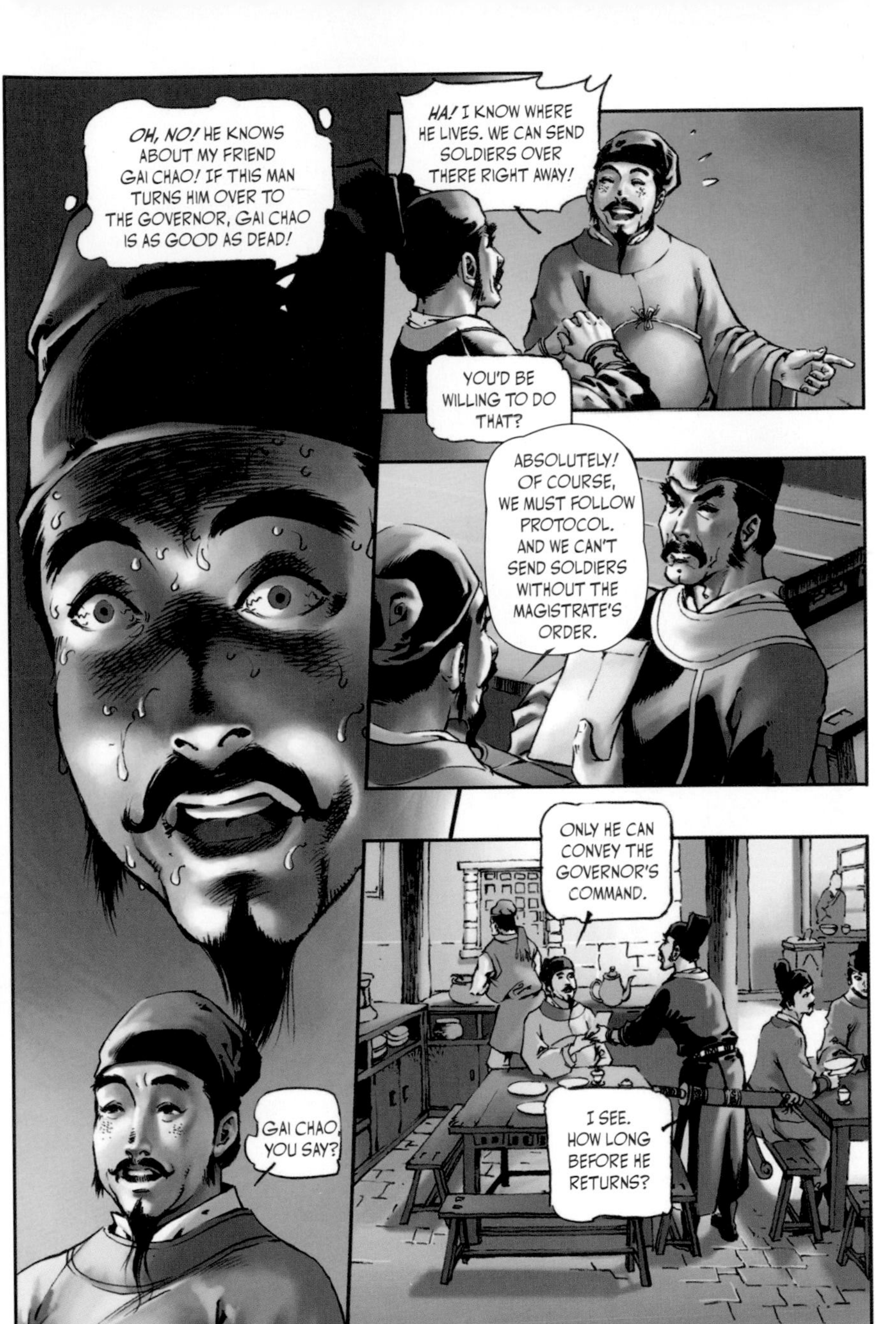
OH, NO! HE KNOWS ABOUT MY FRIEND GAI CHAO! IF THIS MAN TURNS HIM OVER TO THE GOVERNOR, GAI CHAO IS AS GOOD AS DEAD!
HA! I KNOW WHERE HE LIVES. WE CAN SEND SOLDIERS OVER THERE RIGHT AWAY!
YOU'D BE WILLING TO DO THAT?
ABSOLUTELY! OF COURSE, WE MUST FOLLOW PROTOCOL. AND WE CAN'T SEND SOLDIERS WITHOUT THE MAGISTRATE'S ORDER.
GAI CHAO, YOU SAY?
ONLY HE CAN CONVEY THE GOVERNOR'S COMMAND.
I SEE. HOW LONG BEFORE HE RETURNS?

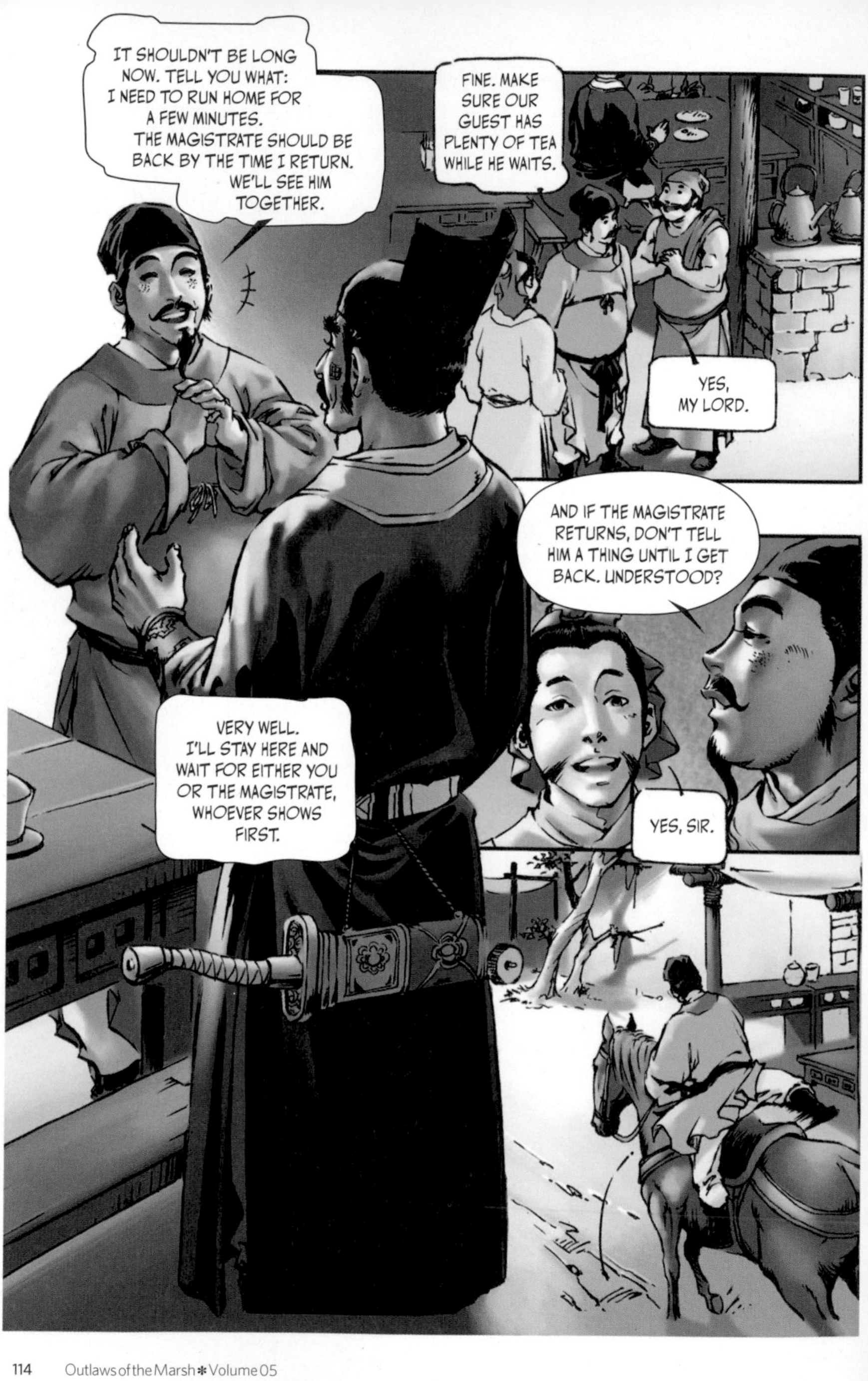
IT SHOULDN'T BE LONG NOW. TELL YOU WHAT: I NEED TO RUN HOME FOR A FEW MINUTES. THE MAGISTRATE SHOULD BE BACK BY THE TIME I RETURN. WE'LL SEE HIM TOGETHER.
FINE. MAKE SURE OUR GUEST HAS PLENTY OF TEA WHILE HE WAITS.
YES, MY LORD.
AND IF THE MAGISTRATE RETURNS, DON'T TELL HIM A THING UNTIL I GET BACK. UNDERSTOOD?
YES, SIR.
VERY WELL. I'LL STAY HERE AND WAIT FOR EITHER YOU OR THE MAGISTRATE, WHOEVER SHOWS FIRST.

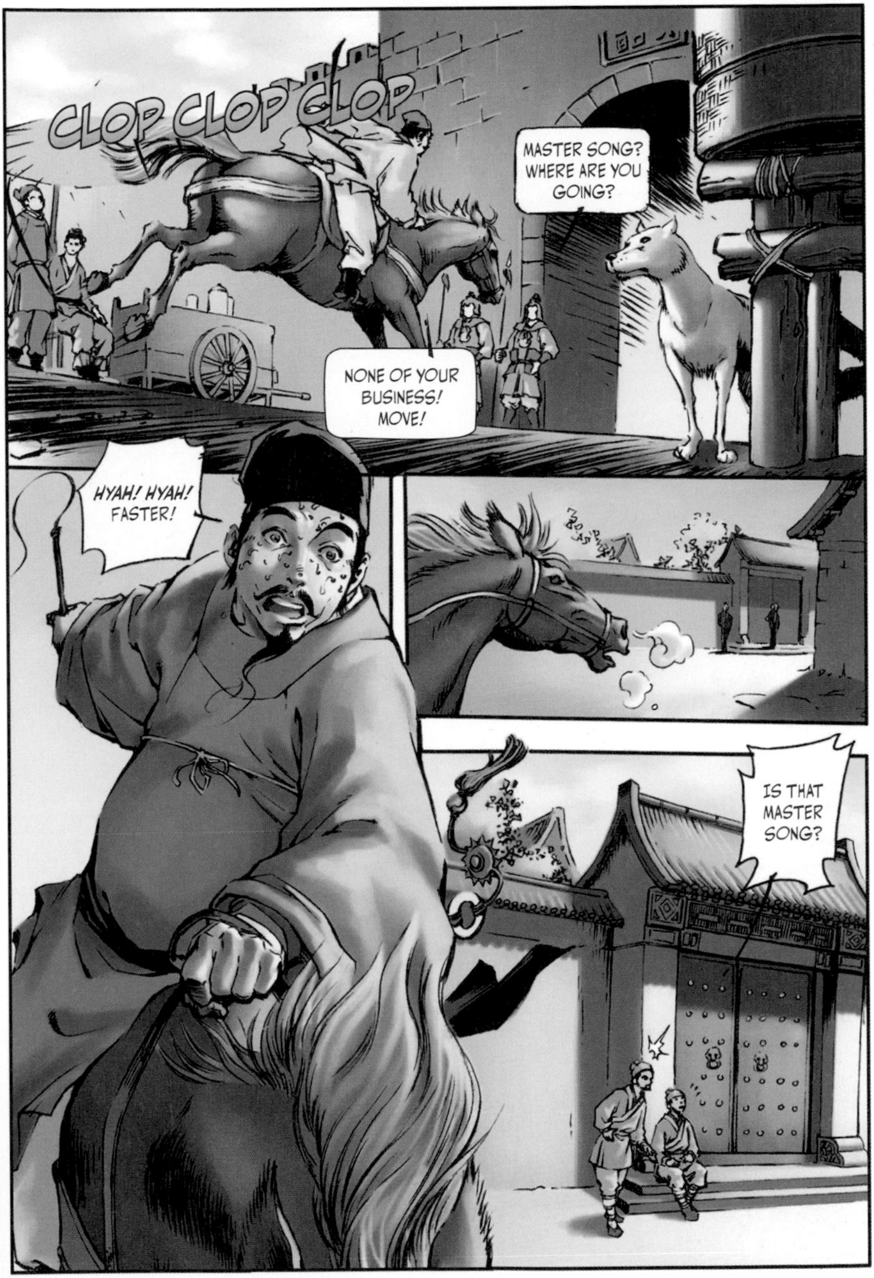

CLOP CLOP CLOP
MASTER SONG? WHERE ARE YOU GOING?
NONE OF YOUR BUSINESS! MOVE!
HYAH! HYAH! FASTER!
IS THAT MASTER SONG?

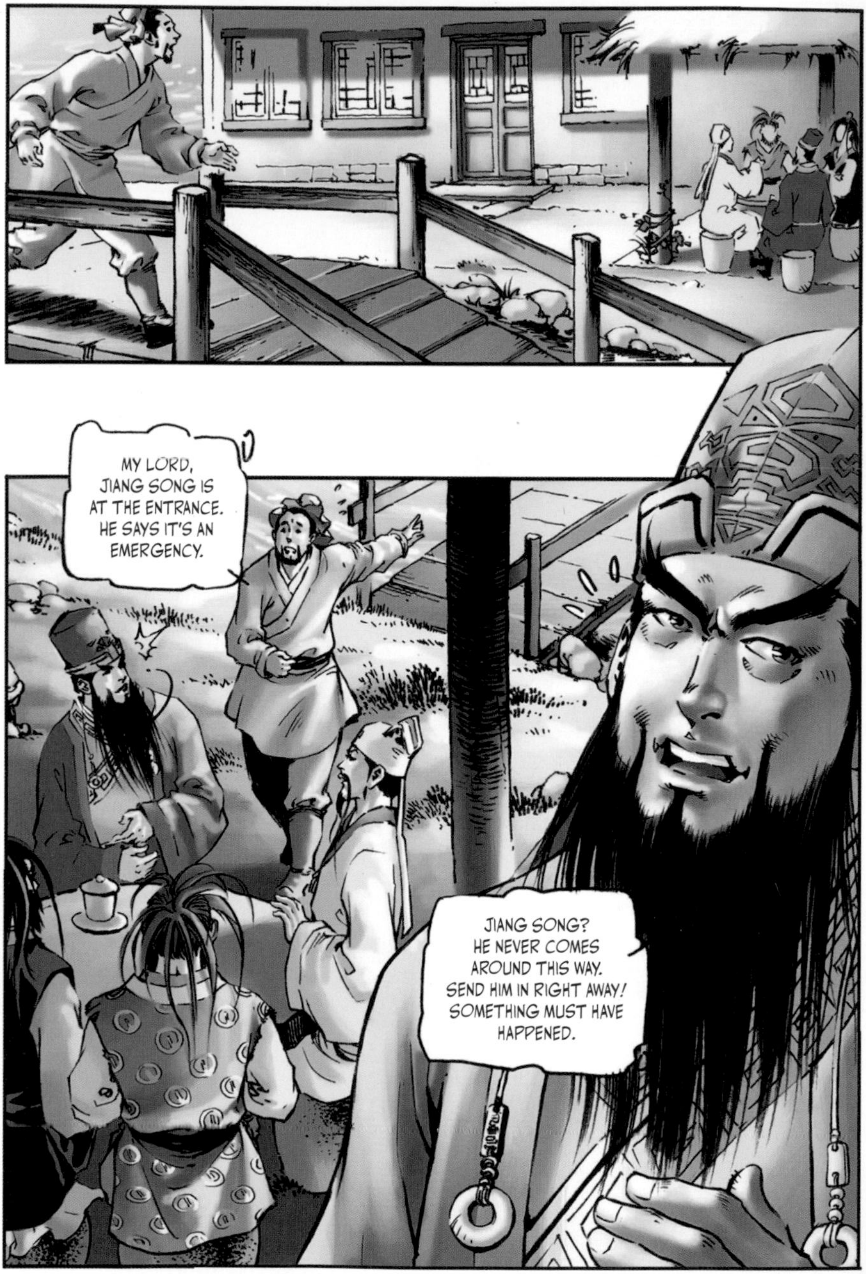
MY LORD, JIANG SONG IS AT THE ENTRANCE. HE SAYS IT'S AN EMERGENCY.
JIANG SONG? HE NEVER COMES AROUND THIS WAY. SEND HIM IN RIGHT AWAY! SOMETHING MUST HAVE HAPPENED.

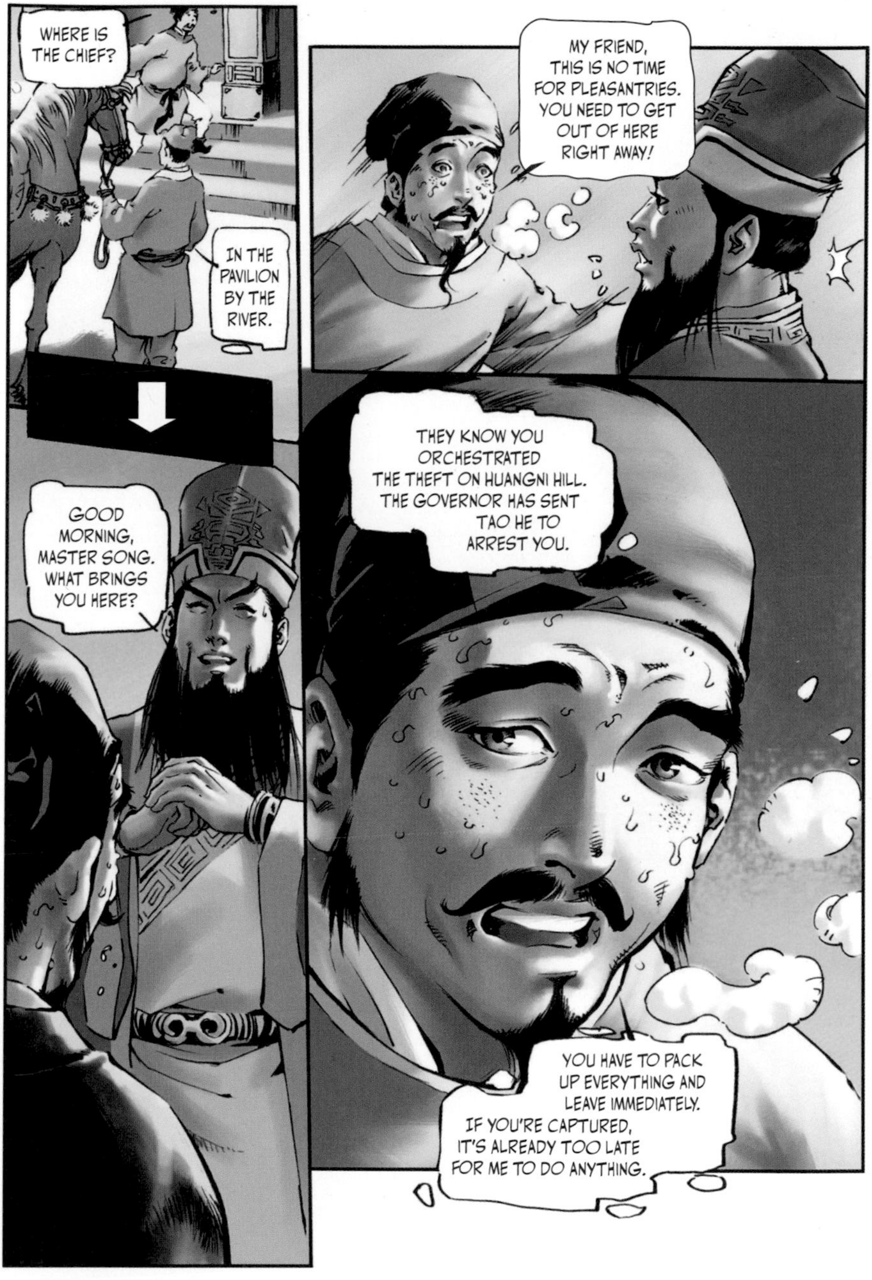
WHERE IS THE CHIEF?
IN THE PAVILION BY THE RIVER.
MY FRIEND, THIS IS NO TIME FOR PLEASANTRIES. YOU NEED TO GET OUT OF HERE RIGHT AWAY!
GOOD MORNING, MASTER SONG. WHAT BRINGS YOU HERE?
THEY KNOW YOU ORCHESTRATED THE THEFT ON HUANGNI HILL. THE GOVERNOR HAS SENT TAO HE TO ARREST YOU.
YOU HAVE TO PACK UP EVERYTHING AND LEAVE IMMEDIATELY. IF YOU'RE CAPTURED, IT'S ALREADY TOO LATE FOR ME TO DO ANYTHING.

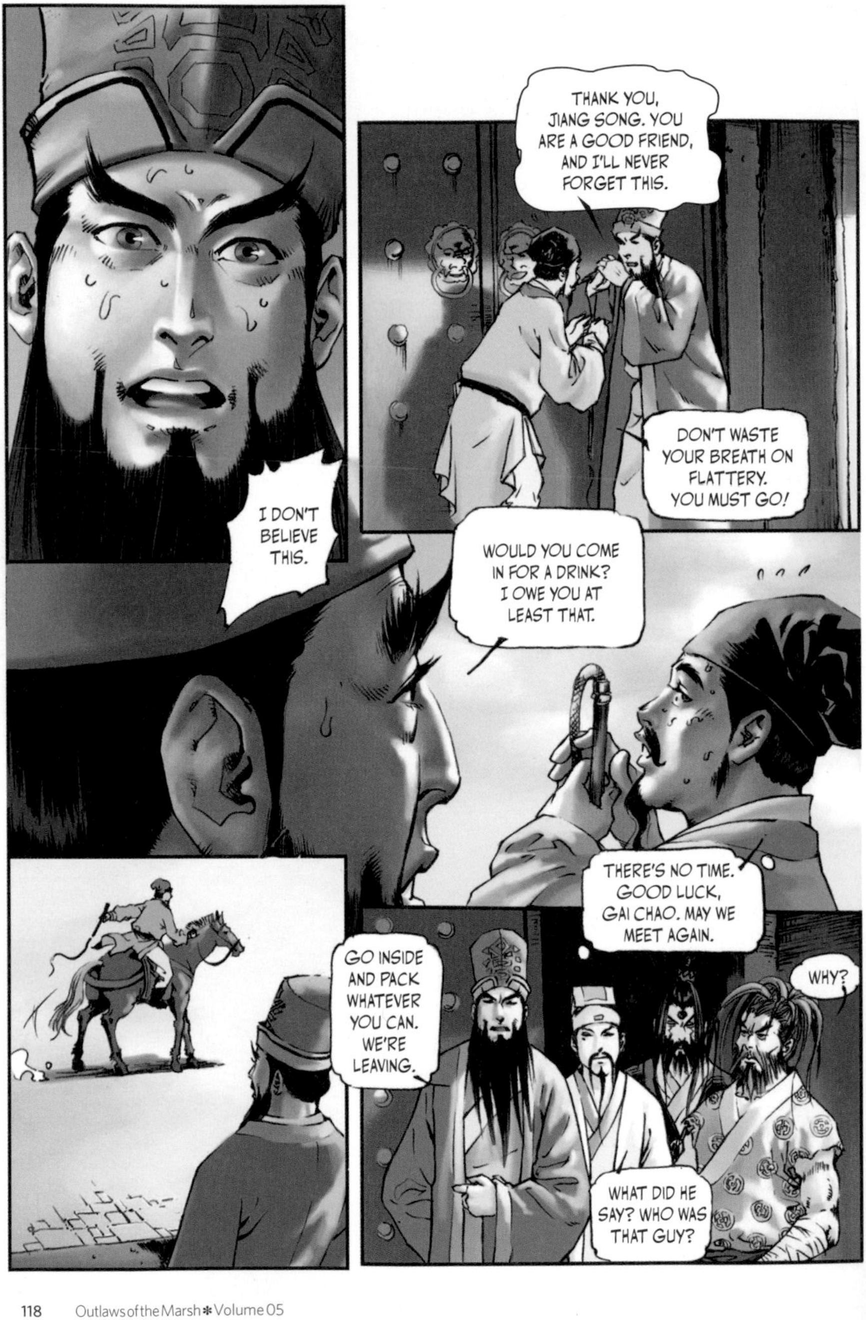

I DON'T BELIEVE THIS.
THANK YOU, JIANG SONG. YOU ARE A GOOD FRIEND, AND I'LL NEVER FORGET THIS.
DON'T WASTE YOUR BREATH ON FLATTERY. YOU MUST GO!
WOULD YOU COME IN FOR A DRINK? I OWE YOU AT LEAST THAT.
THERE'S NO TIME. GOOD LUCK, GAI CHAO. MAY WE MEET AGAIN.
GO INSIDE AND PACK WHATEVER YOU CAN. WE'RE LEAVING.
WHY?
WHAT DID HE SAY? WHO WAS THAT GUY?

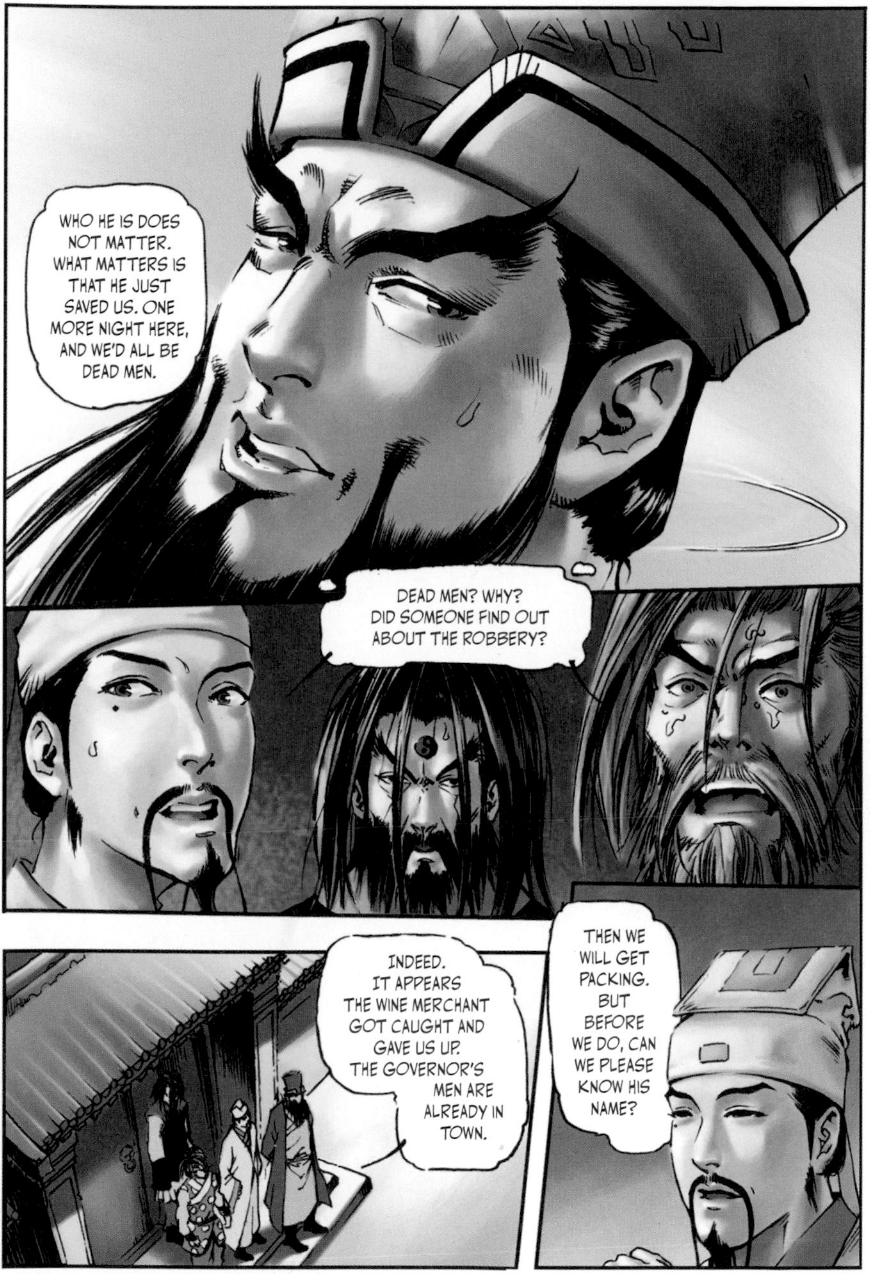
WHO HE IS DOES NOT MATTER. WHAT MATTERS IS THAT HE JUST SAVED US. ONE MORE NIGHT HERE, AND WE'D ALL BE DEAD MEN.
DEAD MEN? WHY? DID SOMEONE FIND OUT ABOUT THE ROBBERY?
INDEED. IT APPEARS THE WINE MERCHANT GOT CAUGHT AND GAVE US UP. THE GOVERNOR'S MEN ARE ALREADY IN TOWN.
THEN WE WILL GET PACKING. BUT BEFORE WE DO, CAN WE PLEASE KNOW HIS NAME?

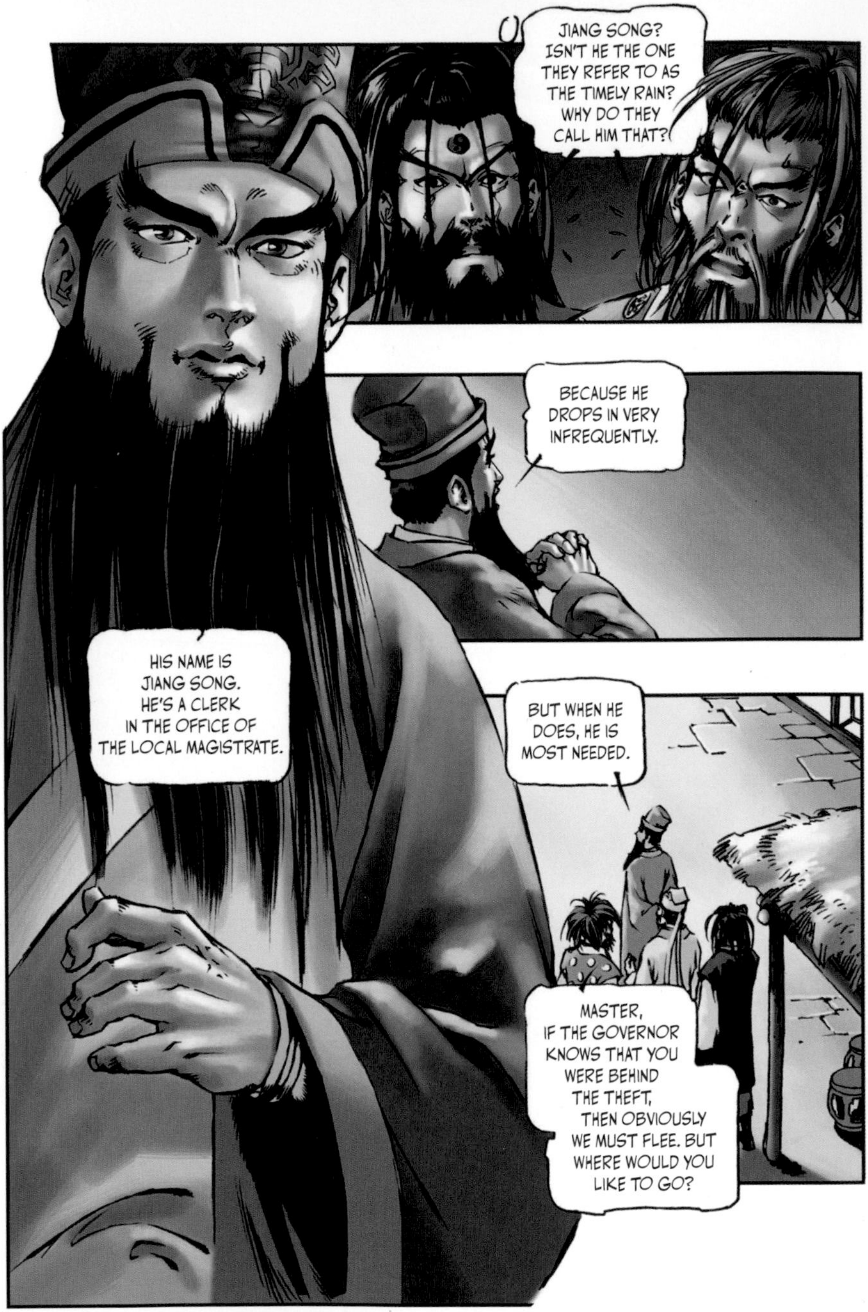
JIANG SONG? ISN'T HE THE ONE THEY REFER TO AS THE TIMELY RAIN? WHY DO THEY CALL HIM THAT?
BECAUSE HE DROPS IN VERY INFREQUENTLY.
HIS NAME IS JIANG SONG. HE'S A CLERK IN THE OFFICE OF THE LOCAL MAGISTRATE.
BUT WHEN HE DOES, HE IS MOST NEEDED.
MASTER, IF THE GOVERNOR KNOWS THAT YOU WERE BEHIND THE THEFT, THEN OBVIOUSLY WE MUST FLEE. BUT WHERE WOULD YOU LIKE TO GO?

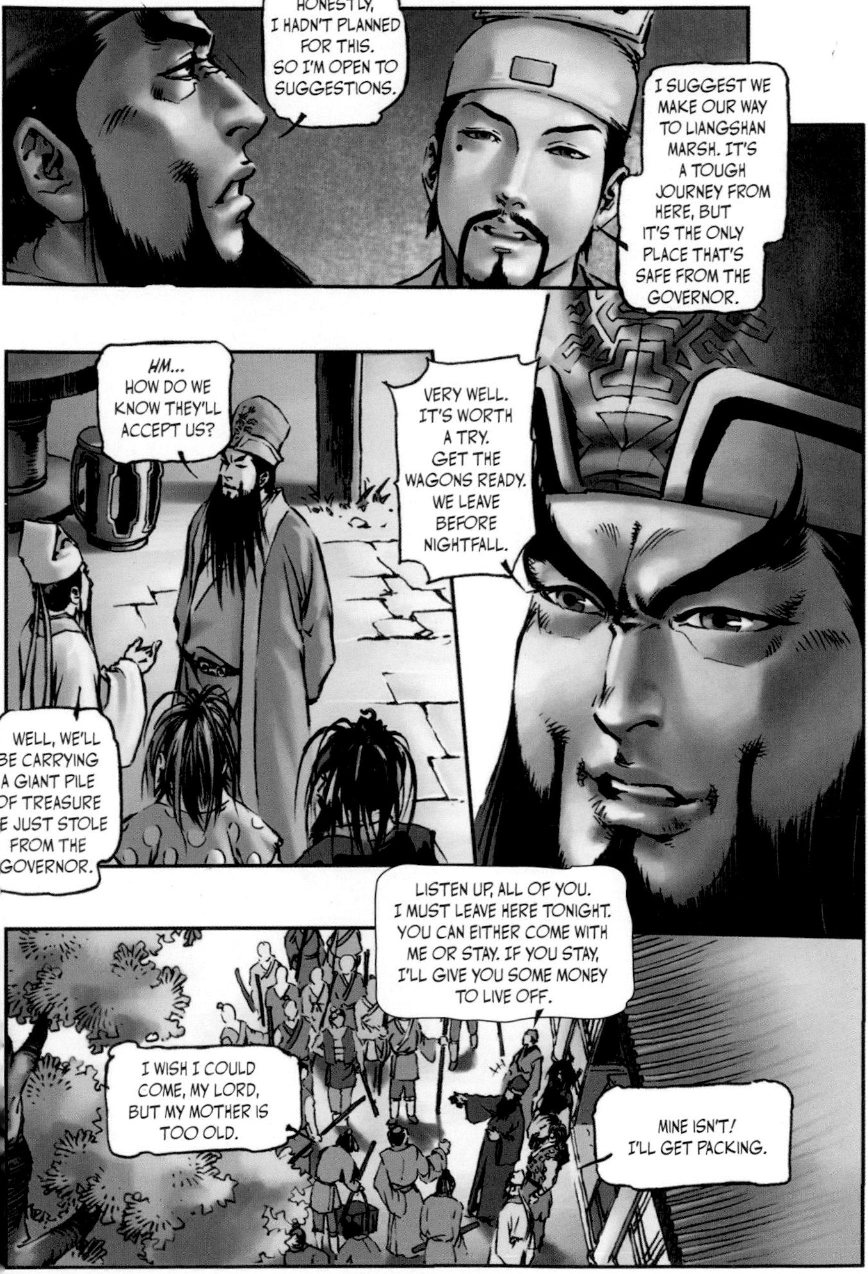
HONESTLY, I HADN'T PLANNED FOR THIS. SO I'M OPEN TO SUGGESTIONS.
I SUGGEST WE MAKE OUR WAY TO LIANGSHAN MARSH. IT'S A TOUGH JOURNEY FROM HERE, BUT IT'S THE ONLY PLACE THAT'S SAFE FROM THE GOVERNOR.
HM... HOW DO WE KNOW THEY'LL ACCEPT US?
WELL, WE'LL BE CARRYING A GIANT PILE OF TREASURE E JUST STOLE FROM THE GOVERNOR.
VERY WELL. IT'S WORTH A TRY. GET THE WAGONS READY. WE LEAVE BEFORE NIGHTFALL.
LISTEN UP, ALL OF YOU. I MUST LEAVE HERE TONIGHT. YOU CAN EITHER COME WITH ME OR STAY. IF YOU STAY, I'LL GIVE YOU SOME MONEY TO LIVE OFF.
I WISH I COULD COME, MY LORD, BUT MY MOTHER IS TOO OLD.
MINE ISN'T! I'LL GET PACKING.

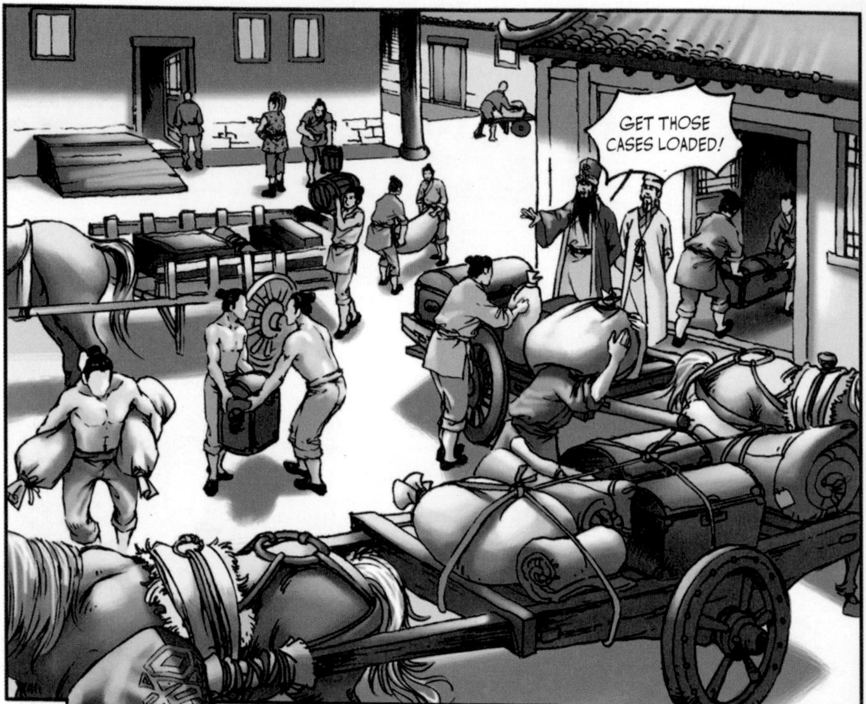
GET THOSE CASES LOADED!

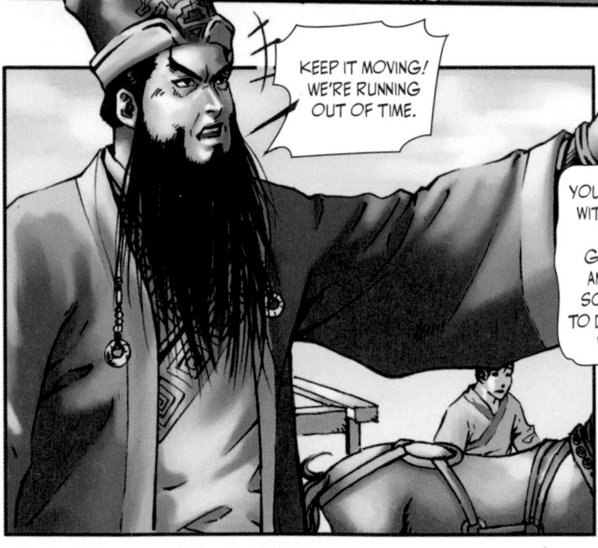
KEEP IT MOVING! WE'RE RUNNING OUT OF TIME.

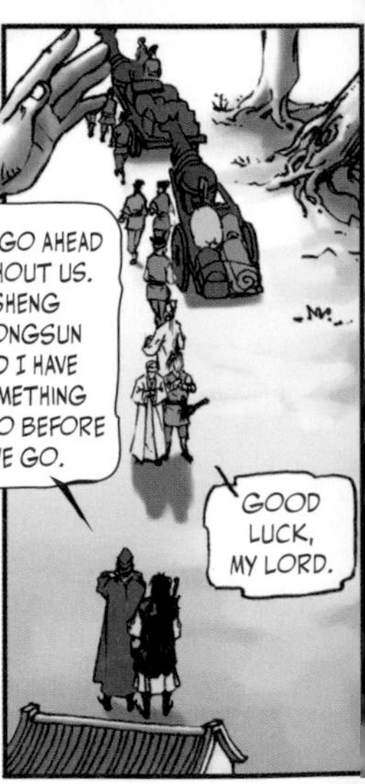
YOU GO AHEAD WITHOUT US. SHENG GONGSUN AND I HAVE SOMETHING TO DO BEFORE WE GO.
GOOD LUCK, MY LORD.

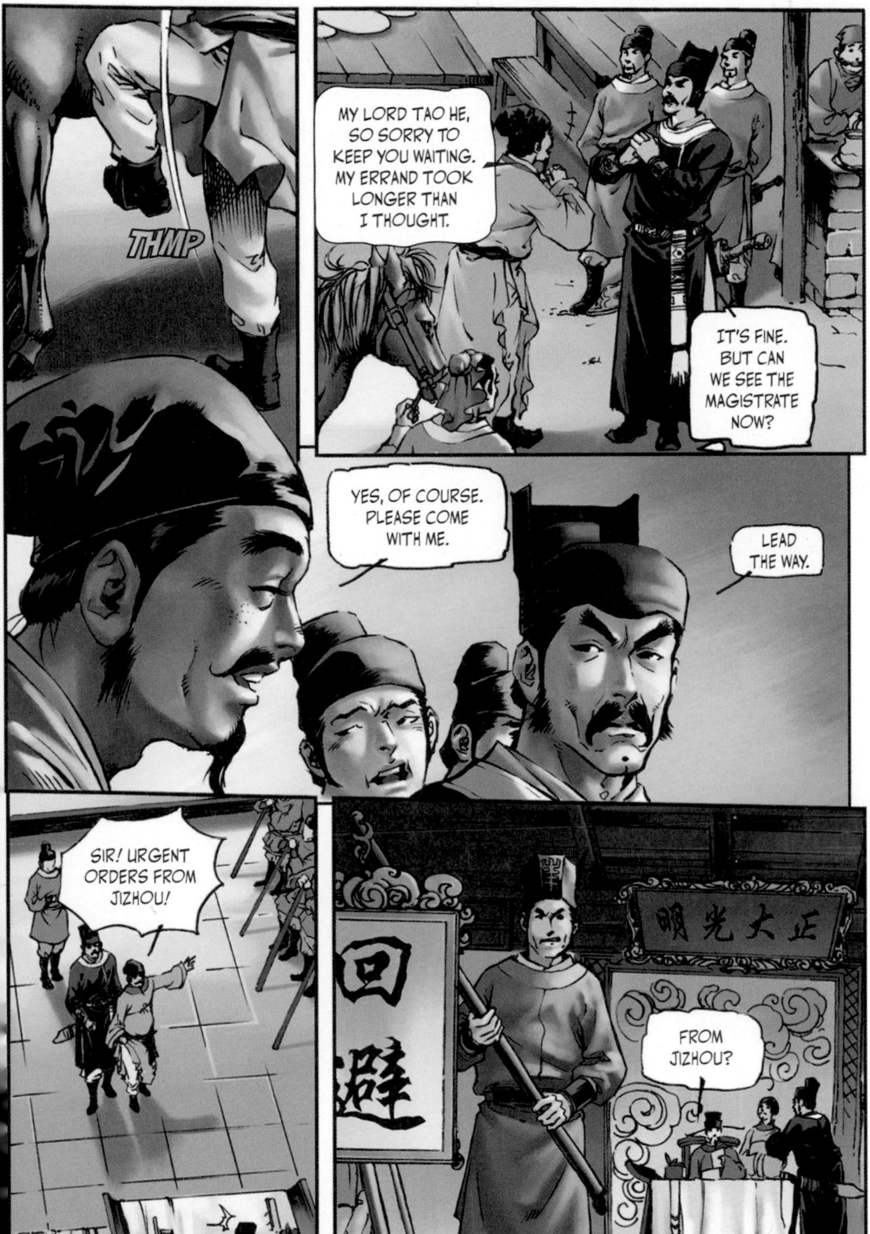
THMP
MY LORD TAO HE, SO SORRY TO KEEP YOU WAITING. MY ERRAND TOOK LONGER THAN I THOUGHT.
IT'S FINE. BUT CAN WE SEE THE MAGISTRATE NOW?
YES, OF COURSE. PLEASE COME WITH ME.
LEAD THE WAY.
SIR! URGENT ORDERS FROM JIZHOU!
回避
正大光明
FROM JIZHOU?

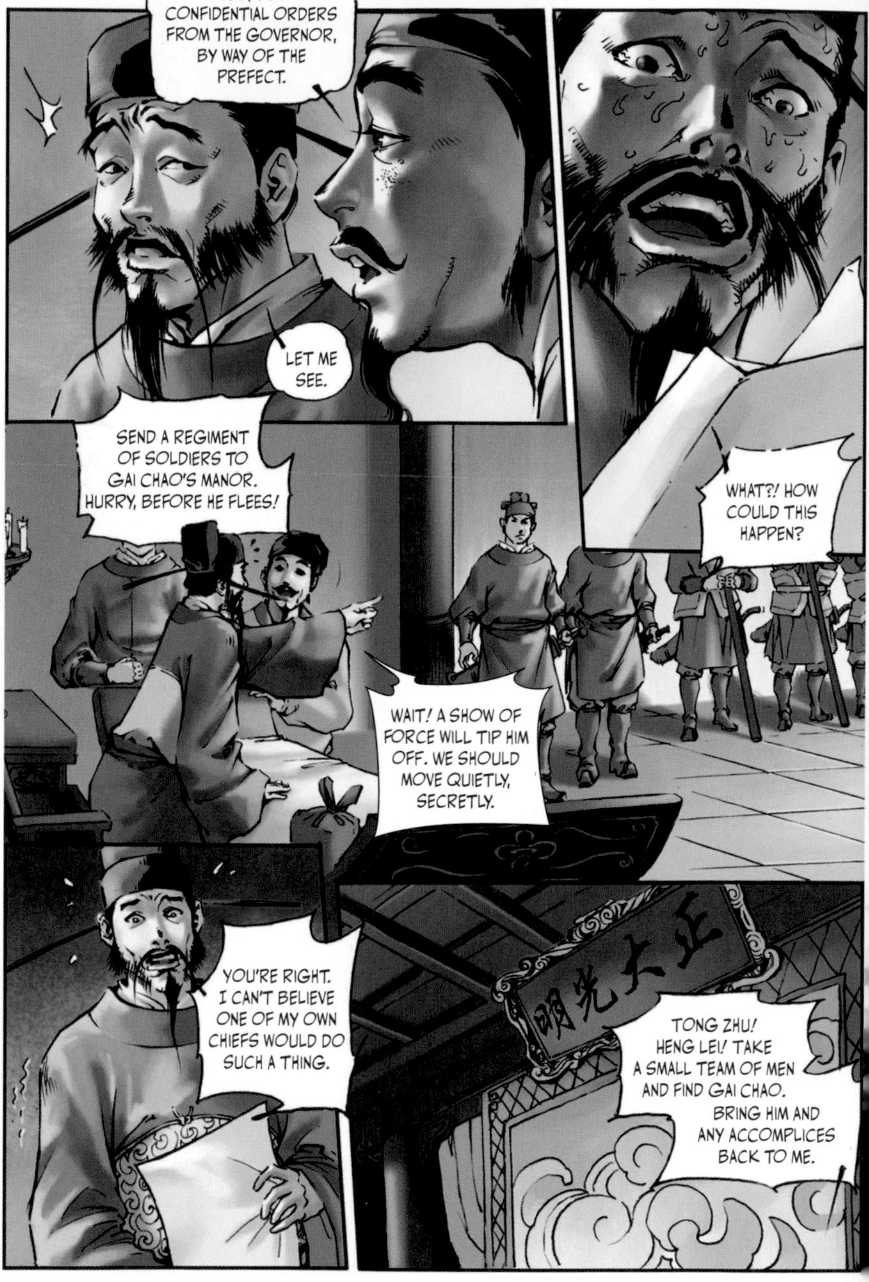
YES, SIR. CONFIDENTIAL ORDERS FROM THE GOVERNOR, BY WAY OF THE PREFECT.
LET ME SEE.
WHAT?! HOW COULD THIS HAPPEN?
SEND A REGIMENT OF SOLDIERS TO GAI CHAO'S MANOR. HURRY, BEFORE HE FLEES!
WAIT! A SHOW OF FORCE WILL TIP HIM OFF. WE SHOULD MOVE QUIETLY, SECRETLY.
YOU'RE RIGHT. I CAN'T BELIEVE ONE OF MY OWN CHIEFS WOULD DO SUCH A THING.
正大光明
TONG ZHU! HENG LEI! TAKE A SMALL TEAM OF MEN AND FIND GAI CHAO.
BRING HIM AND ANY ACCOMPLICES BACK TO ME.

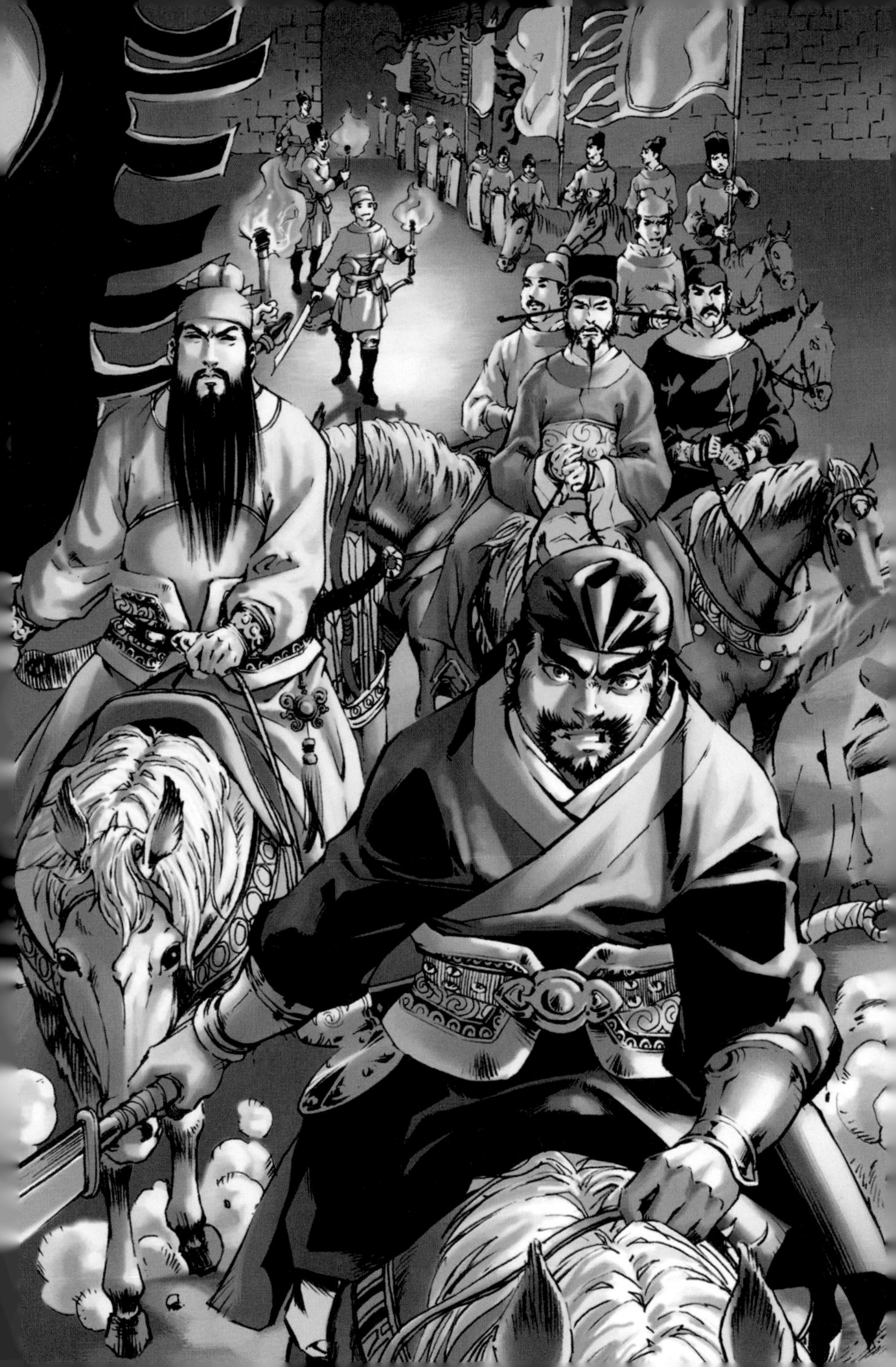

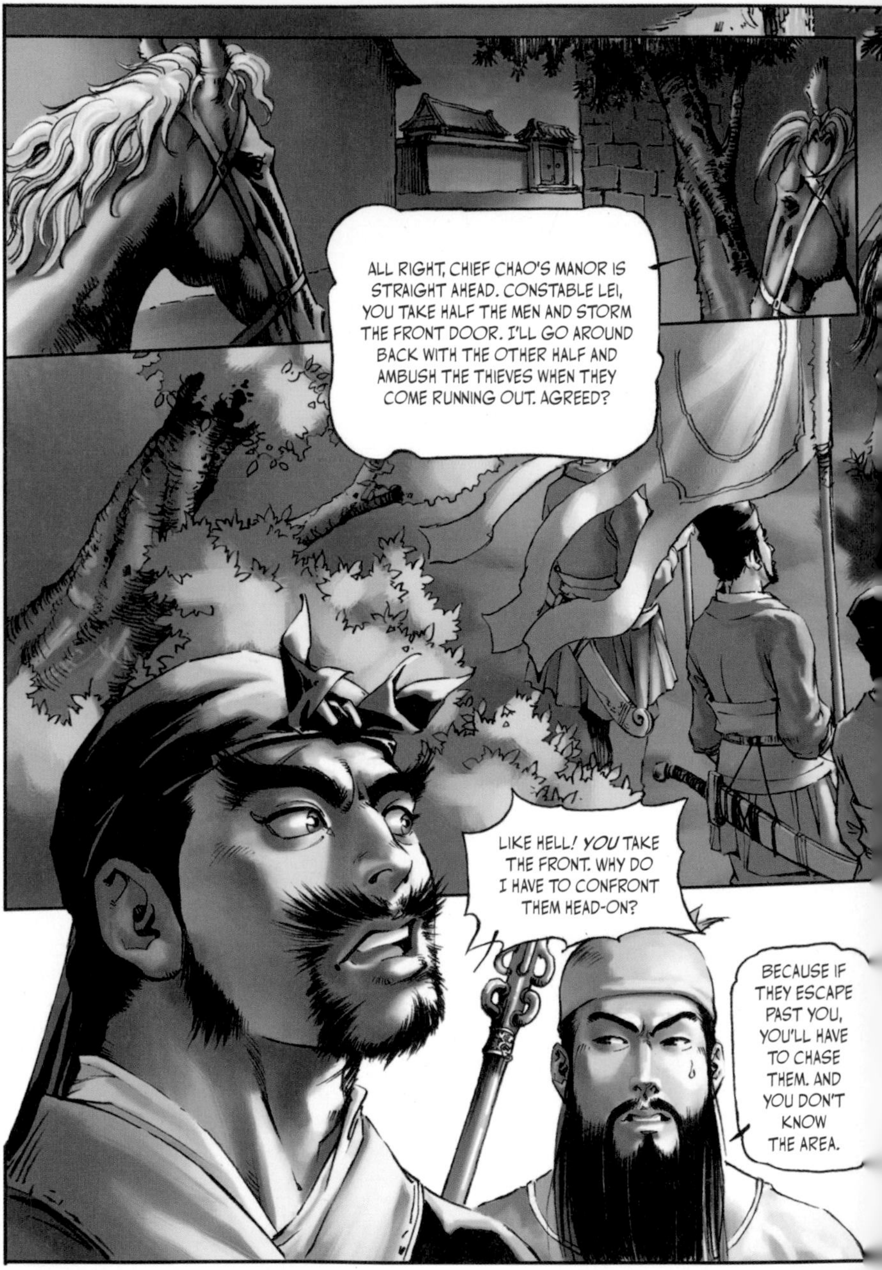
ALL RIGHT, CHIEF CHAO'S MANOR IS STRAIGHT AHEAD. CONSTABLE LEI, YOU TAKE HALF THE MEN AND STORM THE FRONT DOOR. I'LL GO AROUND BACK WITH THE OTHER HALF AND AMBUSH THE THIEVES WHEN THEY COME RUNNING OUT. AGREED?
LIKE HELL! *YOU* TAKE THE FRONT. WHY DO I HAVE TO CONFRONT THEM HEAD-ON?
BECAUSE IF THEY ESCAPE PAST YOU, YOU'LL HAVE TO CHASE THEM. AND YOU DON'T KNOW THE AREA.

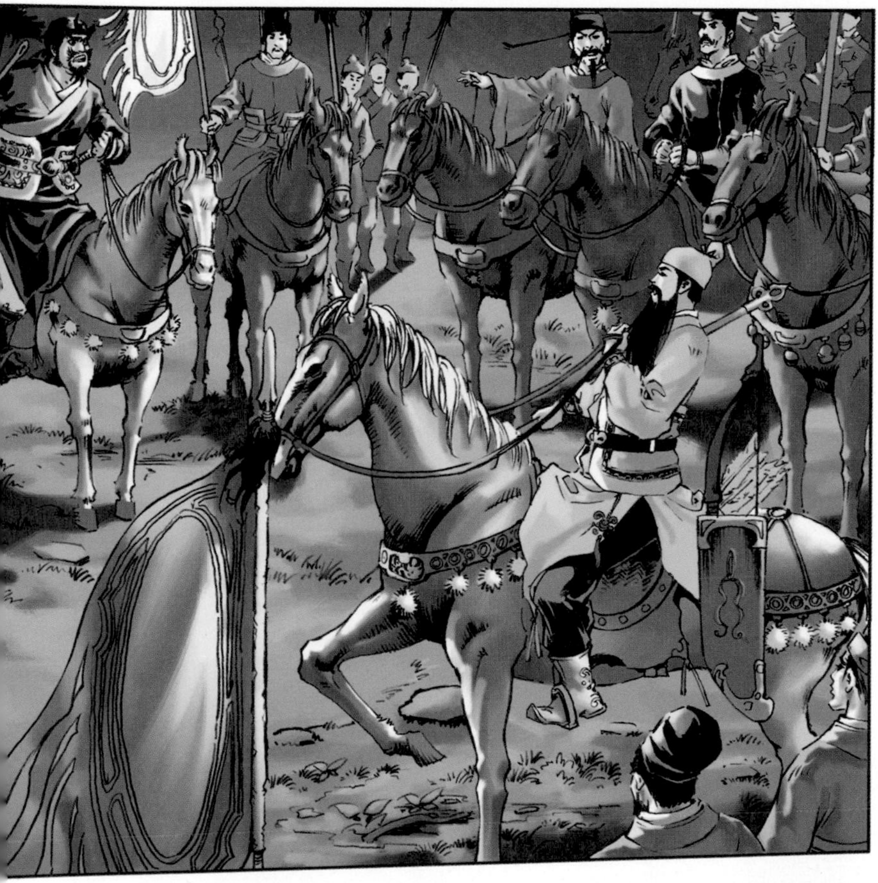

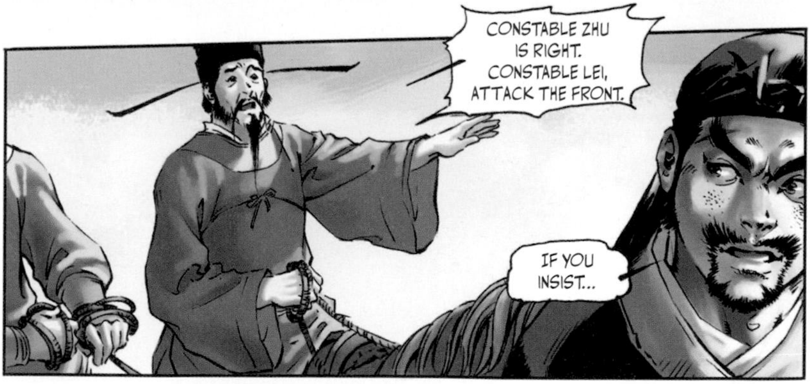
CONSTABLE ZHU IS RIGHT. CONSTABLE LEI, ATTACK THE FRONT.
IF YOU INSIST...

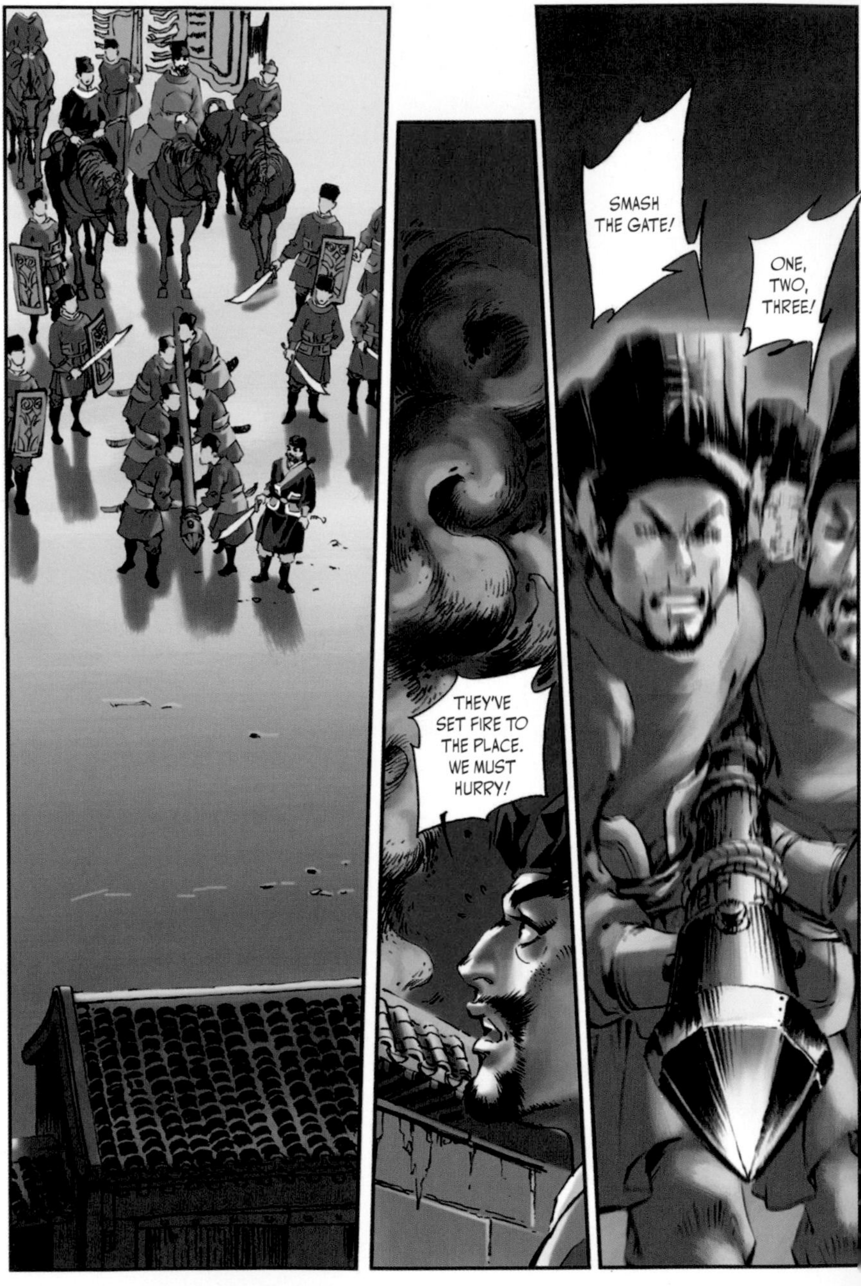
THEY'VE SET FIRE TO THE PLACE. WE MUST HURRY!
SMASH THE GATE!
ONE, TWO, THREE!

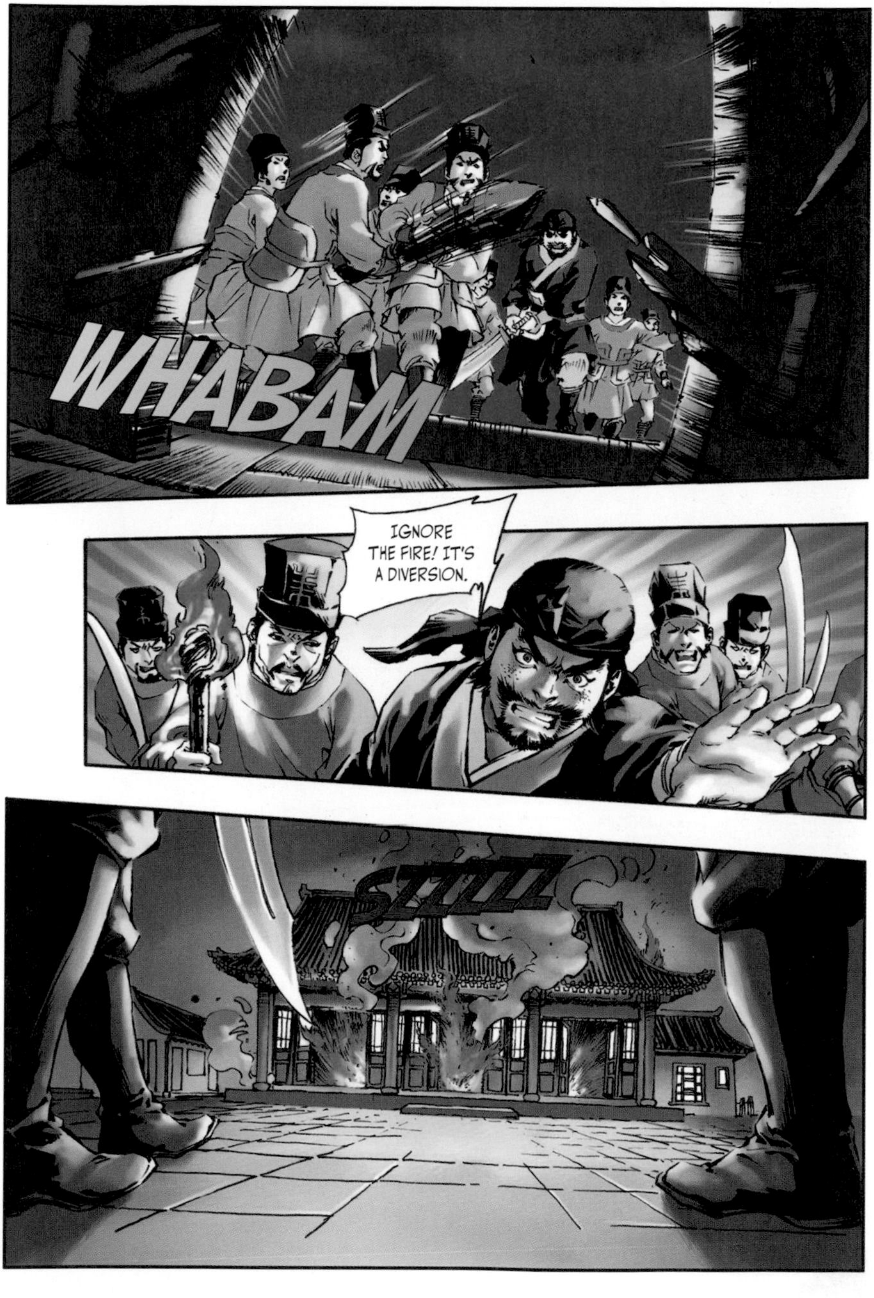
WHABAM
IGNORE THE FIRE! IT'S A DIVERSION.
SZZZZ

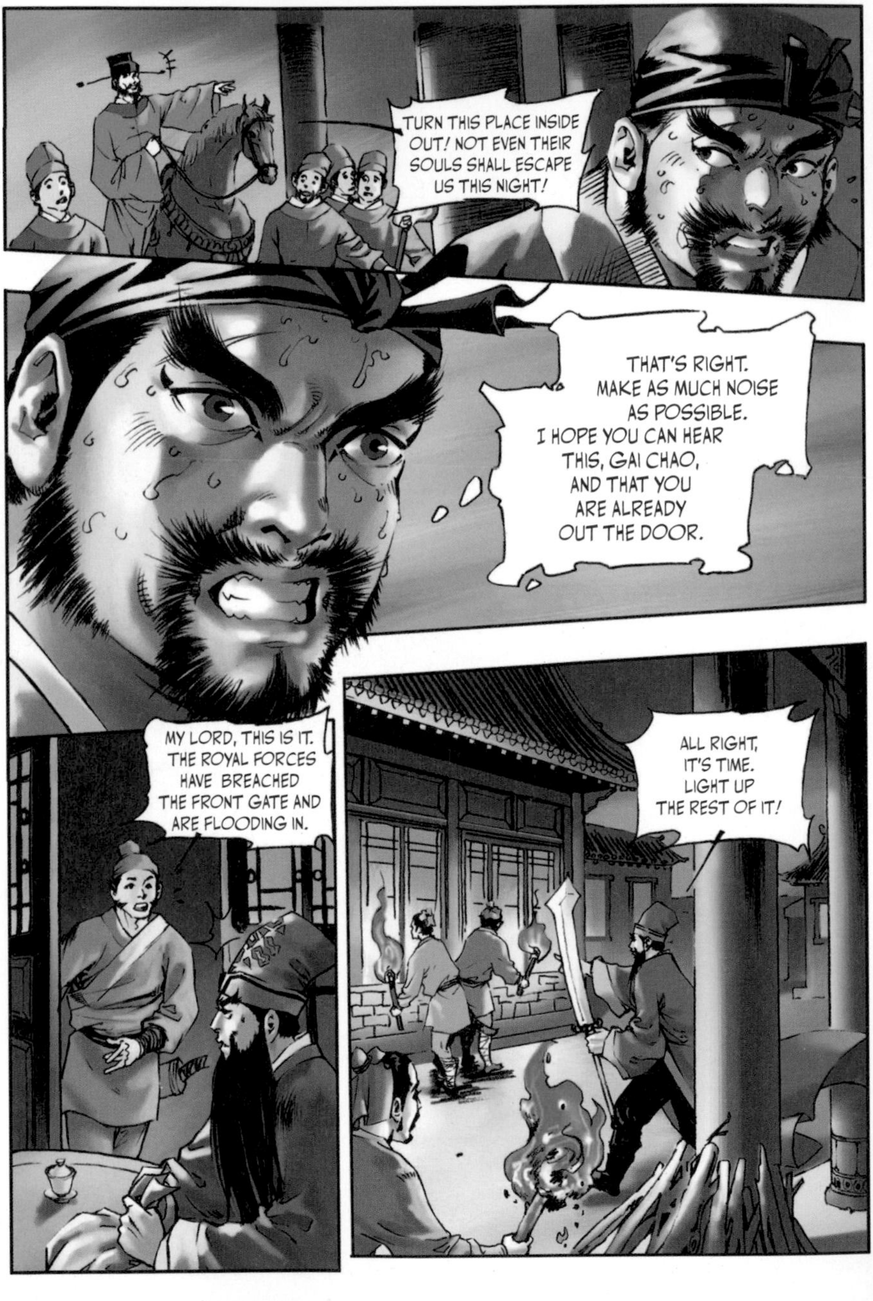
TURN THIS PLACE INSIDE OUT! NOT EVEN THEIR SOULS SHALL ESCAPE US THIS NIGHT!
THAT'S RIGHT. MAKE AS MUCH NOISE AS POSSIBLE. I HOPE YOU CAN HEAR THIS, GAI CHAO, AND THAT YOU ARE ALREADY OUT THE DOOR.
MY LORD, THIS IS IT. THE ROYAL FORCES HAVE BREACHED THE FRONT GATE AND ARE FLOODING IN.
ALL RIGHT, IT'S TIME. LIGHT UP THE REST OF IT!

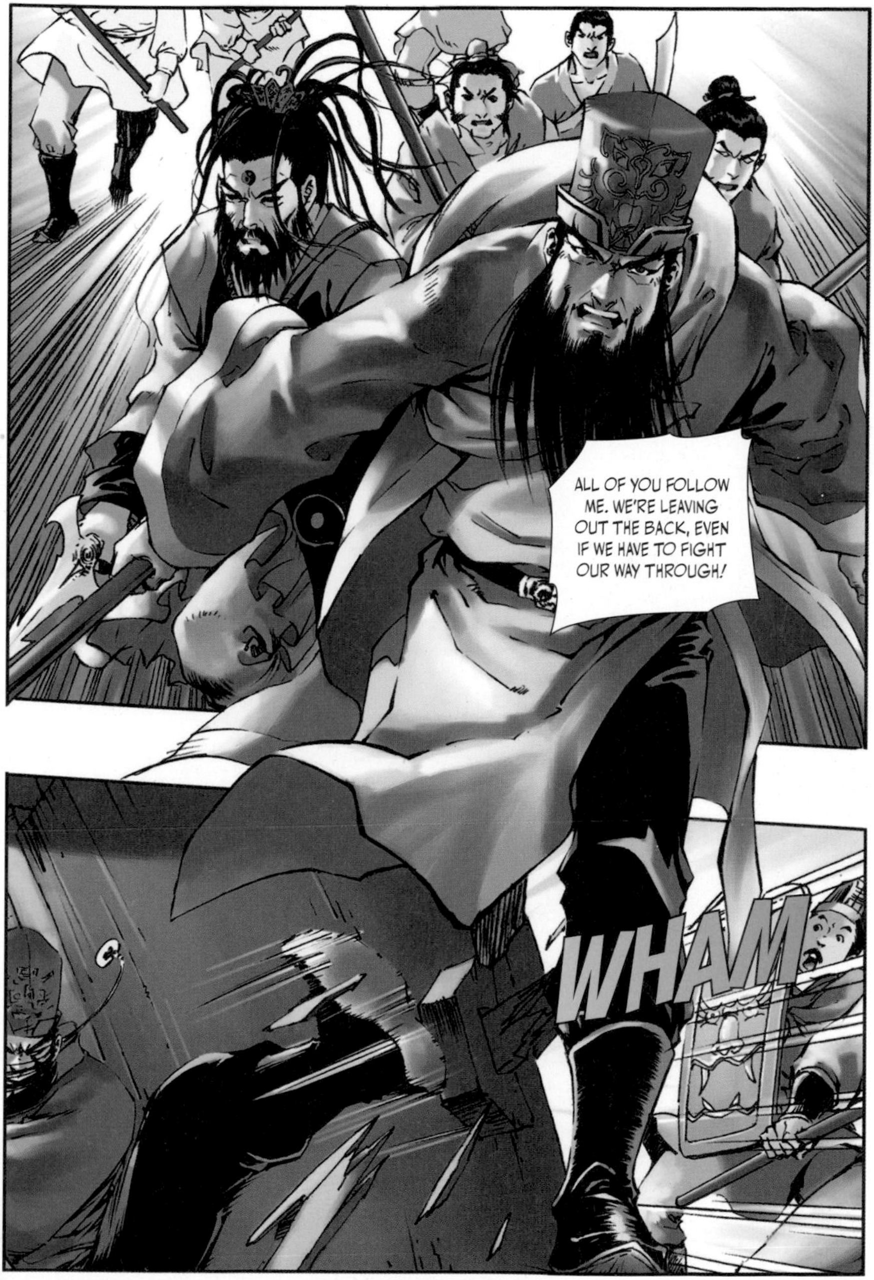
ALL OF YOU FOLLOW ME. WE'RE LEAVING OUT THE BACK, EVEN IF WE HAVE TO FIGHT OUR WAY THROUGH!
WHAM

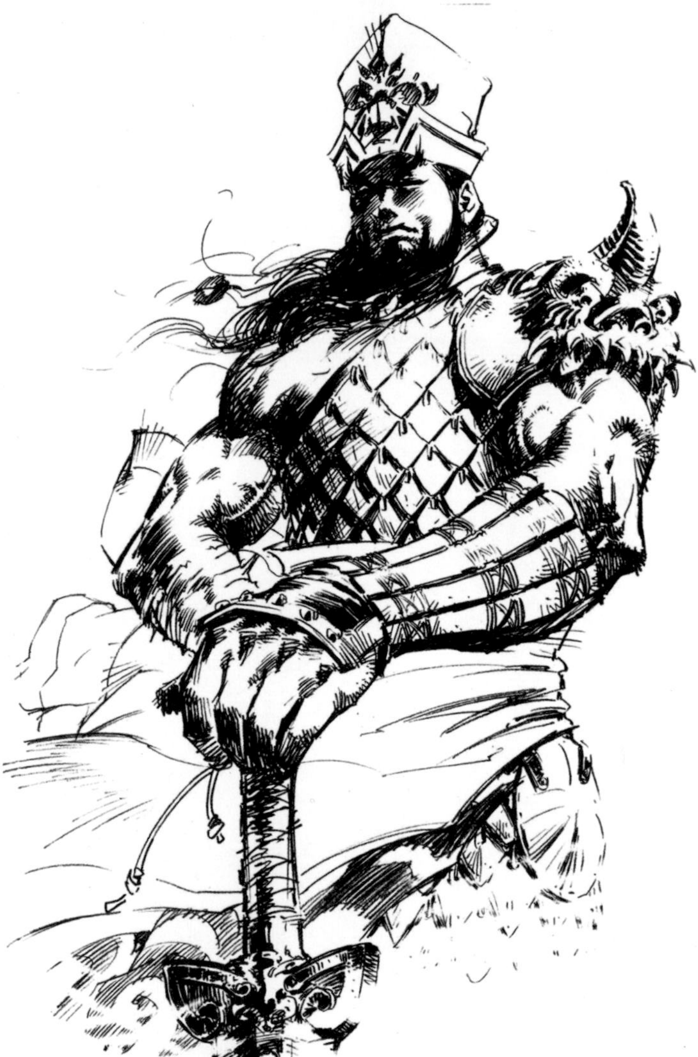

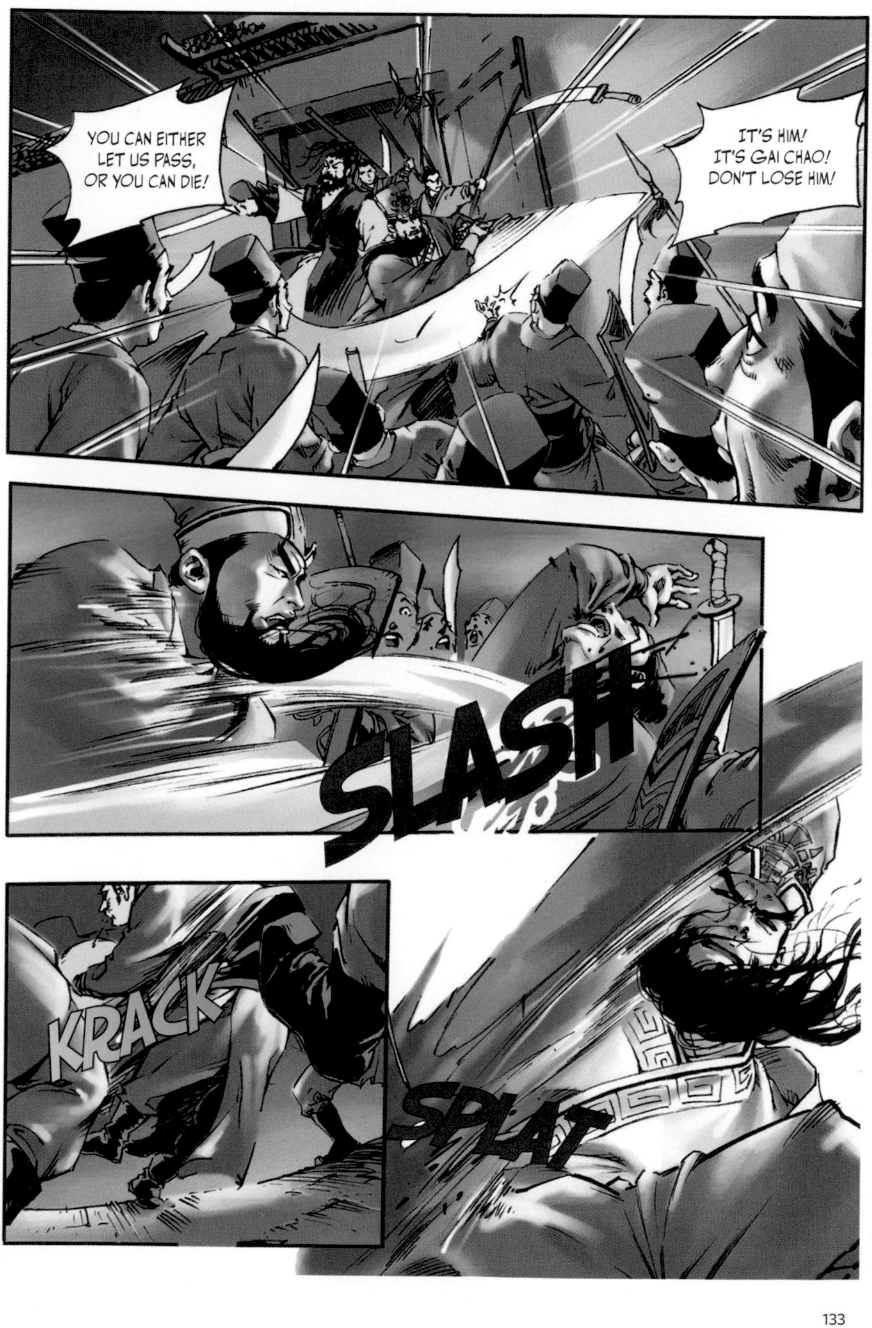
YOU CAN EITHER LET US PASS, OR YOU CAN DIE!
IT'S HIM! IT'S GAI CHAO! DON'T LOSE HIM!
SLASH
KRACK
SPLAT

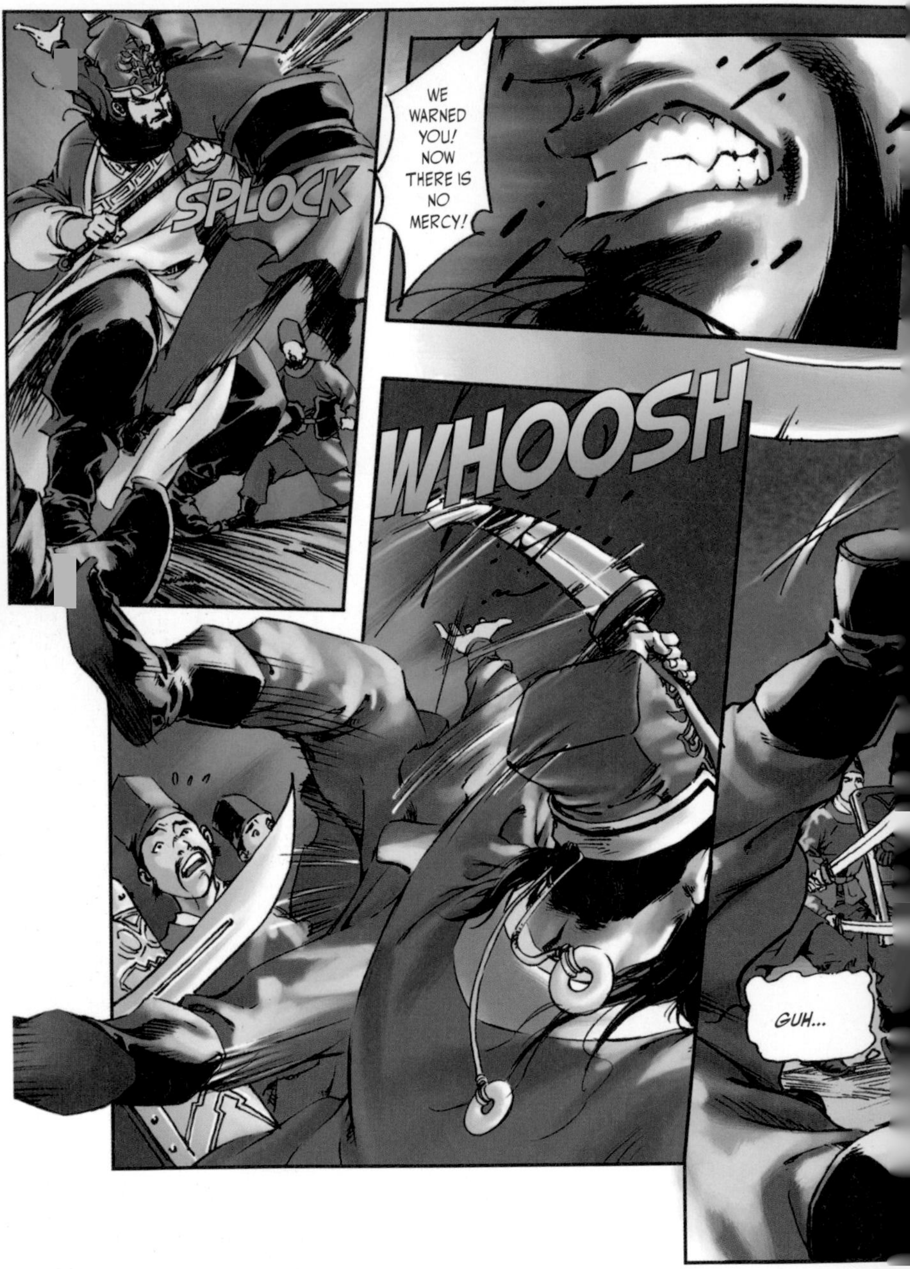
SPLOCK
WE WARNED YOU! NOW THERE IS NO MERCY!
WHOOSH
GUH...

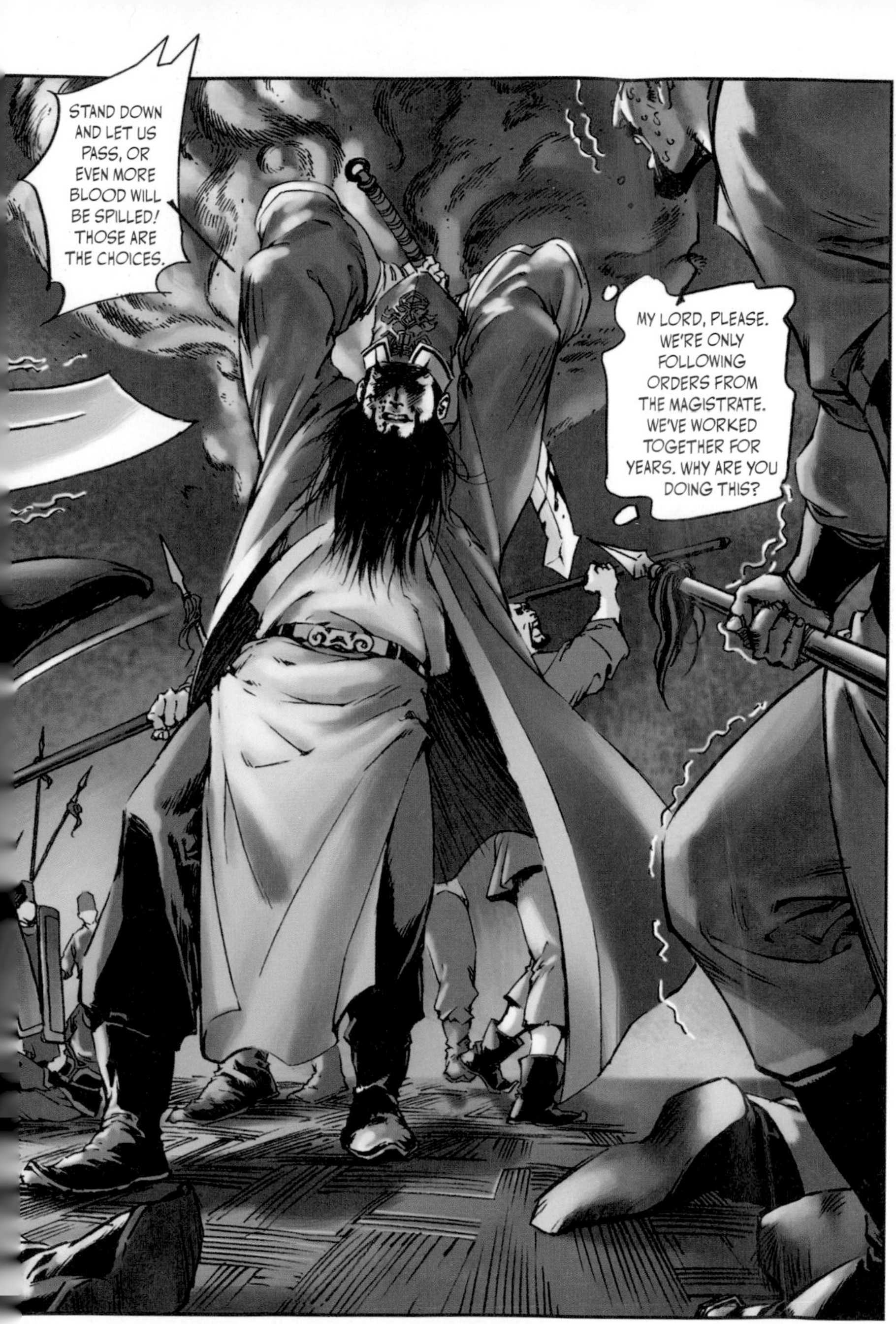
STAND DOWN AND LET US PASS, OR EVEN MORE BLOOD WILL BE SPILLED! THOSE ARE THE CHOICES.
MY LORD, PLEASE. WE'RE ONLY FOLLOWING ORDERS FROM THE MAGISTRATE. WE'VE WORKED TOGETHER FOR YEARS. WHY ARE YOU DOING THIS?

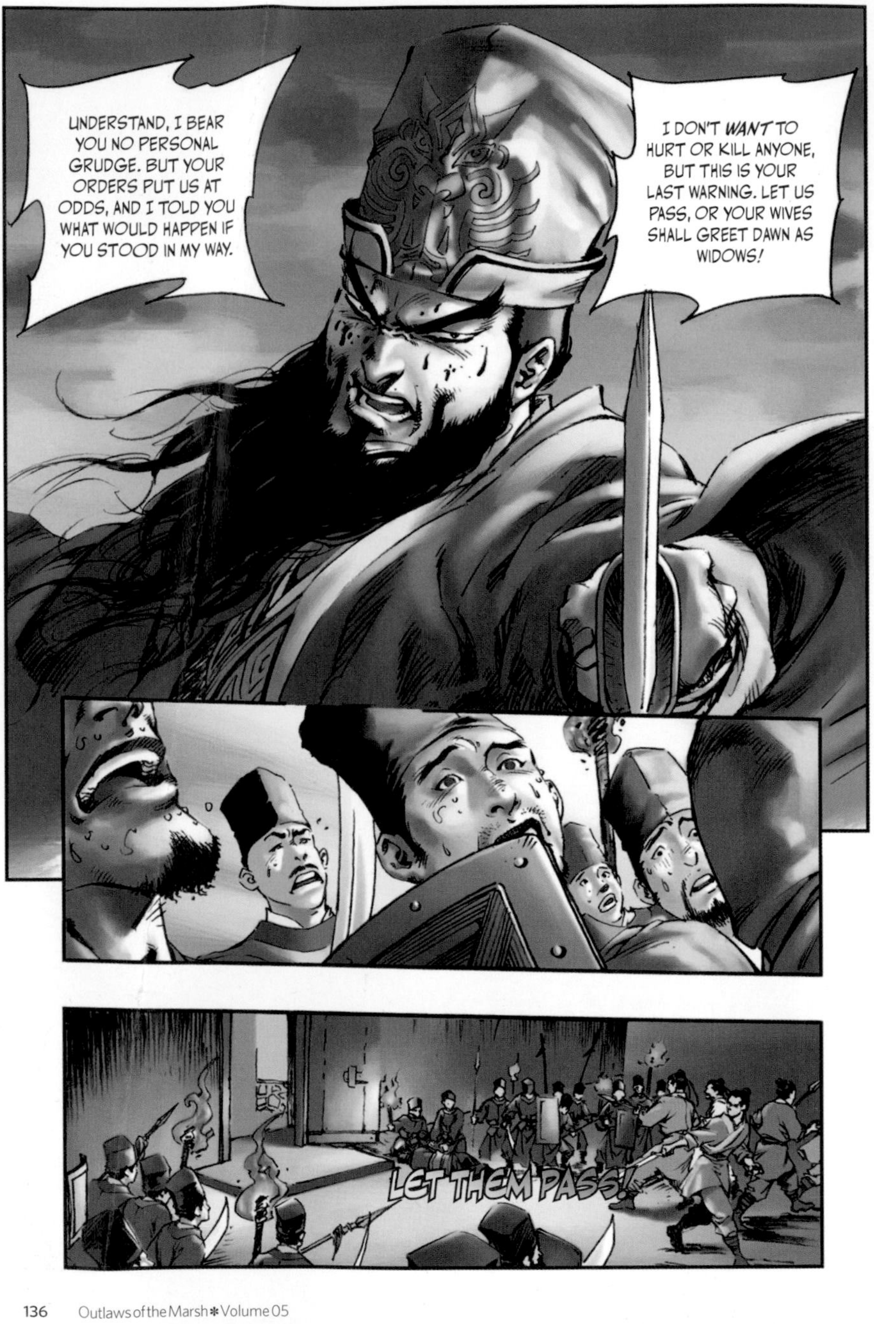
UNDERSTAND, I BEAR YOU NO PERSONAL GRUDGE. BUT YOUR ORDERS PUT US AT ODDS, AND I TOLD YOU WHAT WOULD HAPPEN IF YOU STOOD IN MY WAY.
I DON'T *WANT* TO HURT OR KILL ANYONE, BUT THIS IS YOUR LAST WARNING. LET US PASS, OR YOUR WIVES SHALL GREET DAWN AS WIDOWS!
LET THEM PASS!

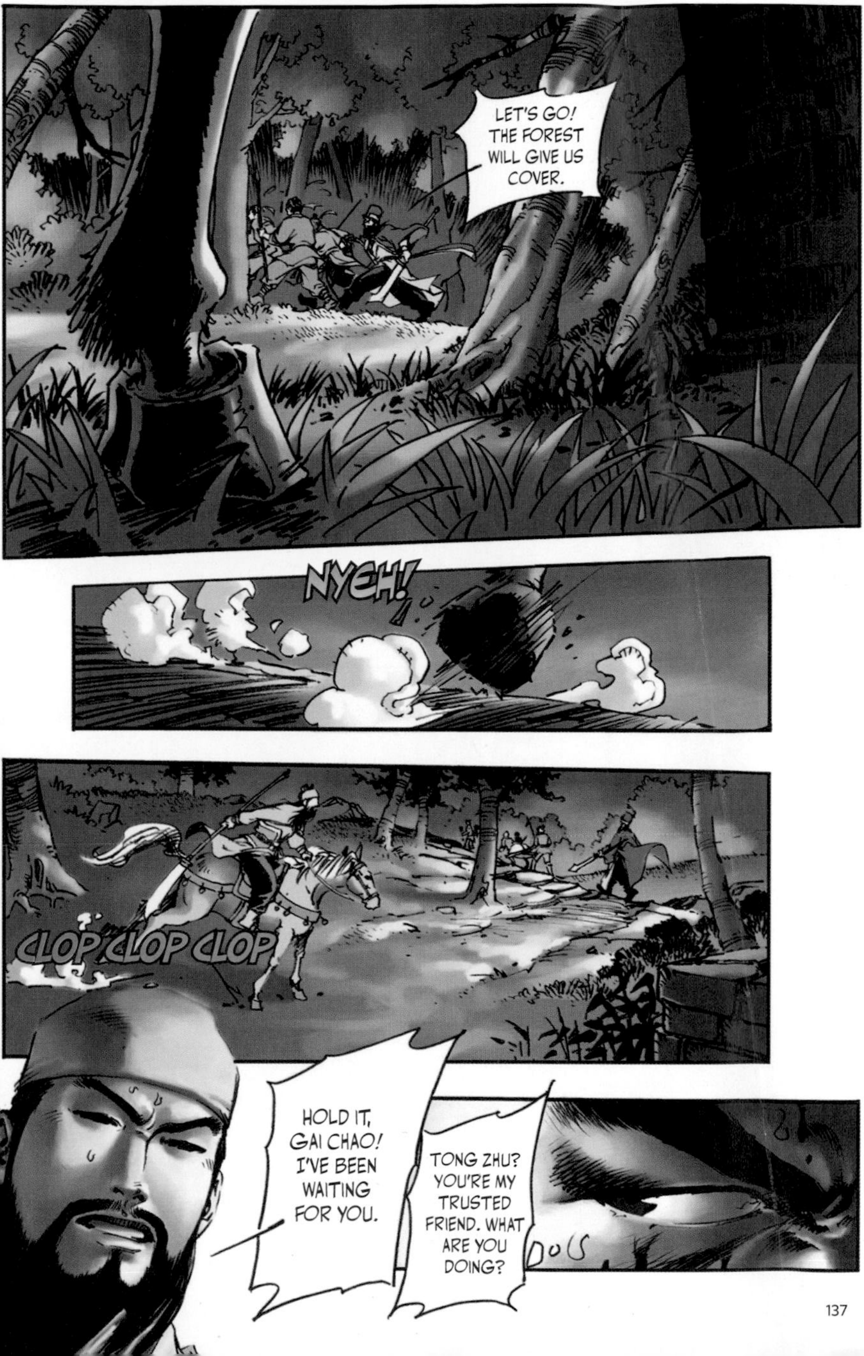
LET'S GO! THE FOREST WILL GIVE US COVER.
NYEH!
CLOP CLOP CLOP
HOLD IT, GAI CHAO! I'VE BEEN WAITING FOR YOU.
TONG ZHU? YOU'RE MY TRUSTED FRIEND. WHAT ARE YOU DOING?

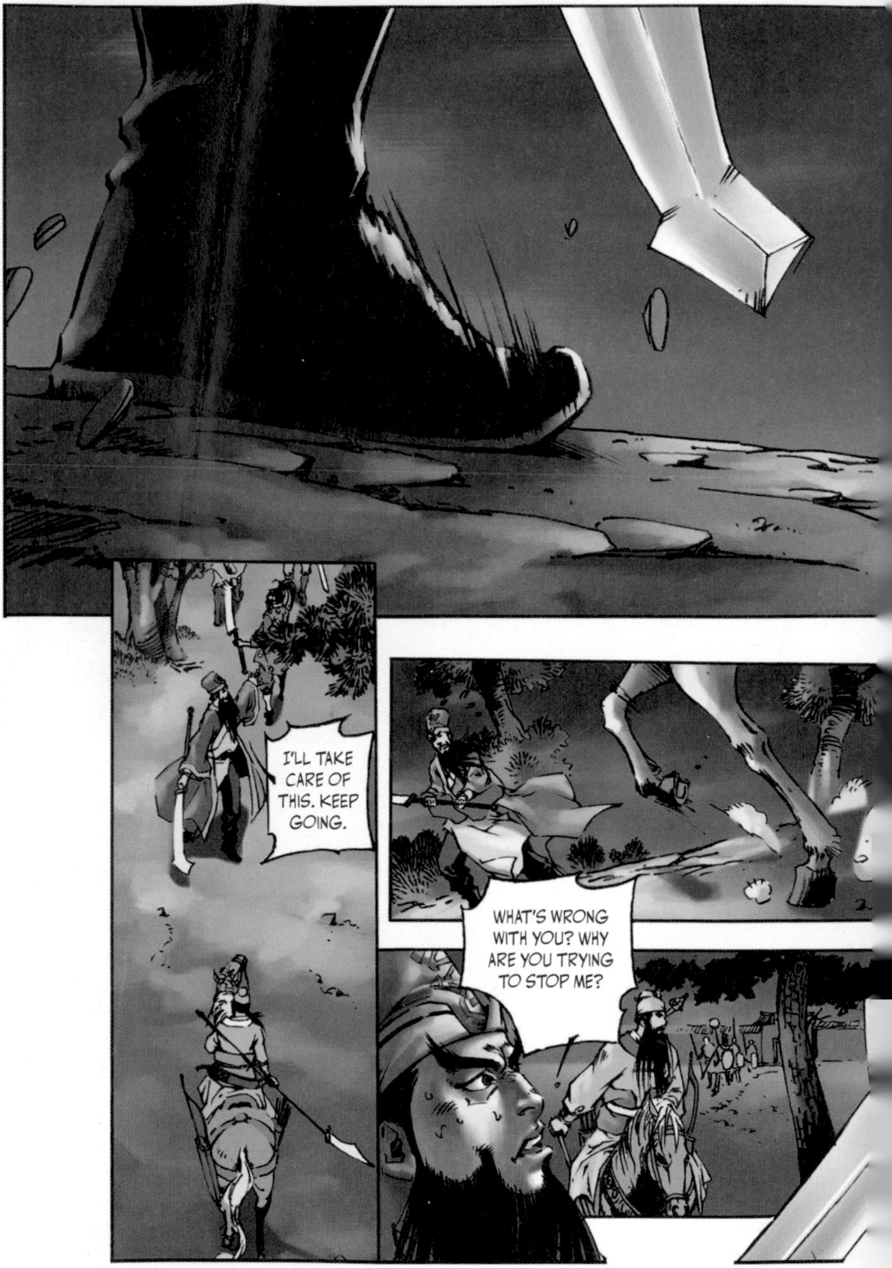
I'LL TAKE CARE OF THIS. KEEP GOING.
WHAT'S WRONG WITH YOU? WHY ARE YOU TRYING TO STOP ME?

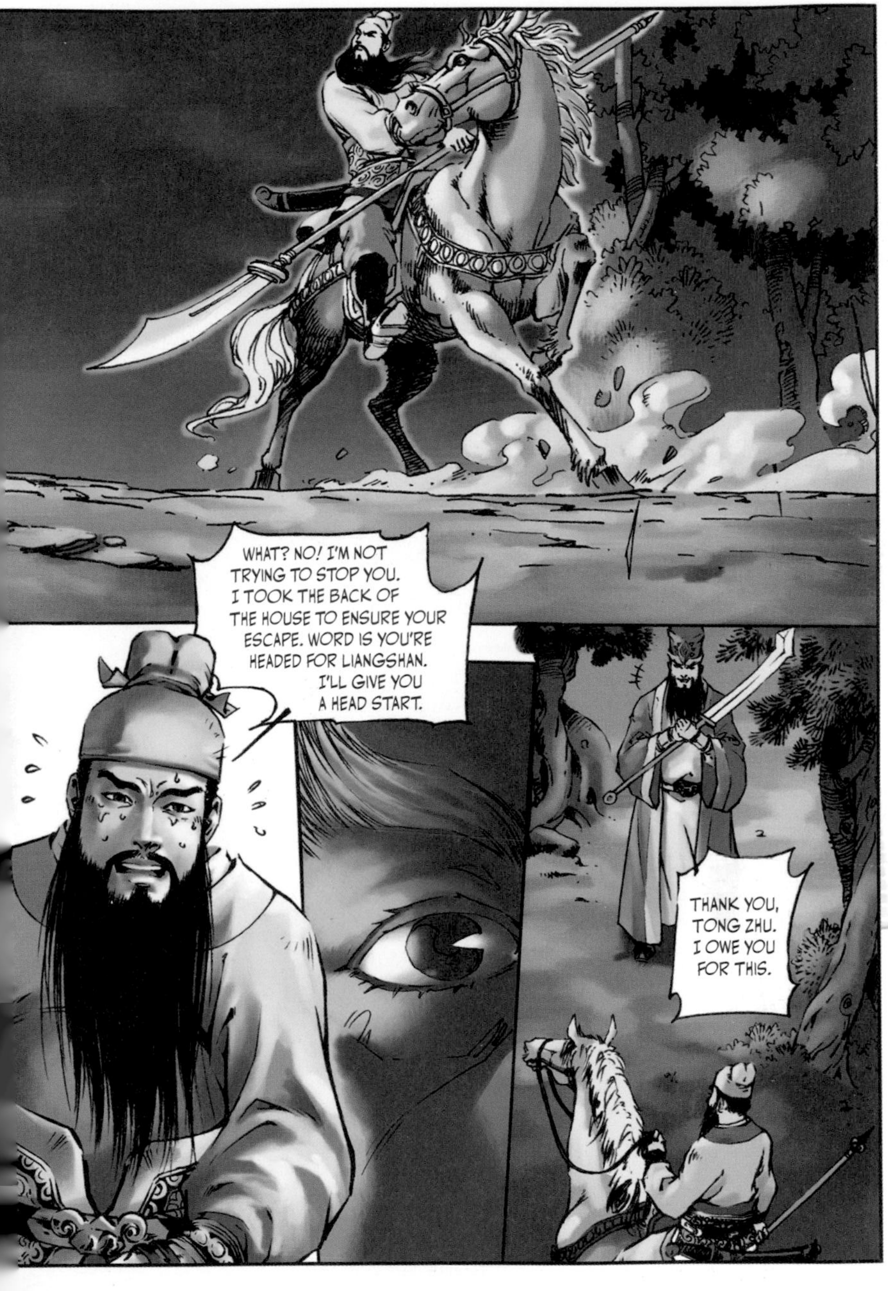
WHAT? NO! I'M NOT TRYING TO STOP YOU. I TOOK THE BACK OF THE HOUSE TO ENSURE YOUR ESCAPE. WORD IS YOU'RE HEADED FOR LIANGSHAN. I'LL GIVE YOU A HEAD START.
THANK YOU, TONG ZHU. I OWE YOU FOR THIS.

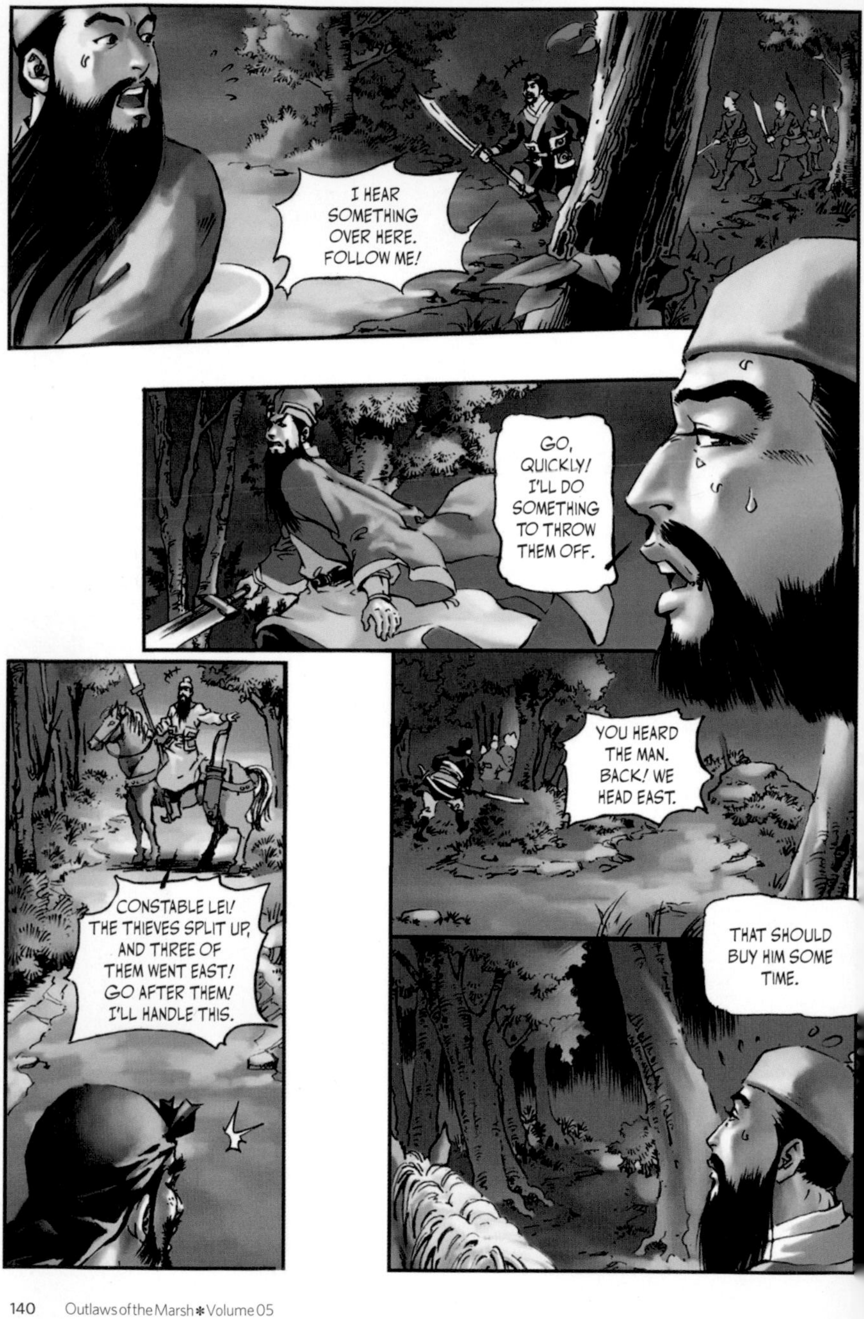
I HEAR SOMETHING OVER HERE. FOLLOW ME!
GO, QUICKLY! I'LL DO SOMETHING TO THROW THEM OFF.
YOU HEARD THE MAN. BACK! WE HEAD EAST.
CONSTABLE LEI! THE THIEVES SPLIT UP, AND THREE OF THEM WENT EAST! GO AFTER THEM! I'LL HANDLE THIS.
THAT SHOULD BUY HIM SOME TIME.

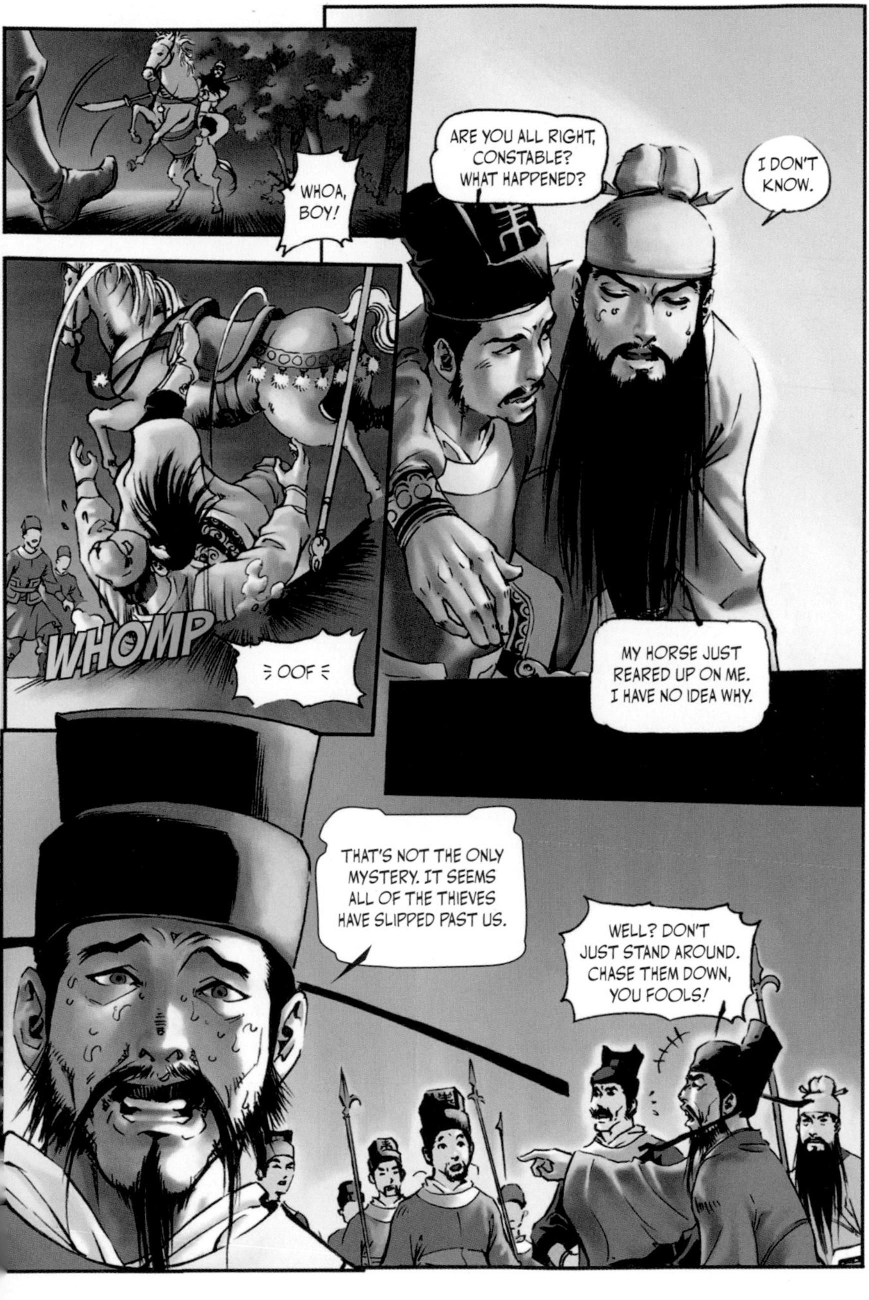
WHOA, BOY!
ARE YOU ALL RIGHT, CONSTABLE? WHAT HAPPENED?
I DON'T KNOW.
WHOMP
OOF
MY HORSE JUST REARED UP ON ME. I HAVE NO IDEA WHY.
THAT'S NOT THE ONLY MYSTERY. IT SEEMS ALL OF THE THIEVES HAVE SLIPPED PAST US.
WELL? DON'T JUST STAND AROUND. CHASE THEM DOWN, YOU FOOLS!

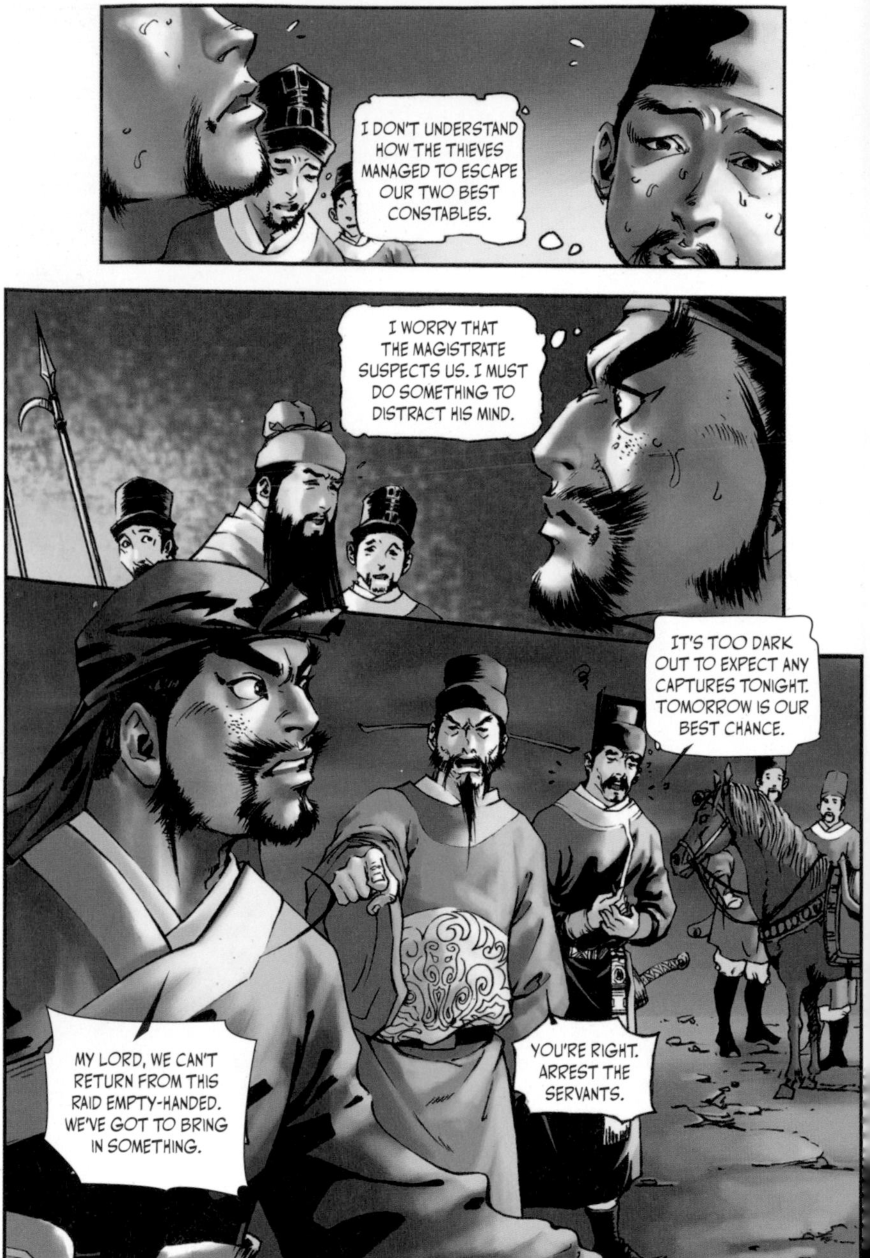
I DON'T UNDERSTAND HOW THE THIEVES MANAGED TO ESCAPE OUR TWO BEST CONSTABLES.
I WORRY THAT THE MAGISTRATE SUSPECTS US. I MUST DO SOMETHING TO DISTRACT HIS MIND.
IT'S TOO DARK OUT TO EXPECT ANY CAPTURES TONIGHT. TOMORROW IS OUR BEST CHANCE.
MY LORD, WE CAN'T RETURN FROM THIS RAID EMPTY-HANDED. WE'VE GOT TO BRING IN SOMETHING.
YOU'RE RIGHT. ARREST THE SERVANTS.

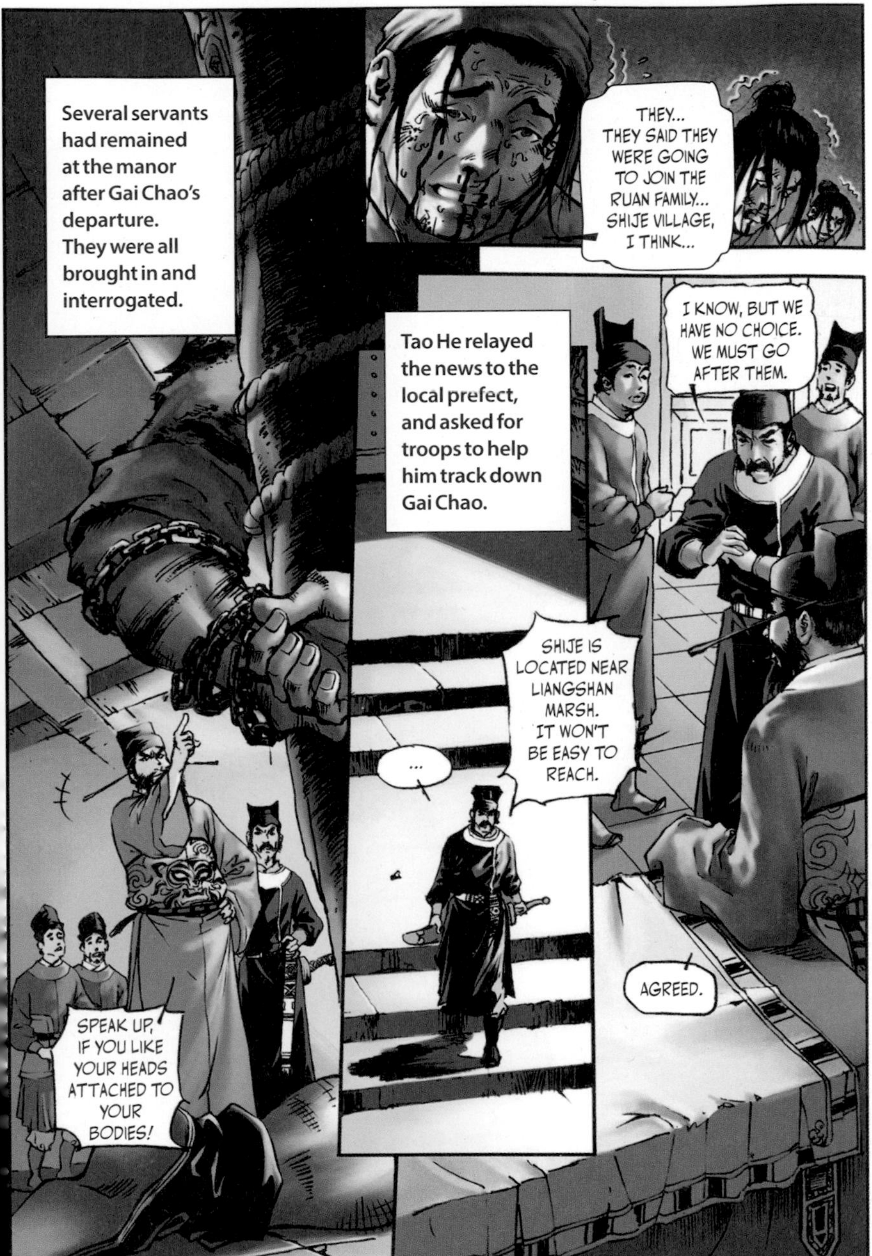
Several servants had remained at the manor after Gai Chao's departure. They were all brought in and interrogated.
SPEAK UP, IF YOU LIKE YOUR HEADS ATTACHED TO YOUR BODIES!
THEY... THEY SAID THEY WERE GOING TO JOIN THE RUAN FAMILY... SHIJE VILLAGE, I THINK...
Tao He relayed the news to the local prefect, and asked for troops to help him track down Gai Chao.
...
SHIJE IS LOCATED NEAR LIANGSHAN MARSH. IT WON'T BE EASY TO REACH.
I KNOW, BUT WE HAVE NO CHOICE. WE MUST GO AFTER THEM.
AGREED.

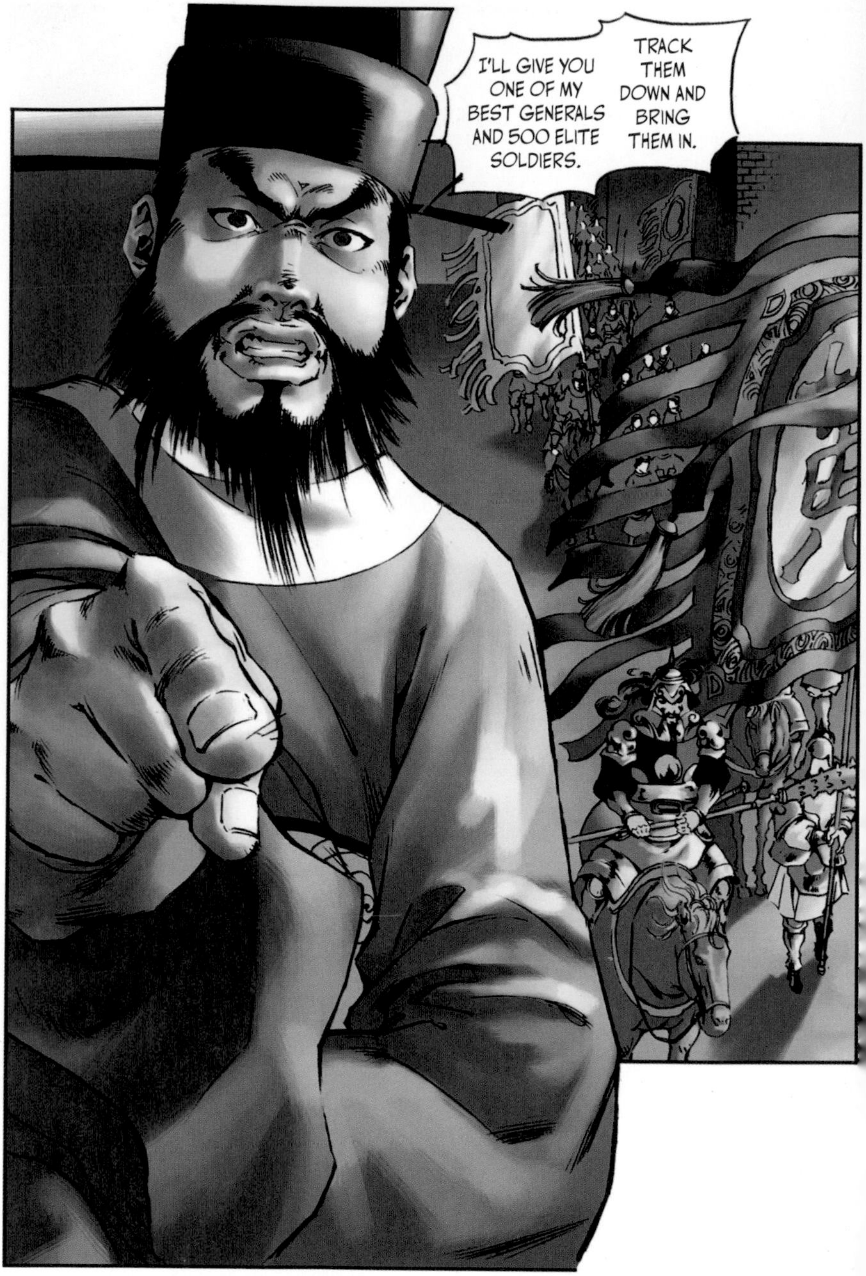
I'LL GIVE YOU ONE OF MY BEST GENERALS AND 500 ELITE SOLDIERS.
TRACK THEM DOWN AND BRING THEM IN.

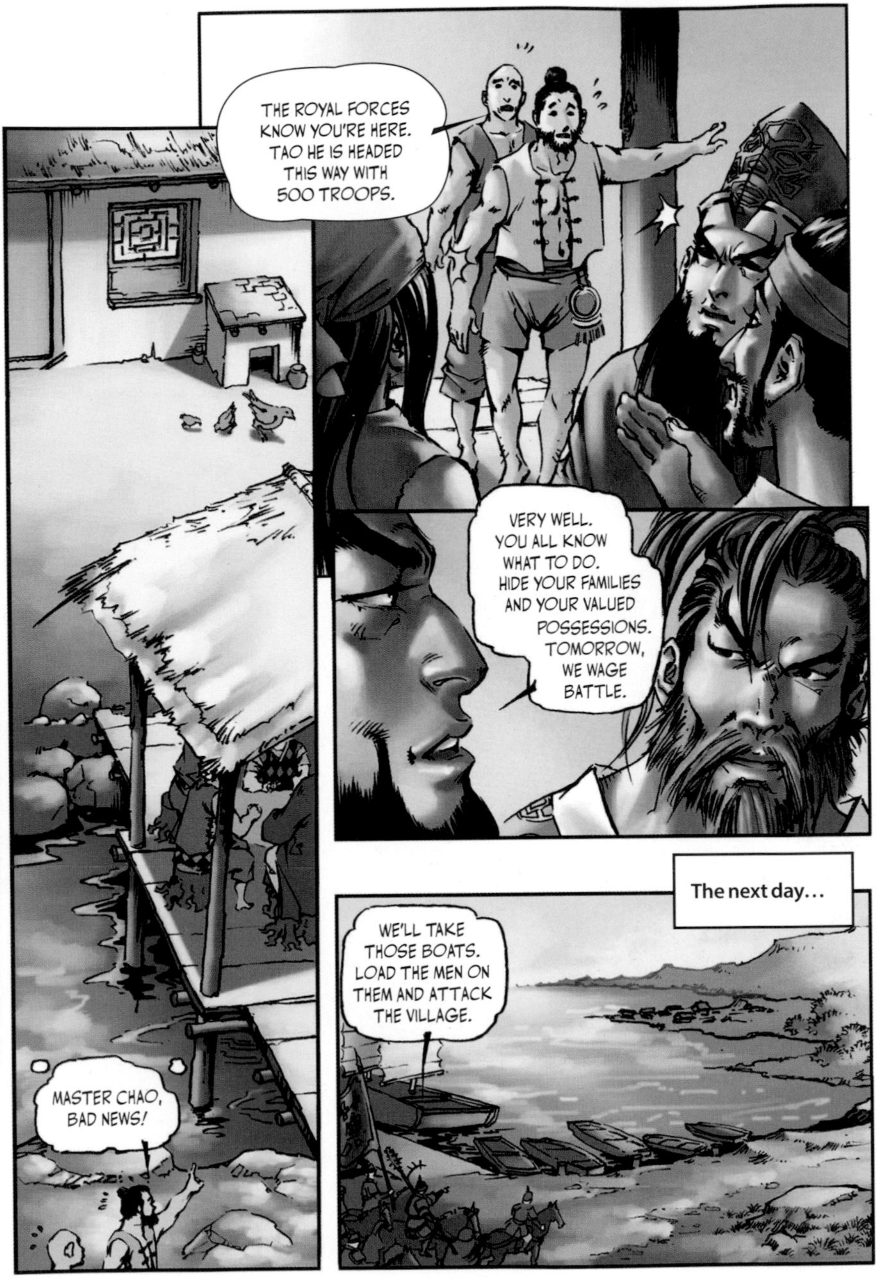
MASTER CHAO, BAD NEWS!
THE ROYAL FORCES KNOW YOU'RE HERE. TAO HE IS HEADED THIS WAY WITH 500 TROOPS.
VERY WELL. YOU ALL KNOW WHAT TO DO. HIDE YOUR FAMILIES AND YOUR VALUED POSSESSIONS. TOMORROW, WE WAGE BATTLE.
The next day...
WE'LL TAKE THOSE BOATS. LOAD THE MEN ON THEM AND ATTACK THE VILLAGE.

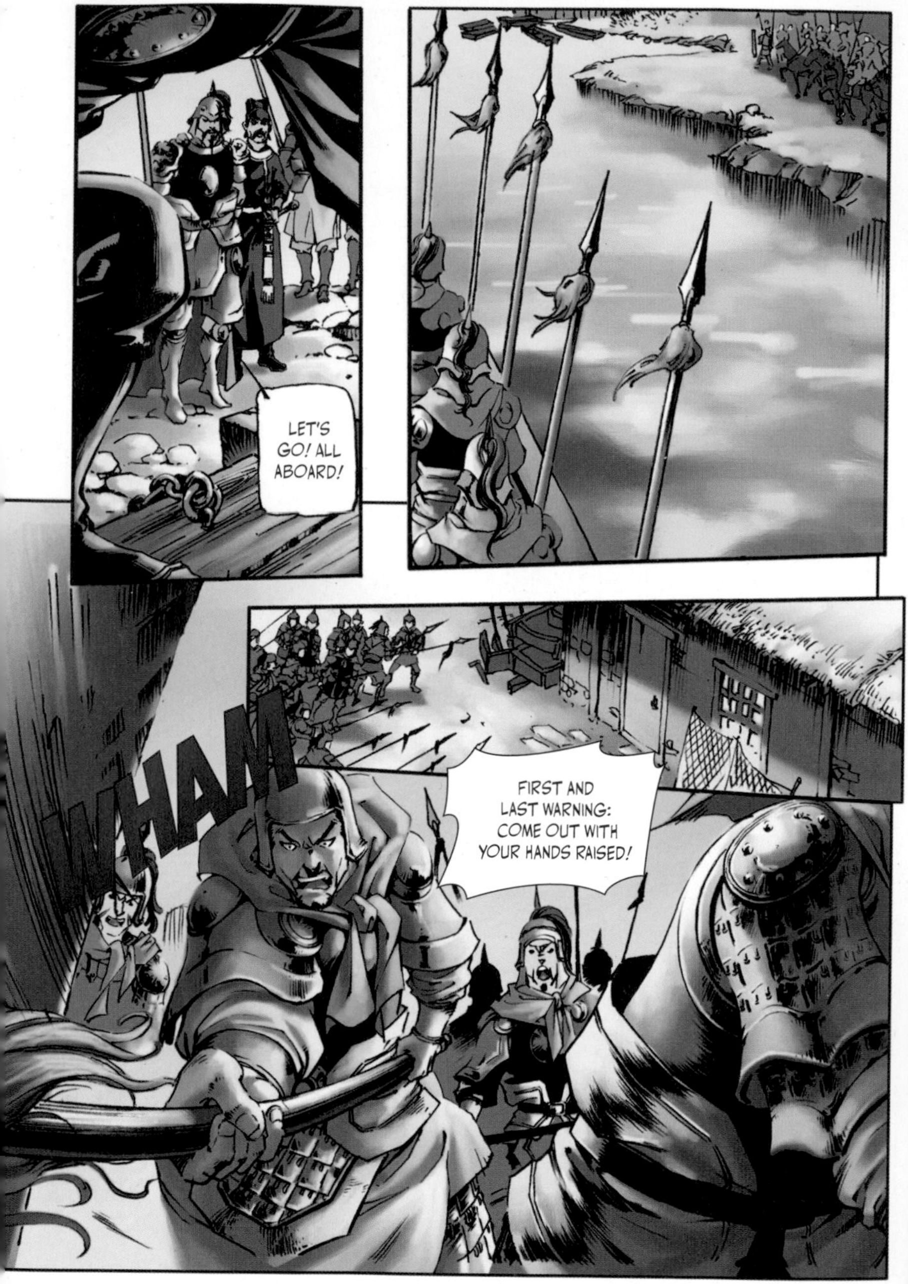
LET'S GO! ALL ABOARD!
WHAM
FIRST AND LAST WARNING: COME OUT WITH YOUR HANDS RAISED!

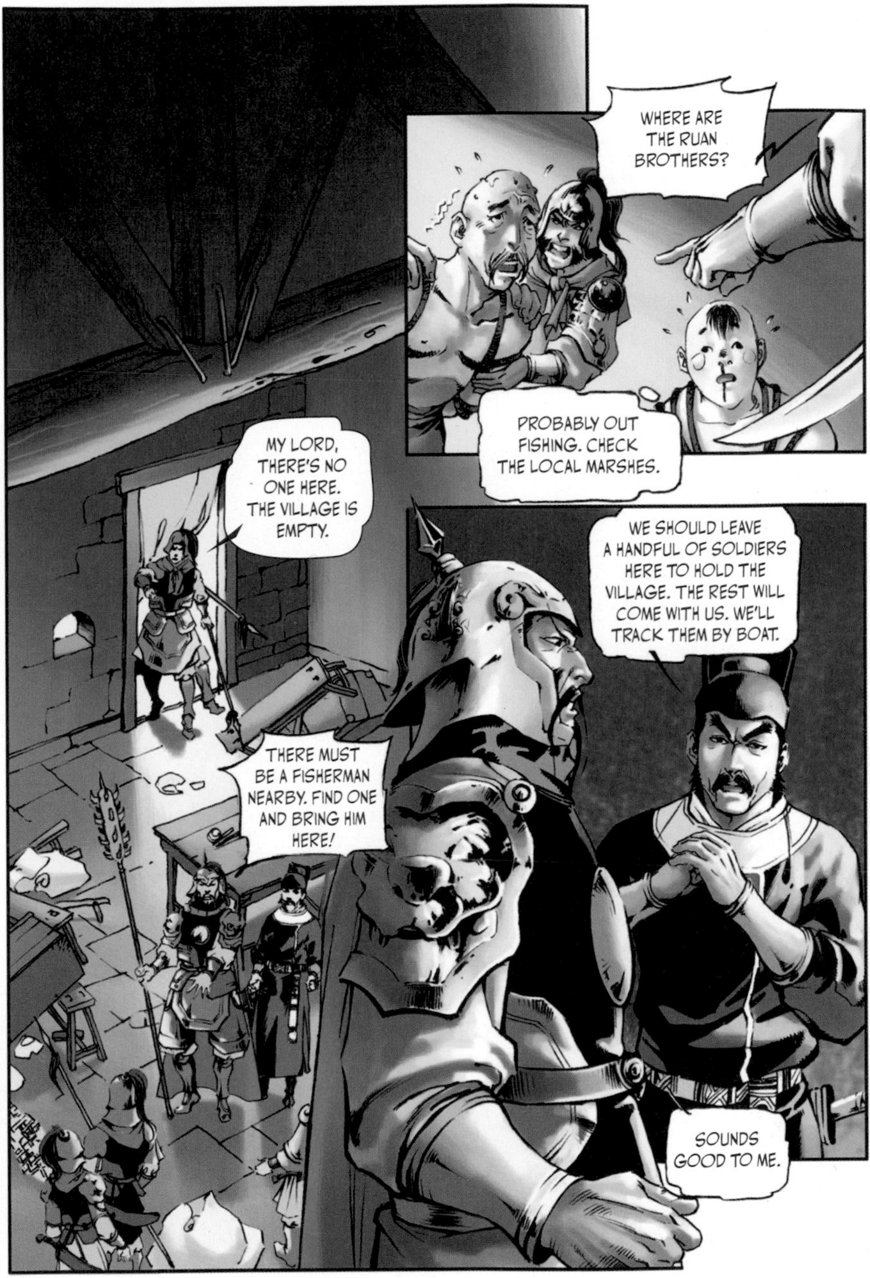
WHERE ARE THE RUAN BROTHERS?
PROBABLY OUT FISHING. CHECK THE LOCAL MARSHES.
MY LORD, THERE'S NO ONE HERE. THE VILLAGE IS EMPTY.
THERE MUST BE A FISHERMAN NEARBY. FIND ONE AND BRING HIM HERE!
WE SHOULD LEAVE A HANDFUL OF SOLDIERS HERE TO HOLD THE VILLAGE. THE REST WILL COME WITH US. WE'LL TRACK THEM BY BOAT.
SOUNDS GOOD TO ME.

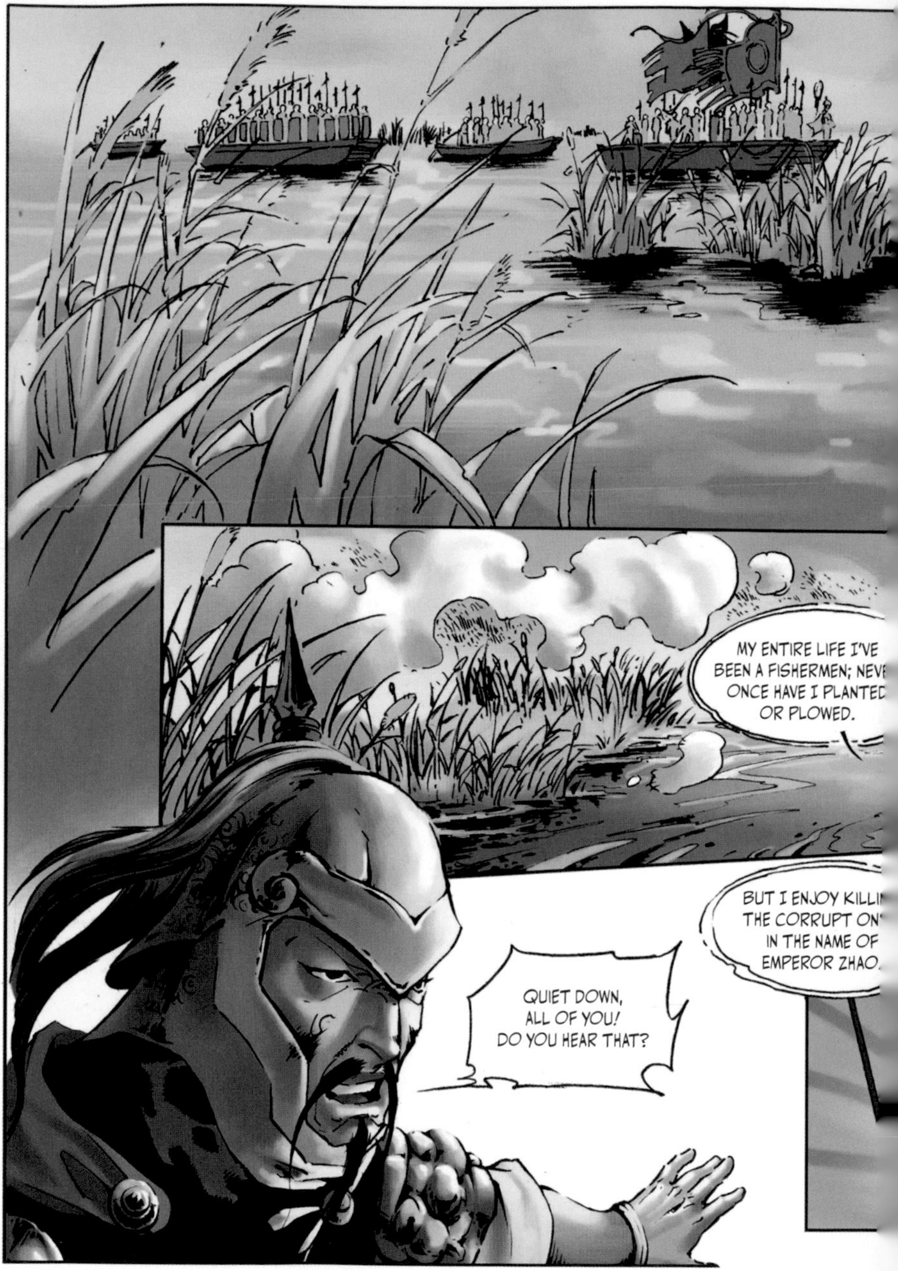
MY ENTIRE LIFE I'VE BEEN A FISHERMEN; NEVE ONCE HAVE I PLANTED OR PLOWED.
BUT I ENJOY KILLI THE CORRUPT ON IN THE NAME OF EMPEROR ZHAO.
QUIET DOWN, ALL OF YOU! DO YOU HEAR THAT?

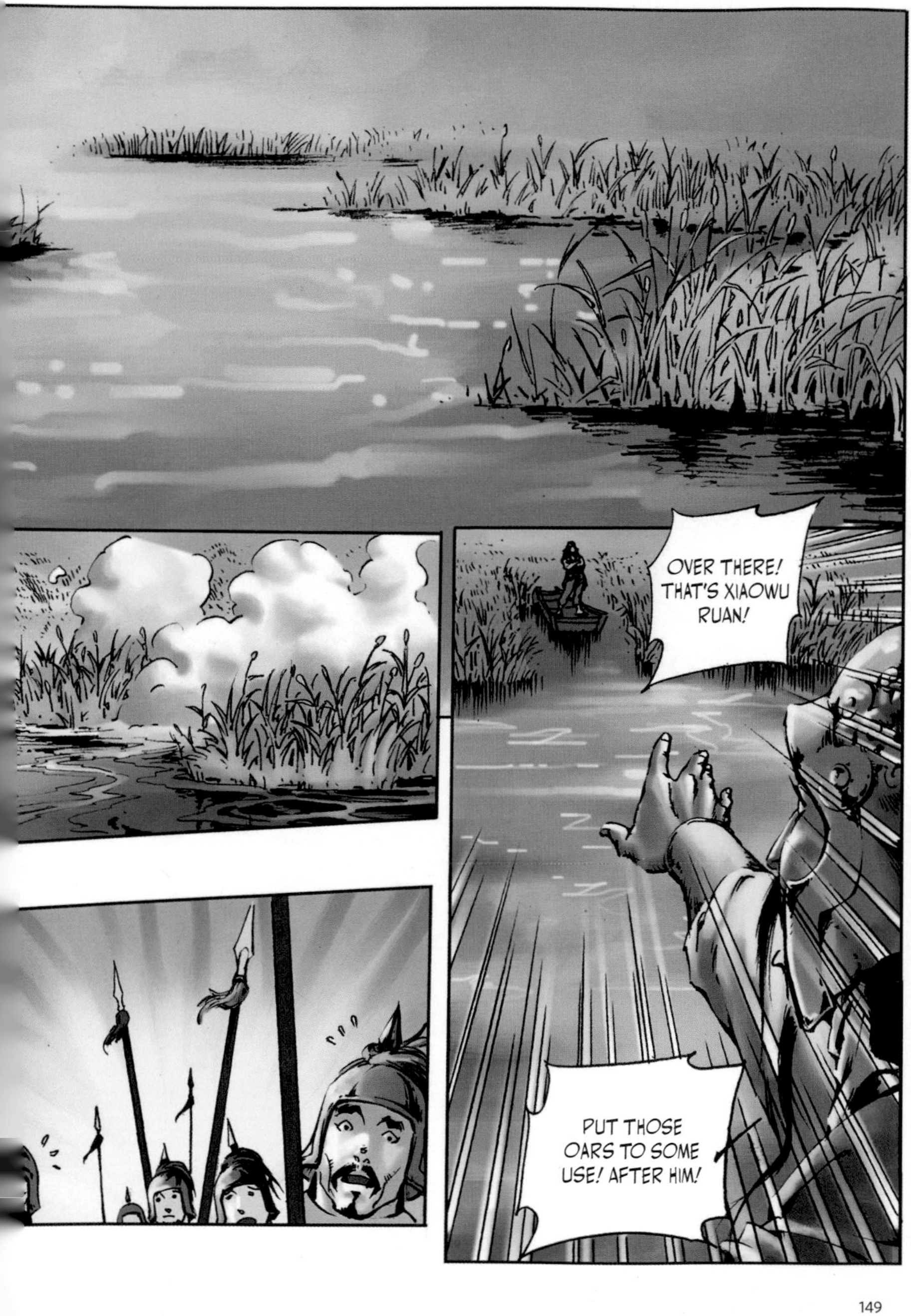
OVER THERE! THAT'S XIAOWU RUAN!
PUT THOSE OARS TO SOME USE! AFTER HIM!

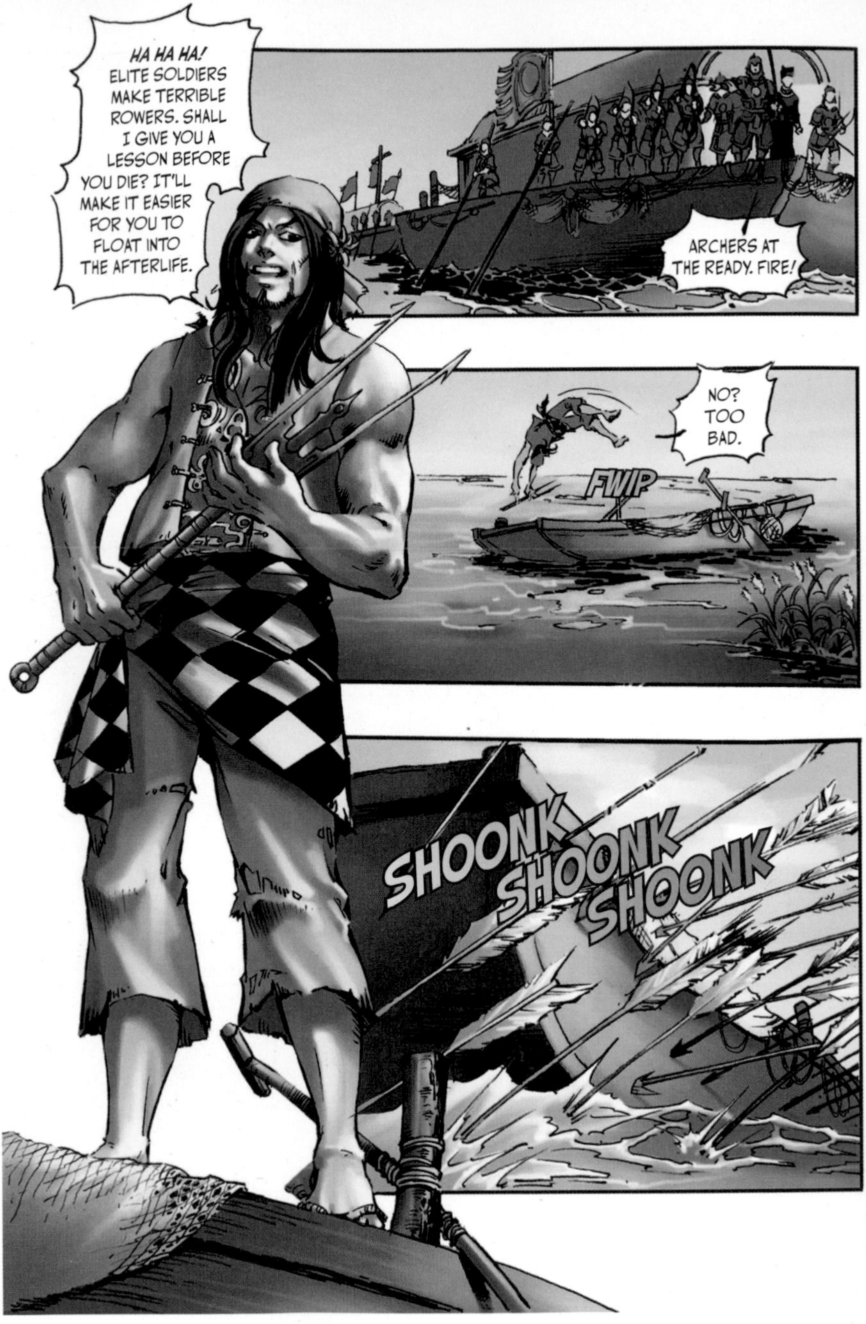
HA HA HA! ELITE SOLDIERS MAKE TERRIBLE ROWERS. SHALL I GIVE YOU A LESSON BEFORE YOU DIE? IT'LL MAKE IT EASIER FOR YOU TO FLOAT INTO THE AFTERLIFE.
ARCHERS AT THE READY. FIRE!
NO? TOO BAD.
FWIP
SHOONK
SHOONK
SHOONK

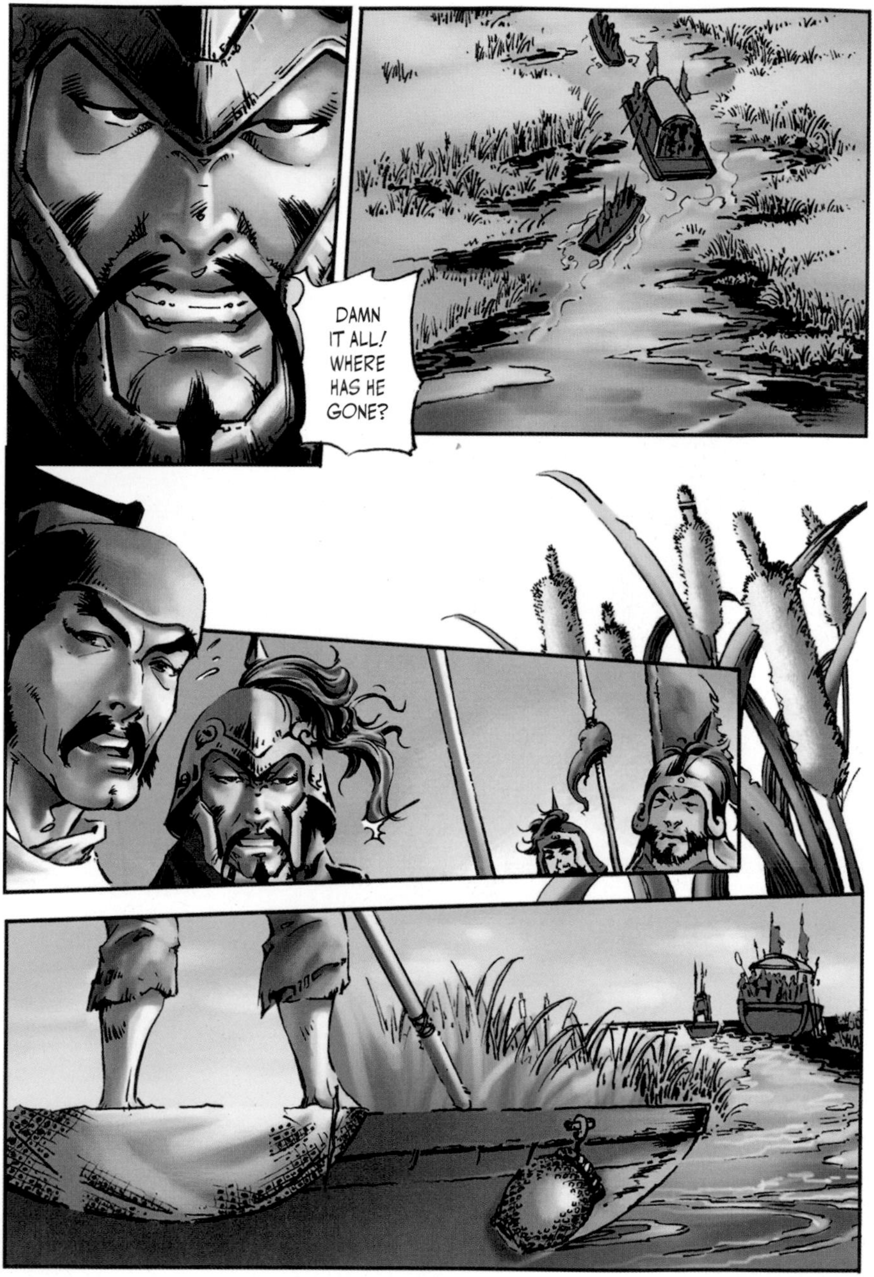
DAMN IT ALL! WHERE HAS HE GONE?

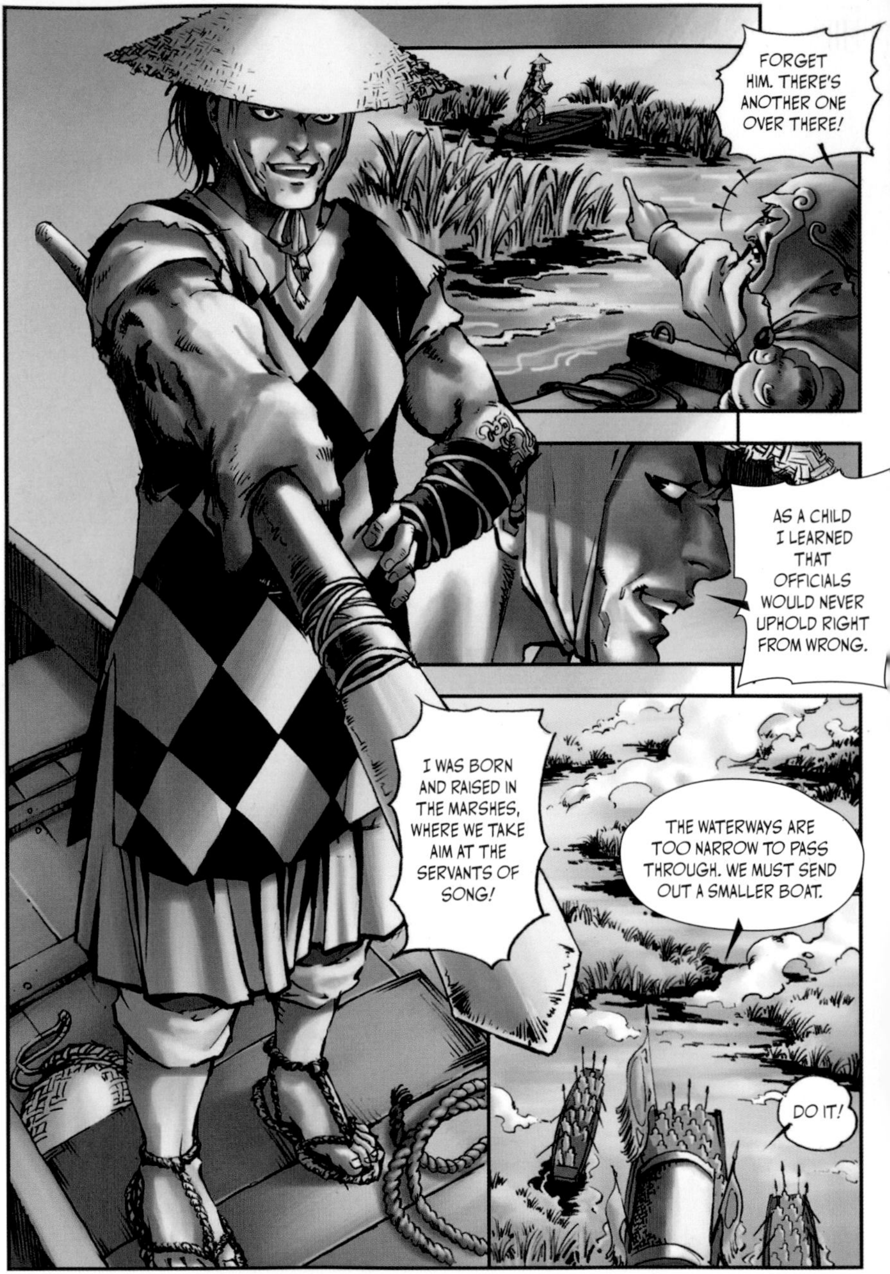
FORGET HIM. THERE'S ANOTHER ONE OVER THERE!
AS A CHILD I LEARNED THAT OFFICIALS WOULD NEVER UPHOLD RIGHT FROM WRONG.
I WAS BORN AND RAISED IN THE MARSHES, WHERE WE TAKE AIM AT THE SERVANTS OF SONG!
THE WATERWAYS ARE TOO NARROW TO PASS THROUGH. WE MUST SEND OUT A SMALLER BOAT.
DO IT!

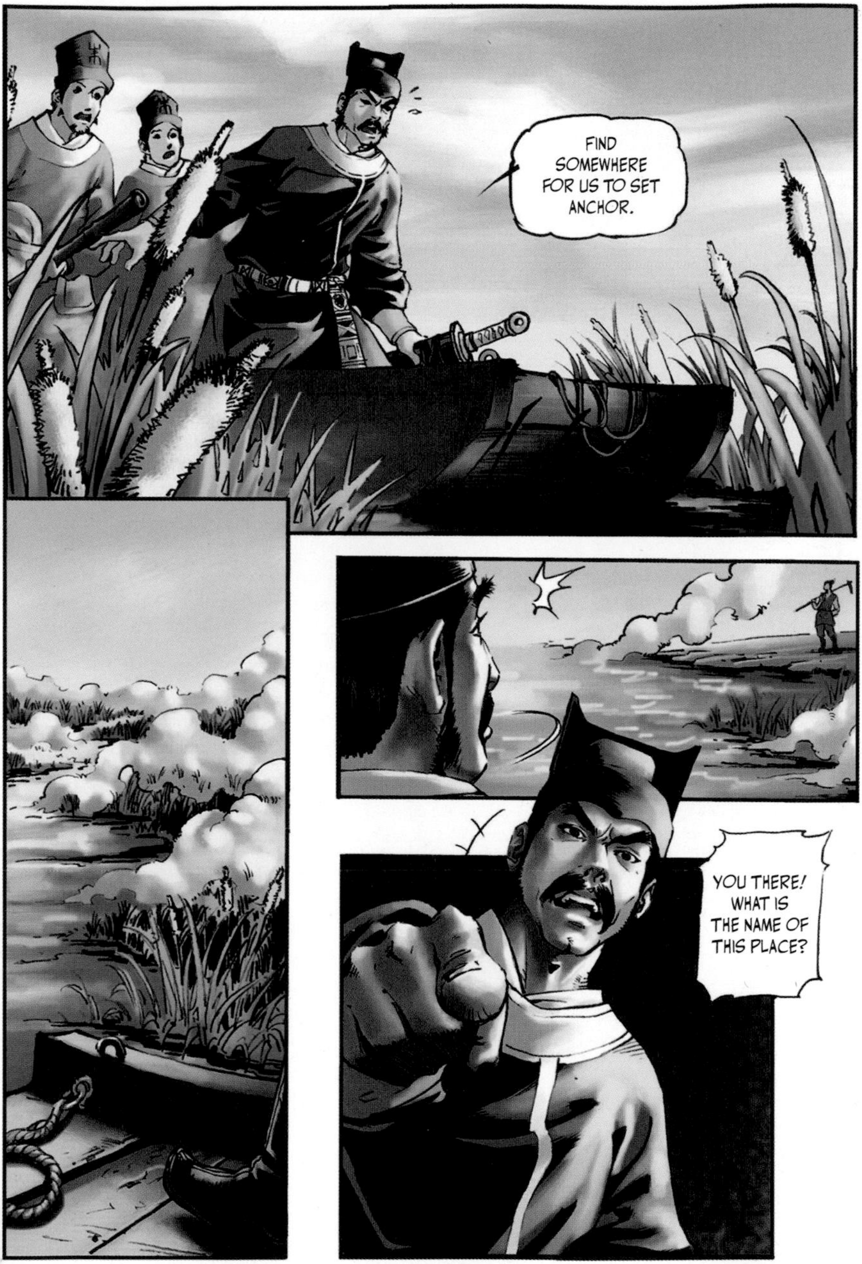
FIND SOMEWHERE FOR US TO SET ANCHOR.
YOU THERE! WHAT IS THE NAME OF THIS PLACE?

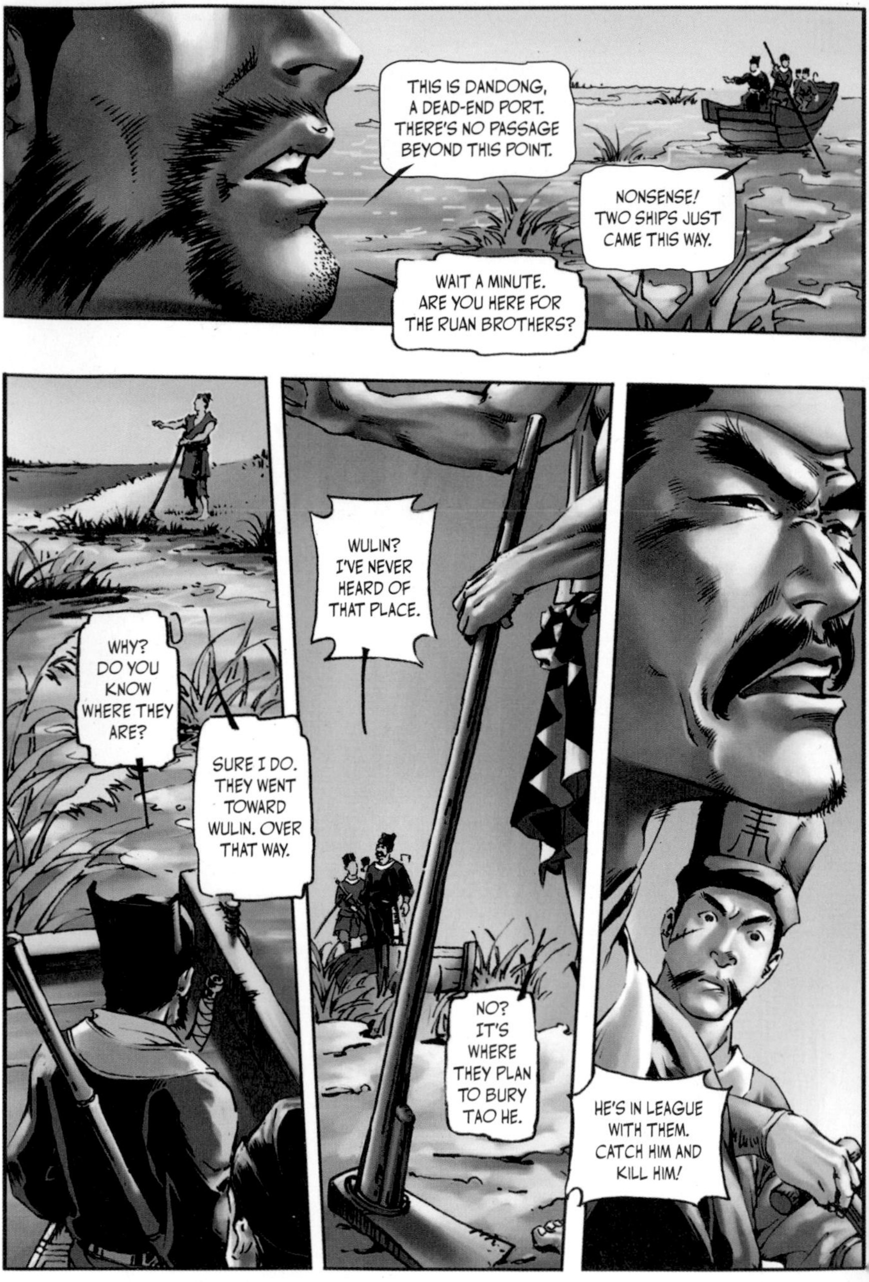
THIS IS DANDONG, A DEAD-END PORT. THERE'S NO PASSAGE BEYOND THIS POINT.
NONSENSE! TWO SHIPS JUST CAME THIS WAY.
WAIT A MINUTE. ARE YOU HERE FOR THE RUAN BROTHERS?
WHY? DO YOU KNOW WHERE THEY ARE?
SURE I DO. THEY WENT TOWARD WULIN. OVER THAT WAY.
WULIN? I'VE NEVER HEARD OF THAT PLACE.
NO? IT'S WHERE THEY PLAN TO BURY TAO HE.
HE'S IN LEAGUE WITH THEM. CATCH HIM AND KILL HIM!

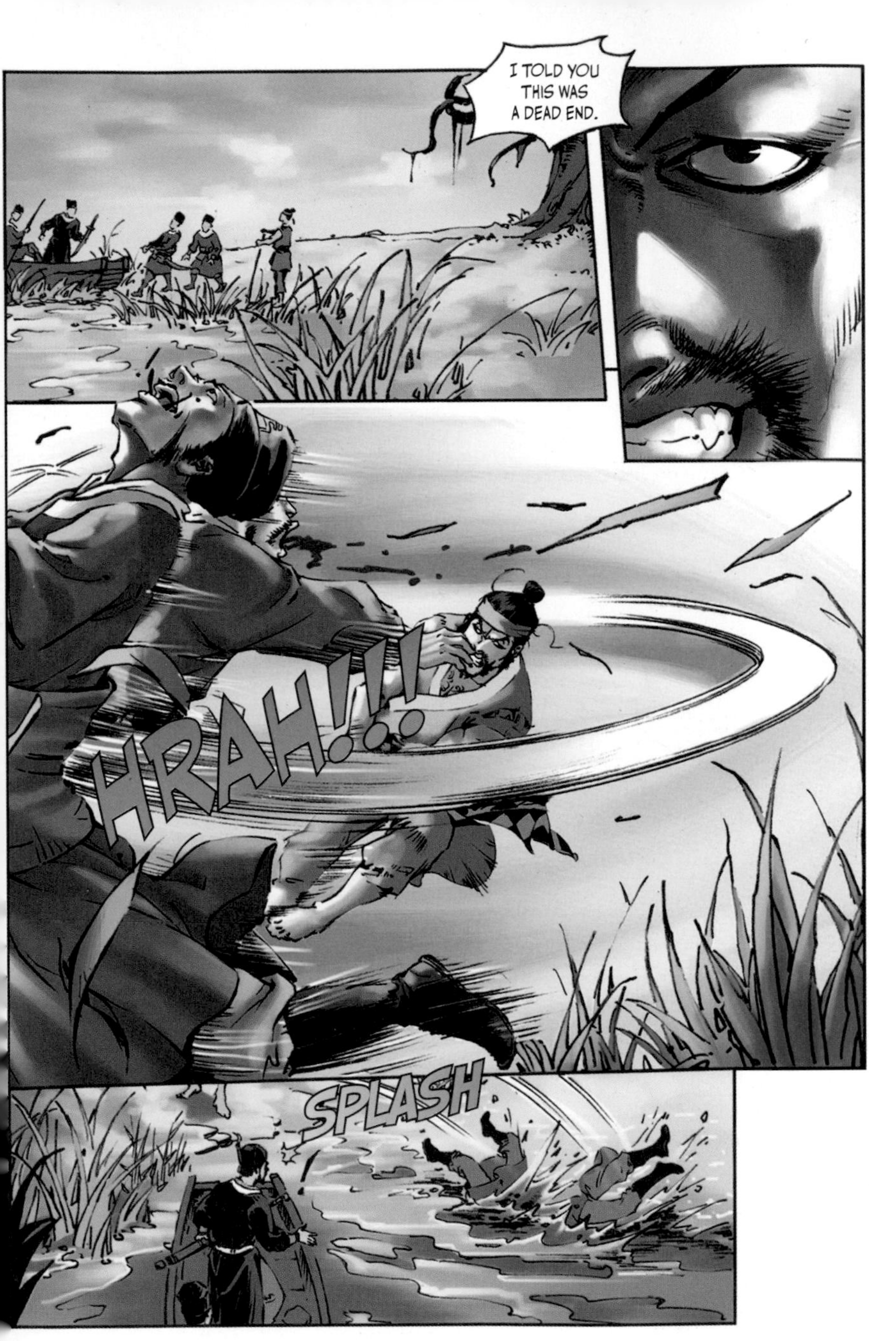
I TOLD YOU
THIS WAS
A DEAD END.
HRAH!!!
SPLASH

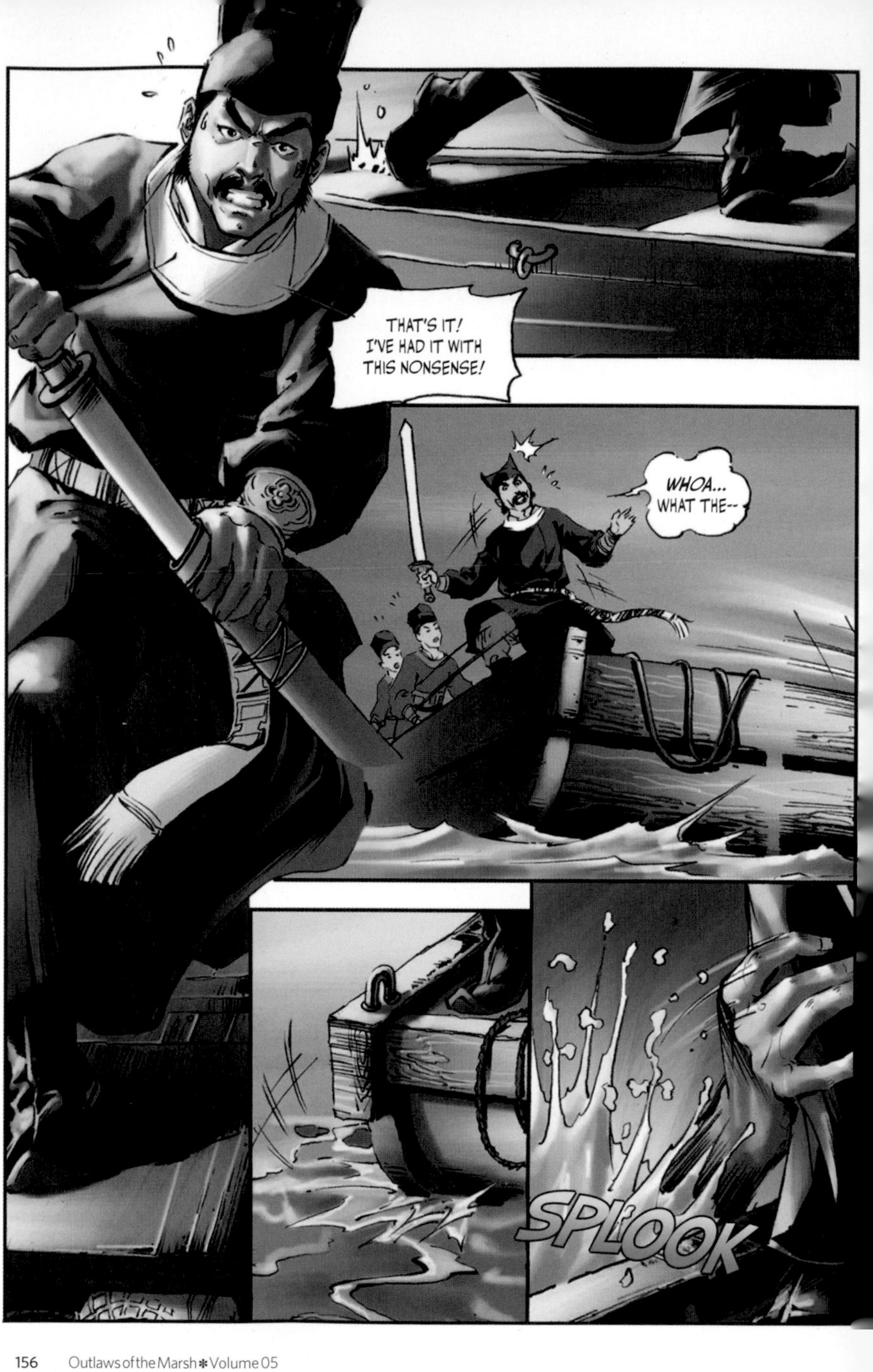
THAT'S IT! I'VE HAD IT WITH THIS NONSENSE!
WHOA... WHAT THE--
SPLOOK

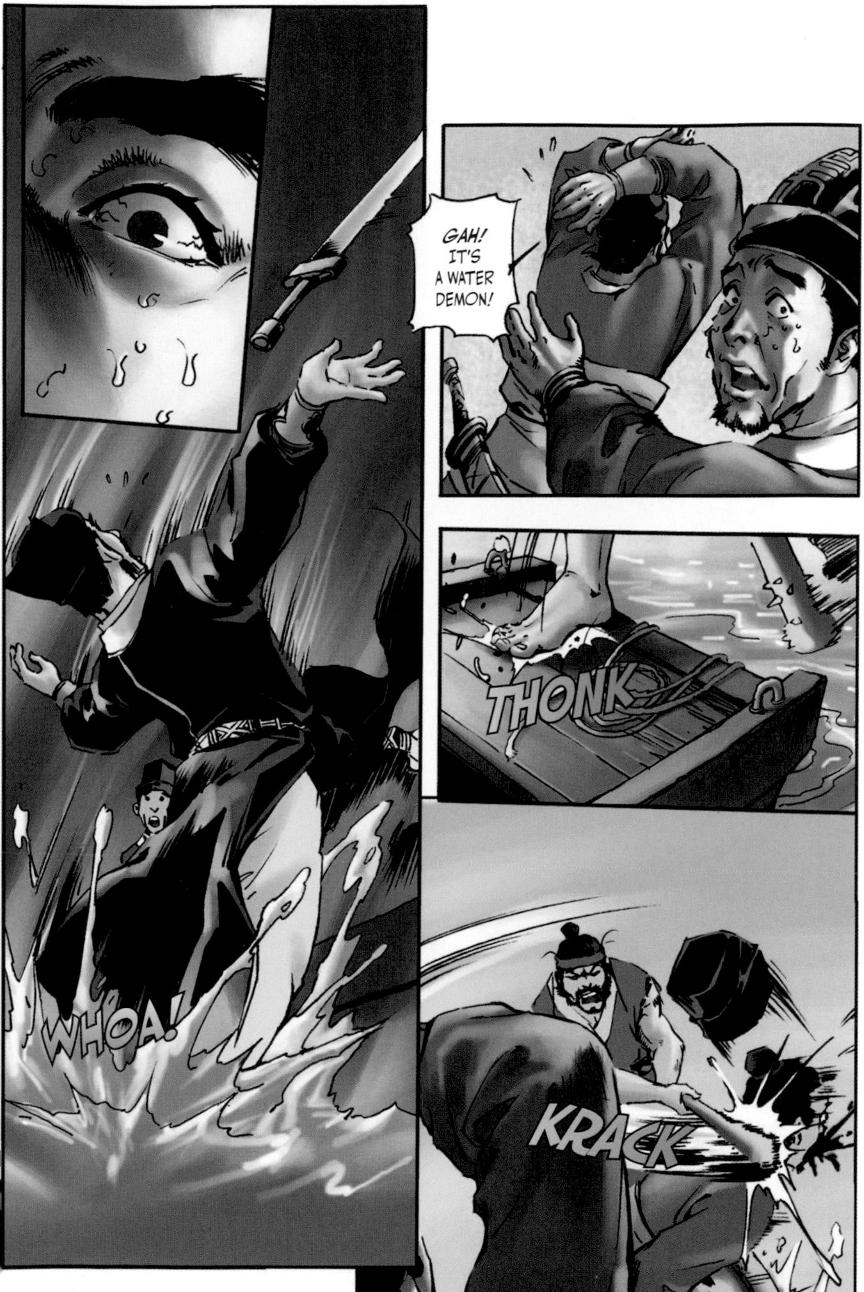
GAH! IT'S A WATER DEMON!
THONK
WHOA!
KRACK

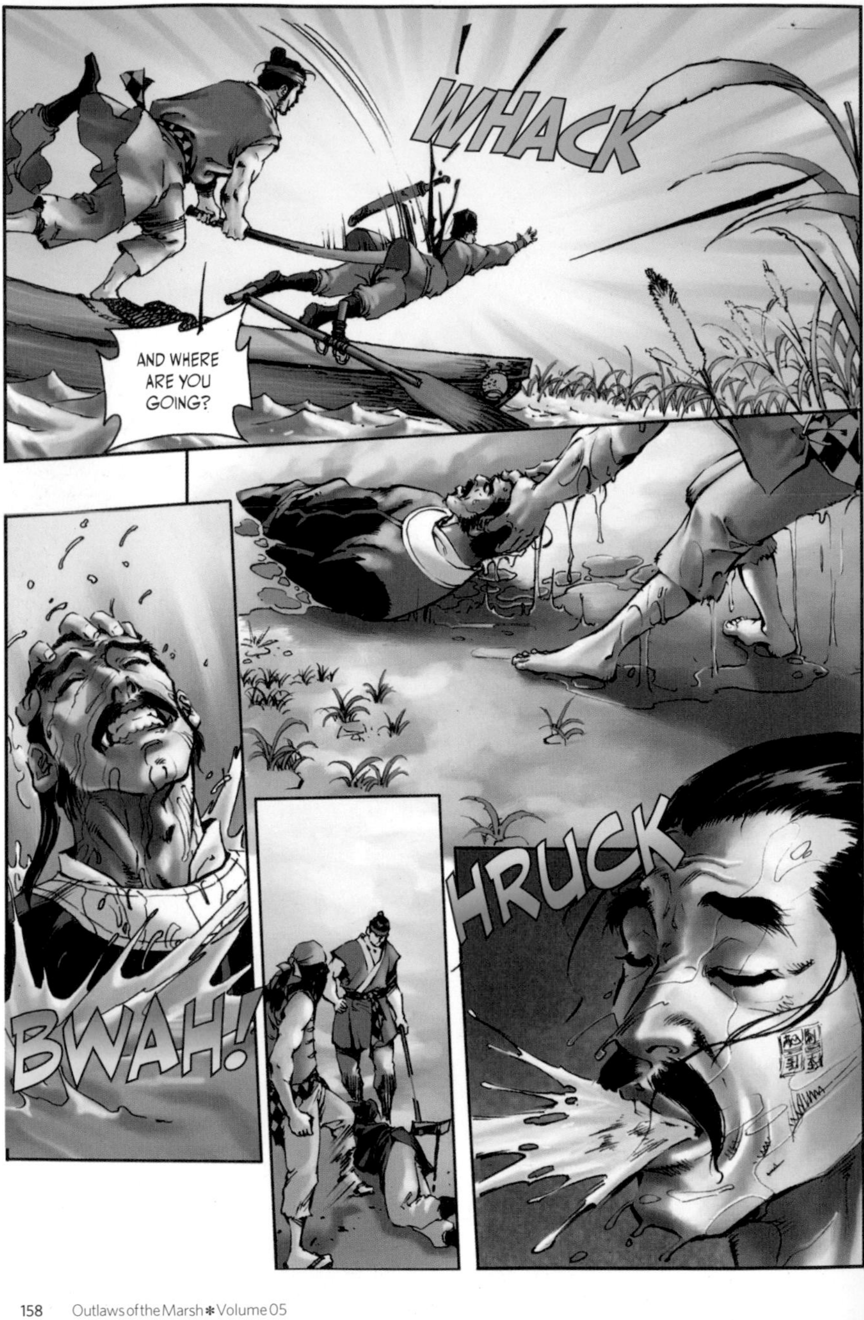
WHACK
AND WHERE ARE YOU GOING?
BWAH!
HRUCK

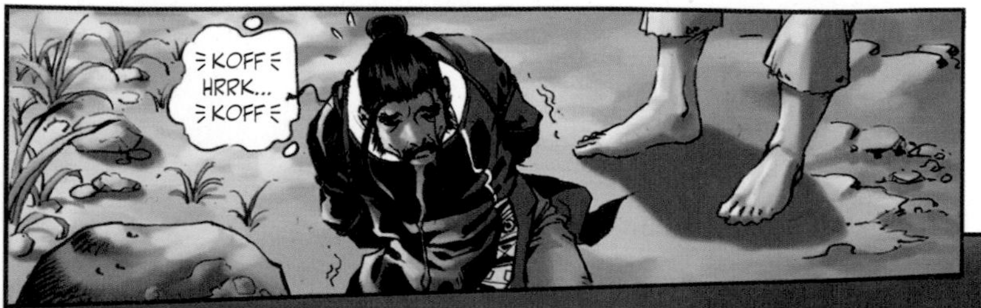
≡KOFF≡ HRRK... ≡KOFF≡

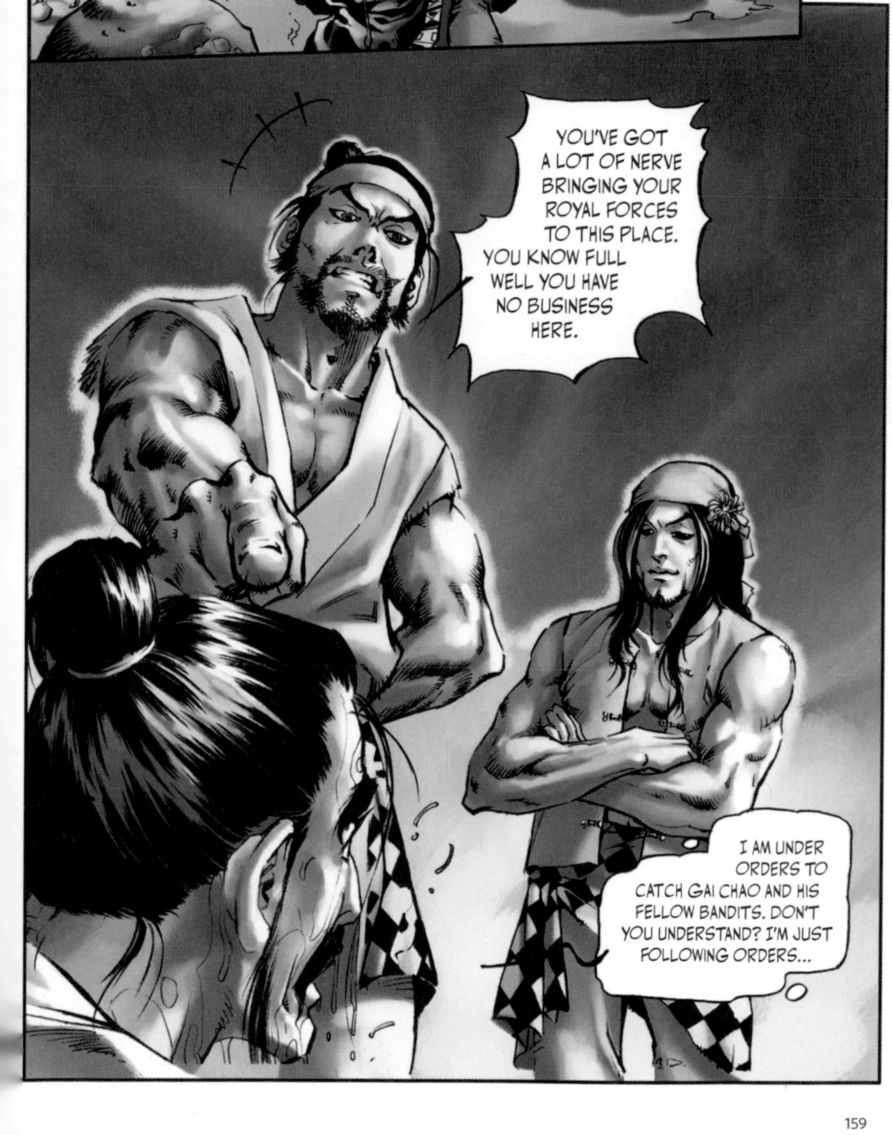
YOU'VE GOT A LOT OF NERVE BRINGING YOUR ROYAL FORCES TO THIS PLACE. YOU KNOW FULL WELL YOU HAVE NO BUSINESS HERE.
I AM UNDER ORDERS TO CATCH GAI CHAO AND HIS FELLOW BANDITS. DON'T YOU UNDERSTAND? I'M JUST FOLLOWING ORDERS...

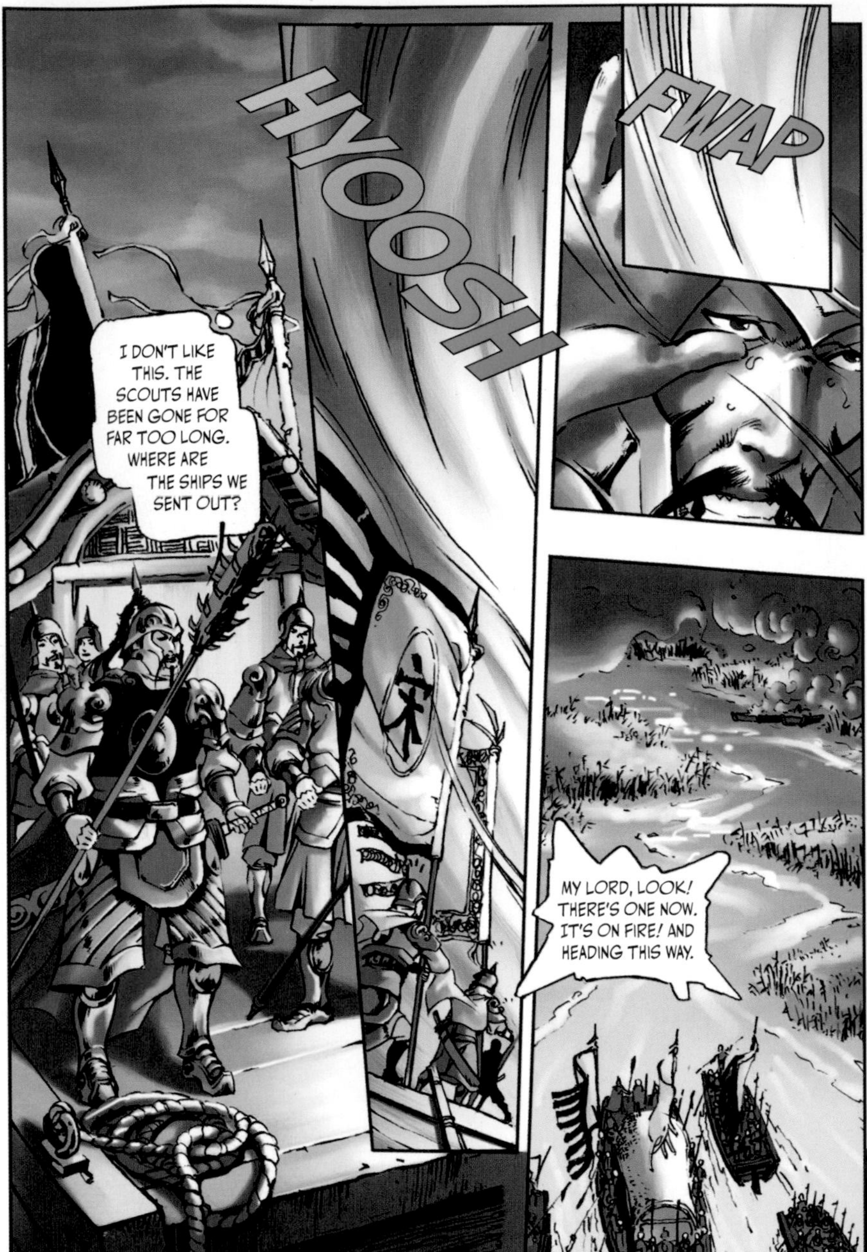
HYOOSH
FWAP
I DON'T LIKE THIS. THE SCOUTS HAVE BEEN GONE FOR FAR TOO LONG. WHERE ARE THE SHIPS WE SENT OUT?
MY LORD, LOOK! THERE'S ONE NOW. IT'S ON FIRE! AND HEADING THIS WAY.

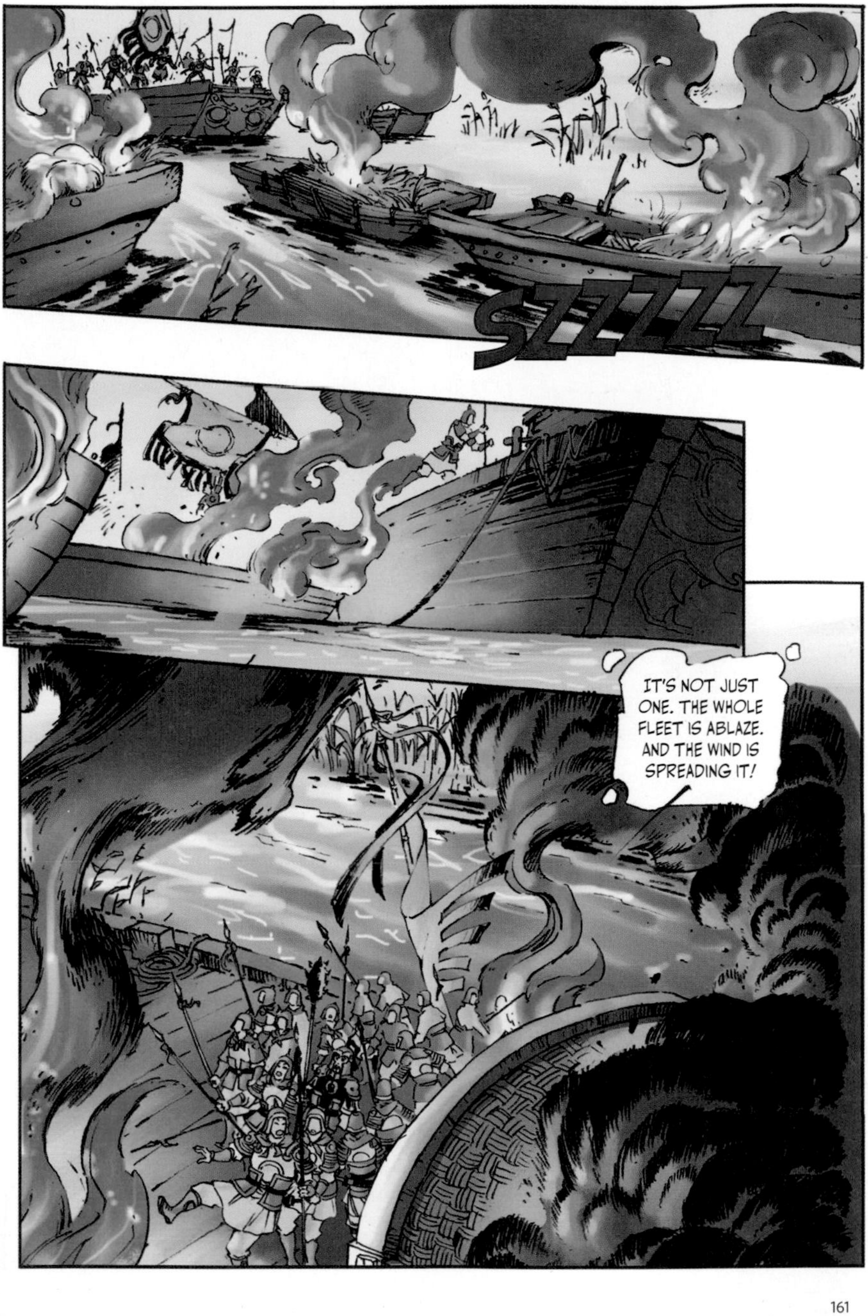
SZZZZZ
IT'S NOT JUST ONE. THE WHOLE FLEET IS ABLAZE. AND THE WIND IS SPREADING IT!

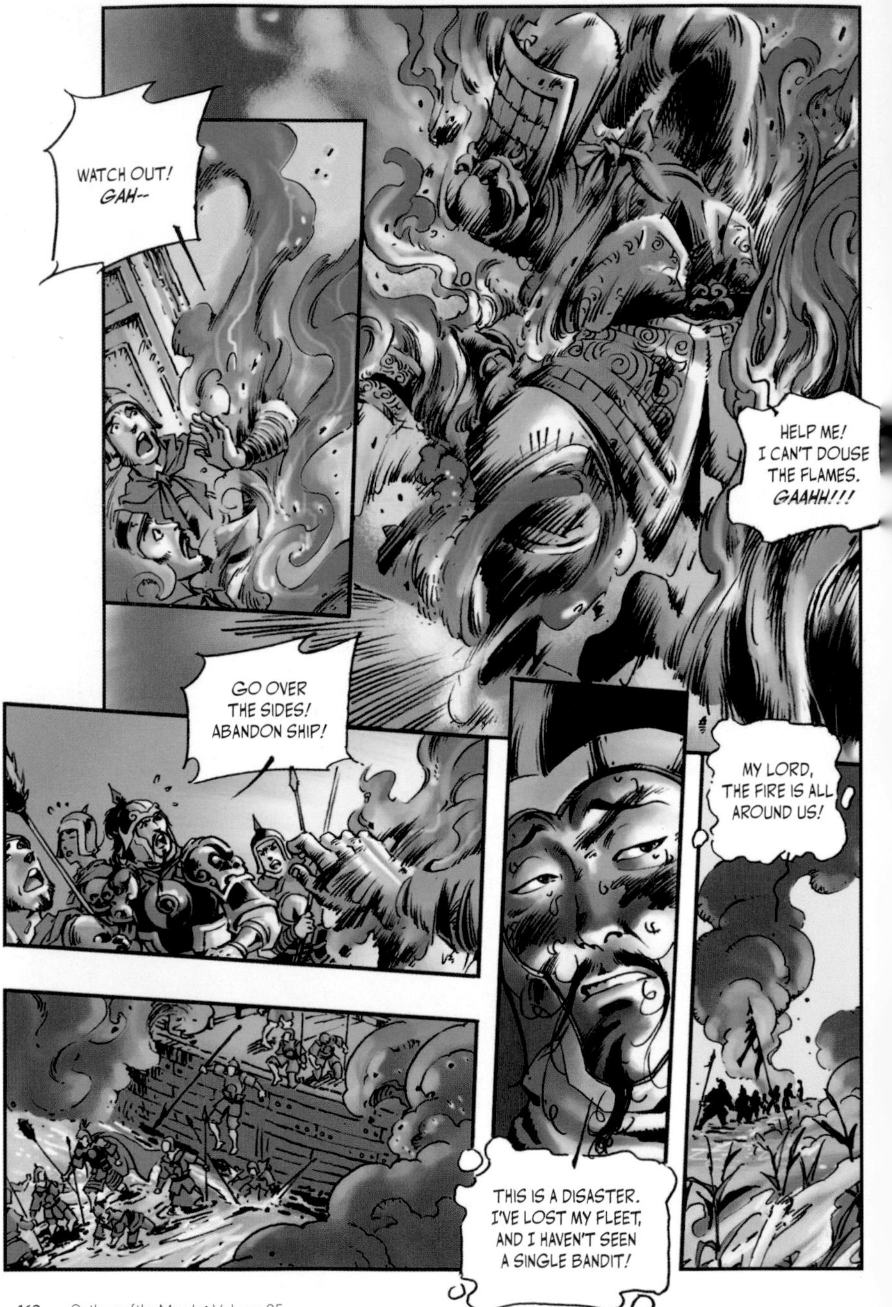
WATCH OUT! GAH--
HELP ME! I CAN'T DOUSE THE FLAMES. GAAHH!!!
GO OVER THE SIDES! ABANDON SHIP!
MY LORD, THE FIRE IS ALL AROUND US!
THIS IS A DISASTER. I'VE LOST MY FLEET, AND I HAVEN'T SEEN A SINGLE BANDIT!

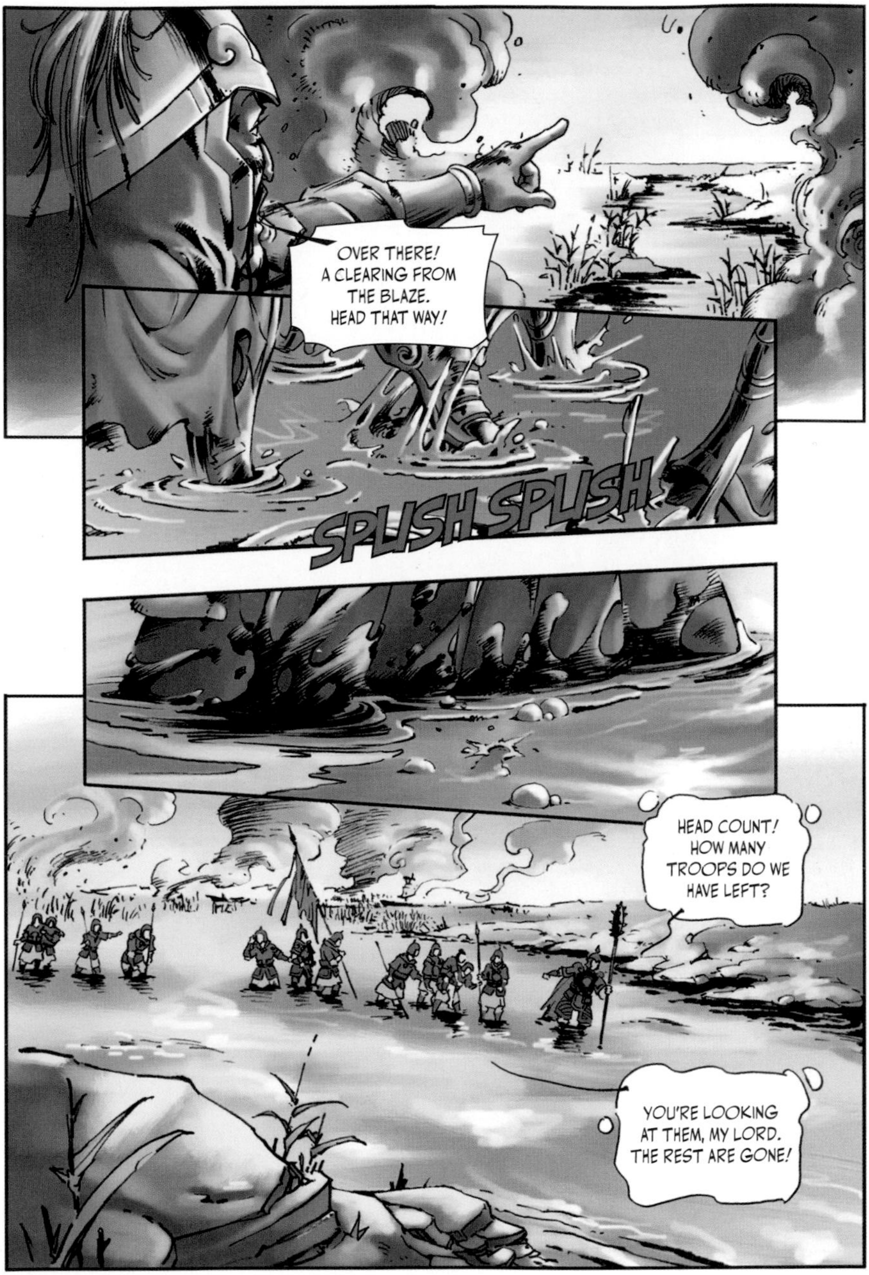
OVER THERE! A CLEARING FROM THE BLAZE. HEAD THAT WAY!
SPLISH SPLISH
HEAD COUNT! HOW MANY TROOPS DO WE HAVE LEFT?
YOU'RE LOOKING AT THEM, MY LORD. THE REST ARE GONE!

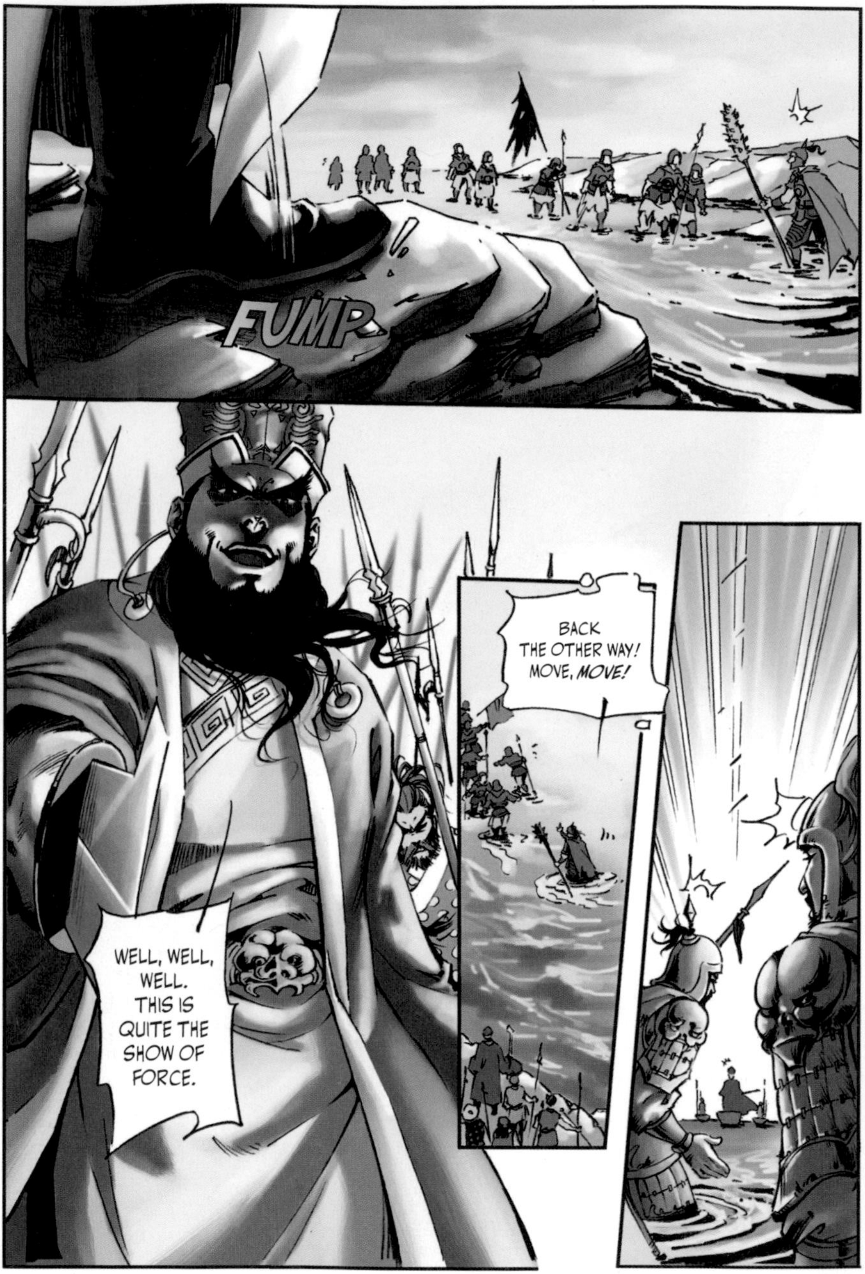
FUMP
WELL, WELL, WELL. THIS IS QUITE THE SHOW OF FORCE.
BACK THE OTHER WAY! MOVE, *MOVE!*

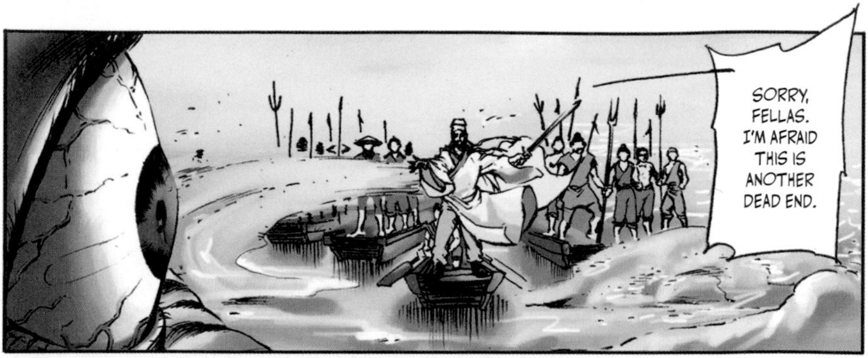
SORRY, FELLAS. I'M AFRAID THIS IS ANOTHER DEAD END.

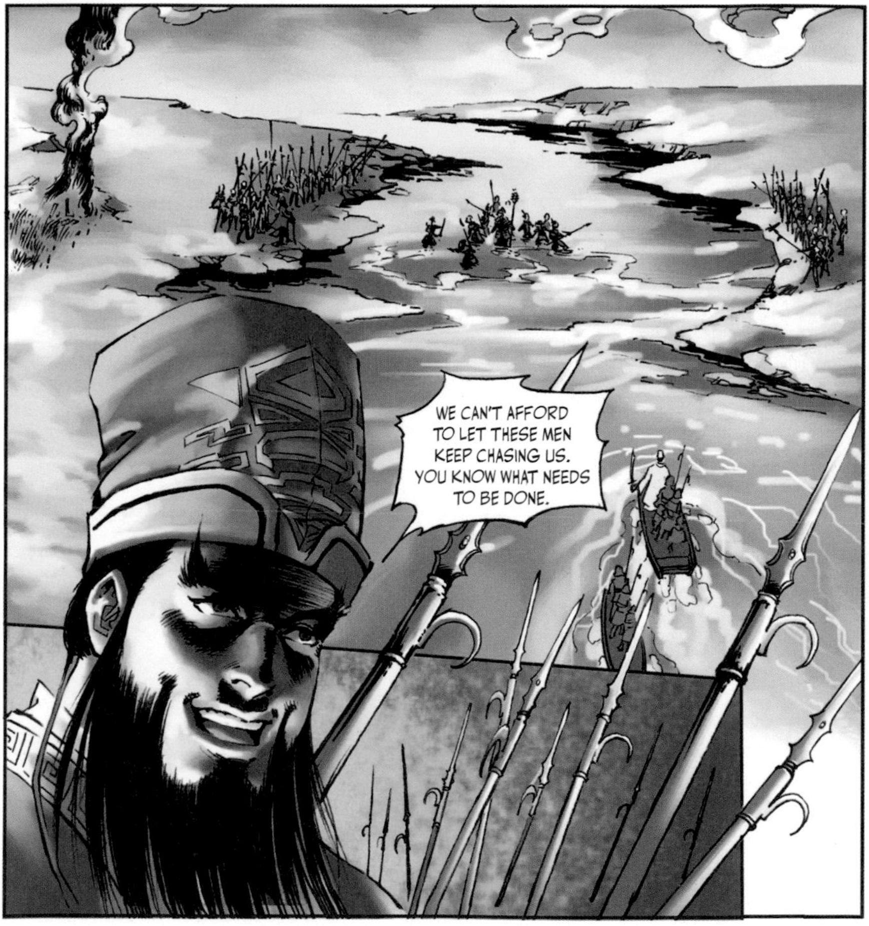
WE CAN'T AFFORD TO LET THESE MEN KEEP CHASING US. YOU KNOW WHAT NEEDS TO BE DONE.

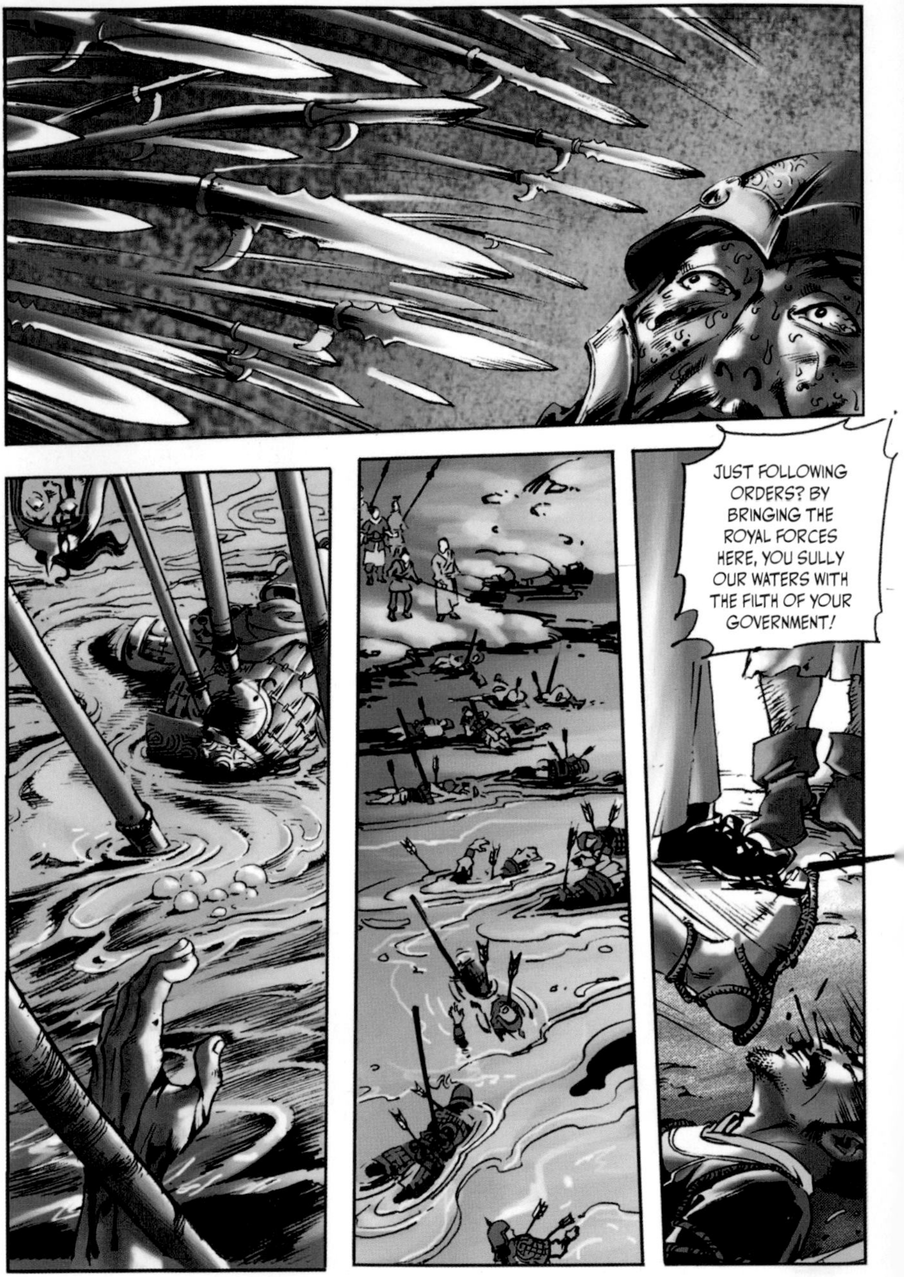
JUST FOLLOWING ORDERS? BY BRINGING THE ROYAL FORCES HERE, YOU SULLY OUR WATERS WITH THE FILTH OF YOUR GOVERNMENT!

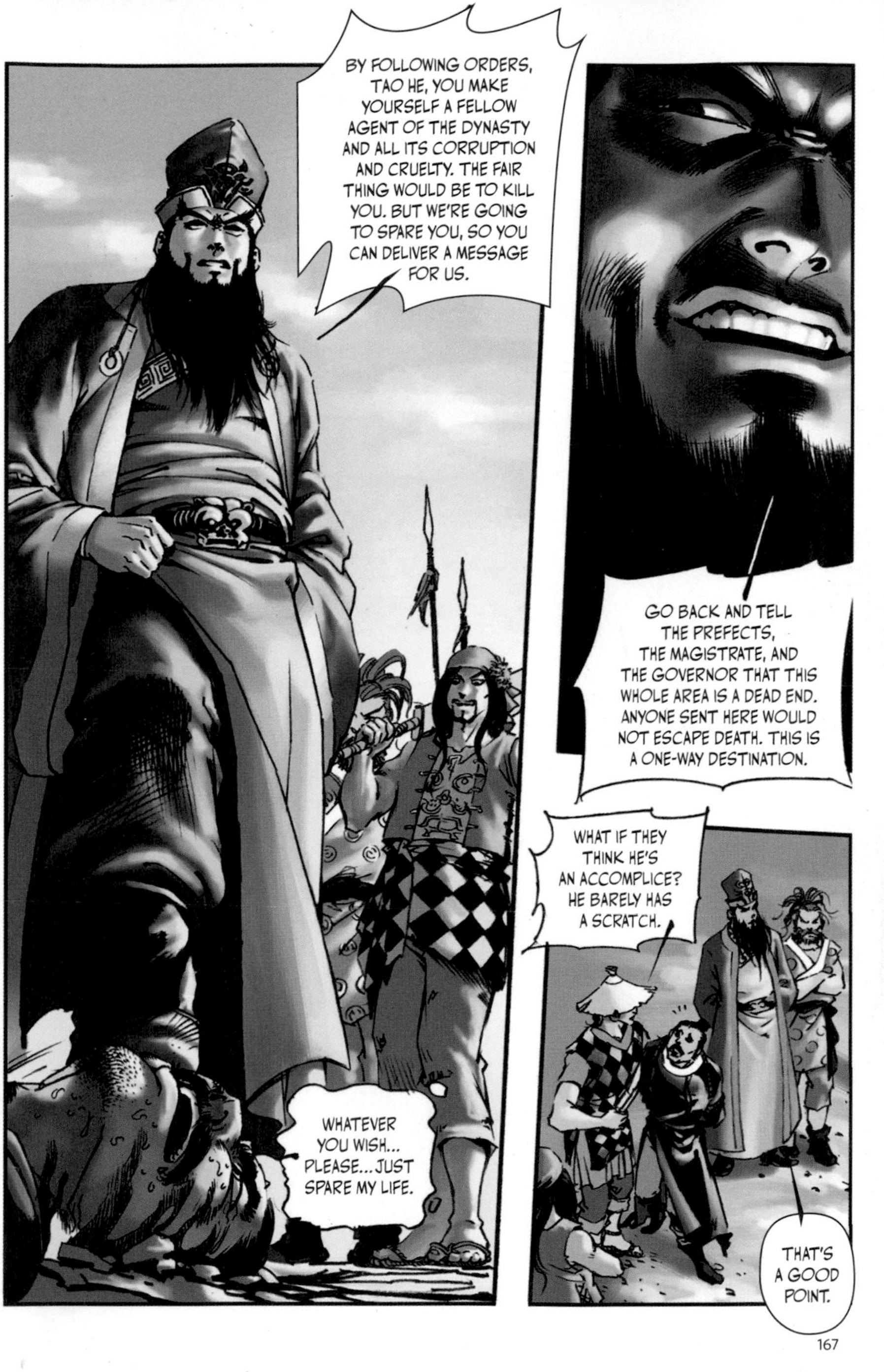
BY FOLLOWING ORDERS, TAO HE, YOU MAKE YOURSELF A FELLOW AGENT OF THE DYNASTY AND ALL ITS CORRUPTION AND CRUELTY. THE FAIR THING WOULD BE TO KILL YOU. BUT WE'RE GOING TO SPARE YOU, SO YOU CAN DELIVER A MESSAGE FOR US.
WHATEVER YOU WISH... PLEASE... JUST SPARE MY LIFE.
GO BACK AND TELL THE PREFECTS, THE MAGISTRATE, AND THE GOVERNOR THAT THIS WHOLE AREA IS A DEAD END. ANYONE SENT HERE WOULD NOT ESCAPE DEATH. THIS IS A ONE-WAY DESTINATION.
WHAT IF THEY THINK HE'S AN ACCOMPLICE? HE BARELY HAS A SCRATCH.
THAT'S A GOOD POINT.

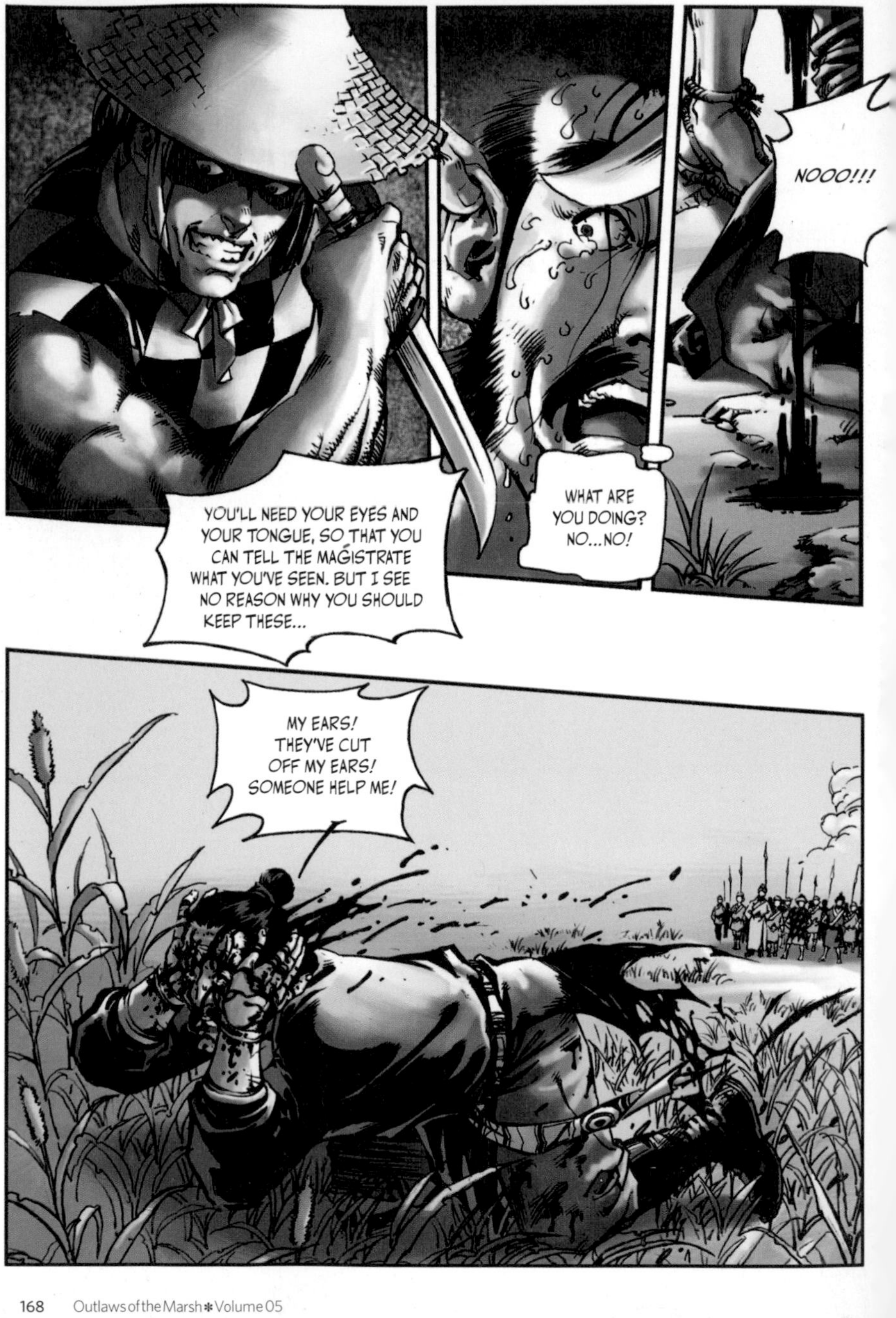
YOU'LL NEED YOUR EYES AND YOUR TONGUE, SO THAT YOU CAN TELL THE MAGISTRATE WHAT YOU'VE SEEN. BUT I SEE NO REASON WHY YOU SHOULD KEEP THESE...
WHAT ARE YOU DOING? NO...NO!
NOOO!!!
MY EARS! THEY'VE CUT OFF MY EARS! SOMEONE HELP ME!

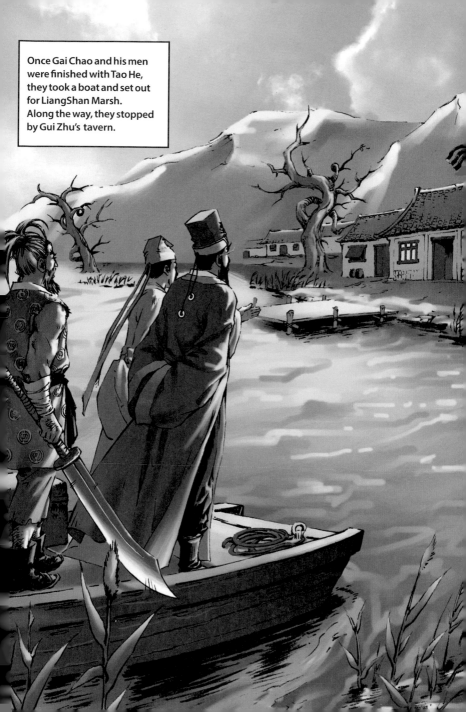

Once Gai Chao and his men were finished with Tao He, they took a boat and set out for LiangShan Marsh. Along the way, they stopped by Gui Zhu's tavern.

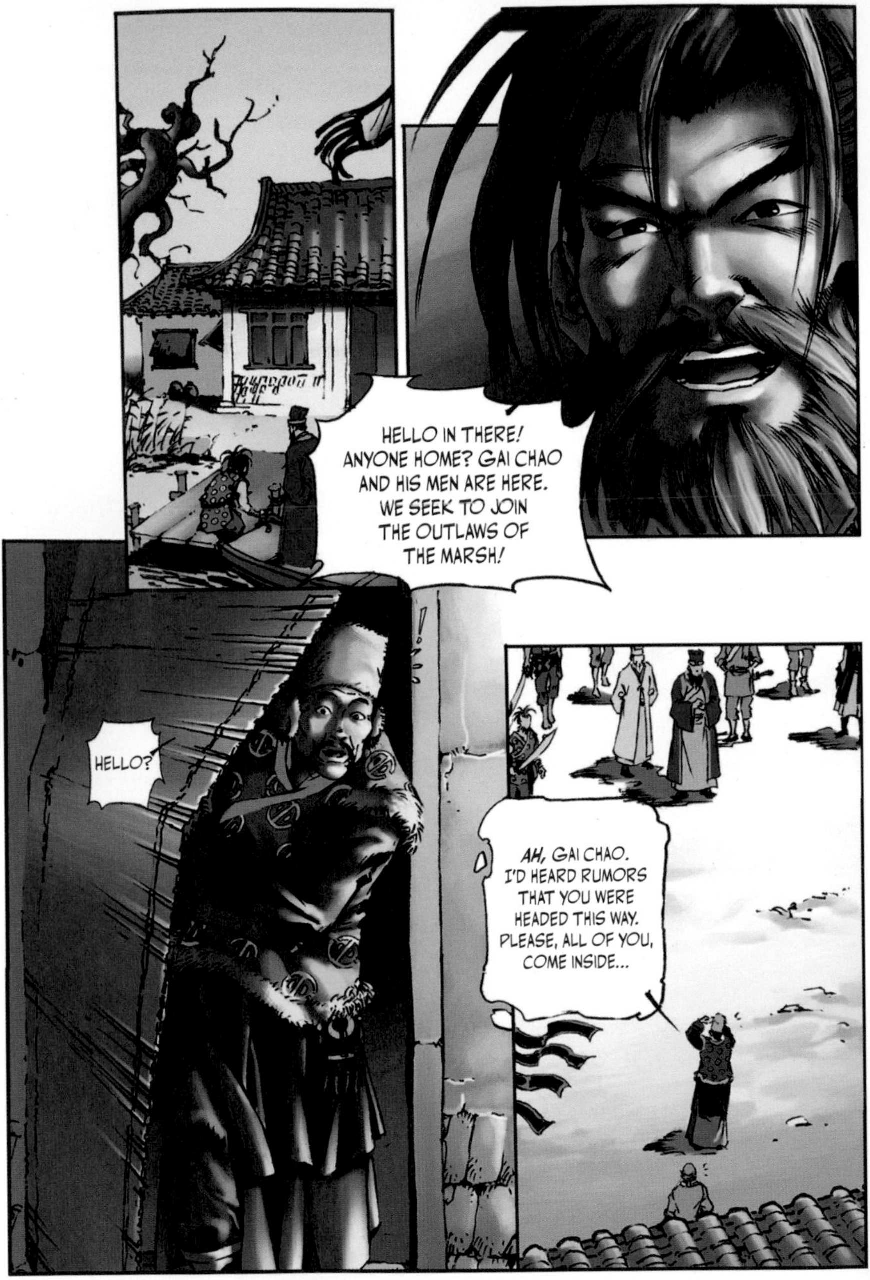
HELLO IN THERE! ANYONE HOME? GAI CHAO AND HIS MEN ARE HERE. WE SEEK TO JOIN THE OUTLAWS OF THE MARSH!
HELLO?
AH, GAI CHAO. I'D HEARD RUMORS THAT YOU WERE HEADED THIS WAY. PLEASE, ALL OF YOU, COME INSIDE...

Violence and Benevolence

Outlaws of the Marsh is a story in which the central governing authority is riddled with corruption and trusted by very few. As a result, the story examines several characters who act as self-appointed authority figures to those around them. With regard to the specific figures of Gai Chao and ZhiShen Lu, the story draws contrasting portraits about the utility of violence in establishing authority. Where one man is quick to use intimidation and violence as a way of winning allies and subordinates, Gai Chao is a more benevolent operator, a man who prefers to extend an open hand rather than a fist – at least until he is backed into a corner, at which point he acts swiftly and violently.

From the time we first meet ZhiShen Lu, as a major in a local police force, it is clear that he operates outside of the system he claims to serve: he acts as a one-man moral authority, as judge, jury, and executioner deciding the fate of anyone who crosses him. It's something of a running gag that the first thing one must do upon meeting ZhiShen is fight him off. If ZhiShen fancies himself a leader (which he clearly does, as he does not hesitate to take over as captain Mount ErLong), he is clearly the kind of leader who prefers the stick to the carrot, who would rather assert his authority by violently subjugating those who would end up serving him, or serving with him. Gai Chao, on the other hand, is a much quieter presence. He cultivates a network of subordinates not through intimidation but through a kind of self-serving altruism: he extends friendship and favor to those who fun afoul of the law, a method that serves him well when he finds himself on the wrong side of the authorities. It's a testament to the success of this method that almost everyone enlisted by the Prefect to capture Gai Chao ends up helping him escape. It is only when Gai Chao and his men are being relentlessly pursued by the royal authorities that his method turns violent. When confronted with the reality that the army dispatched to hunt him down will not give up the pursuit, Gai Chao quickly and ruthlessly determines that the army must be destroyed.

By contrasting the examples of ZhiShen Lu and Gai Chao, we understand how *Outlaws of the Marsh* presents a complex depiction of leadership in a lawless age. The question becomes, though: Which one of these men will benefit in the long run from how he establishes his authority, and which one will be destroyed by it?

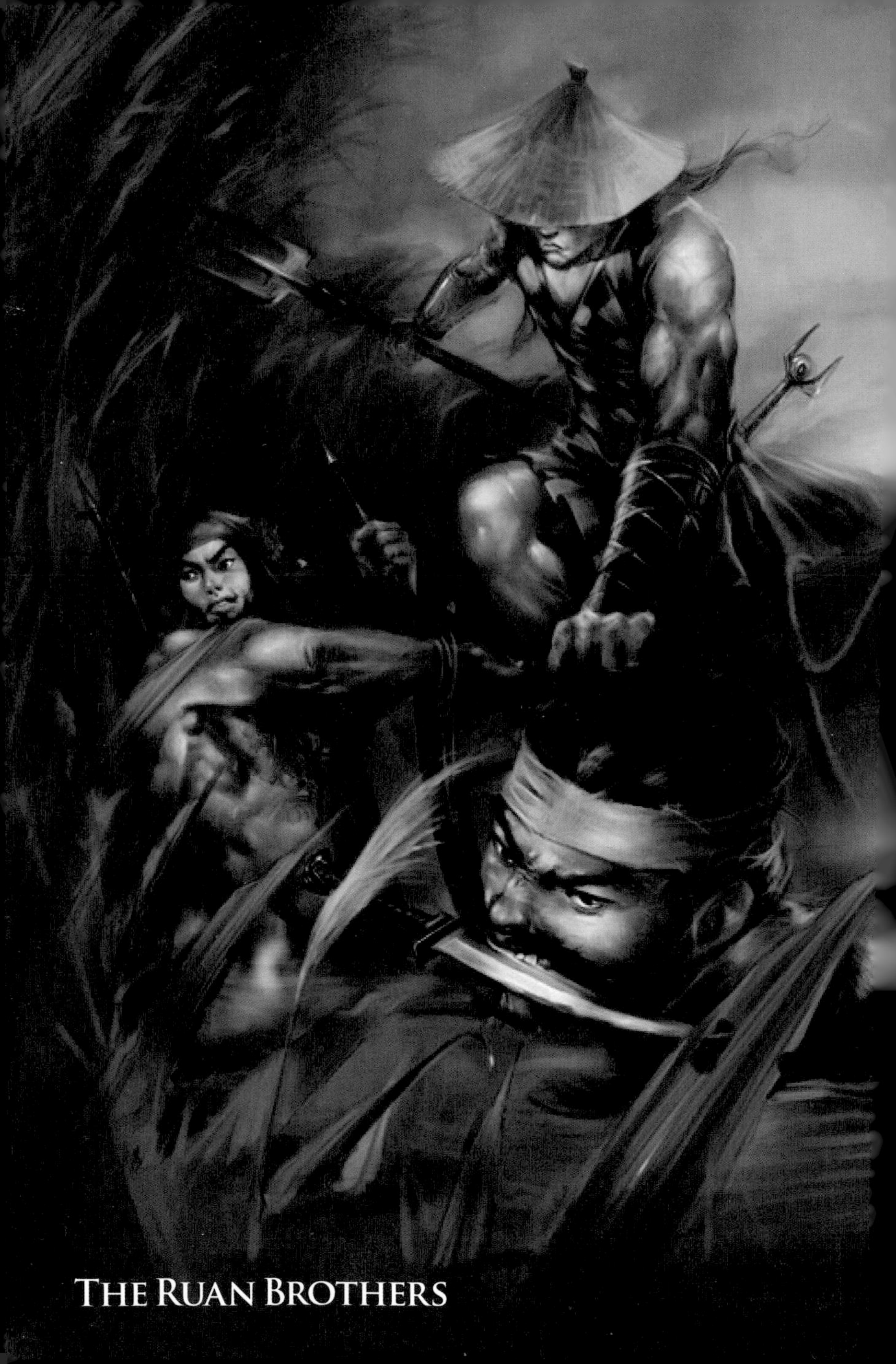

THE RUAN BROTHERS

TALES FROM CHINA

OUTLAWS of the MARSH

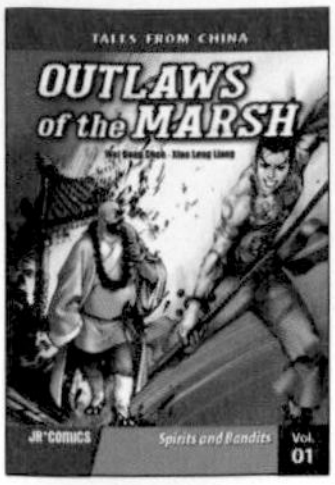
TALES FROM CHINA
OUTLAWS of the MARSH
Spirits and Bandits
Vol. 01
Vol.01

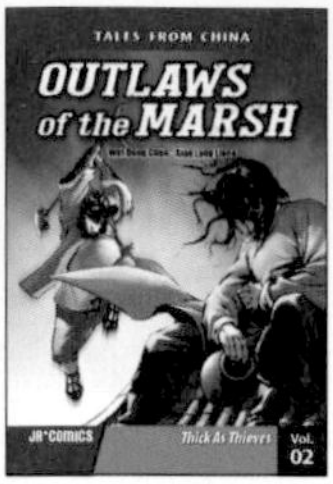
TALES FROM CHINA
OUTLAWS of the MARSH
Thick As Thieves
Vol. 02
Vol.02

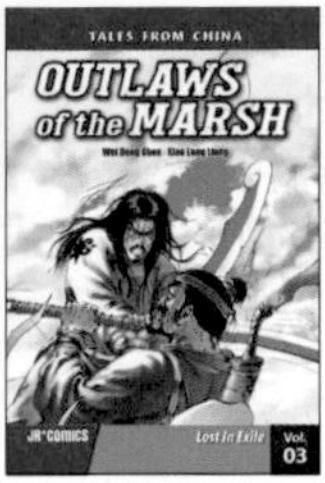
TALES FROM CHINA
OUTLAWS of the MARSH
Lost In Exile
Vol. 03
Vol.03

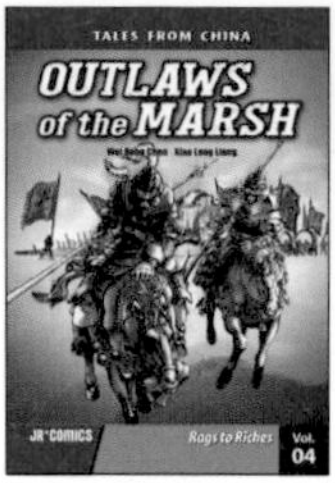
TALES FROM CHINA
OUTLAWS of the MARSH
Rags to Riches
Vol. 04
Vol.04

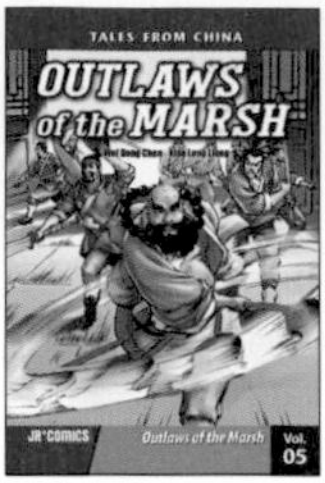
TALES FROM CHINA
OUTLAWS of the MARSH
Outlaws of the Marsh
Vol. 05
Vol.05

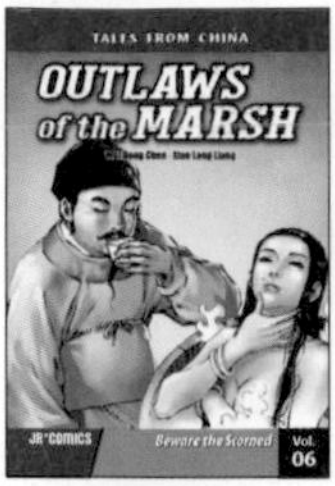
TALES FROM CHINA
OUTLAWS of the MARSH
Beware the Scorned
Vol. 06
Vol.06

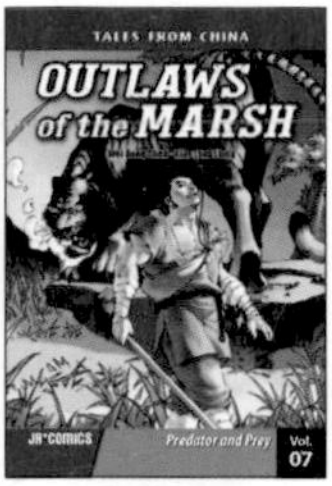
TALES FROM CHINA
OUTLAWS of the MARSH
Predator and Prey
Vol. 07
Vol.07

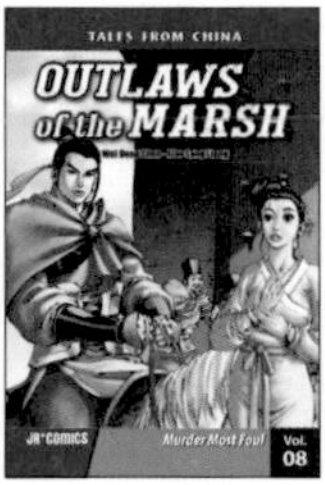
TALES FROM CHINA
OUTLAWS of the MARSH
Murder Most Foul
Vol. 08
Vol.08

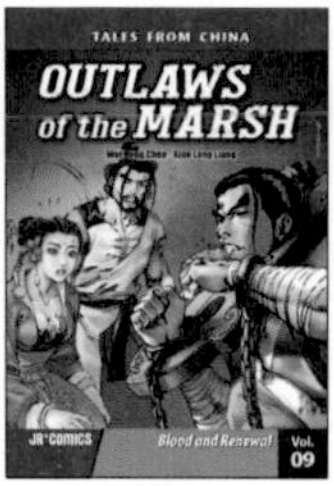
TALES FROM CHINA
OUTLAWS of the MARSH
Blood and Renewal
Vol. 09
Vol.09

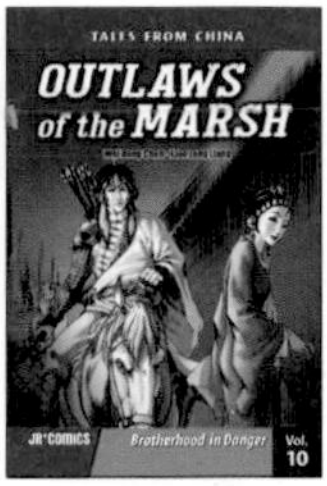
TALES FROM CHINA
OUTLAWS of the MARSH
Brotherhood in Danger
Vol. 10
Vol.10

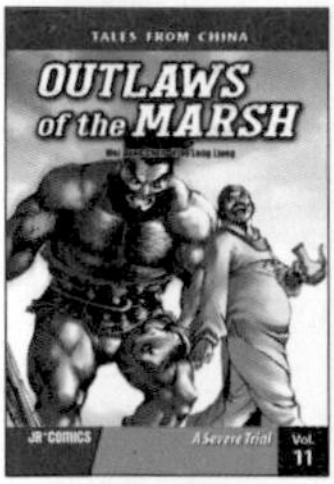
TALES FROM CHINA
OUTLAWS of the MARSH
A Severe Trial
Vol. 11
Vol.11

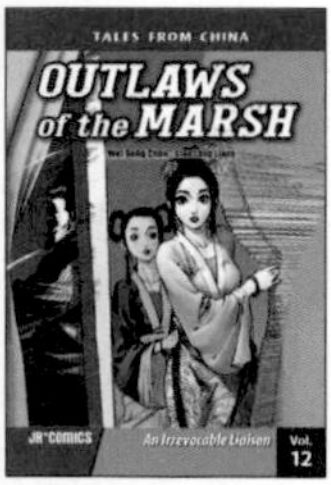
TALES FROM CHINA
OUTLAWS of the MARSH
An Irrevocable Liaison
Vol. 12
Vol.12

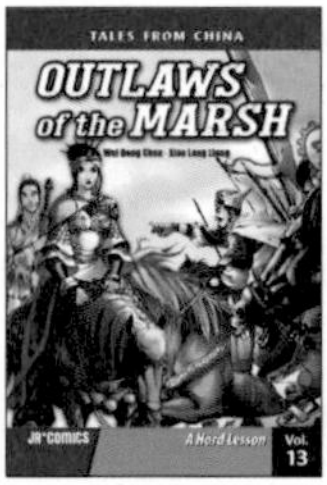
TALES FROM CHINA
OUTLAWS of the MARSH
A Hard Lesson
Vol. 13
Vol.13

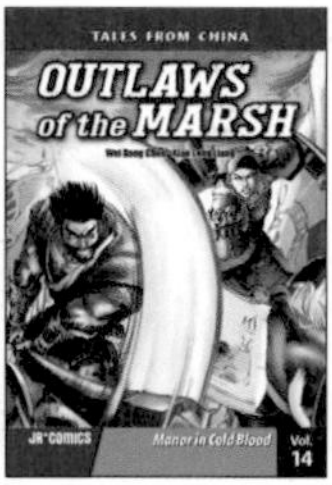
TALES FROM CHINA
OUTLAWS of the MARSH
Manor in Cold Blood
Vol. 14
Vol.14

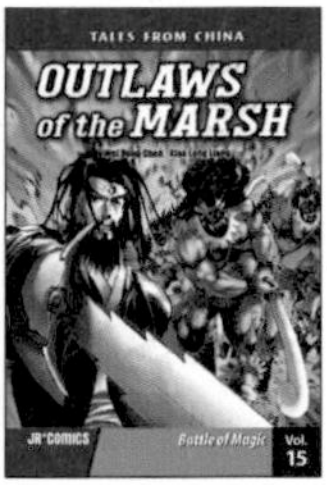
TALES FROM CHINA
OUTLAWS of the MARSH
Battle of Magic
Vol. 15
Vol.15

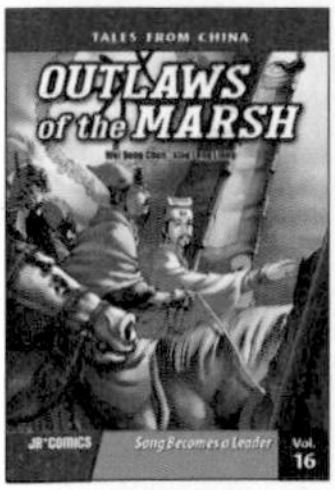
TALES FROM CHINA
OUTLAWS of the MARSH
Song Becomes a Leader
Vol. 16
Vol.16

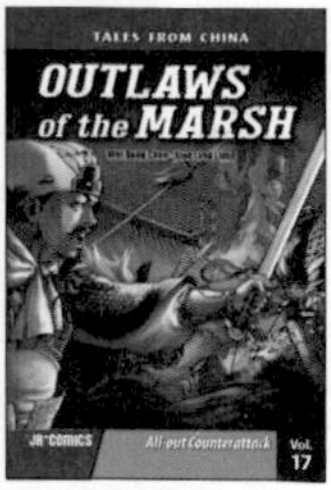
TALES FROM CHINA
OUTLAWS of the MARSH
All-out Counterattack
Vol. 17
Vol.17

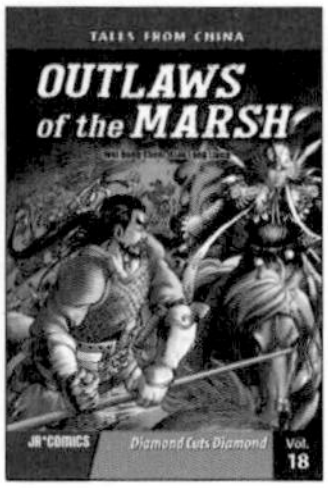
TALES FROM CHINA
OUTLAWS of the MARSH
Diamond Cuts Diamond
Vol. 18
Vol.18

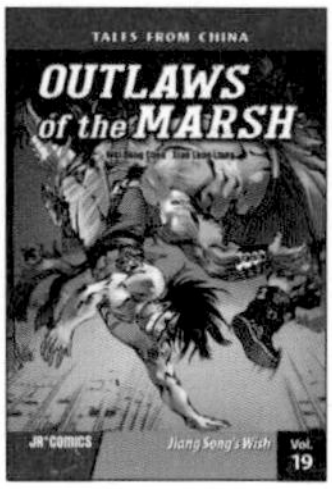
TALES FROM CHINA
OUTLAWS of the MARSH
Jiang Song's Wish
Vol. 19
Vol.19

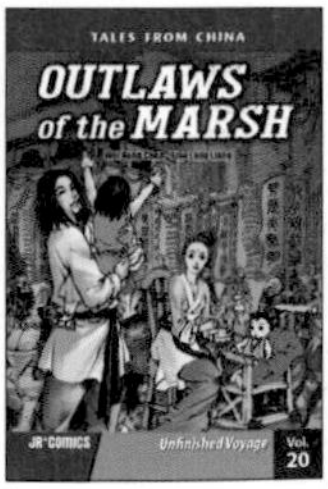
TALES FROM CHINA
OUTLAWS of the MARSH
Unfinished Voyage
Vol. 20
Vol.20

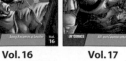